bad kitty

CH.

Bad Kitty Vol. 1: Catnipped
Written and Created by Michele Jaffe
Art by Lince

Lettering - Lucas Rivera
Toning - Jan Michael Aldeguer
Cover Illustration - Ulisses Perez
Cover Design - Jose Macasocol, Jr.

Editor - Bryce P. Coleman
Digital Imaging Manager - Chris Buford
Pre-Production Supervisor - Erika Terriquez
Production Manager - Elisabeth Brizzi
Managing Editor - Vy Nguyen
Creative Director - Anne Marie Horne
Editor-in-Chief - Rob Tokar
Publisher - Mike Kiley
President and C.O.O. - John Parker
C.E.O. and Chief Creative Officer - Stu Levy

A  Manga

TOKYOPOP and are trademarks or registered trademarks of TOKYOPOP Inc.

TOKYOPOP Inc.
5900 Wilshire Blvd. Suite 2000
Los Angeles, CA 90036

E-mail: info@TOKYOPOP.com
Come visit us online at www.TOKYOPOP.com

ISBN 978-0-06-135162-4
Library of Congress catalog card number: 2008924817

1   2   3   4   5   6   7   8   9   10

❖

First Edition

bad kitty

Volume One: Catnipped

Written & Created by
Michele Jaffe

Art by
Lince

HAMBURG // LONDON // LOS ANGELES // TOKYO

HarperCollins*Publishers*

Contents

Chapter One

Jasmine Callihan

HAIR: Safe

PORES: Small to Medium

HEART: FULL!!

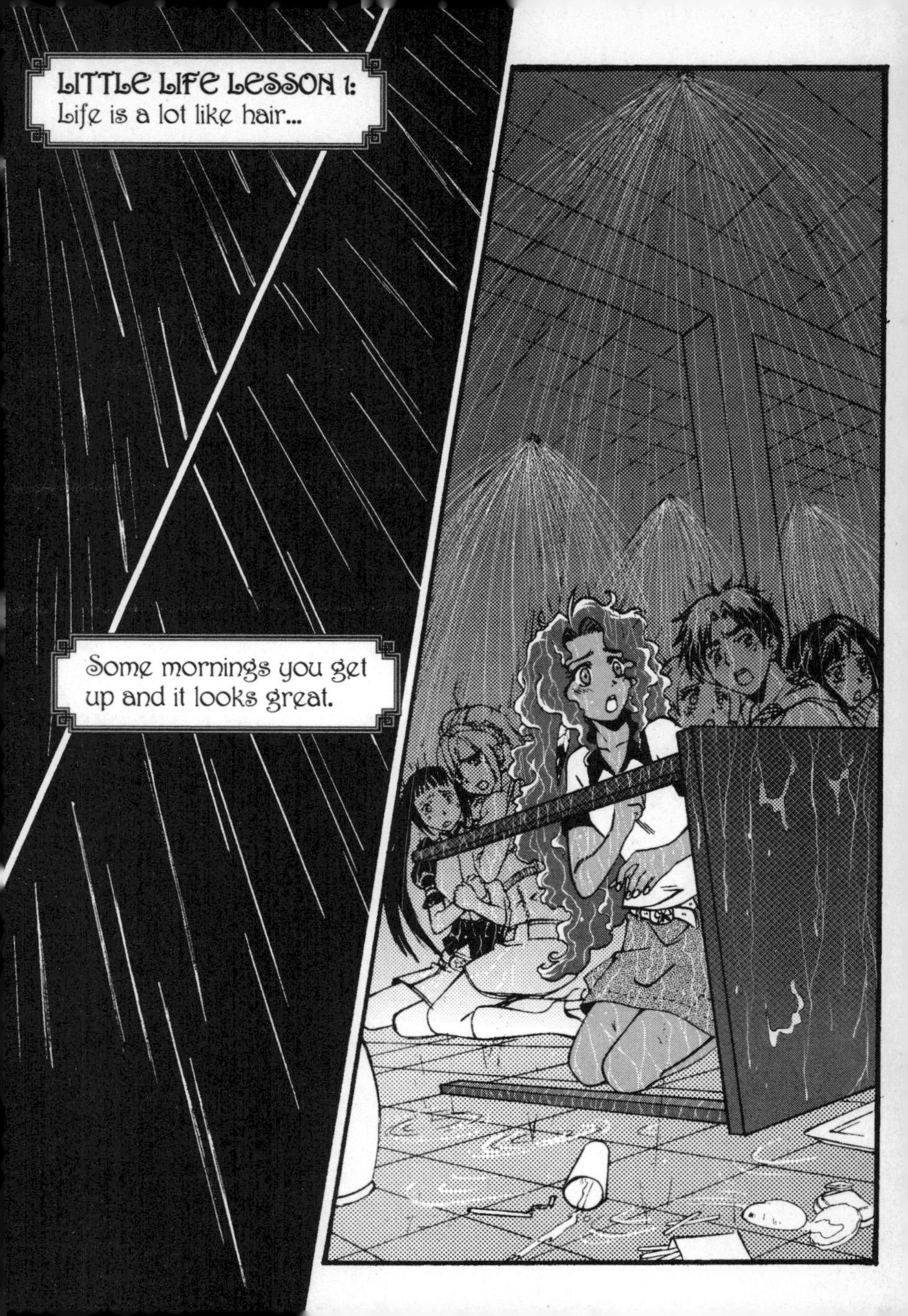
LITTLE LIFE LESSON 1:
Life is a lot like hair...
Some mornings you get up and it looks great.

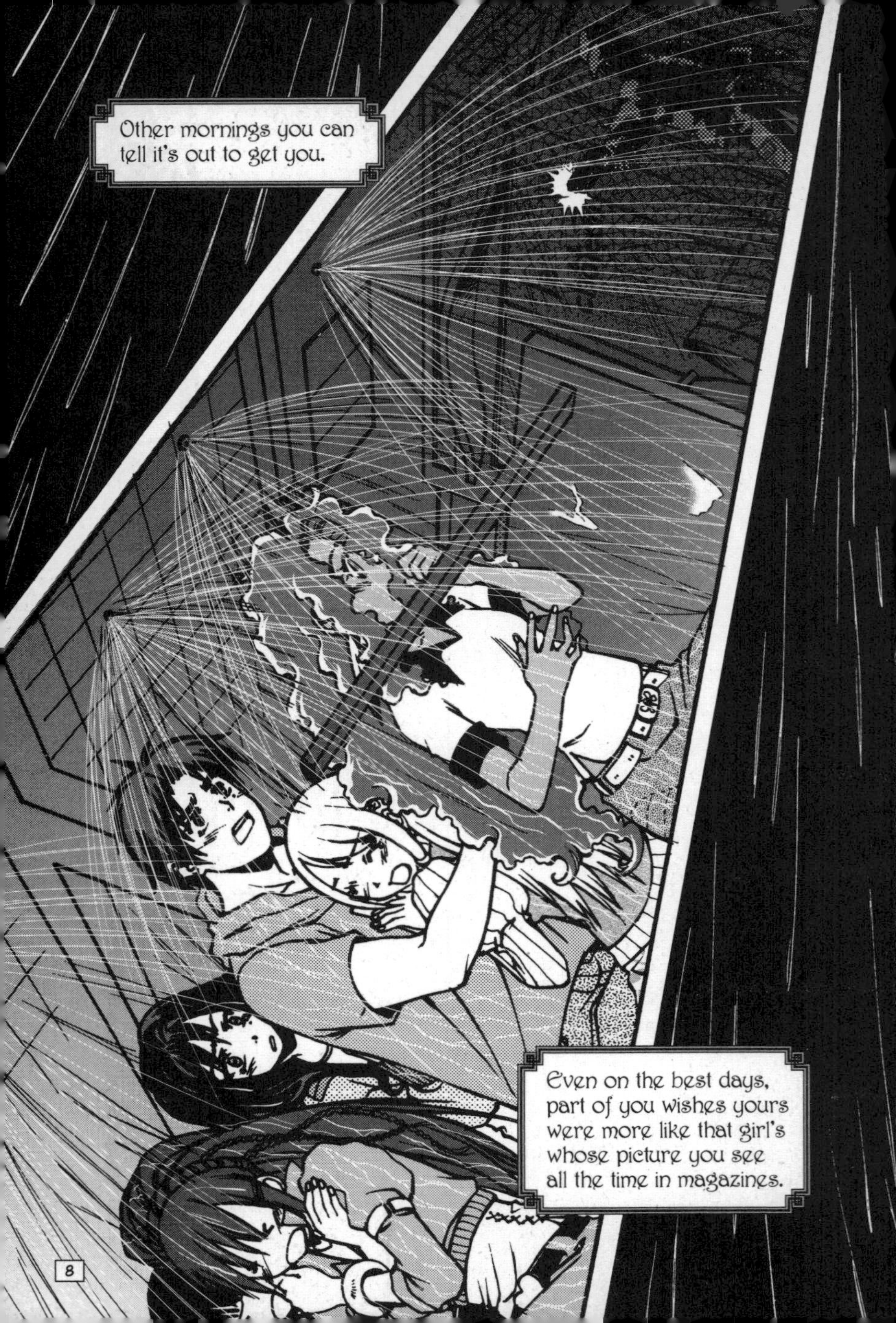

Other mornings you can tell it's out to get you.
Even on the best days, part of you wishes yours were more like that girl's whose picture you see all the time in magazines.

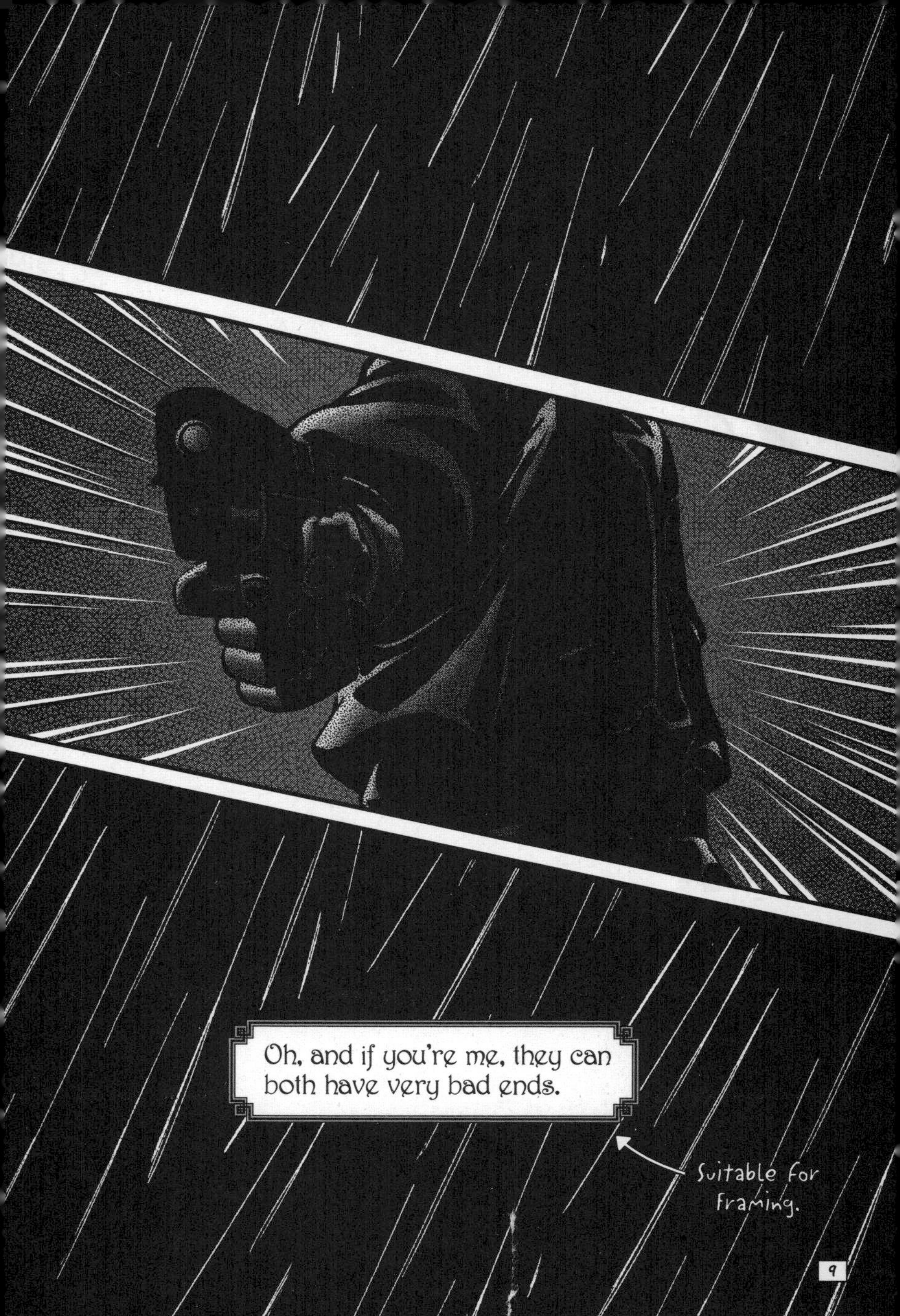
Oh, and if you're me, they can both have very bad ends.
Suitable for Framing.

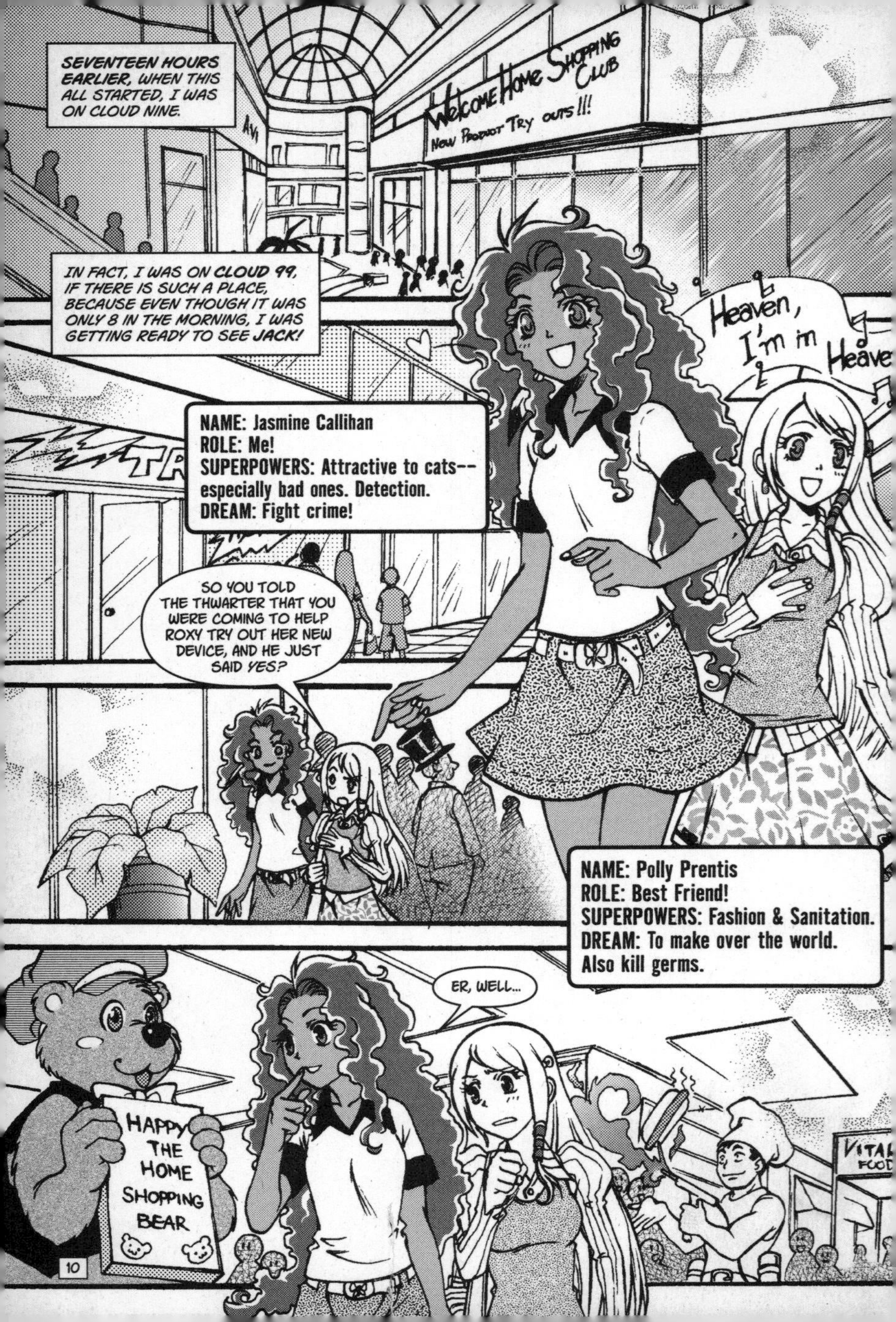
SEVENTEEN HOURS EARLIER, WHEN THIS ALL STARTED, I WAS ON CLOUD NINE.
Welcome Home Shopping Club
New Product Try outs!!!
IN FACT, I WAS ON CLOUD 99, IF THERE IS SUCH A PLACE, BECAUSE EVEN THOUGH IT WAS ONLY 8 IN THE MORNING, I WAS GETTING READY TO SEE JACK!
NAME: Jasmine Callihan
ROLE: Me!
SUPERPOWERS: Attractive to cats--especially bad ones. Detection.
DREAM: Fight crime!
Heaven, I'm in Heave
SO YOU TOLD THE THWARTER THAT YOU WERE COMING TO HELP ROXY TRY OUT HER NEW DEVICE, AND HE JUST SAID YES?
NAME: Polly Prentis
ROLE: Best Friend!
SUPERPOWERS: Fashion & Sanitation.
DREAM: To make over the world. Also kill germs.
ER, WELL...
HAPPY THE HOME SHOPPING BEAR

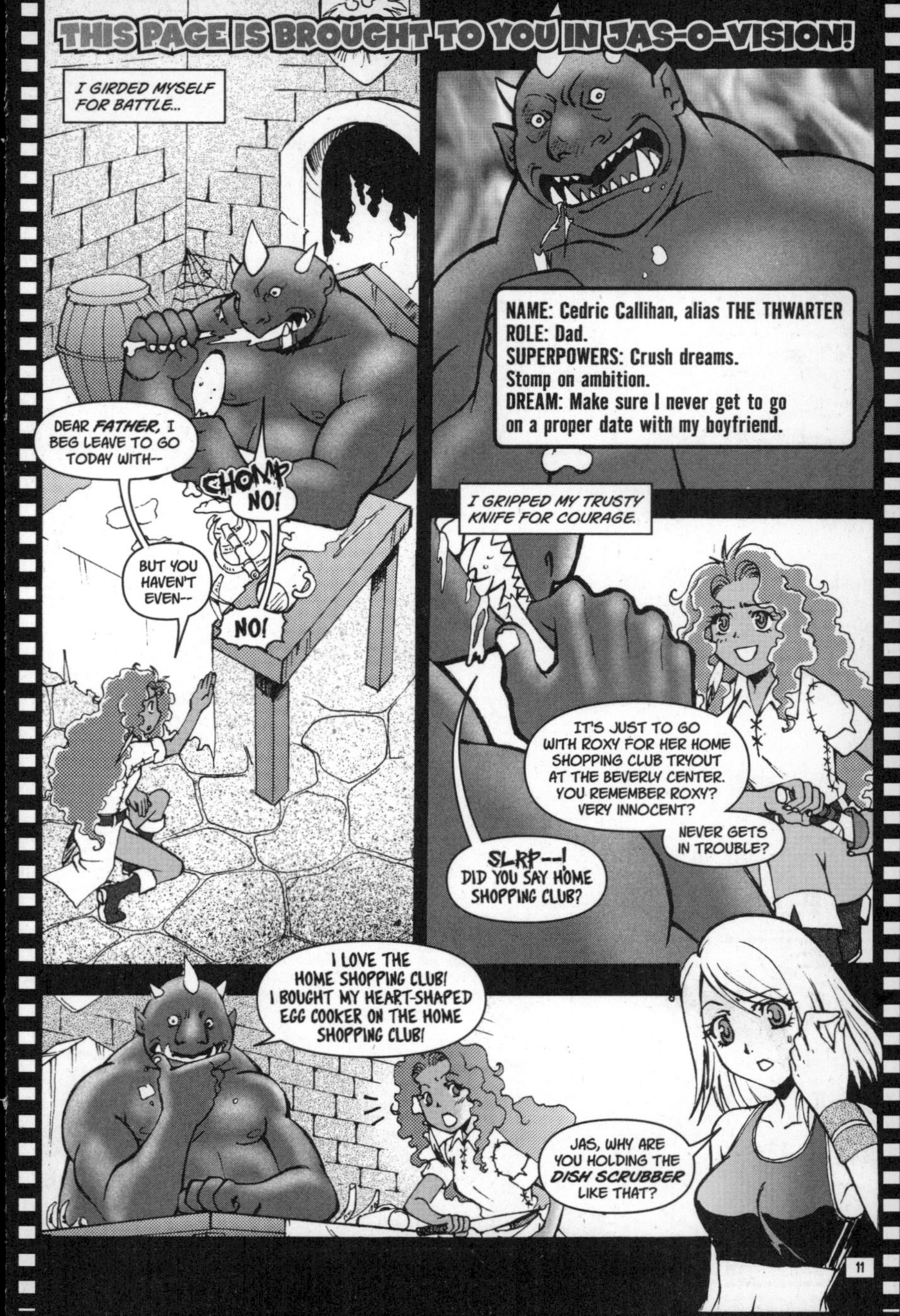
THIS PAGE IS BROUGHT TO YOU IN JAS-O-VISION!
I GIRDED MYSELF FOR BATTLE...
DEAR *FATHER,* I BEG LEAVE TO GO TODAY WITH--
CHOMP
NO!
BUT YOU HAVEN'T EVEN--
NO!
NAME: Cedric Callihan, alias THE THWARTER
ROLE: Dad.
SUPERPOWERS: Crush dreams.
Stomp on ambition.
DREAM: Make sure I never get to go on a proper date with my boyfriend.
I GRIPPED MY TRUSTY KNIFE FOR COURAGE.
IT'S JUST TO GO WITH ROXY FOR HER HOME SHOPPING CLUB TRYOUT AT THE BEVERLY CENTER. YOU REMEMBER ROXY? VERY INNOCENT?
NEVER GETS IN TROUBLE?
SLRP--! DID YOU SAY HOME SHOPPING CLUB?
I LOVE THE HOME SHOPPING CLUB! I BOUGHT MY HEART-SHAPED EGG COOKER ON THE HOME SHOPPING CLUB!
JAS, WHY ARE YOU HOLDING THE *DISH SCRUBBER* LIKE THAT?

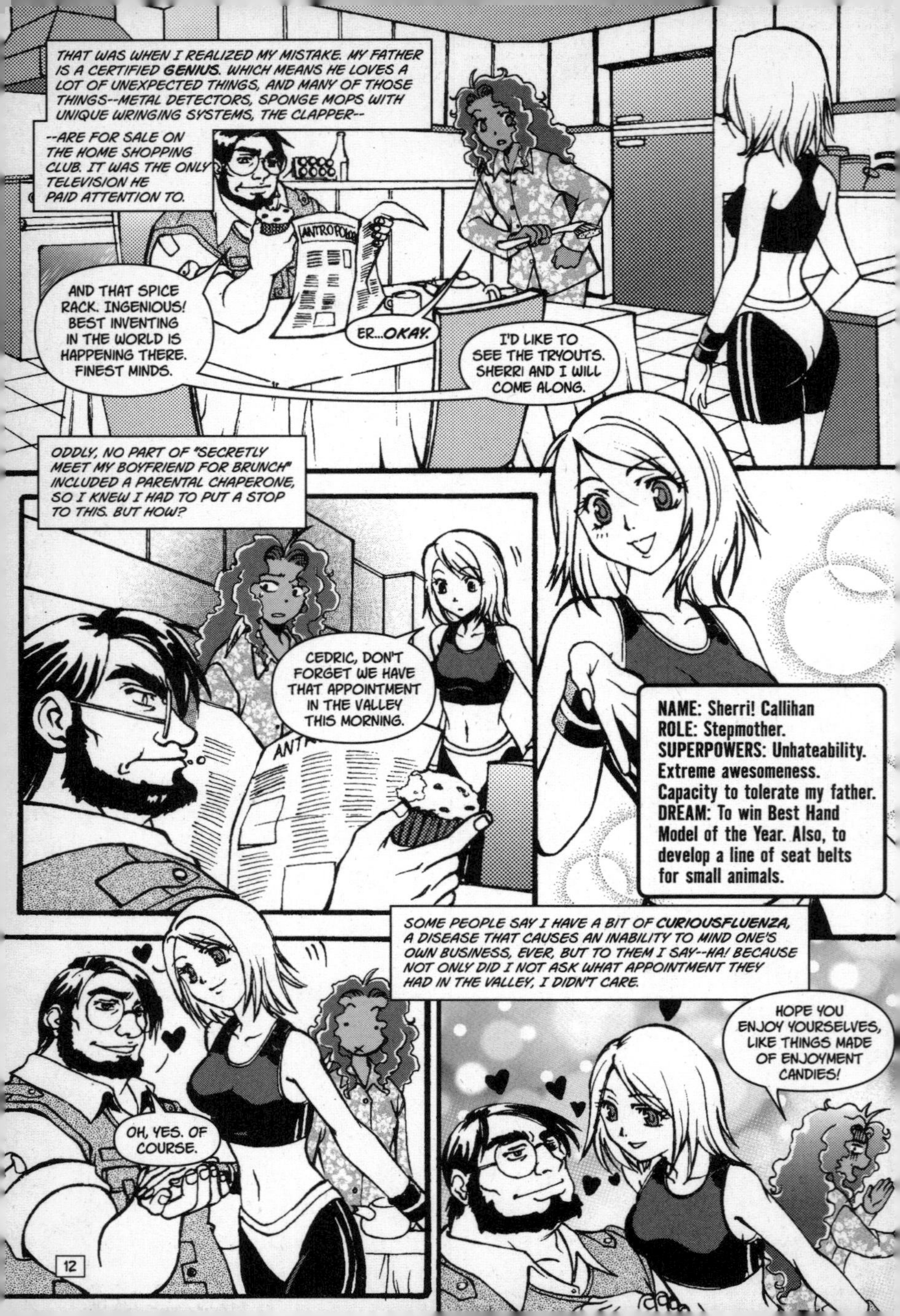
THAT WAS WHEN I REALIZED MY MISTAKE. MY FATHER IS A CERTIFIED GENIUS. WHICH MEANS HE LOVES A LOT OF UNEXPECTED THINGS, AND MANY OF THOSE THINGS--METAL DETECTORS, SPONGE MOPS WITH UNIQUE WRINGING SYSTEMS, THE CLAPPER--
--ARE FOR SALE ON THE HOME SHOPPING CLUB. IT WAS THE ONLY TELEVISION HE PAID ATTENTION TO.
AND THAT SPICE RACK. INGENIOUS! BEST INVENTING IN THE WORLD IS HAPPENING THERE. FINEST MINDS.
ER...OKAY.
I'D LIKE TO SEE THE TRYOUTS. SHERRI AND I WILL COME ALONG.
ODDLY, NO PART OF "SECRETLY MEET MY BOYFRIEND FOR BRUNCH" INCLUDED A PARENTAL CHAPERONE, SO I KNEW I HAD TO PUT A STOP TO THIS. BUT HOW?
CEDRIC, DON'T FORGET WE HAVE THAT APPOINTMENT IN THE VALLEY THIS MORNING.
NAME: Sherri! Callihan
ROLE: Stepmother.
SUPERPOWERS: Unhateability. Extreme awesomeness. Capacity to tolerate my father.
DREAM: To win Best Hand Model of the Year. Also, to develop a line of seat belts for small animals.
OH, YES. OF COURSE.
SOME PEOPLE SAY I HAVE A BIT OF CURIOUSFLUENZA, A DISEASE THAT CAUSES AN INABILITY TO MIND ONE'S OWN BUSINESS, EVER, BUT TO THEM I SAY--HA! BECAUSE NOT ONLY DID I NOT ASK WHAT APPOINTMENT THEY HAD IN THE VALLEY, I DIDN'T CARE.
HOPE YOU ENJOY YOURSELVES, LIKE THINGS MADE OF ENJOYMENT CANDIES!

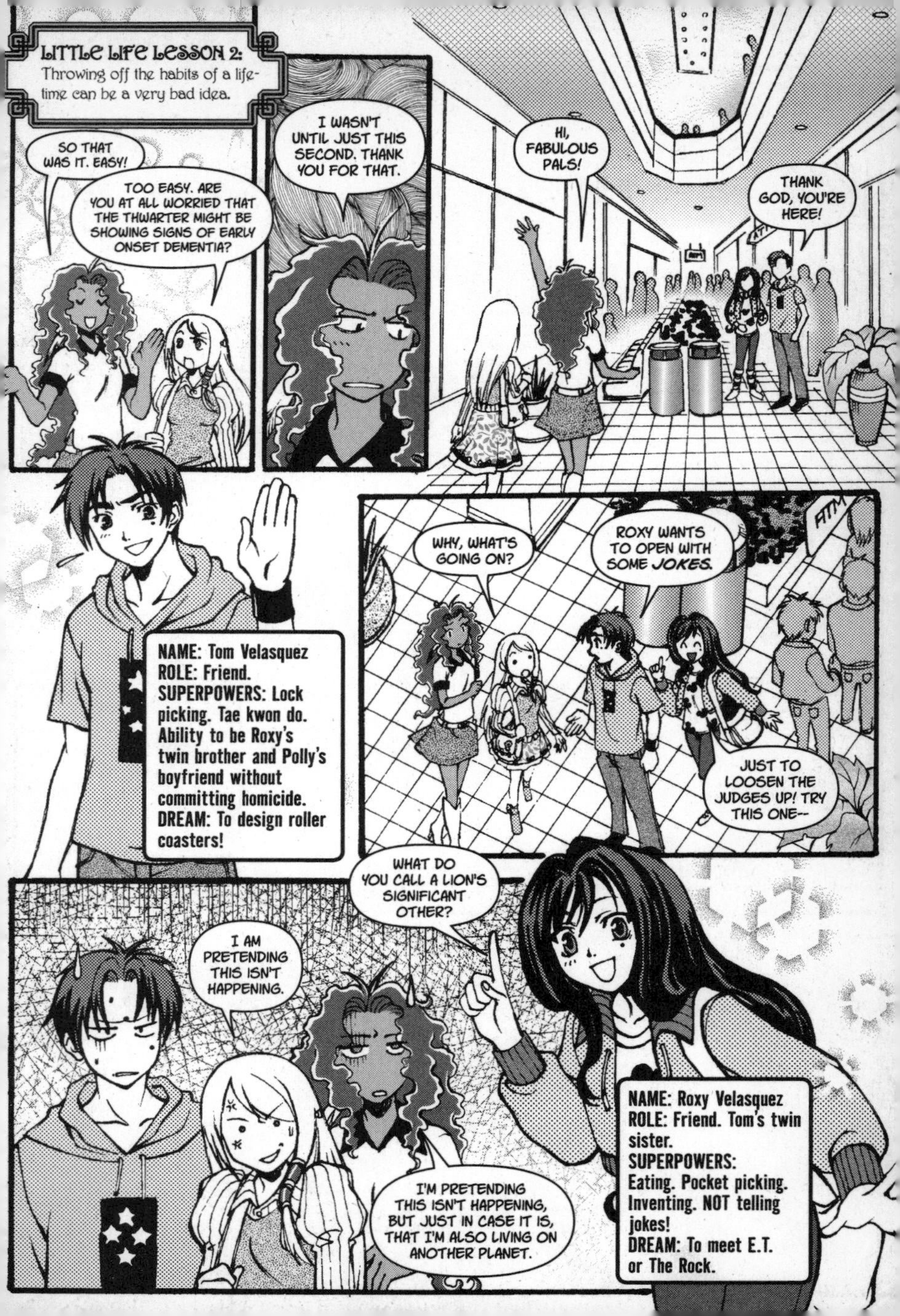
LITTLE LIFE LESSON 2:
Throwing off the habits of a lifetime can be a very bad idea.
SO THAT WAS IT. EASY!
TOO EASY. ARE YOU AT ALL WORRIED THAT THE THWARTER MIGHT BE SHOWING SIGNS OF EARLY ONSET DEMENTIA?
I WASN'T UNTIL JUST THIS SECOND. THANK YOU FOR THAT.
HI, FABULOUS PALS!
THANK GOD, YOU'RE HERE!
NAME: Tom Velasquez
ROLE: Friend.
SUPERPOWERS: Lock picking. Tae kwon do. Ability to be Roxy's twin brother and Polly's boyfriend without committing homicide.
DREAM: To design roller coasters!
WHY, WHAT'S GOING ON?
ROXY WANTS TO OPEN WITH SOME JOKES.
ATM
JUST TO LOOSEN THE JUDGES UP! TRY THIS ONE--
WHAT DO YOU CALL A LION'S SIGNIFICANT OTHER?
I AM PRETENDING THIS ISN'T HAPPENING.
I'M PRETENDING THIS ISN'T HAPPENING, BUT JUST IN CASE IT IS, THAT I'M ALSO LIVING ON ANOTHER PLANET.
NAME: Roxy Velasquez
ROLE: Friend. Tom's twin sister.
SUPERPOWERS: Eating. Pocket picking. Inventing. NOT telling jokes!
DREAM: To meet E.T. or The Rock.

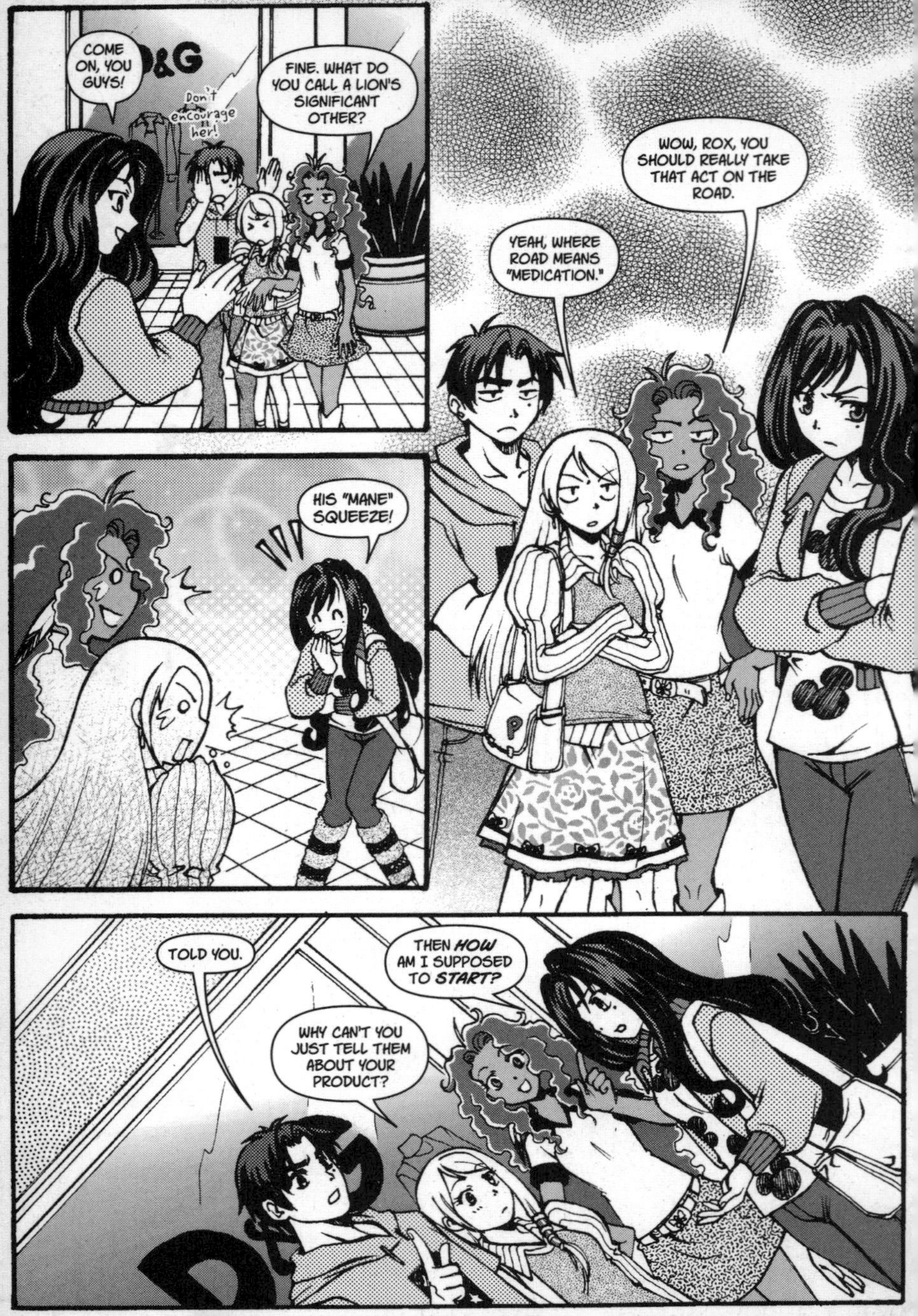
COME ON, YOU GUYS!
D&G
Don't encourage her!
FINE. WHAT DO YOU CALL A LION'S SIGNIFICANT OTHER?
HIS "MANE" SQUEEZE!
YEAH, WHERE ROAD MEANS "MEDICATION."
WOW, ROX, YOU SHOULD REALLY TAKE THAT ACT ON THE ROAD.
TOLD YOU.
THEN HOW AM I SUPPOSED TO START?
WHY CAN'T YOU JUST TELL THEM ABOUT YOUR PRODUCT?

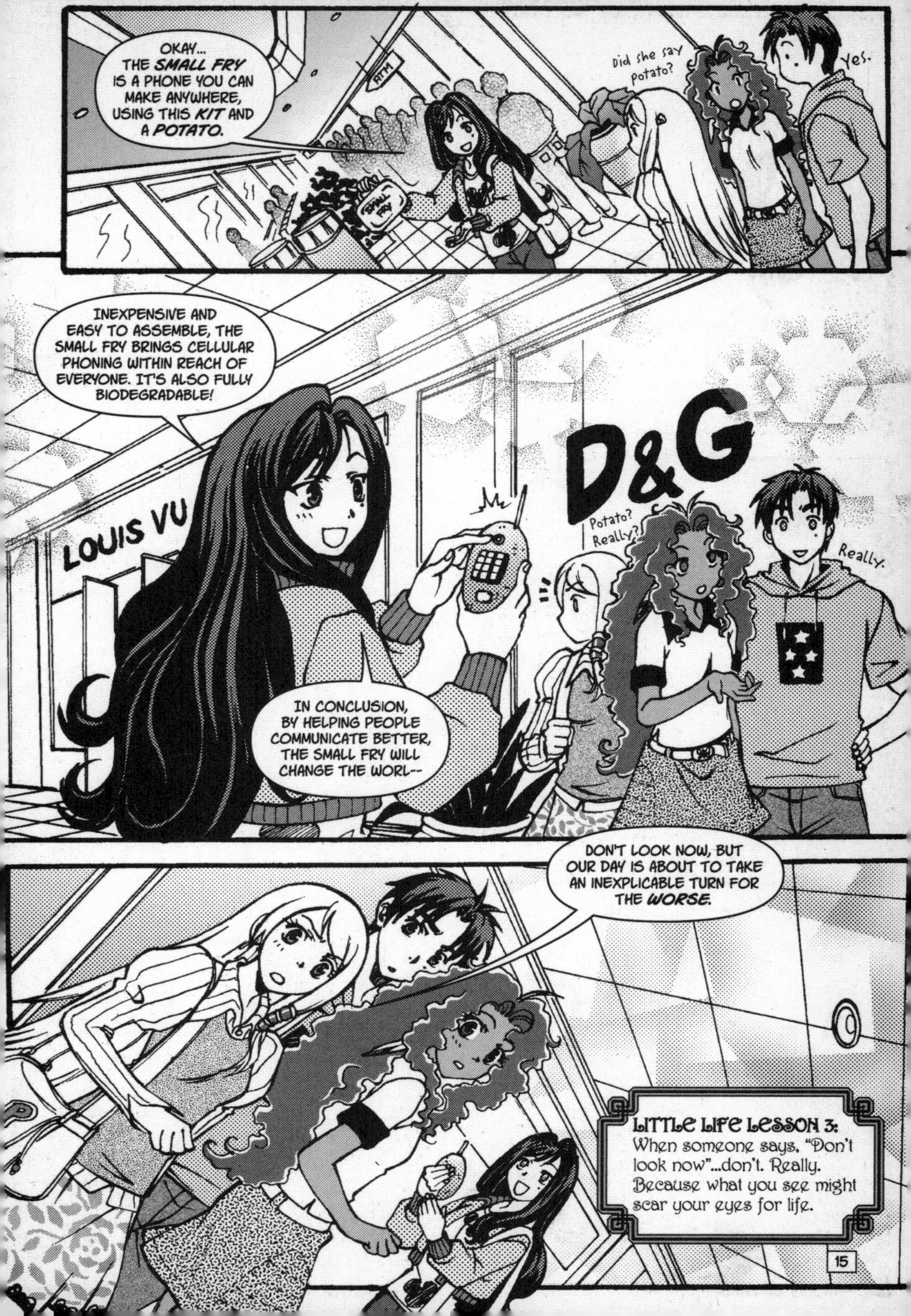
OKAY... THE SMALL FRY IS A PHONE YOU CAN MAKE ANYWHERE, USING THIS KIT AND A POTATO.
ATM
SMALL FRY
Did she say potato?
Yes.
INEXPENSIVE AND EASY TO ASSEMBLE, THE SMALL FRY BRINGS CELLULAR PHONING WITHIN REACH OF EVERYONE. IT'S ALSO FULLY BIODEGRADABLE!
LOUIS VU
D&G
Potato? Really?!
Really.
IN CONCLUSION, BY HELPING PEOPLE COMMUNICATE BETTER, THE SMALL FRY WILL CHANGE THE WORL--
DON'T LOOK NOW, BUT OUR DAY IS ABOUT TO TAKE AN INEXPLICABLE TURN FOR THE WORSE.
LITTLE LIFE LESSON 3:
When someone says, "Don't look now"...don't. Really. Because what you see might scar your eyes for life.

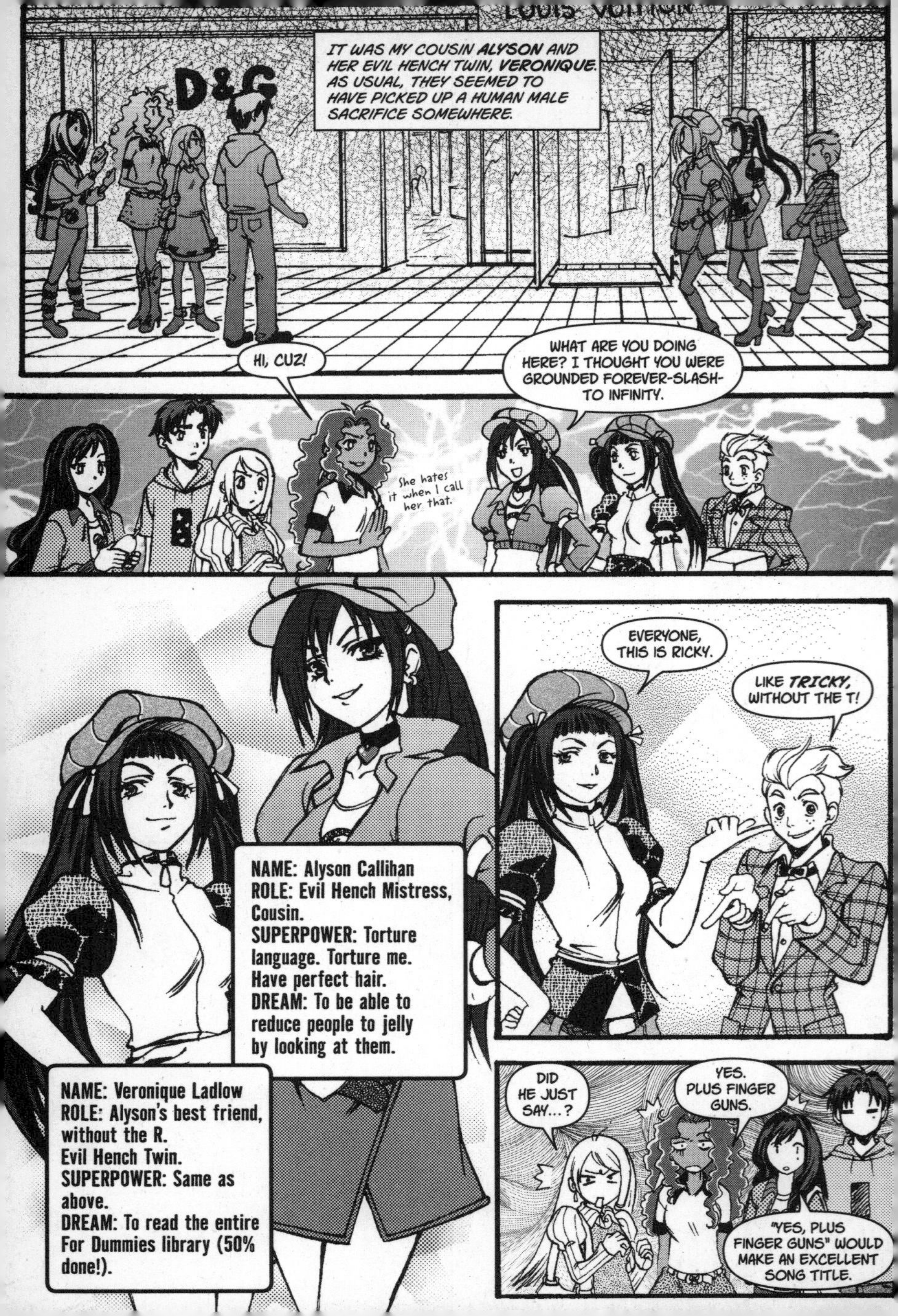

IT WAS MY COUSIN ALYSON AND HER EVIL HENCH TWIN, VERONIQUE. AS USUAL, THEY SEEMED TO HAVE PICKED UP A HUMAN MALE SACRIFICE SOMEWHERE.
D&G
HI, CUZ!
WHAT ARE YOU DOING HERE? I THOUGHT YOU WERE GROUNDED FOREVER-SLASH-TO INFINITY.
She hates it when I call her that.
NAME: Alyson Callihan
ROLE: Evil Hench Mistress, Cousin.
SUPERPOWER: Torture language. Torture me. Have perfect hair.
DREAM: To be able to reduce people to jelly by looking at them.
NAME: Veronique Ladlow
ROLE: Alyson's best friend, without the R. Evil Hench Twin.
SUPERPOWER: Same as above.
DREAM: To read the entire For Dummies library (50% done!).
EVERYONE, THIS IS RICKY.
LIKE TRICKY, WITHOUT THE T!
DID HE JUST SAY...?
YES. PLUS FINGER GUNS.
"YES, PLUS FINGER GUNS" WOULD MAKE AN EXCELLENT SONG TITLE.

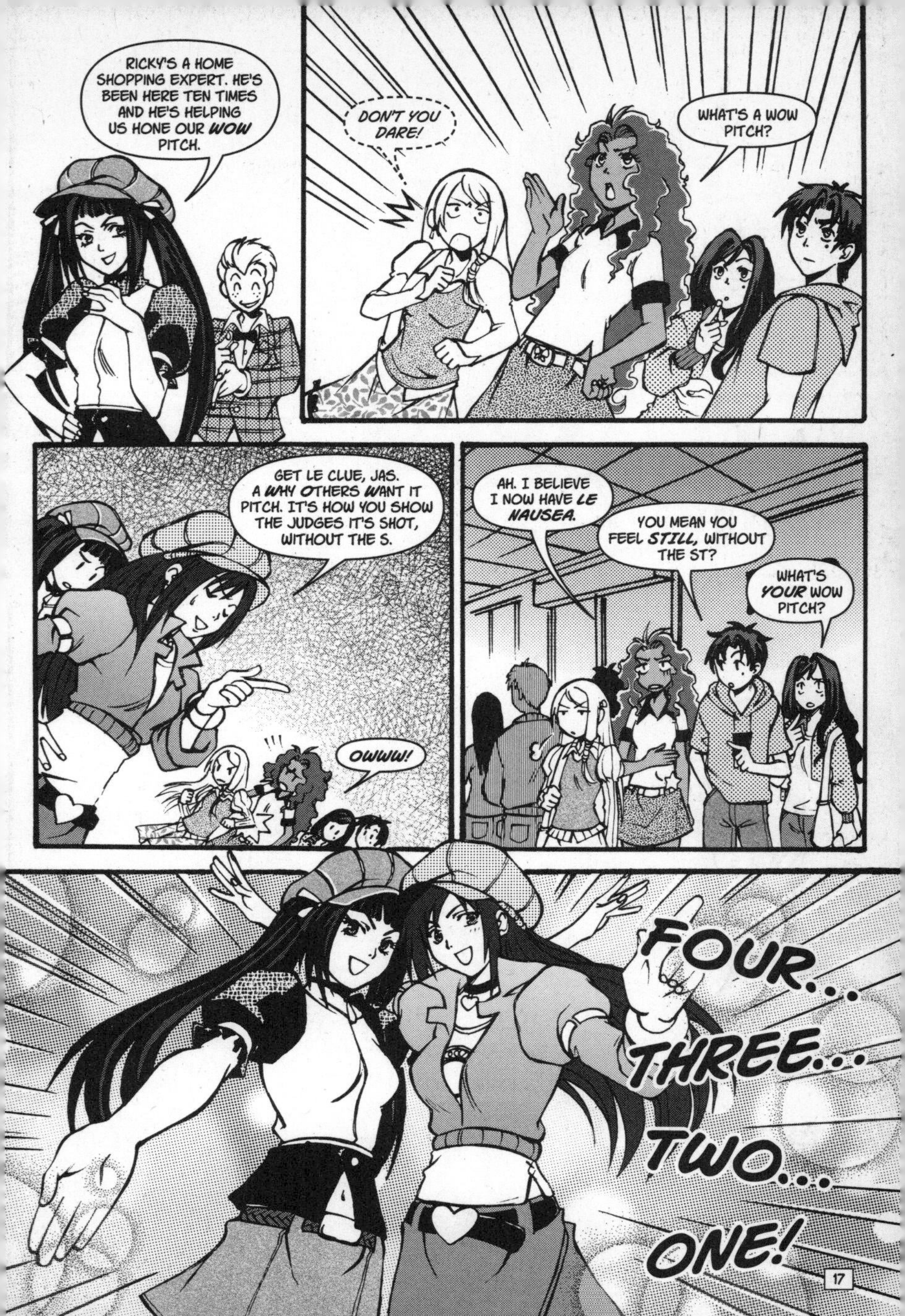

RICKY'S A HOME SHOPPING EXPERT. HE'S BEEN HERE TEN TIMES AND HE'S HELPING US HONE OUR WOW PITCH.
DON'T YOU DARE!
WHAT'S A WOW PITCH?
GET LE CLUE, JAS. A WHY OTHERS WANT IT PITCH. IT'S HOW YOU SHOW THE JUDGES IT'S SHOT, WITHOUT THE S.
!!!
OWWW!
AH. I BELIEVE I NOW HAVE LE NAUSEA.
YOU MEAN YOU FEEL STILL, WITHOUT THE ST?
WHAT'S YOUR WOW PITCH?
FOUR...
THREE...
TWO...
ONE!

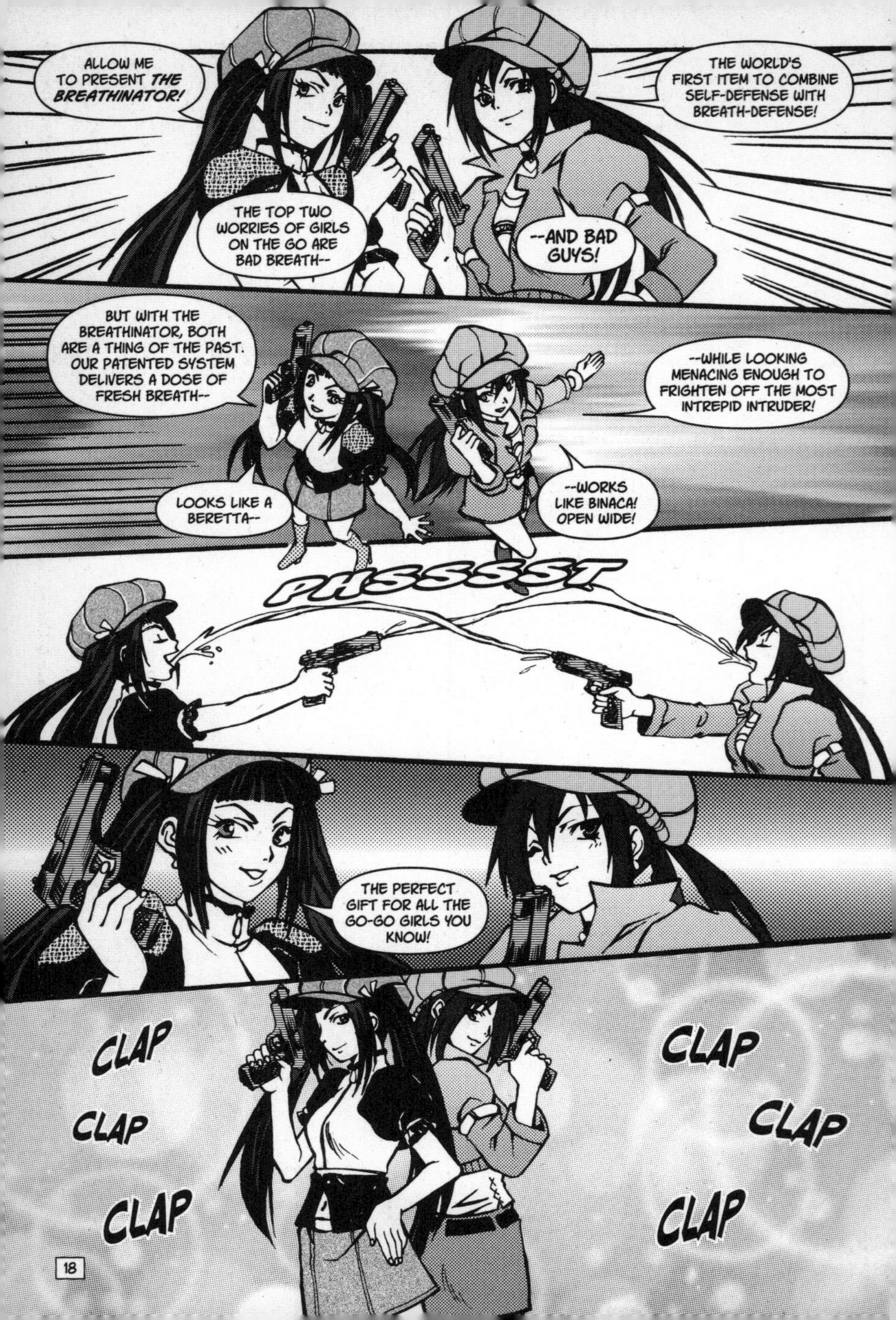
ALLOW ME TO PRESENT *THE BREATHINATOR!*
THE WORLD'S FIRST ITEM TO COMBINE SELF-DEFENSE WITH BREATH-DEFENSE!
THE TOP TWO WORRIES OF GIRLS ON THE GO ARE BAD BREATH--
--AND BAD GUYS!
BUT WITH THE BREATHINATOR, BOTH ARE A THING OF THE PAST. OUR PATENTED SYSTEM DELIVERS A DOSE OF FRESH BREATH--
--WHILE LOOKING MENACING ENOUGH TO FRIGHTEN OFF THE MOST INTREPID INTRUDER!
LOOKS LIKE A BERETTA--
--WORKS LIKE BINACA! OPEN WIDE!
PHSSSST
THE PERFECT GIFT FOR ALL THE GO-GO GIRLS YOU KNOW!
CLAP
CLAP
CLAP
CLAP
CLAP
CLAP

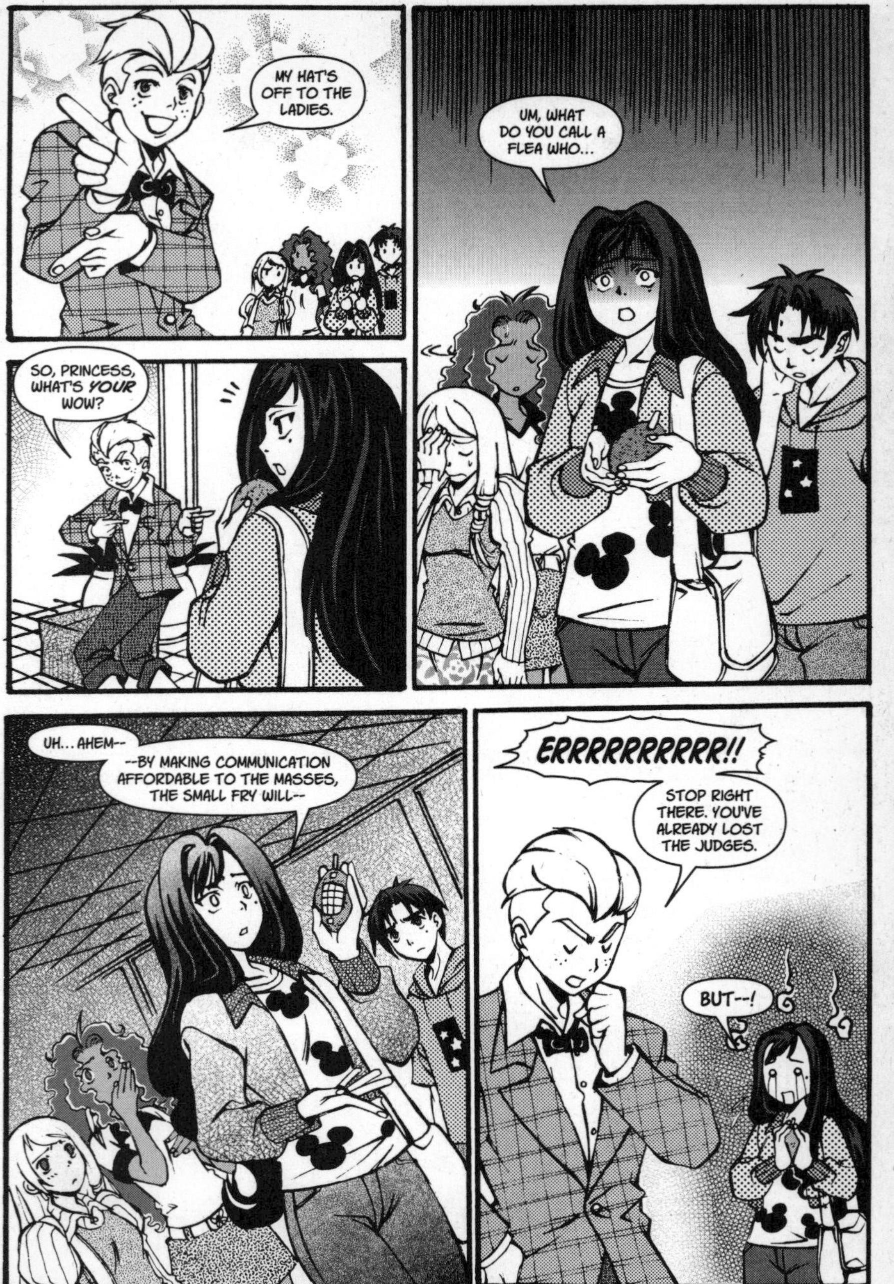
MY HAT'S OFF TO THE LADIES.
UM, WHAT DO YOU CALL A FLEA WHO...
SO, PRINCESS, WHAT'S *YOUR* WOW?
UH... AHEM--
--BY MAKING COMMUNICATION AFFORDABLE TO THE MASSES, THE SMALL FRY WILL--
ERRRRRRRRRR!!
STOP RIGHT THERE. YOU'VE ALREADY LOST THE JUDGES.
BUT--!

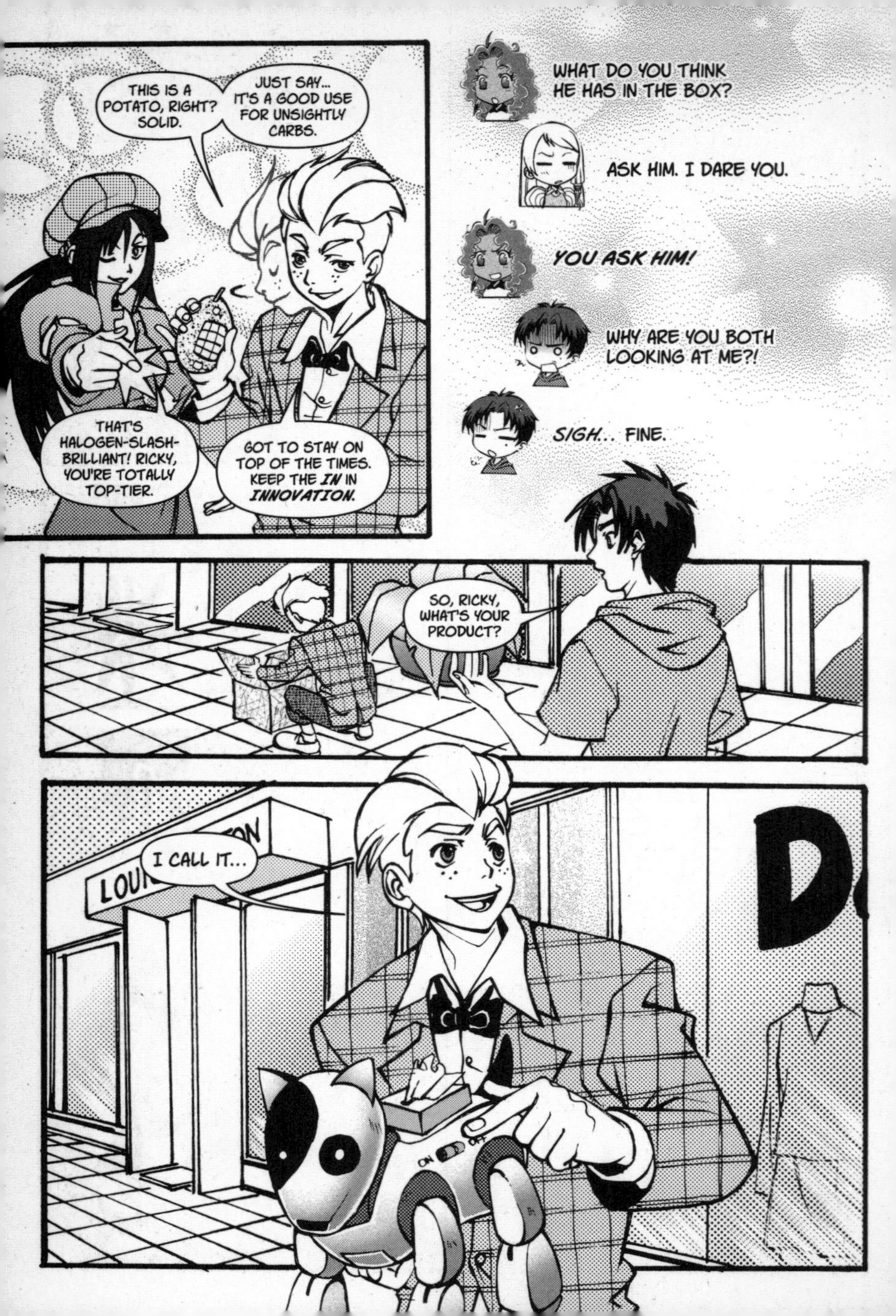
THIS IS A POTATO, RIGHT? SOLID.
JUST SAY... IT'S A GOOD USE FOR UNSIGHTLY CARBS.
THAT'S HALOGEN-SLASH-BRILLIANT! RICKY, YOU'RE TOTALLY TOP-TIER.
GOT TO STAY ON TOP OF THE TIMES. KEEP THE *IN* IN *INNOVATION*.
WHAT DO YOU THINK HE HAS IN THE BOX?
ASK HIM. I DARE YOU.
YOU ASK HIM!
WHY ARE YOU BOTH LOOKING AT ME?!
SIGH... FINE.
SO, RICKY, WHAT'S YOUR PRODUCT?
I CALL IT...
ON
OFF

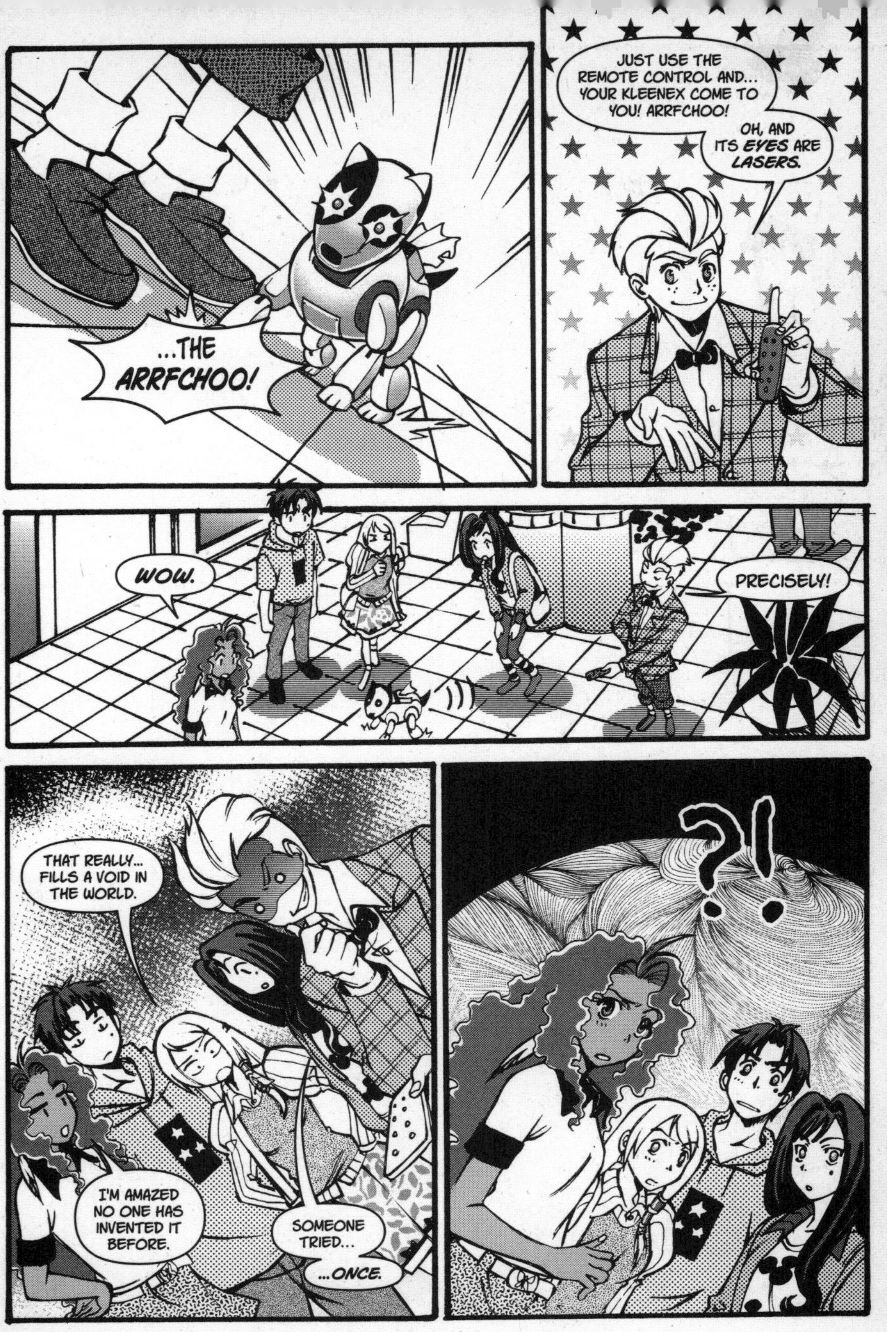
...THE ARRFCHOO!
JUST USE THE REMOTE CONTROL AND... YOUR KLEENEX COME TO YOU! ARRFCHOO!
OH, AND ITS EYES ARE LASERS.
WOW.
PRECISELY!
THAT REALLY... FILLS A VOID IN THE WORLD.
I'M AMAZED NO ONE HAS INVENTED IT BEFORE.
SOMEONE TRIED...
...ONCE.
?!

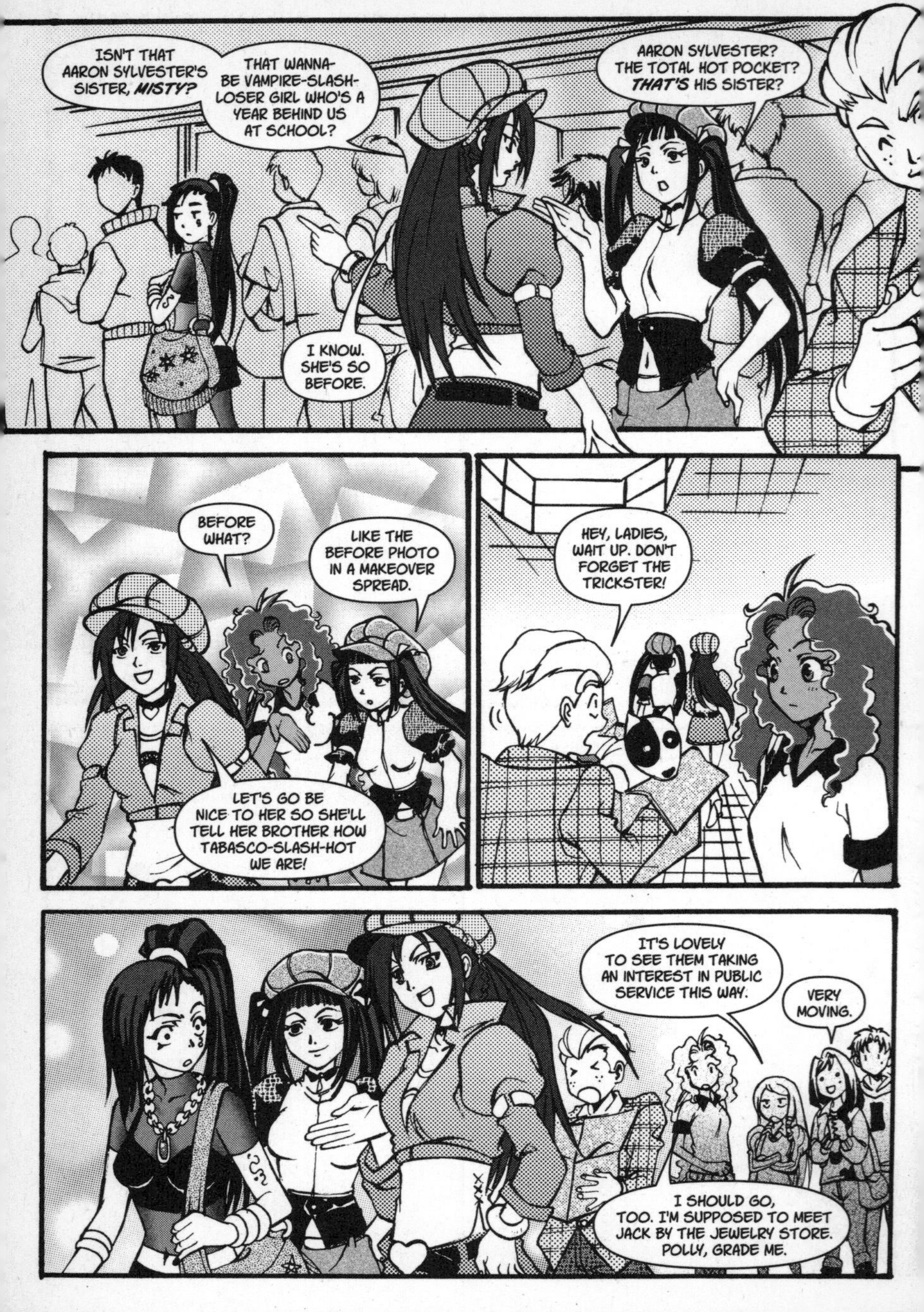
ISN'T THAT AARON SYLVESTER'S SISTER, *MISTY?*
THAT WANNA-BE VAMPIRE-SLASH-LOSER GIRL WHO'S A YEAR BEHIND US AT SCHOOL?
AARON SYLVESTER? THE TOTAL HOT POCKET? *THAT'S* HIS SISTER?
I KNOW. SHE'S SO BEFORE.
BEFORE WHAT?
LIKE THE BEFORE PHOTO IN A MAKEOVER SPREAD.
LET'S GO BE NICE TO HER SO SHE'LL TELL HER BROTHER HOW TABASCO-SLASH-HOT WE ARE!
HEY, LADIES, WAIT UP. DON'T FORGET THE TRICKSTER!
IT'S LOVELY TO SEE THEM TAKING AN INTEREST IN PUBLIC SERVICE THIS WAY.
VERY MOVING.
I SHOULD GO, TOO. I'M SUPPOSED TO MEET JACK BY THE JEWELRY STORE. POLLY, GRADE ME.

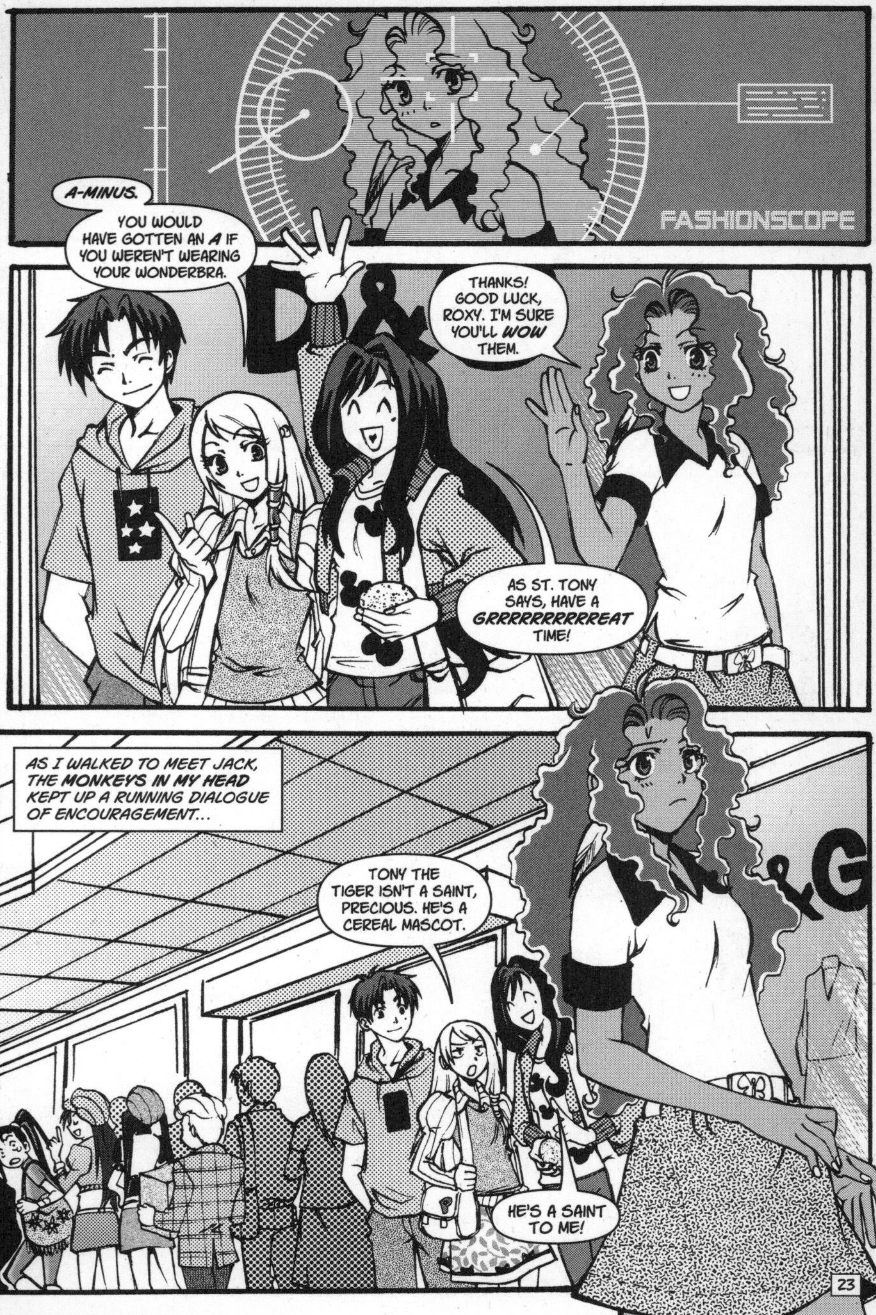
FASHIONSCOPE
A-MINUS.
YOU WOULD HAVE GOTTEN AN *A* IF YOU WEREN'T WEARING YOUR WONDERBRA.
THANKS! GOOD LUCK, ROXY. I'M SURE YOU'LL *WOW* THEM.
AS ST. TONY SAYS, HAVE A *GRRRRRRRRRREAT* TIME!
AS I WALKED TO MEET JACK, THE **MONKEYS IN MY HEAD** KEPT UP A RUNNING DIALOGUE OF ENCOURAGEMENT...
TONY THE TIGER ISN'T A SAINT, PRECIOUS. HE'S A CEREAL MASCOT.
HE'S A SAINT TO ME!

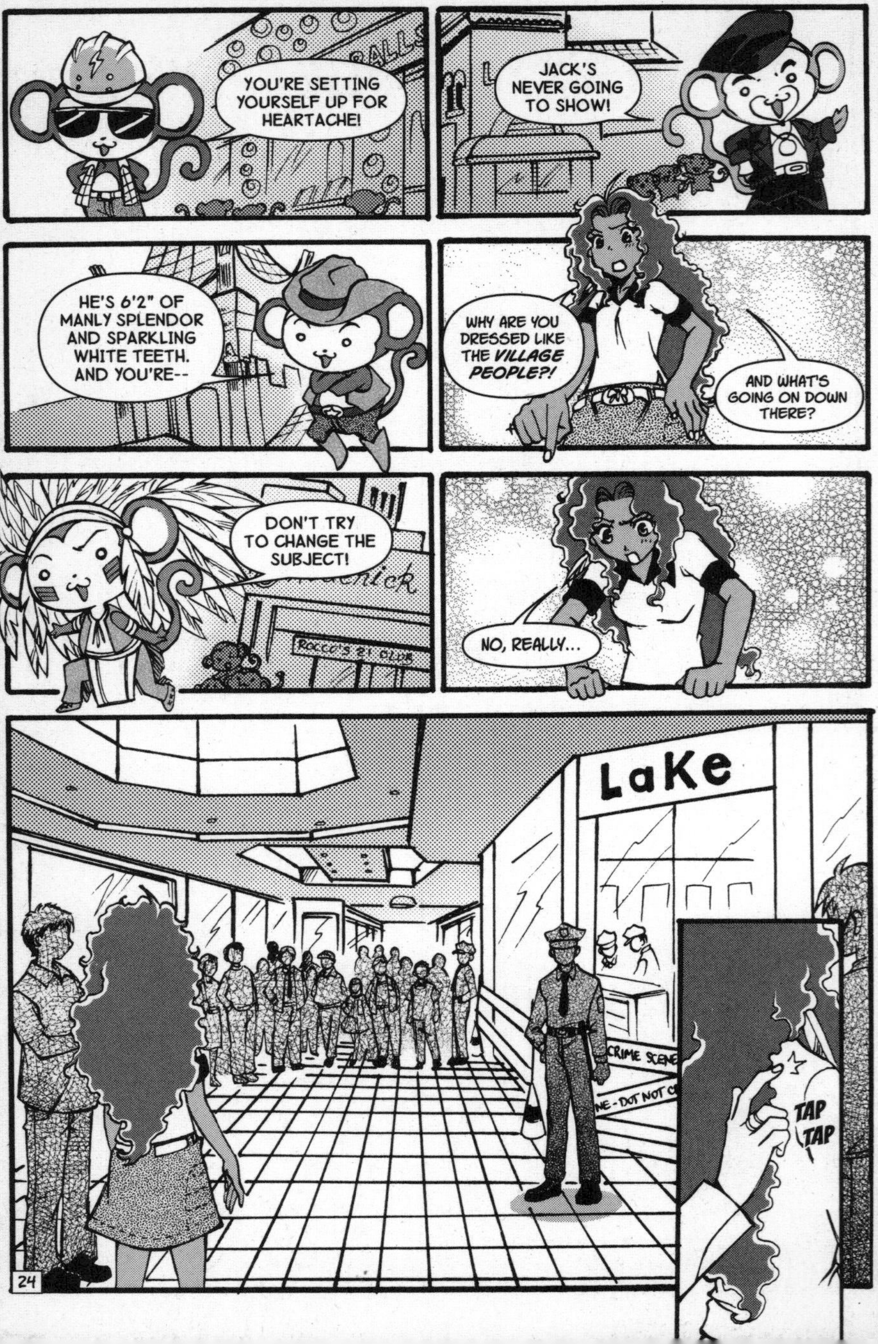
YOU'RE SETTING YOURSELF UP FOR HEARTACHE!
JACK'S NEVER GOING TO SHOW!
HE'S 6'2" OF MANLY SPLENDOR AND SPARKLING WHITE TEETH. AND YOU'RE--
WHY ARE YOU DRESSED LIKE THE *VILLAGE PEOPLE?!*
AND WHAT'S GOING ON DOWN THERE?
DON'T TRY TO CHANGE THE SUBJECT!
NO, REALLY...
LaKe
CRIME SCENE
TAP TAP

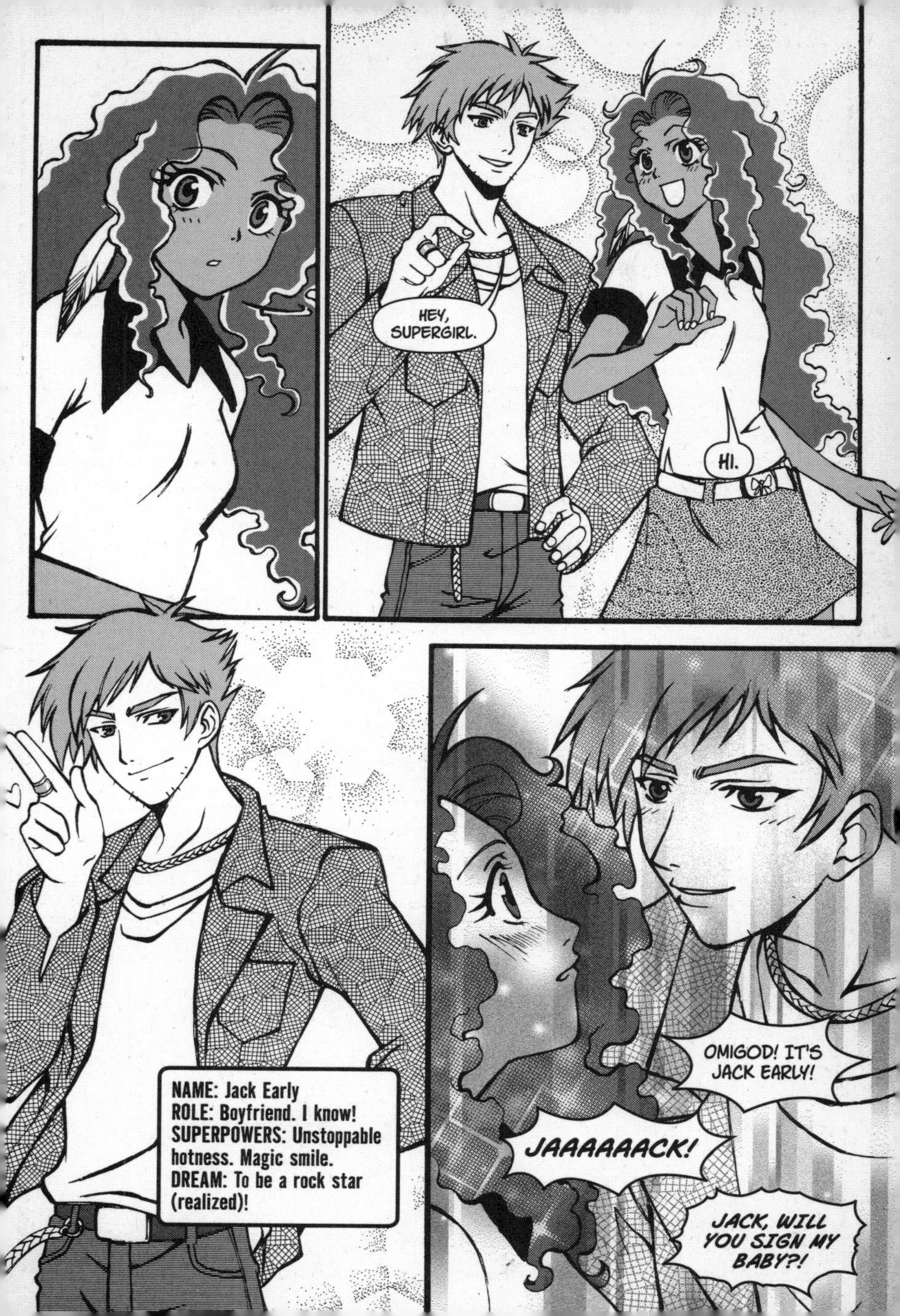
HEY, SUPERGIRL.
HI.
NAME: Jack Early
ROLE: Boyfriend. I know!
SUPERPOWERS: Unstoppable hotness. Magic smile.
DREAM: To be a rock star (realized)!
OMIGOD! IT'S JACK EARLY!
JAAAAAACK!
JACK, WILL YOU SIGN MY BABY?!

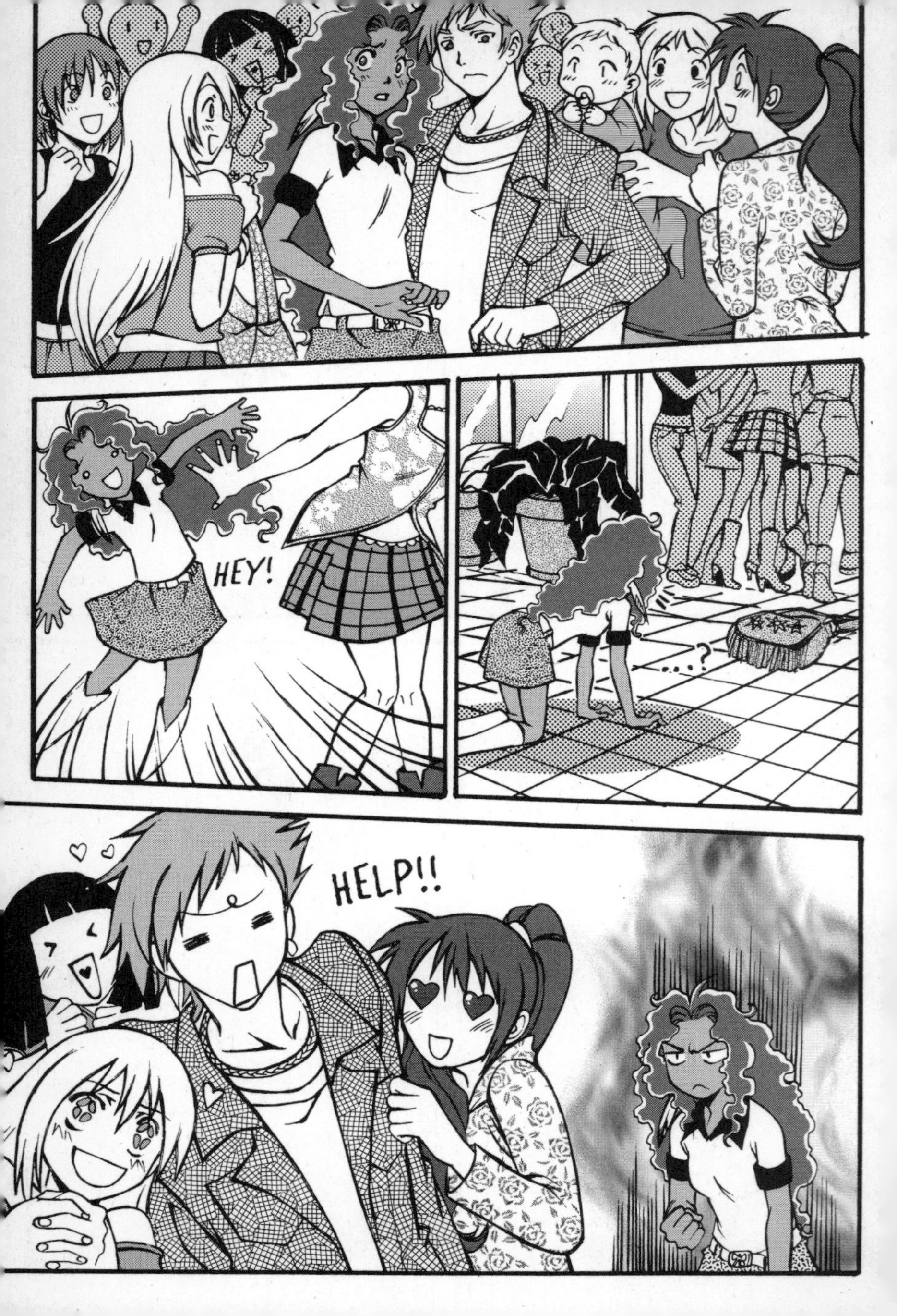
HEY!
...?
HELP!!

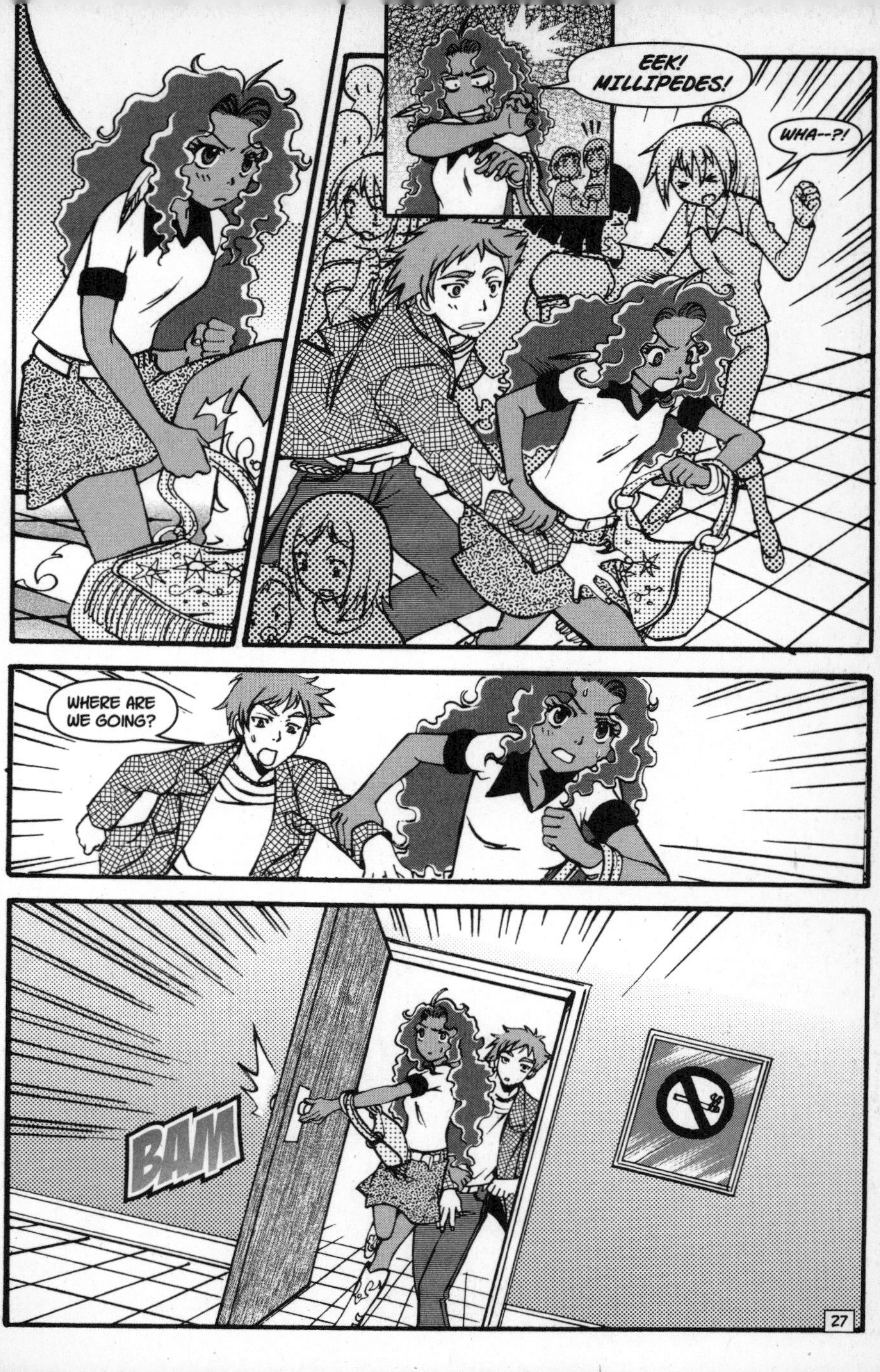
EEK! MILLIPEDES!
WHA--?!
WHERE ARE WE GOING?
BAM

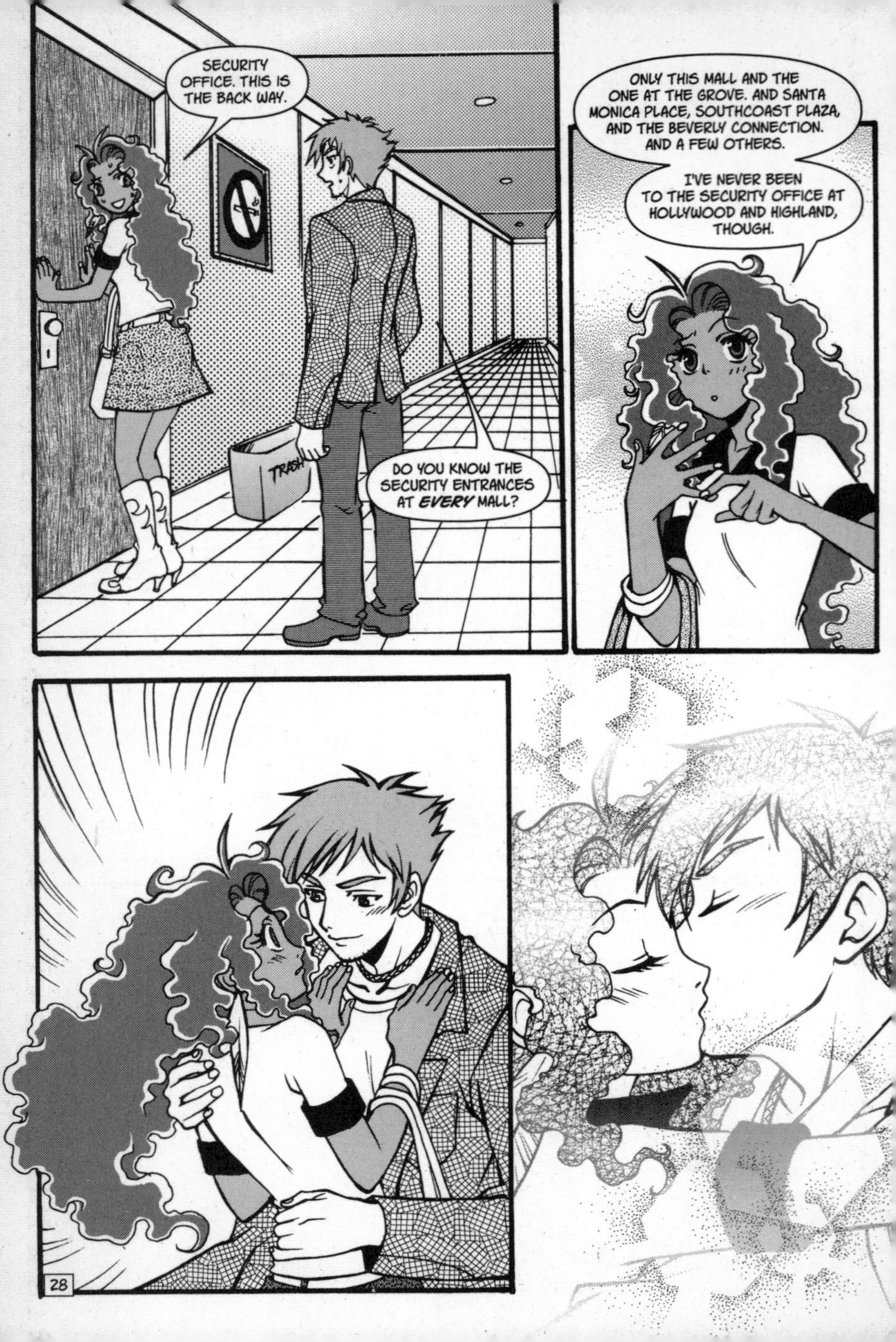
SECURITY OFFICE. THIS IS THE BACK WAY.
TRASH
DO YOU KNOW THE SECURITY ENTRANCES AT *EVERY* MALL?
ONLY THIS MALL AND THE ONE AT THE GROVE. AND SANTA MONICA PLACE, SOUTHCOAST PLAZA, AND THE BEVERLY CONNECTION. AND A FEW OTHERS.
I'VE NEVER BEEN TO THE SECURITY OFFICE AT HOLLYWOOD AND HIGHLAND, THOUGH.

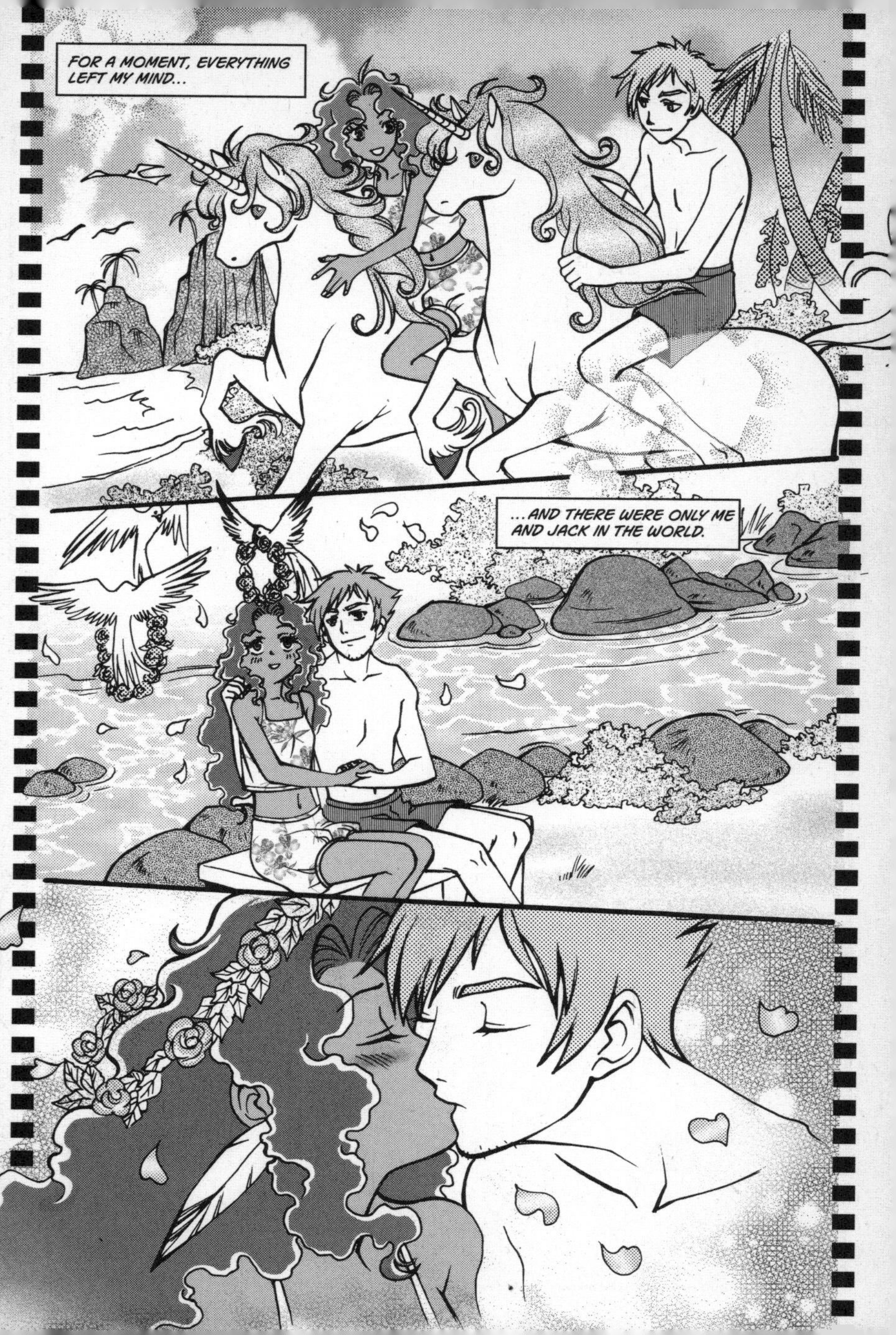
FOR A MOMENT, EVERYTHING LEFT MY MIND...
...AND THERE WERE ONLY ME AND JACK IN THE WORLD.

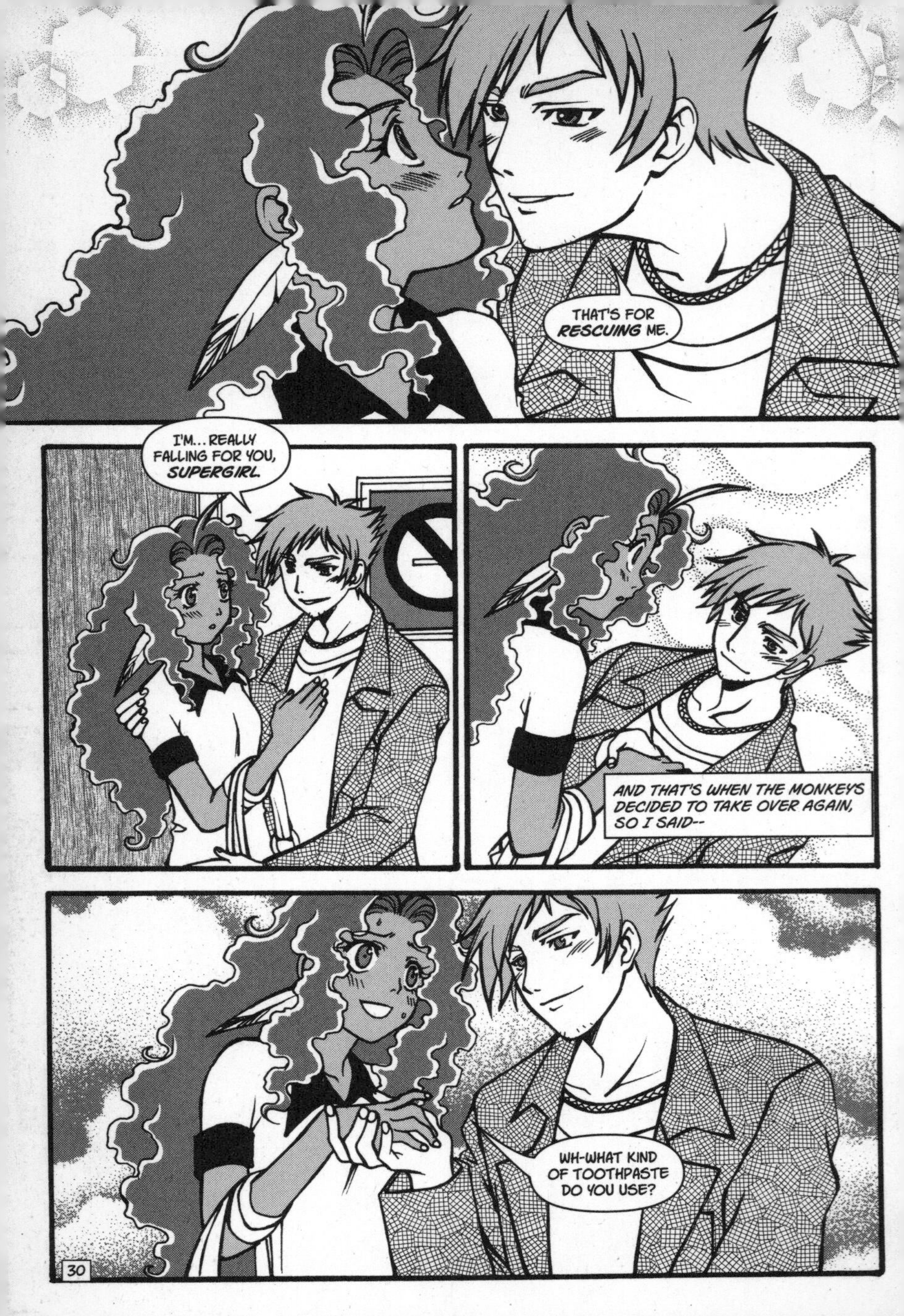
THAT'S FOR *RESCUING* ME.
I'M... REALLY FALLING FOR YOU, *SUPERGIRL.*
AND THAT'S WHEN THE MONKEYS DECIDED TO TAKE OVER AGAIN, SO I SAID--
WH-WHAT KIND OF TOOTHPASTE DO YOU USE?

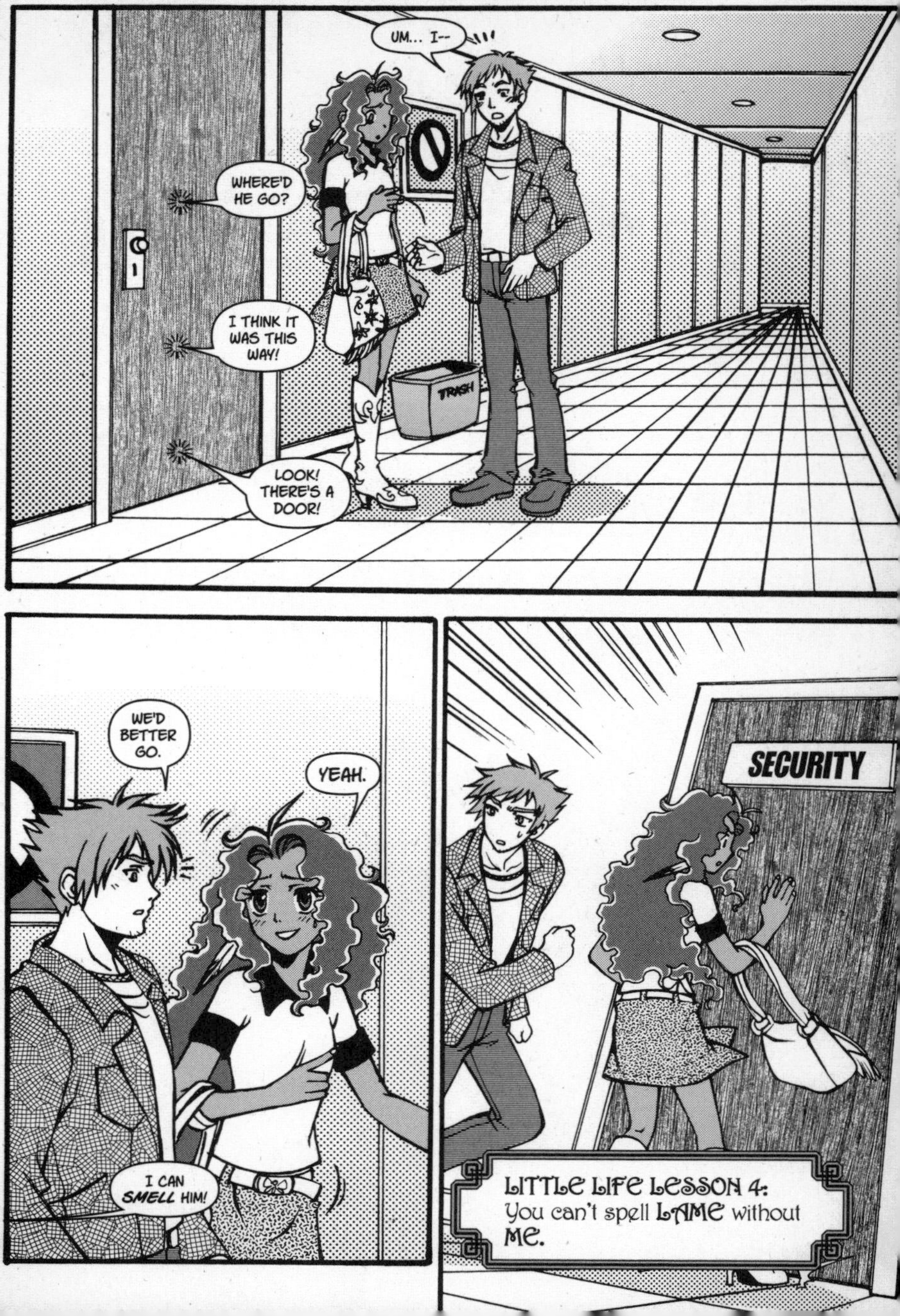
UM... I--
WHERE'D HE GO?
I THINK IT WAS THIS WAY!
TRASH
LOOK! THERE'S A DOOR!
WE'D BETTER GO.
YEAH.
I CAN SMELL HIM!
SECURITY
LITTLE LIFE LESSON 4:
You can't spell LAME without ME.

Chapter Two

Jasmine Callihan

HAIR: Attack Mode!

PORES: Medium

HEART: FALLING

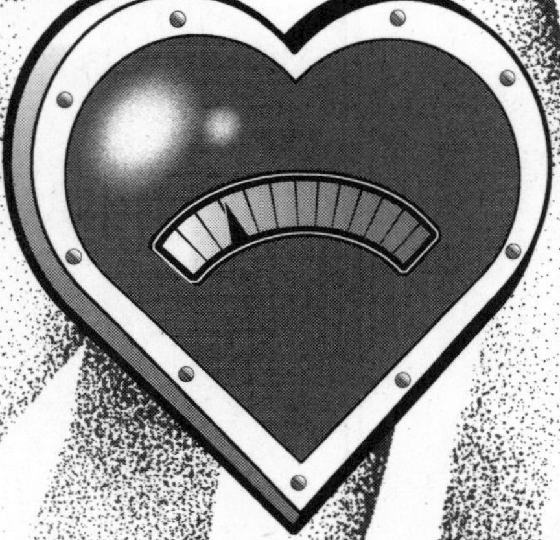

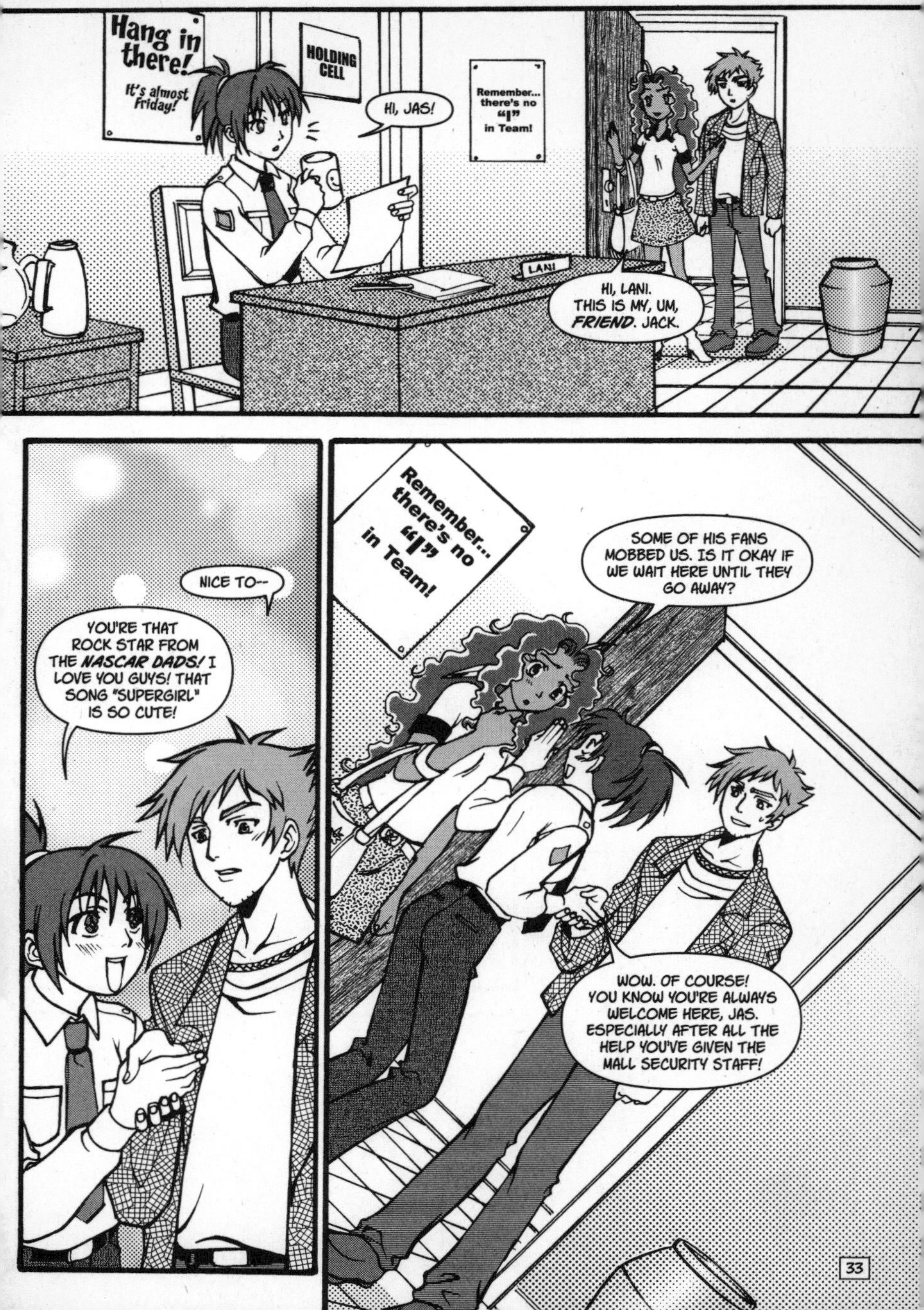
Hang in there!
It's almost Friday!
HOLDING CELL
HI, JAS!
Remember... there's no "I" in Team!
LANI
HI, LANI. THIS IS MY, UM, FRIEND. JACK.
NICE TO--
YOU'RE THAT ROCK STAR FROM THE NASCAR DADS! I LOVE YOU GUYS! THAT SONG "SUPERGIRL" IS SO CUTE!
Remember... there's no "I" in Team!
SOME OF HIS FANS MOBBED US. IS IT OKAY IF WE WAIT HERE UNTIL THEY GO AWAY?
WOW. OF COURSE! YOU KNOW YOU'RE ALWAYS WELCOME HERE, JAS. ESPECIALLY AFTER ALL THE HELP YOU'VE GIVEN THE MALL SECURITY STAFF!

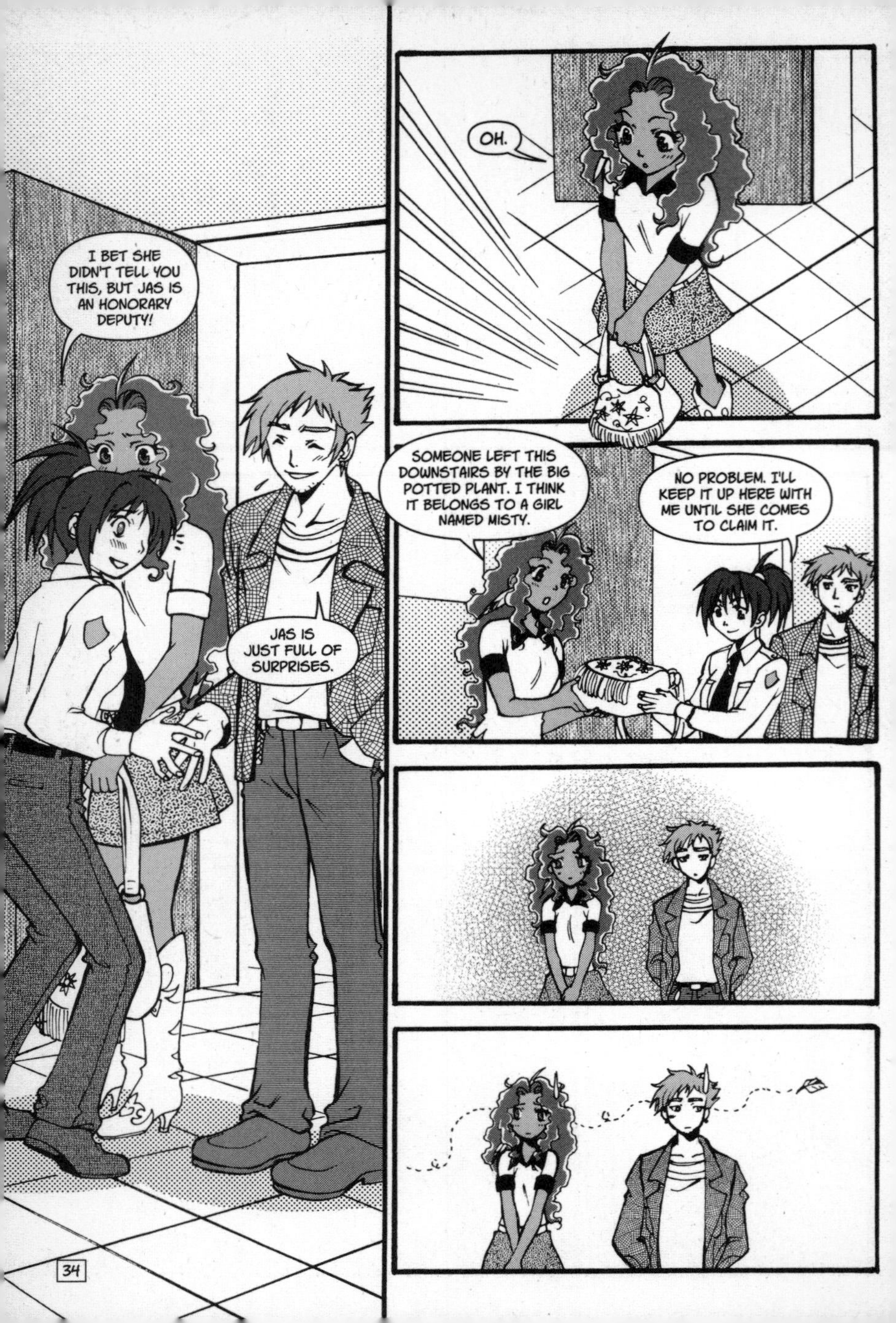
I BET SHE DIDN'T TELL YOU THIS, BUT JAS IS AN HONORARY DEPUTY!
JAS IS JUST FULL OF SURPRISES.
OH.
SOMEONE LEFT THIS DOWNSTAIRS BY THE BIG POTTED PLANT. I THINK IT BELONGS TO A GIRL NAMED MISTY.
NO PROBLEM. I'LL KEEP IT UP HERE WITH ME UNTIL SHE COMES TO CLAIM IT.

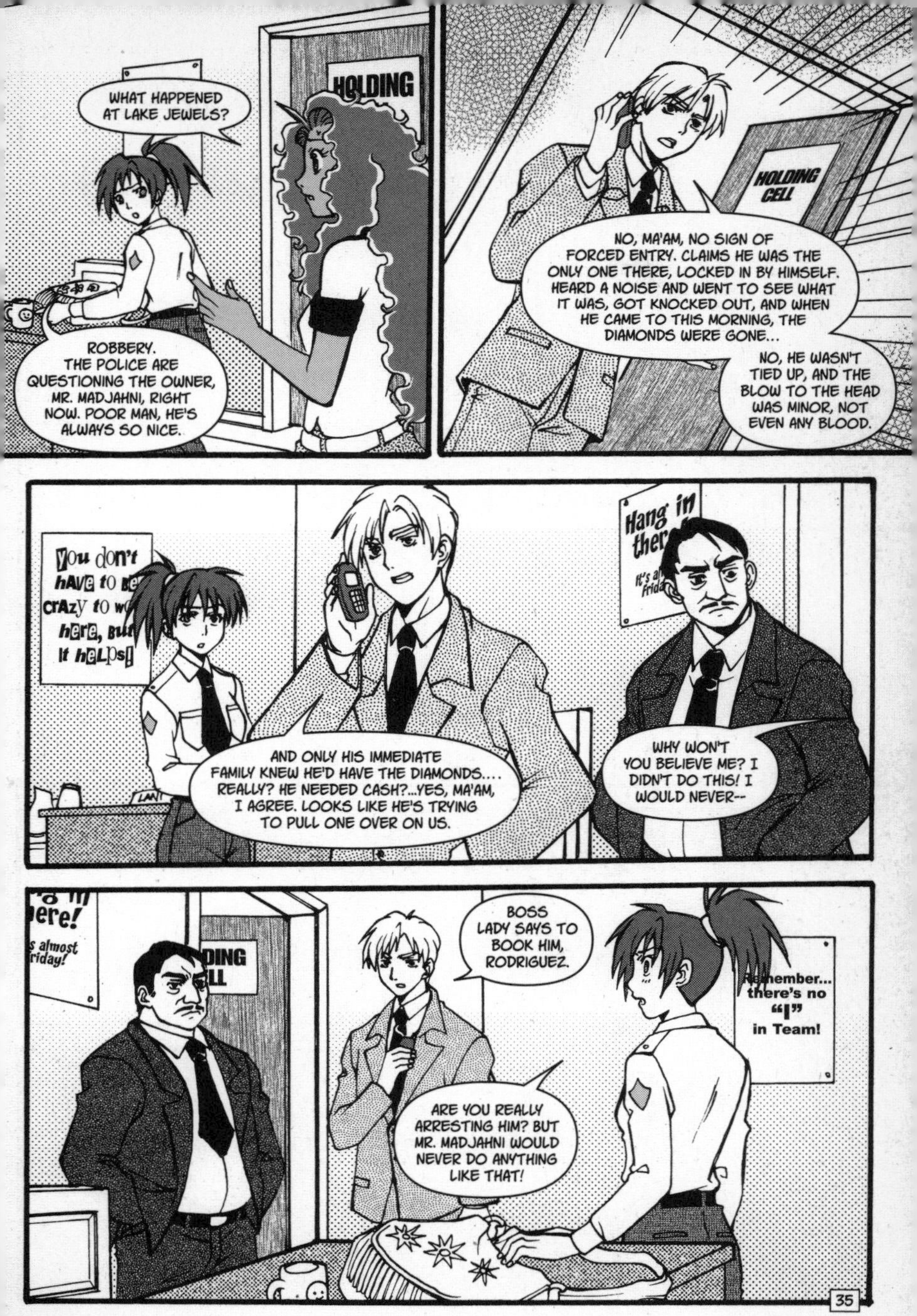
HOLDING
WHAT HAPPENED AT LAKE JEWELS?
ROBBERY. THE POLICE ARE QUESTIONING THE OWNER, MR. MADJAHNI, RIGHT NOW. POOR MAN, HE'S ALWAYS SO NICE.
HOLDING CELL
NO, MA'AM, NO SIGN OF FORCED ENTRY. CLAIMS HE WAS THE ONLY ONE THERE, LOCKED IN BY HIMSELF. HEARD A NOISE AND WENT TO SEE WHAT IT WAS, GOT KNOCKED OUT, AND WHEN HE CAME TO THIS MORNING, THE DIAMONDS WERE GONE...
NO, HE WASN'T TIED UP, AND THE BLOW TO THE HEAD WAS MINOR, NOT EVEN ANY BLOOD.
AND ONLY HIS IMMEDIATE FAMILY KNEW HE'D HAVE THE DIAMONDS.... REALLY? HE NEEDED CASH?...YES, MA'AM, I AGREE. LOOKS LIKE HE'S TRYING TO PULL ONE OVER ON US.
WHY WON'T YOU BELIEVE ME? I DIDN'T DO THIS! I WOULD NEVER--
BOSS LADY SAYS TO BOOK HIM, RODRIGUEZ.
ARE YOU REALLY ARRESTING HIM? BUT MR. MADJAHNI WOULD NEVER DO ANYTHING LIKE THAT!

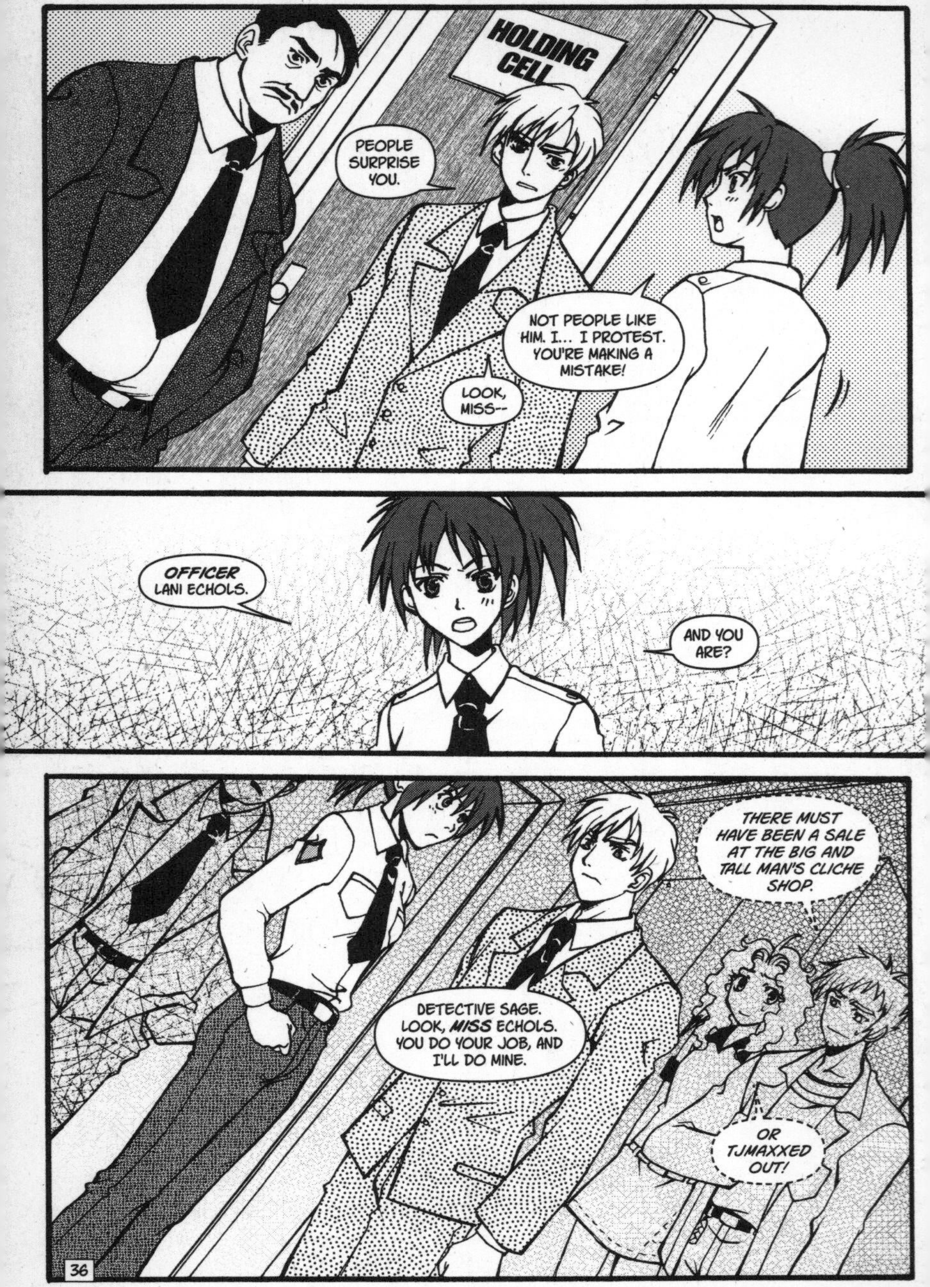
HOLDING CELL
PEOPLE SURPRISE YOU.
NOT PEOPLE LIKE HIM. I... I PROTEST. YOU'RE MAKING A MISTAKE!
LOOK, MISS--
OFFICER LANI ECHOLS.
AND YOU ARE?
DETECTIVE SAGE. LOOK, MISS ECHOLS. YOU DO YOUR JOB, AND I'LL DO MINE.
THERE MUST HAVE BEEN A SALE AT THE BIG AND TALL MAN'S CLICHE SHOP.
OR TJMAXXED OUT!

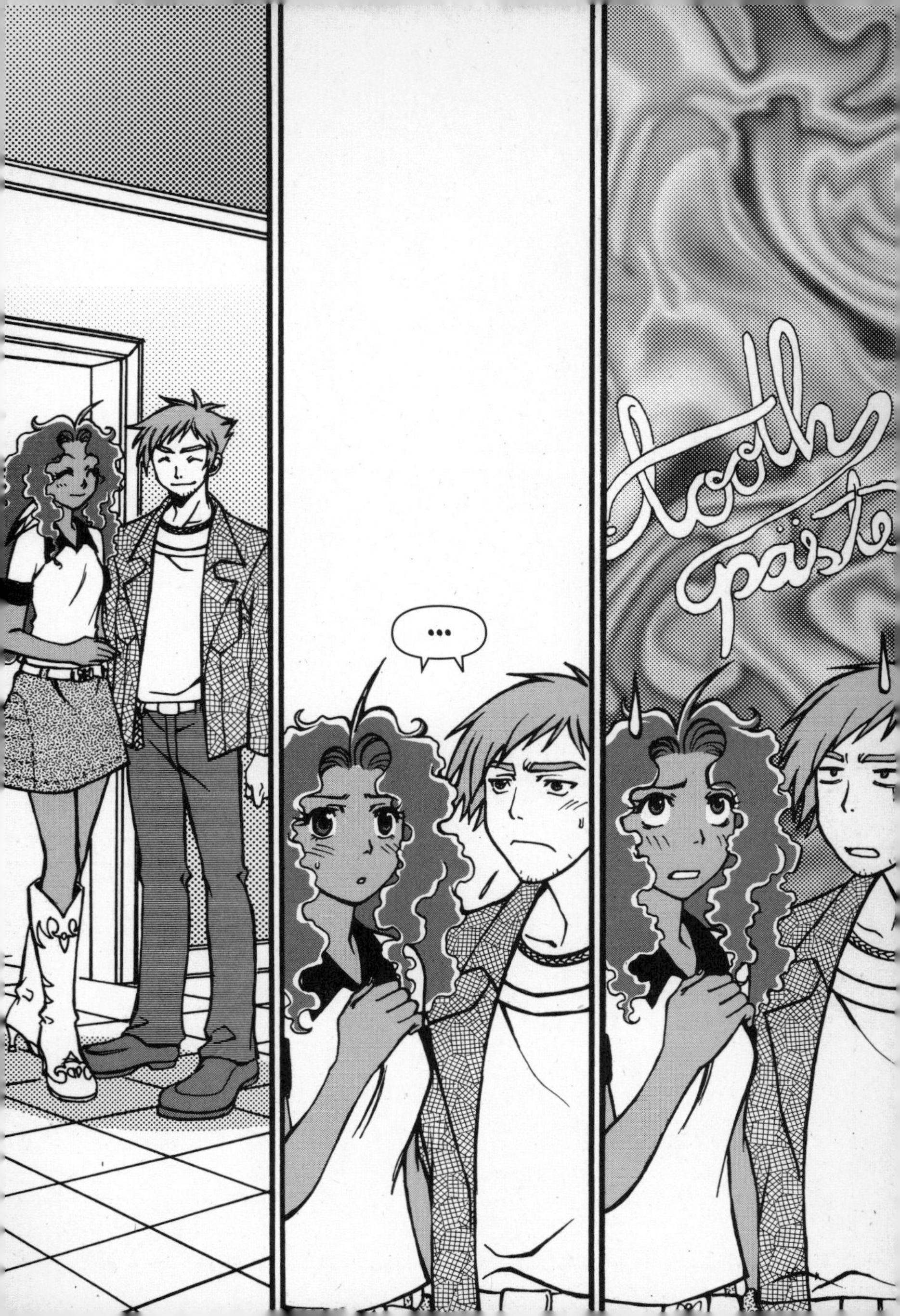
...
tooth paste

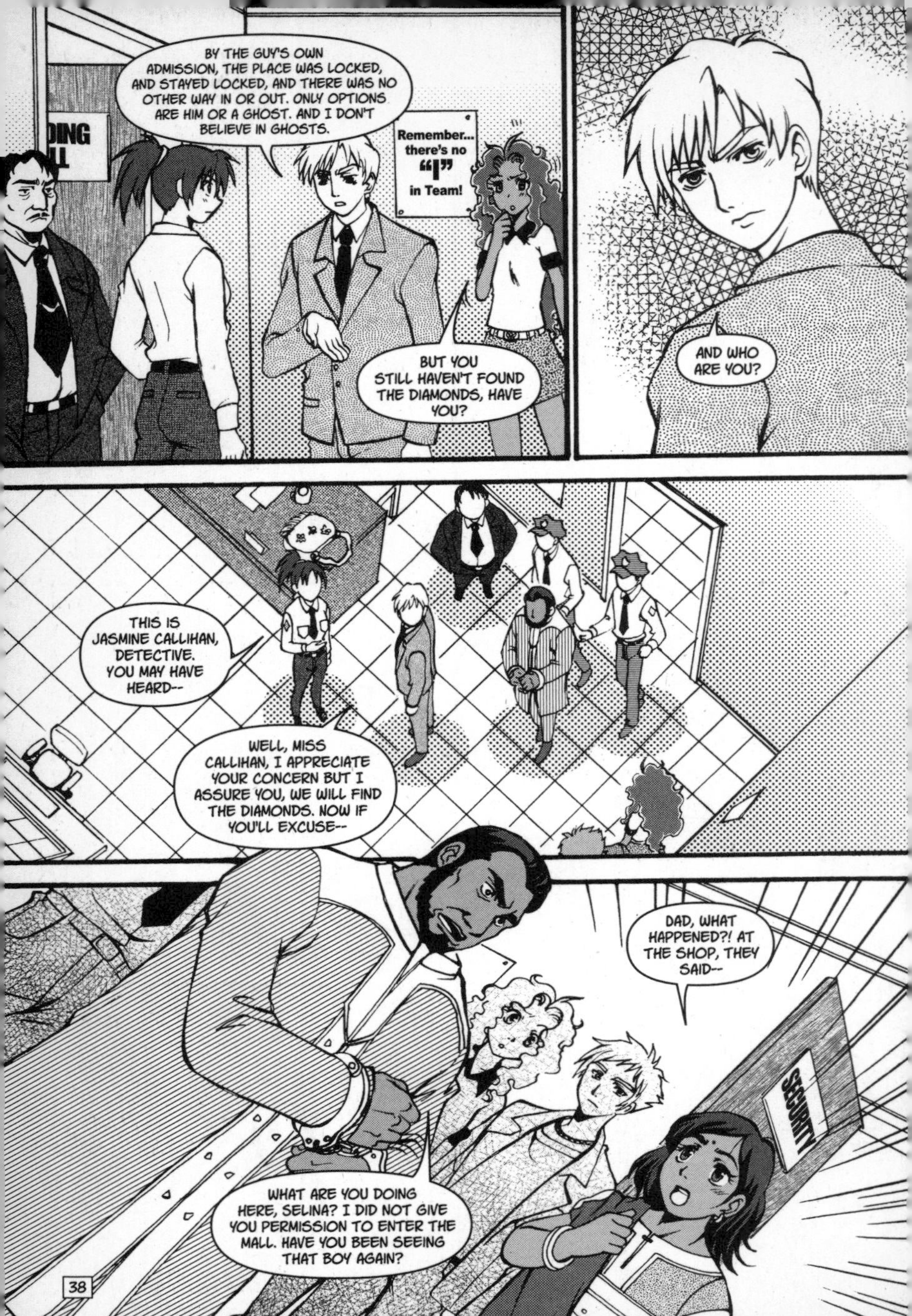

DOING
BY THE GUY'S OWN ADMISSION, THE PLACE WAS LOCKED, AND STAYED LOCKED, AND THERE WAS NO OTHER WAY IN OR OUT. ONLY OPTIONS ARE HIM OR A GHOST. AND I DON'T BELIEVE IN GHOSTS.
Remember... there's no "I" in Team!
BUT YOU STILL HAVEN'T FOUND THE DIAMONDS, HAVE YOU?
AND WHO ARE YOU?
THIS IS JASMINE CALLIHAN, DETECTIVE. YOU MAY HAVE HEARD--
WELL, MISS CALLIHAN, I APPRECIATE YOUR CONCERN BUT I ASSURE YOU, WE WILL FIND THE DIAMONDS. NOW IF YOU'LL EXCUSE--
DAD, WHAT HAPPENED?! AT THE SHOP, THEY SAID--
SECURITY
WHAT ARE YOU DOING HERE, SELINA? I DID NOT GIVE YOU PERMISSION TO ENTER THE MALL. HAVE YOU BEEN SEEING THAT BOY AGAIN?

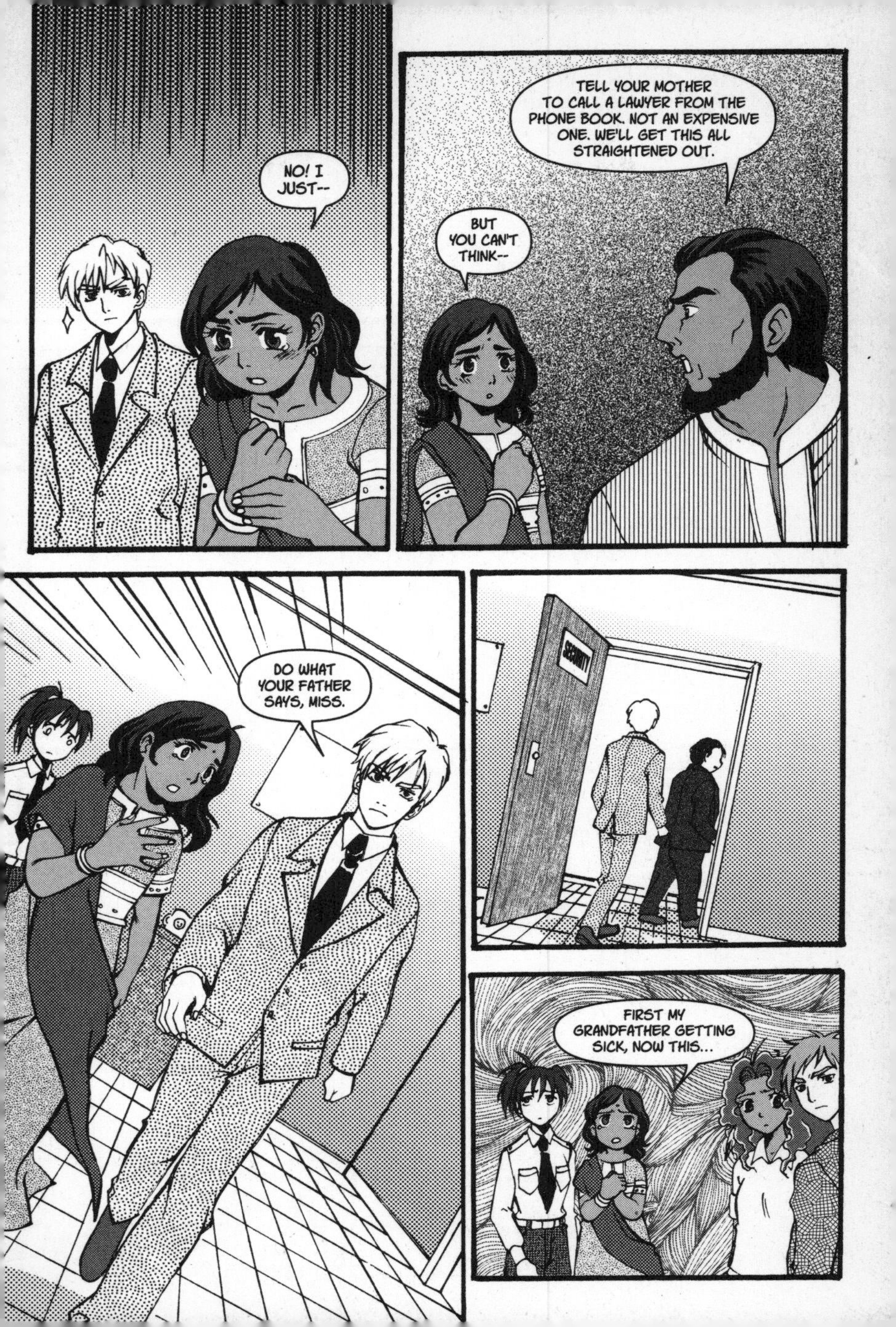
NO! I JUST--
TELL YOUR MOTHER TO CALL A LAWYER FROM THE PHONE BOOK. NOT AN EXPENSIVE ONE. WE'LL GET THIS ALL STRAIGHTENED OUT.
BUT YOU CAN'T THINK--
DO WHAT YOUR FATHER SAYS, MISS.
SECURITY
FIRST MY GRANDFATHER GETTING SICK, NOW THIS...

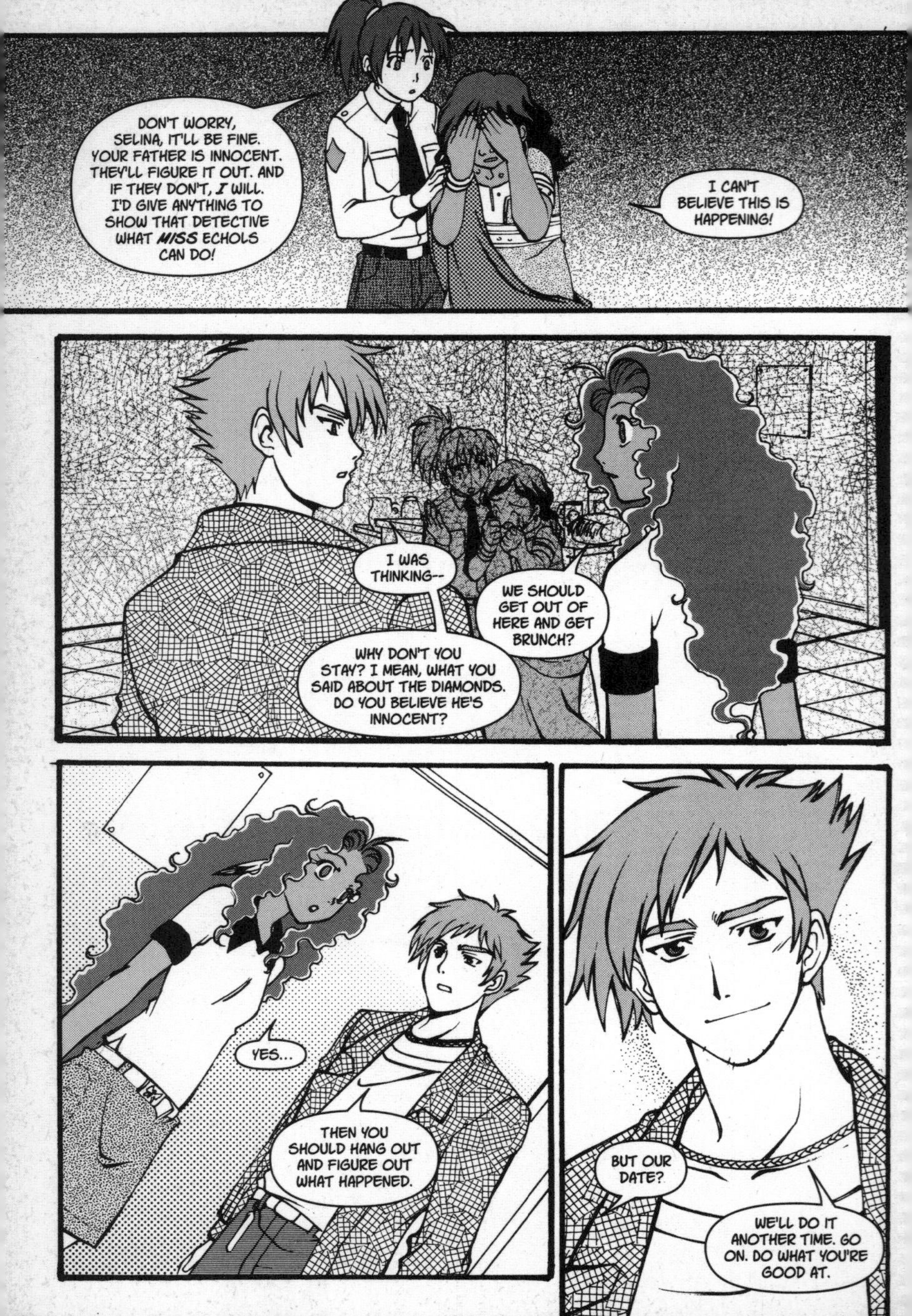
DON'T WORRY, SELINA, IT'LL BE FINE. YOUR FATHER IS INNOCENT. THEY'LL FIGURE IT OUT. AND IF THEY DON'T, I WILL. I'D GIVE ANYTHING TO SHOW THAT DETECTIVE WHAT MISS ECHOLS CAN DO!
I CAN'T BELIEVE THIS IS HAPPENING!
I WAS THINKING--
WE SHOULD GET OUT OF HERE AND GET BRUNCH?
WHY DON'T YOU STAY? I MEAN, WHAT YOU SAID ABOUT THE DIAMONDS. DO YOU BELIEVE HE'S INNOCENT?
YES...
THEN YOU SHOULD HANG OUT AND FIGURE OUT WHAT HAPPENED.
BUT OUR DATE?
WE'LL DO IT ANOTHER TIME. GO ON. DO WHAT YOU'RE GOOD AT.

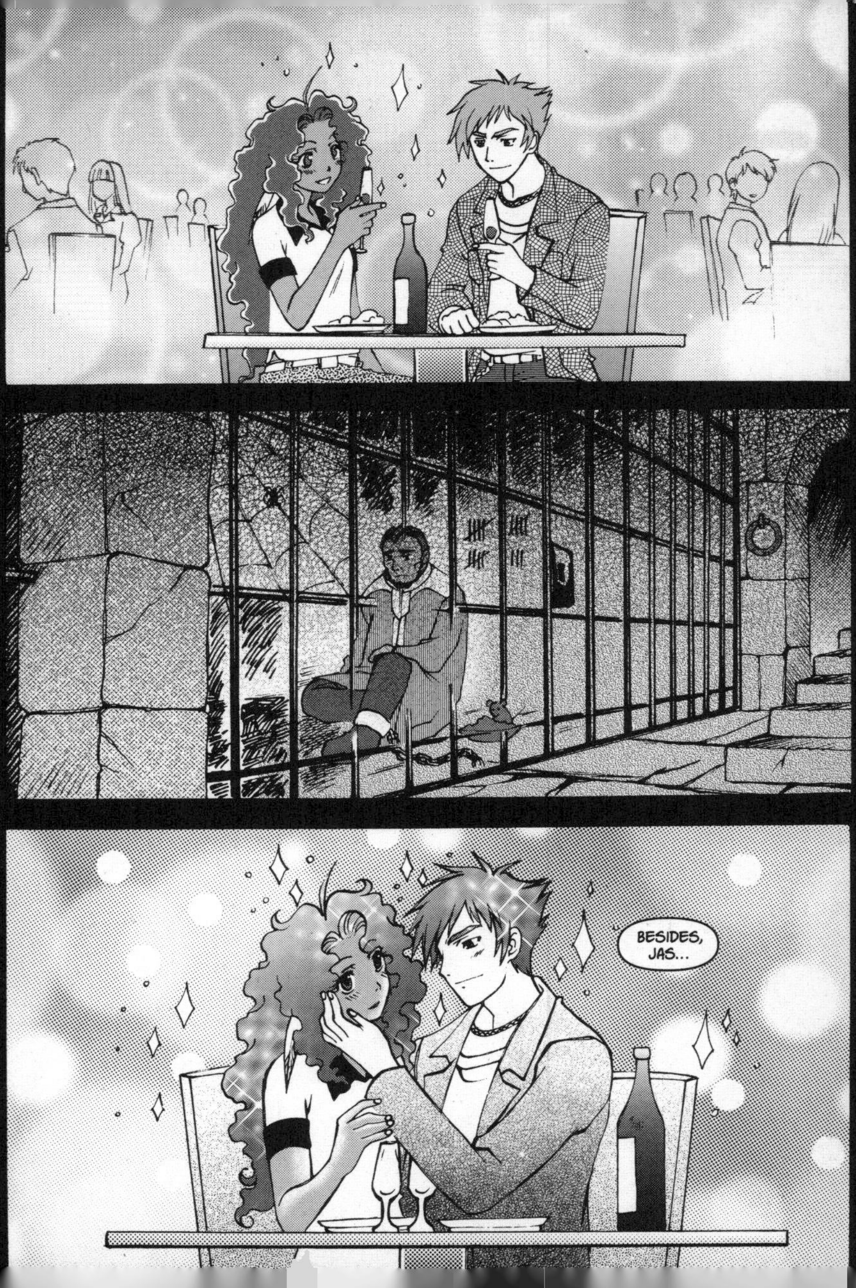
BESIDES, JAS...

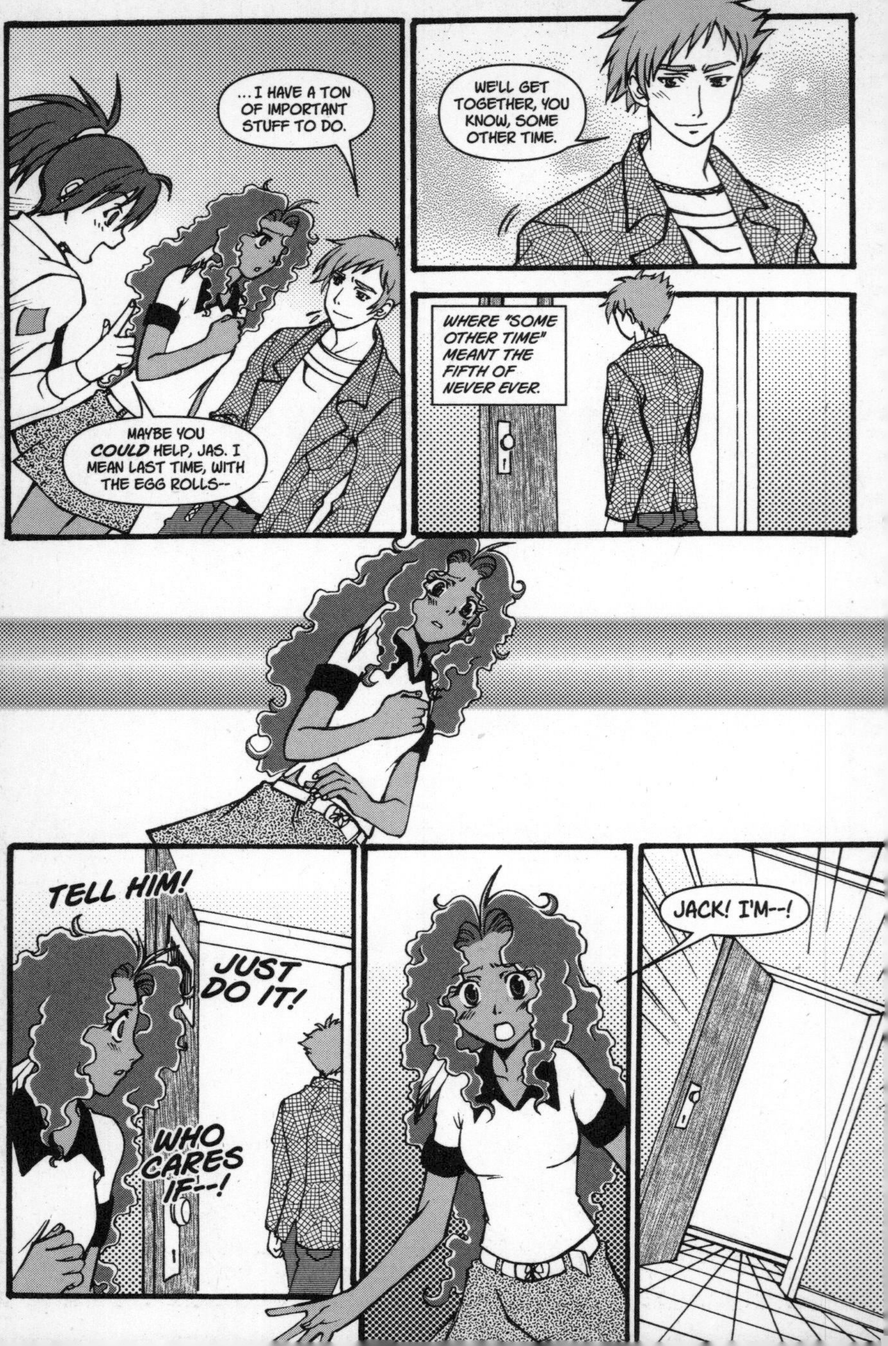
...I HAVE A TON OF IMPORTANT STUFF TO DO.
MAYBE YOU COULD HELP, JAS. I MEAN LAST TIME, WITH THE EGG ROLLS--
WE'LL GET TOGETHER, YOU KNOW, SOME OTHER TIME.
WHERE "SOME OTHER TIME" MEANT THE FIFTH OF NEVER EVER.
TELL HIM!
JUST DO IT!
WHO CARES IF--!
JACK! I'M--!

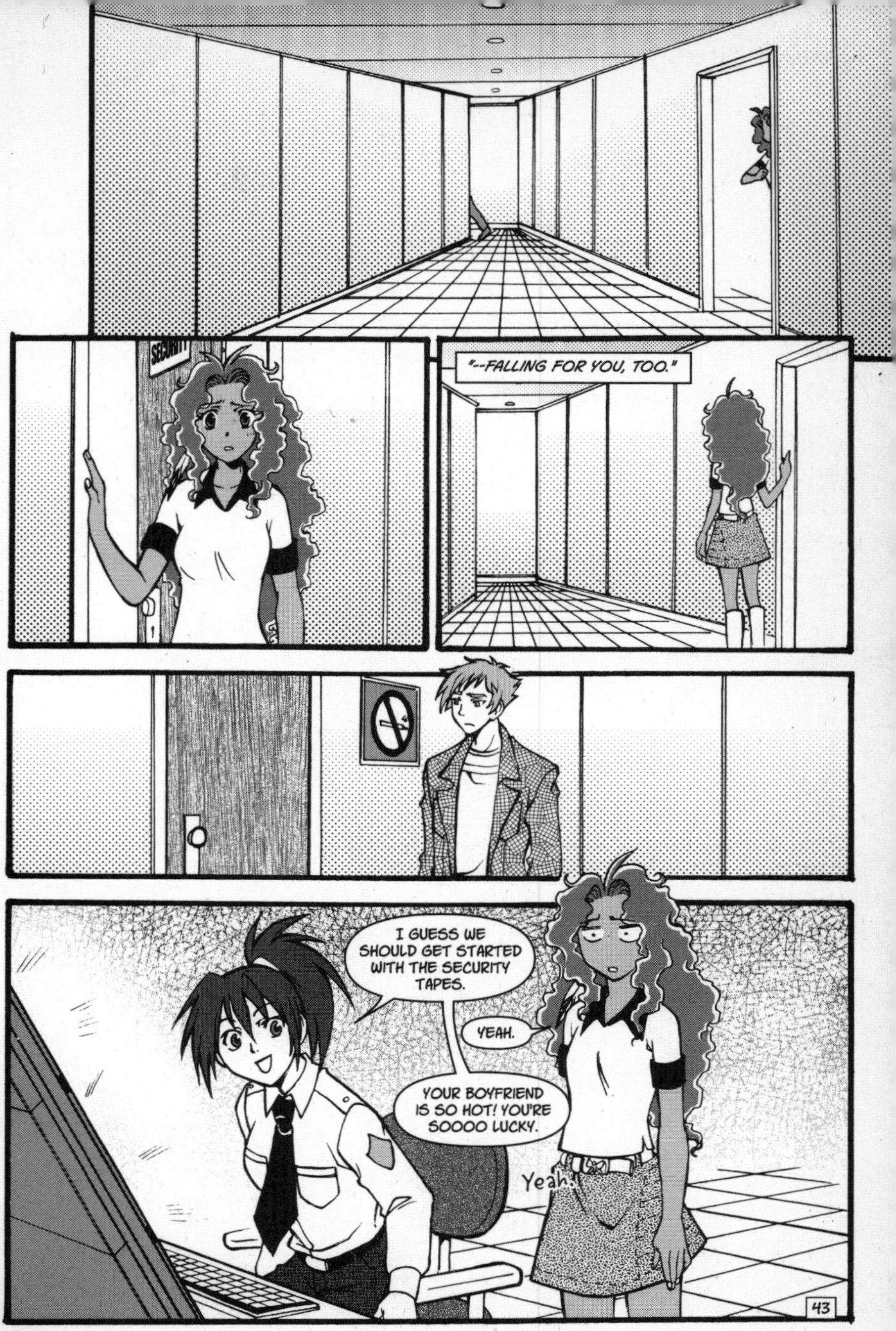

SECURITY
"--FALLING FOR YOU, TOO."
I GUESS WE SHOULD GET STARTED WITH THE SECURITY TAPES.
YEAH.
YOUR BOYFRIEND IS SO HOT! YOU'RE SOOOO LUCKY.
Yeah.

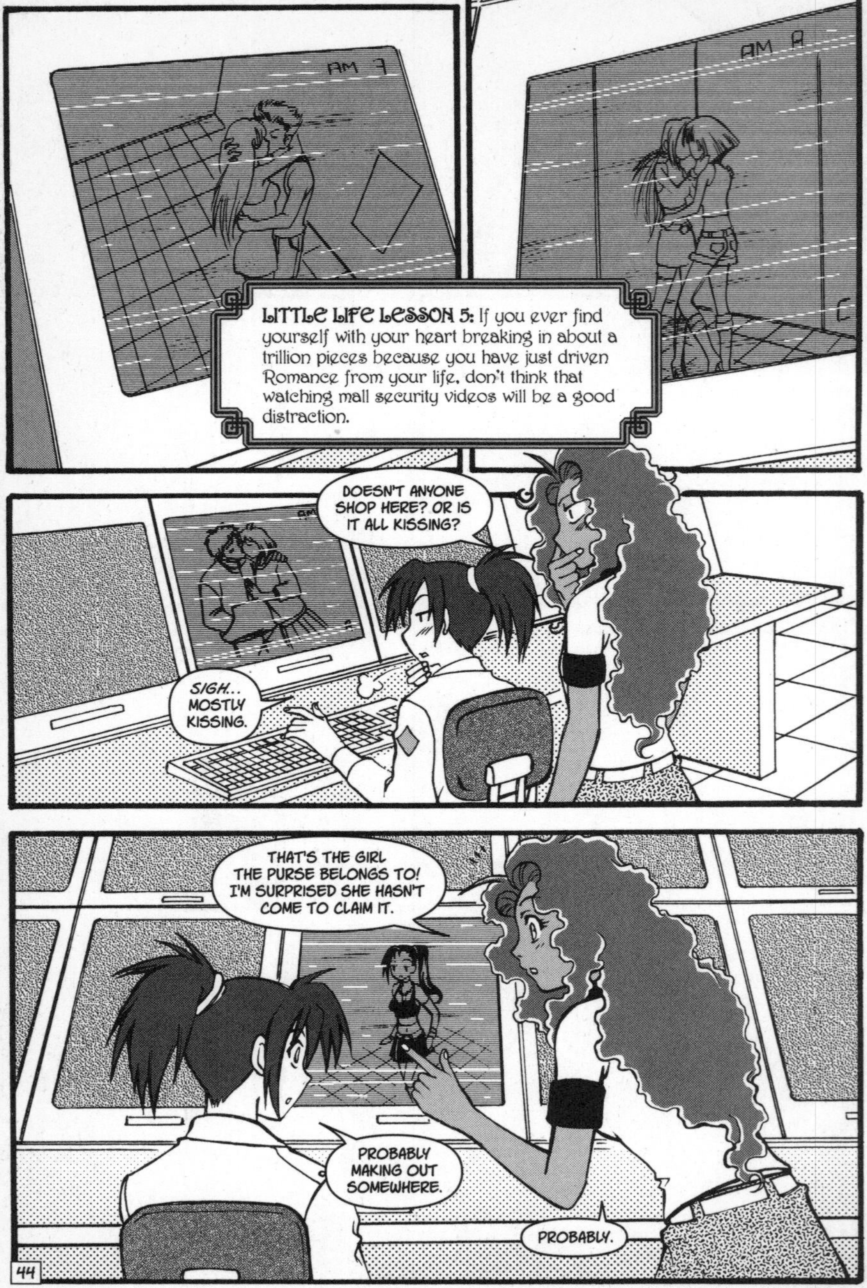

LITTLE LIFE LESSON 5: If you ever find yourself with your heart breaking in about a trillion pieces because you have just driven Romance from your life, don't think that watching mall security videos will be a good distraction.
DOESN'T ANYONE SHOP HERE? OR IS IT ALL KISSING?
SIGH... MOSTLY KISSING.
THAT'S THE GIRL THE PURSE BELONGS TO! I'M SURPRISED SHE HASN'T COME TO CLAIM IT.
PROBABLY MAKING OUT SOMEWHERE.
PROBABLY.

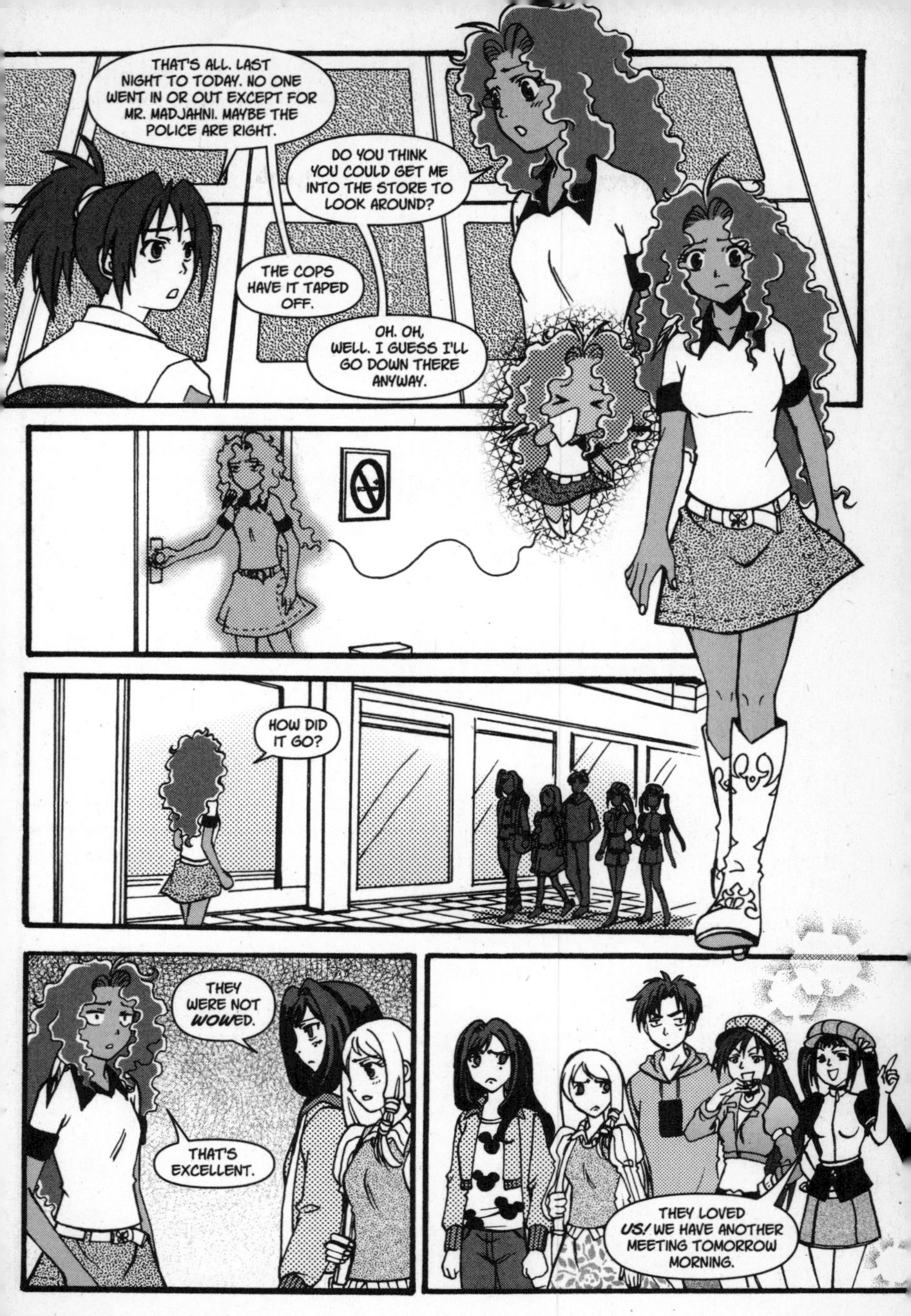
THAT'S ALL. LAST NIGHT TO TODAY. NO ONE WENT IN OR OUT EXCEPT FOR MR. MADJAHNI. MAYBE THE POLICE ARE RIGHT.
DO YOU THINK YOU COULD GET ME INTO THE STORE TO LOOK AROUND?
THE COPS HAVE IT TAPED OFF.
OH. OH, WELL. I GUESS I'LL GO DOWN THERE ANYWAY.
HOW DID IT GO?
THEY WERE NOT *WOWED*.
THAT'S EXCELLENT.
THEY LOVED *US!* WE HAVE ANOTHER MEETING TOMORROW MORNING.

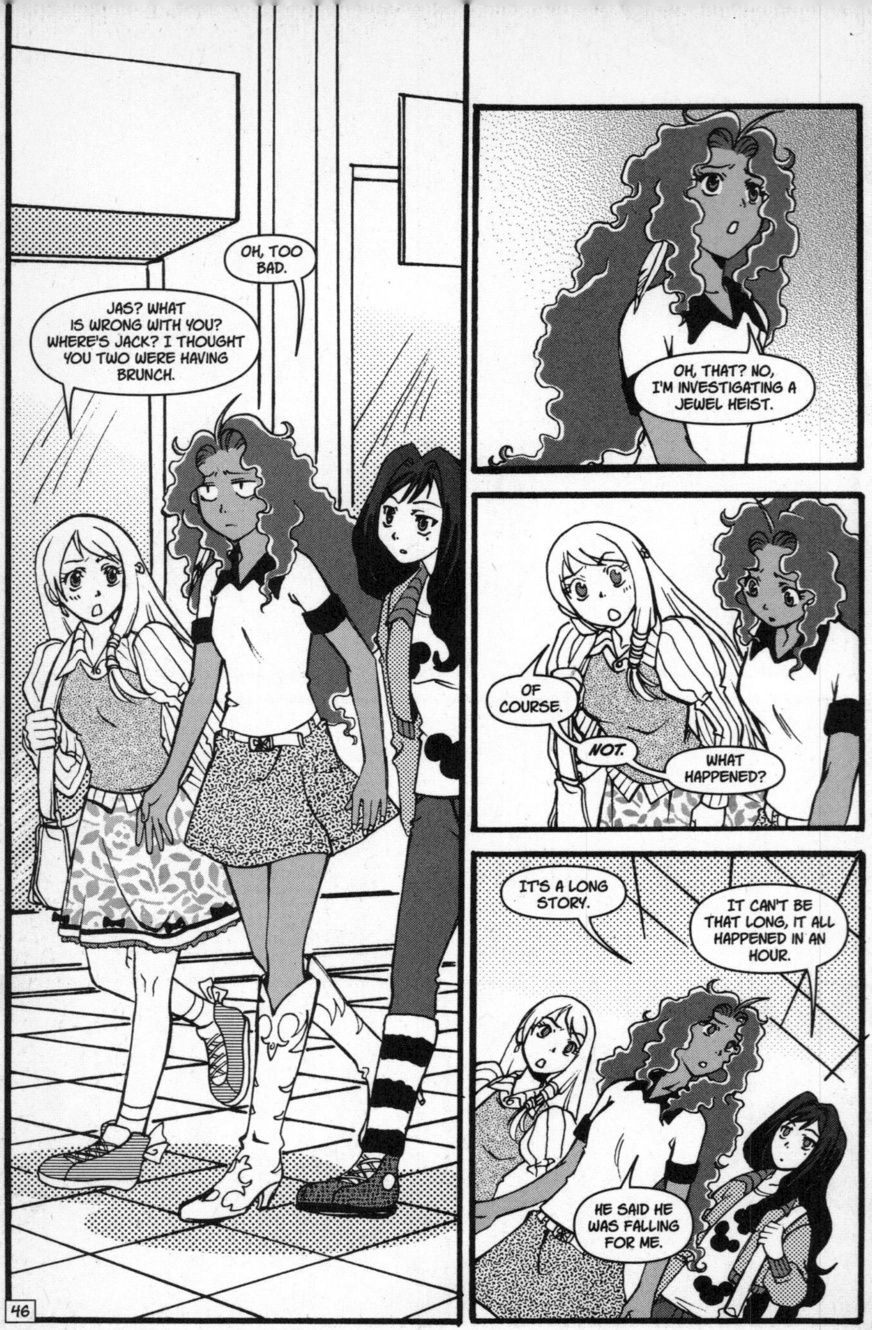
JAS? WHAT IS WRONG WITH YOU? WHERE'S JACK? I THOUGHT YOU TWO WERE HAVING BRUNCH.
OH, TOO BAD.
OH, THAT? NO, I'M INVESTIGATING A JEWEL HEIST.
OF COURSE.
NOT.
WHAT HAPPENED?
IT'S A LONG STORY.
IT CAN'T BE THAT LONG, IT ALL HAPPENED IN AN HOUR.
HE SAID HE WAS FALLING FOR ME.

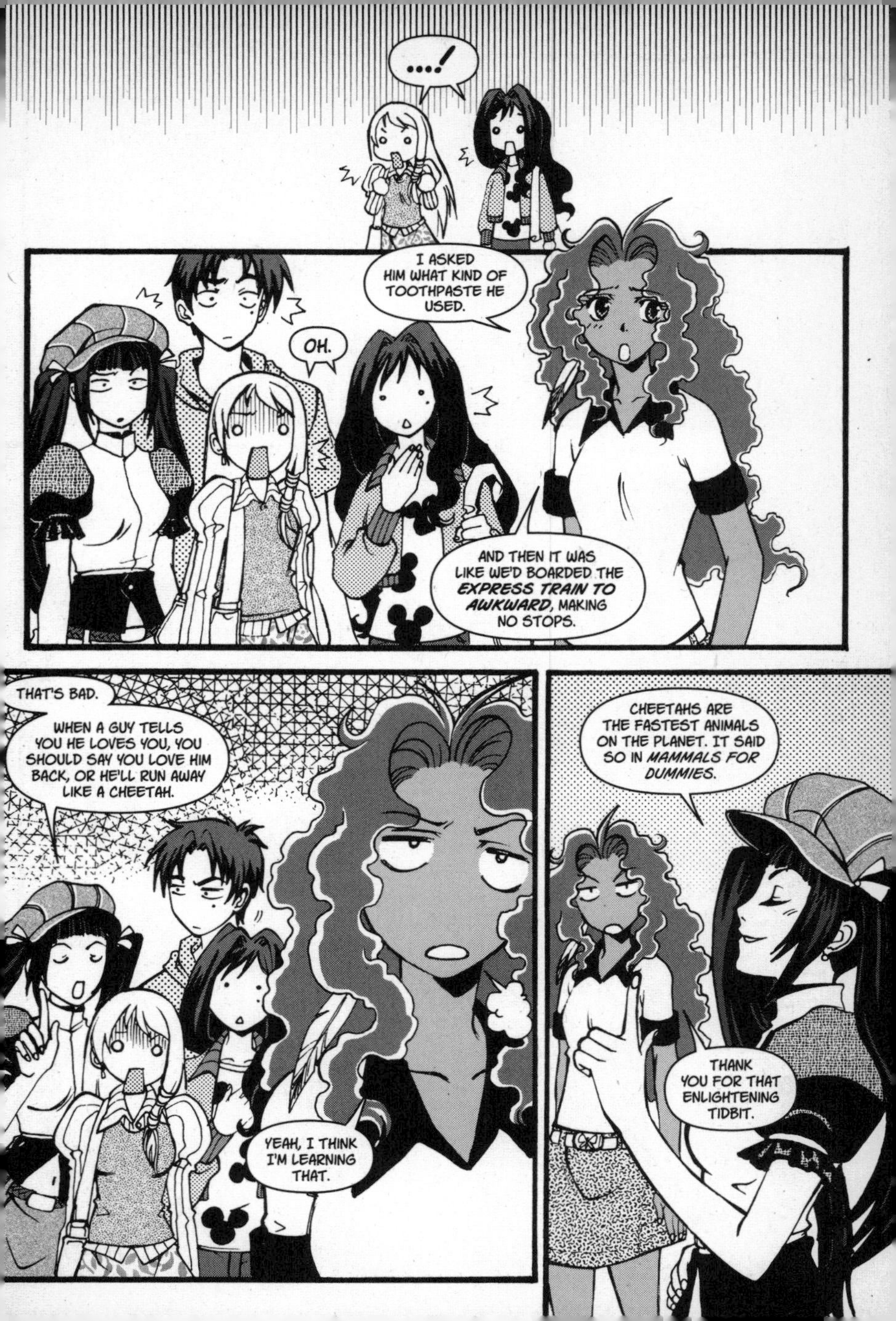
....!
I ASKED HIM WHAT KIND OF TOOTHPASTE HE USED.
OH.
AND THEN IT WAS LIKE WE'D BOARDED THE *EXPRESS TRAIN TO AWKWARD*, MAKING NO STOPS.
THAT'S BAD.
WHEN A GUY TELLS YOU HE LOVES YOU, YOU SHOULD SAY YOU LOVE HIM BACK, OR HE'LL RUN AWAY LIKE A CHEETAH.
YEAH, I THINK I'M LEARNING THAT.
CHEETAHS ARE THE FASTEST ANIMALS ON THE PLANET. IT SAID SO IN *MAMMALS FOR DUMMIES*.
THANK YOU FOR THAT ENLIGHTENING TIDBIT.

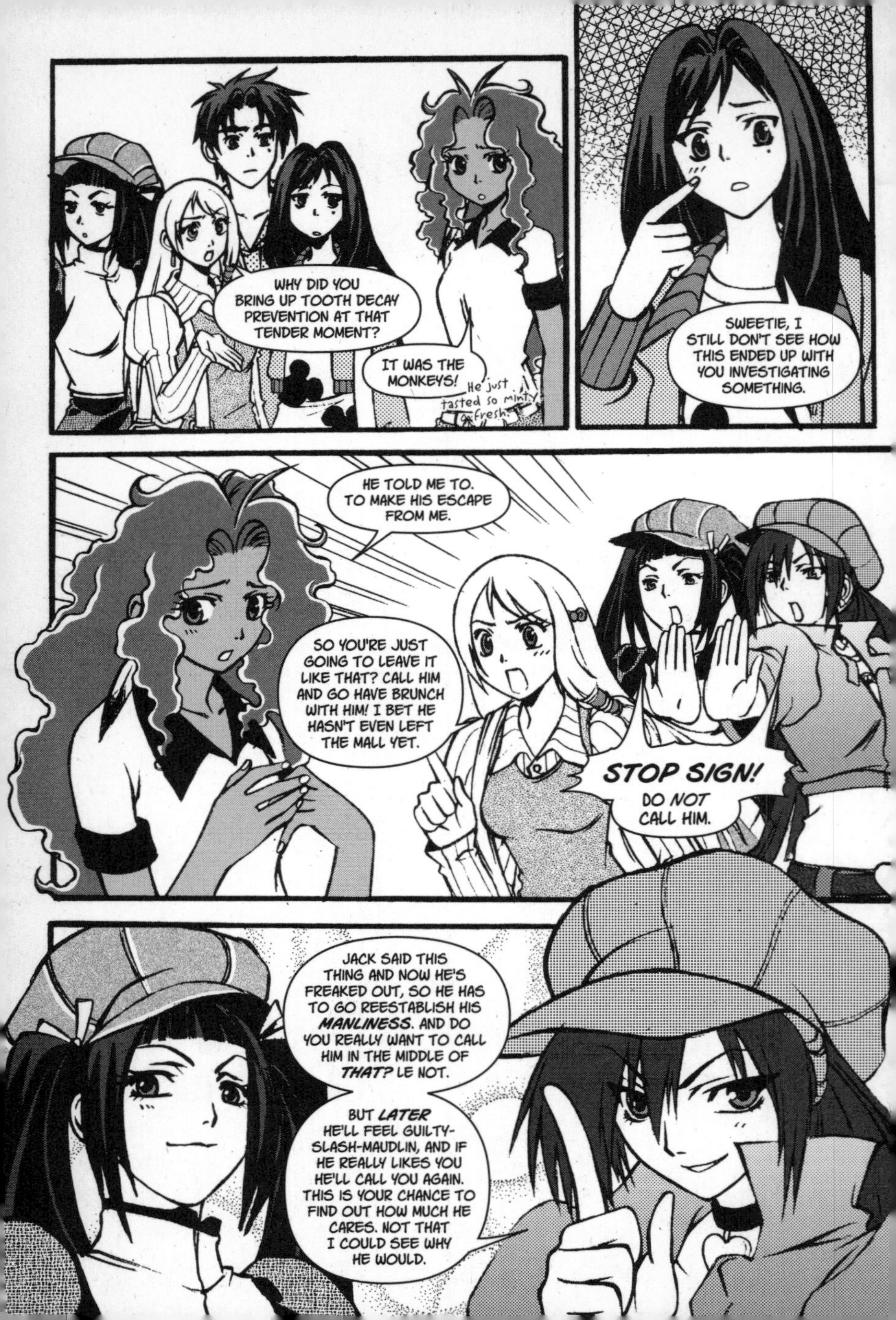
WHY DID YOU BRING UP TOOTH DECAY PREVENTION AT THAT TENDER MOMENT?
IT WAS THE MONKEYS!
He just tasted so minty fresh!
SWEETIE, I STILL DON'T SEE HOW THIS ENDED UP WITH YOU INVESTIGATING SOMETHING.
HE TOLD ME TO. TO MAKE HIS ESCAPE FROM ME.
SO YOU'RE JUST GOING TO LEAVE IT LIKE THAT? CALL HIM AND GO HAVE BRUNCH WITH HIM! I BET HE HASN'T EVEN LEFT THE MALL YET.
STOP SIGN! DO NOT CALL HIM.
JACK SAID THIS THING AND NOW HE'S FREAKED OUT, SO HE HAS TO GO REESTABLISH HIS MANLINESS. AND DO YOU REALLY WANT TO CALL HIM IN THE MIDDLE OF THAT? LE NOT.
BUT LATER HE'LL FEEL GUILTY-SLASH-MAUDLIN, AND IF HE REALLY LIKES YOU HE'LL CALL YOU AGAIN. THIS IS YOUR CHANCE TO FIND OUT HOW MUCH HE CARES. NOT THAT I COULD SEE WHY HE WOULD.

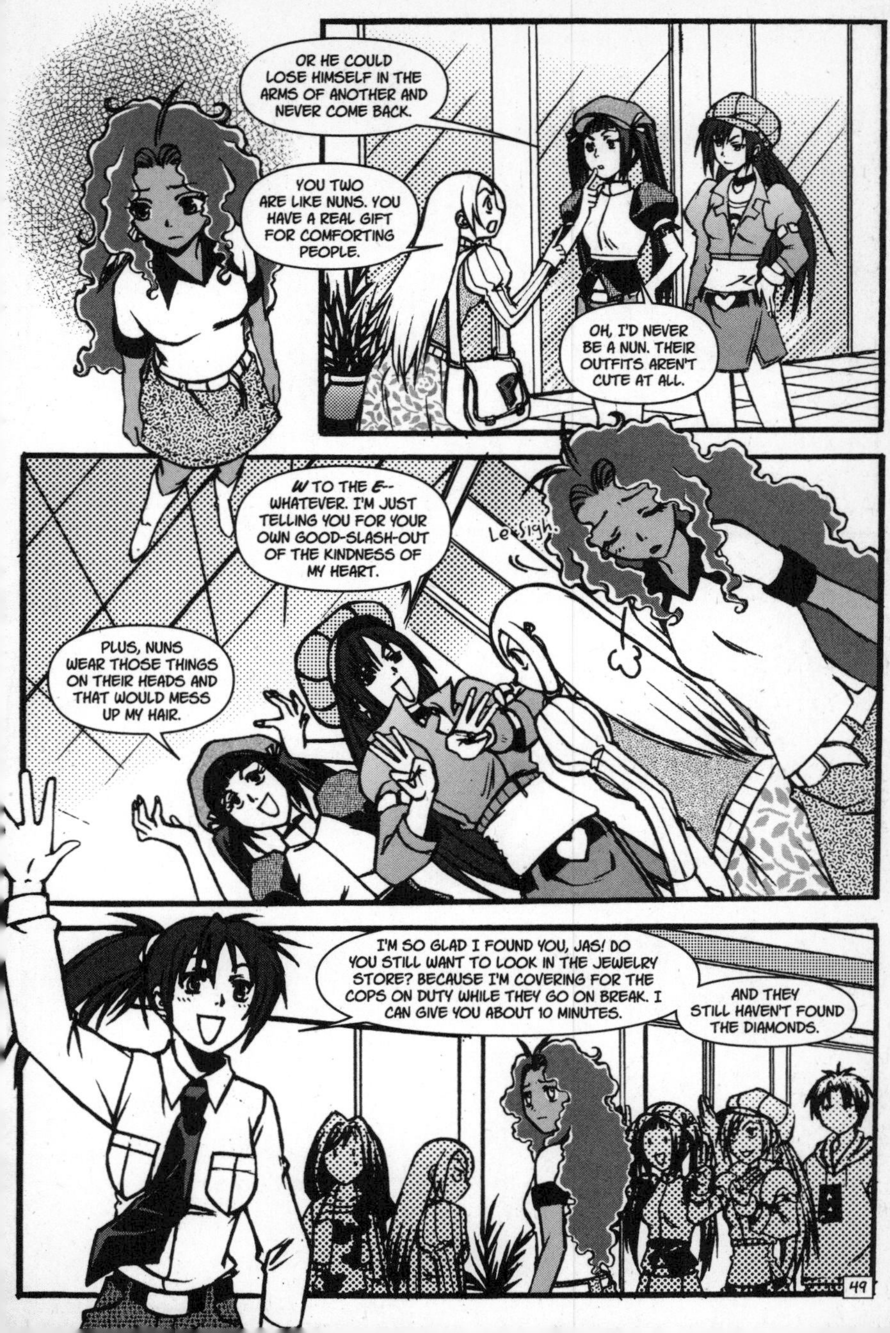
OR HE COULD LOSE HIMSELF IN THE ARMS OF ANOTHER AND NEVER COME BACK.
YOU TWO ARE LIKE NUNS. YOU HAVE A REAL GIFT FOR COMFORTING PEOPLE.
OH, I'D NEVER BE A NUN. THEIR OUTFITS AREN'T CUTE AT ALL.
PLUS, NUNS WEAR THOSE THINGS ON THEIR HEADS AND THAT WOULD MESS UP MY HAIR.
W TO THE *E*-- WHATEVER. I'M JUST TELLING YOU FOR YOUR OWN GOOD-SLASH-OUT OF THE KINDNESS OF MY HEART.
Le Sigh.
I'M SO GLAD I FOUND YOU, JAS! DO YOU STILL WANT TO LOOK IN THE JEWELRY STORE? BECAUSE I'M COVERING FOR THE COPS ON DUTY WHILE THEY GO ON BREAK. I CAN GIVE YOU ABOUT 10 MINUTES.
AND THEY STILL HAVEN'T FOUND THE DIAMONDS.

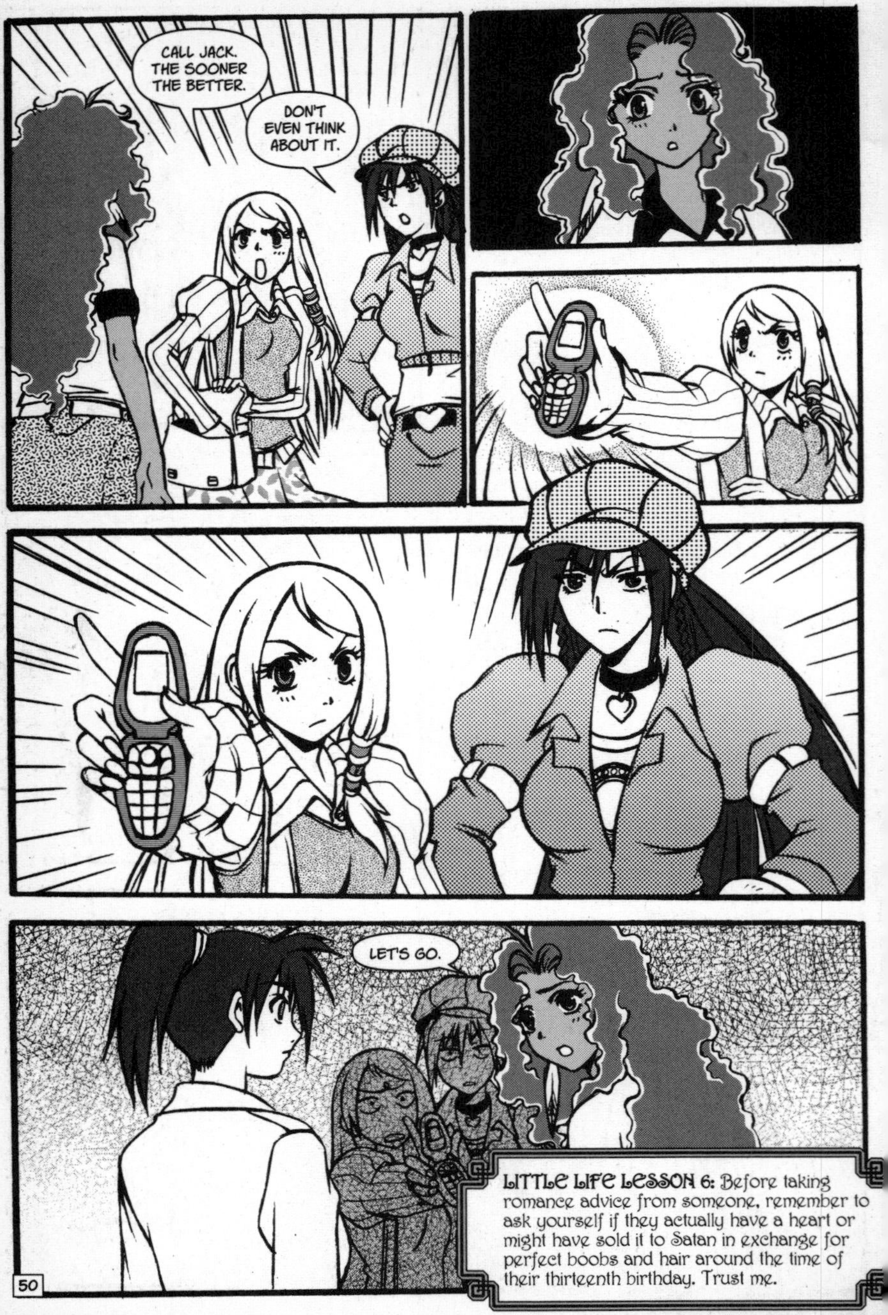
CALL JACK. THE SOONER THE BETTER.
DON'T EVEN THINK ABOUT IT.
LET'S GO.
LITTLE LIFE LESSON 6: Before taking romance advice from someone, remember to ask yourself if they actually have a heart or might have sold it to Satan in exchange for perfect boobs and hair around the time of their thirteenth birthday. Trust me.

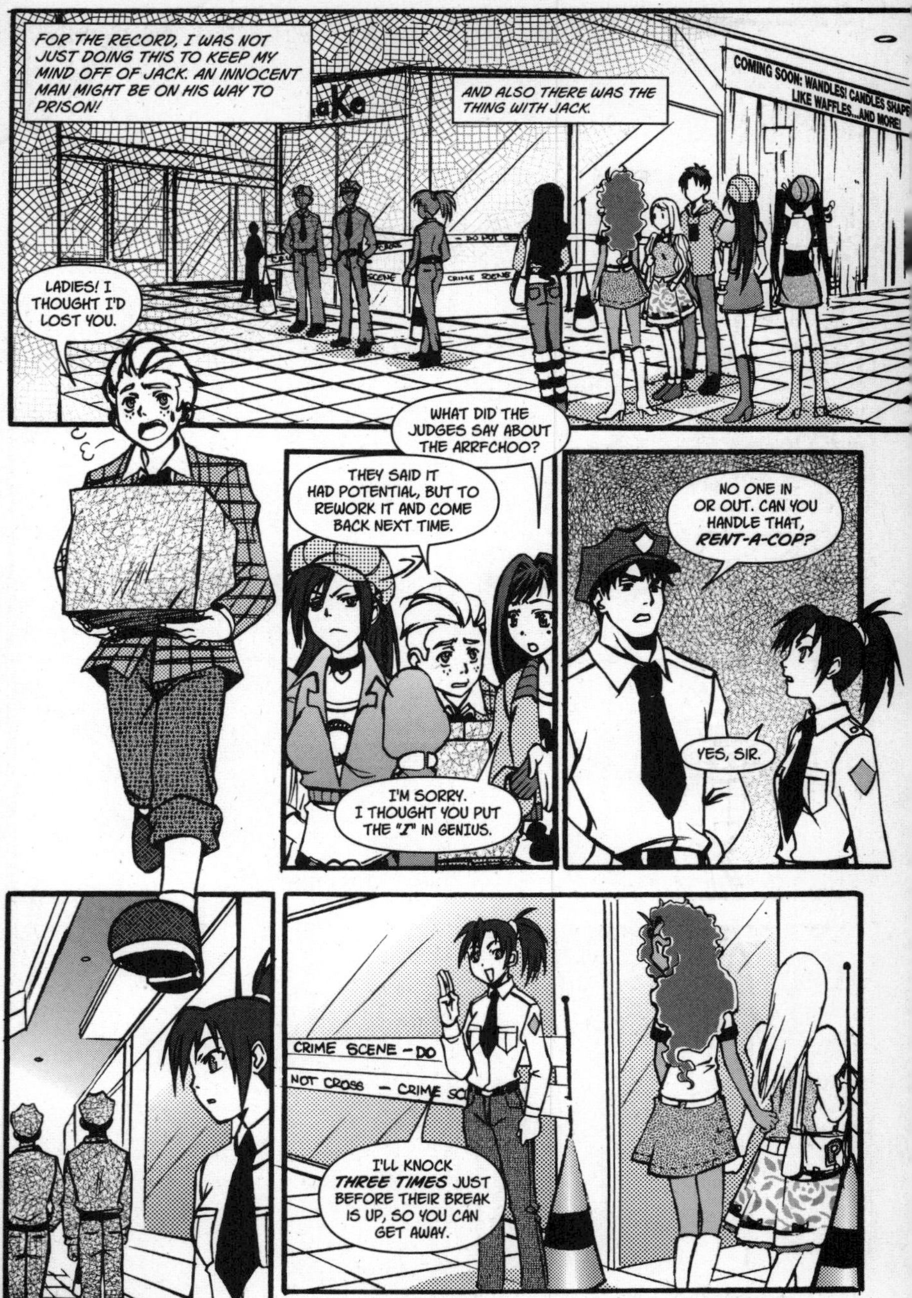
FOR THE RECORD, I WAS NOT JUST DOING THIS TO KEEP MY MIND OFF OF JACK. AN INNOCENT MAN MIGHT BE ON HIS WAY TO PRISON!
AND ALSO THERE WAS THE THING WITH JACK.
COMING SOON: WANDLES! CANDLES SHAPE LIKE WAFFLES...AND MORE!
CRIME SCENE
LADIES! I THOUGHT I'D LOST YOU.
WHAT DID THE JUDGES SAY ABOUT THE ARRFCHOO?
THEY SAID IT HAD POTENTIAL, BUT TO REWORK IT AND COME BACK NEXT TIME.
I'M SORRY. I THOUGHT YOU PUT THE "I" IN GENIUS.
NO ONE IN OR OUT. CAN YOU HANDLE THAT, RENT-A-COP?
YES, SIR.
CRIME SCENE - DO
NOT CROSS - CRIME SC
I'LL KNOCK THREE TIMES JUST BEFORE THEIR BREAK IS UP, SO YOU CAN GET AWAY.

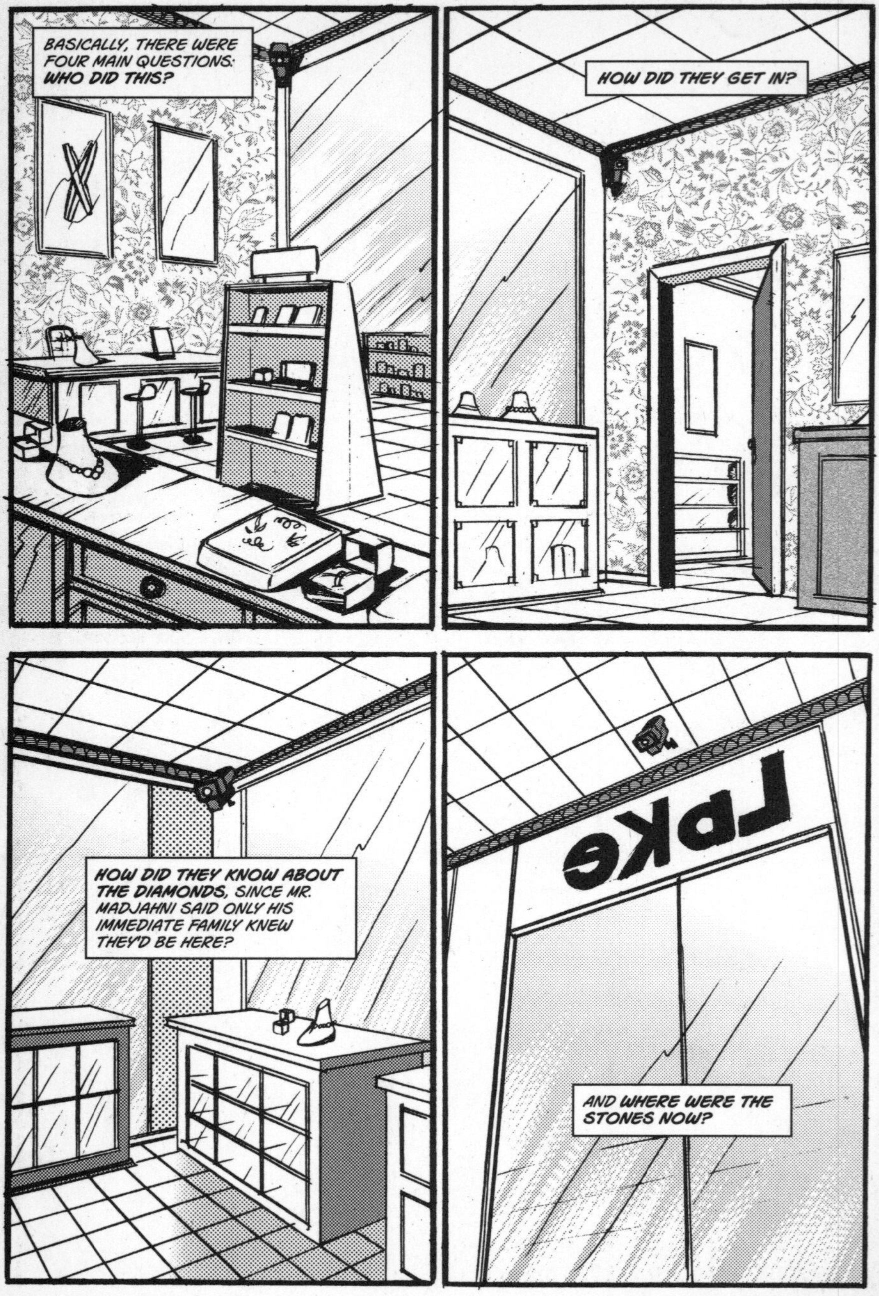
BASICALLY, THERE WERE FOUR MAIN QUESTIONS: **WHO DID THIS?**
HOW DID THEY GET IN?
HOW DID THEY KNOW ABOUT THE DIAMONDS, SINCE MR. MADJAHNI SAID ONLY HIS IMMEDIATE FAMILY KNEW THEY'D BE HERE?
AND WHERE WERE THE STONES NOW?

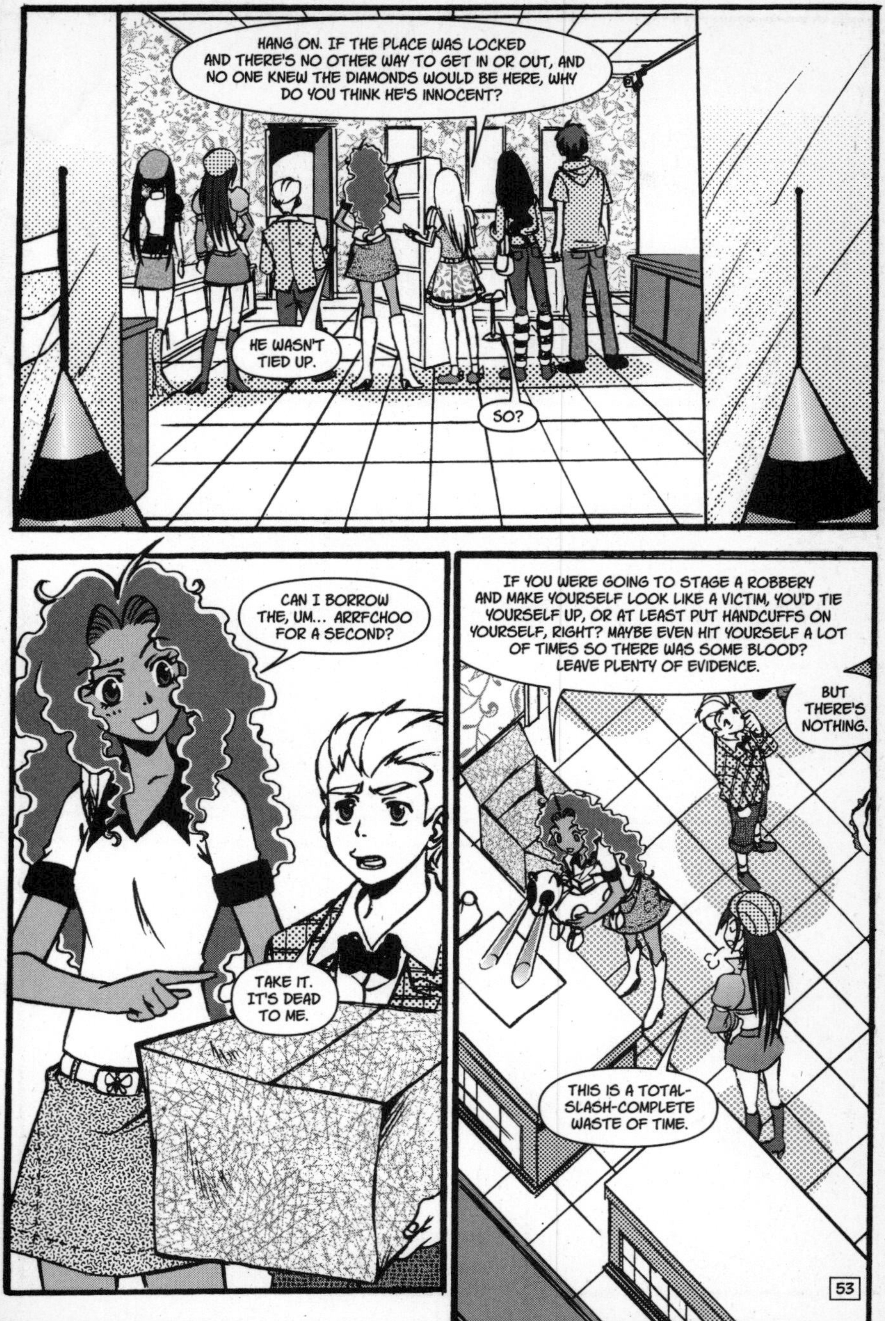
HANG ON. IF THE PLACE WAS LOCKED AND THERE'S NO OTHER WAY TO GET IN OR OUT, AND NO ONE KNEW THE DIAMONDS WOULD BE HERE, WHY DO YOU THINK HE'S INNOCENT?
HE WASN'T TIED UP.
SO?
CAN I BORROW THE, UM... ARRFCHOO FOR A SECOND?
TAKE IT. IT'S DEAD TO ME.
IF YOU WERE GOING TO STAGE A ROBBERY AND MAKE YOURSELF LOOK LIKE A VICTIM, YOU'D TIE YOURSELF UP, OR AT LEAST PUT HANDCUFFS ON YOURSELF, RIGHT? MAYBE EVEN HIT YOURSELF A LOT OF TIMES SO THERE WAS SOME BLOOD? LEAVE PLENTY OF EVIDENCE.
BUT THERE'S NOTHING.
THIS IS A TOTAL-SLASH-COMPLETE WASTE OF TIME.

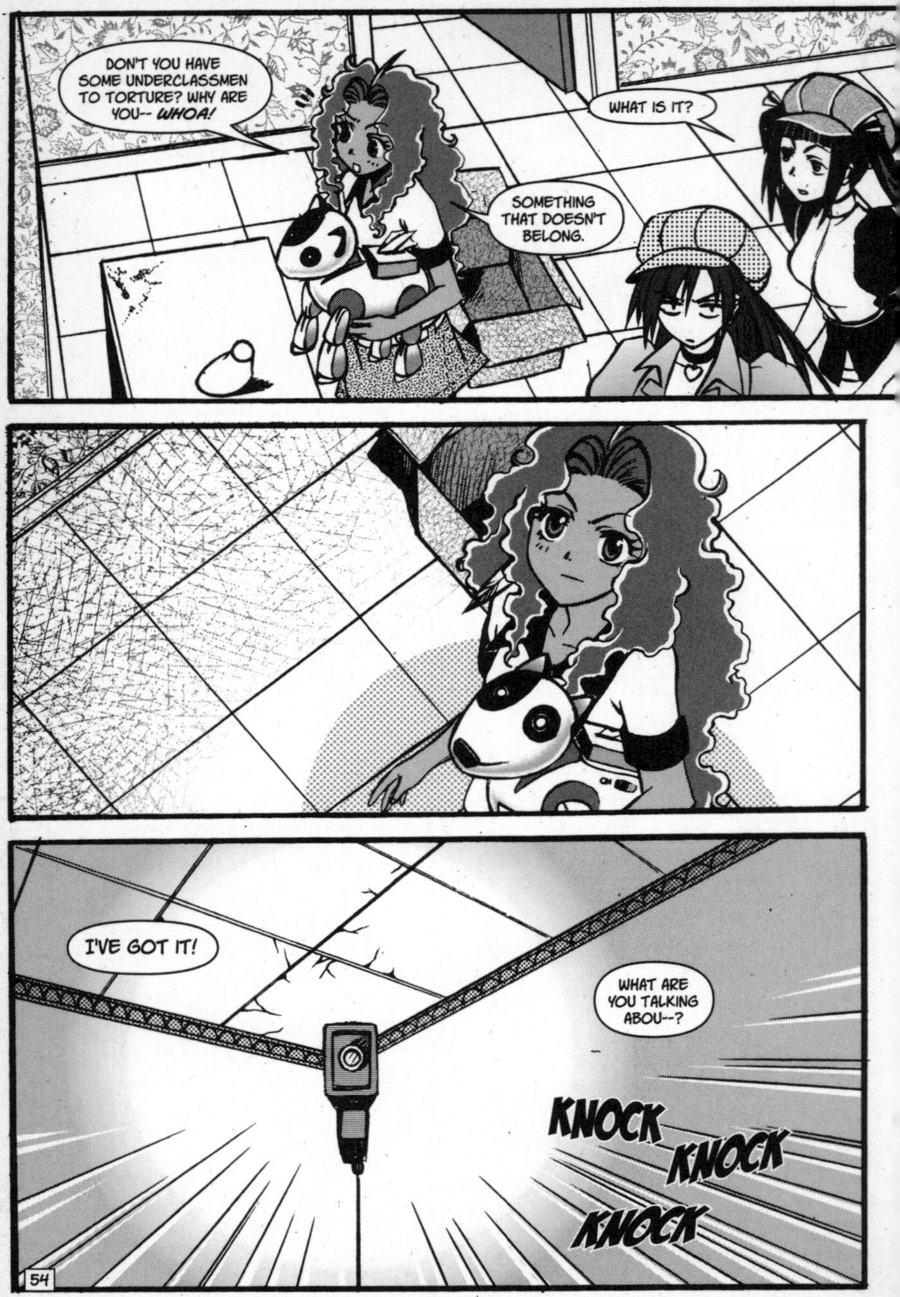
DON'T YOU HAVE SOME UNDERCLASSMEN TO TORTURE? WHY ARE YOU-- WHOA!
WHAT IS IT?
SOMETHING THAT DOESN'T BELONG.
I'VE GOT IT!
WHAT ARE YOU TALKING ABOU--?
KNOCK
KNOCK
KNOCK

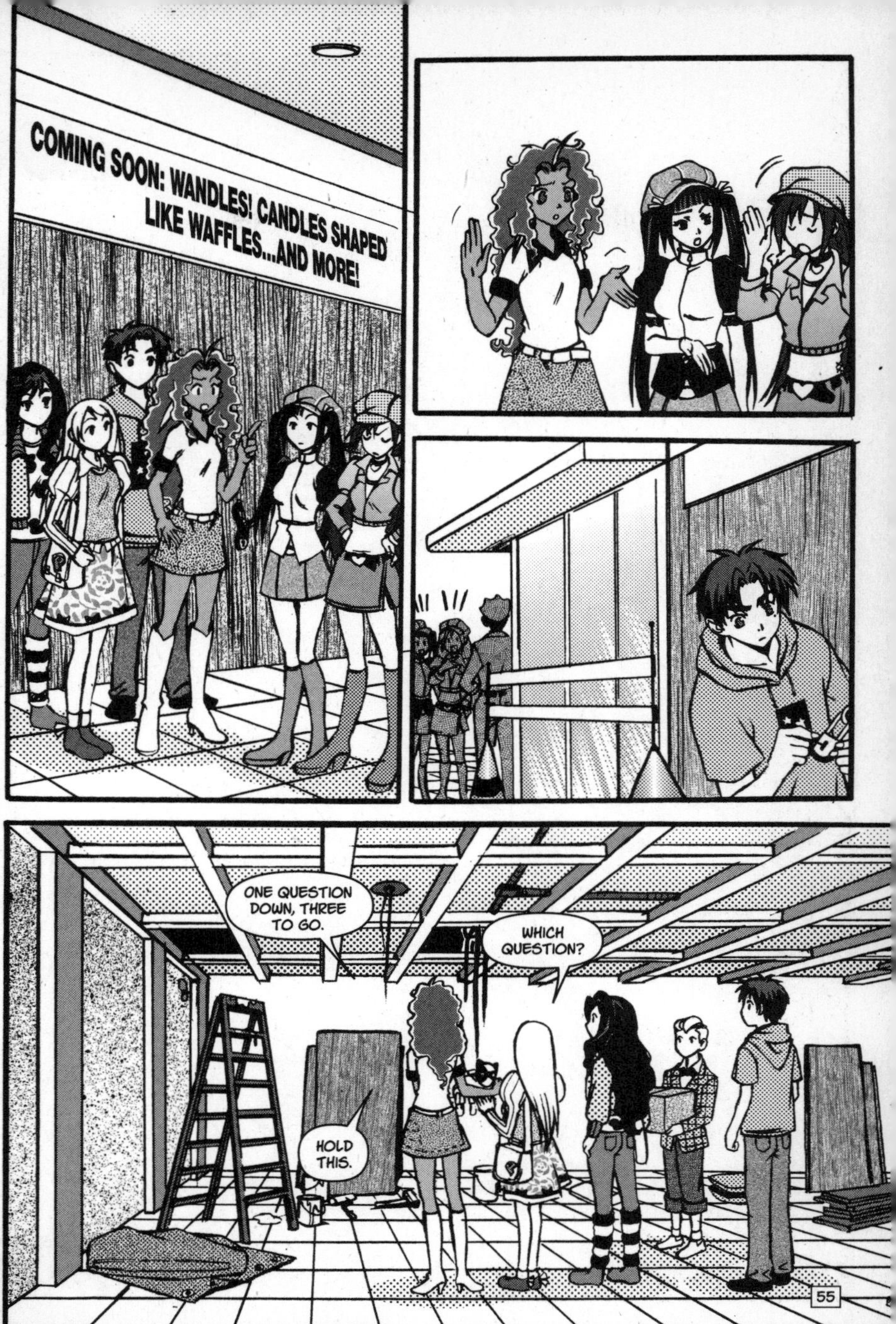

COMING SOON: WANDLES! CANDLES SHAPED LIKE WAFFLES...AND MORE!
ONE QUESTION DOWN, THREE TO GO.
WHICH QUESTION?
HOLD THIS.

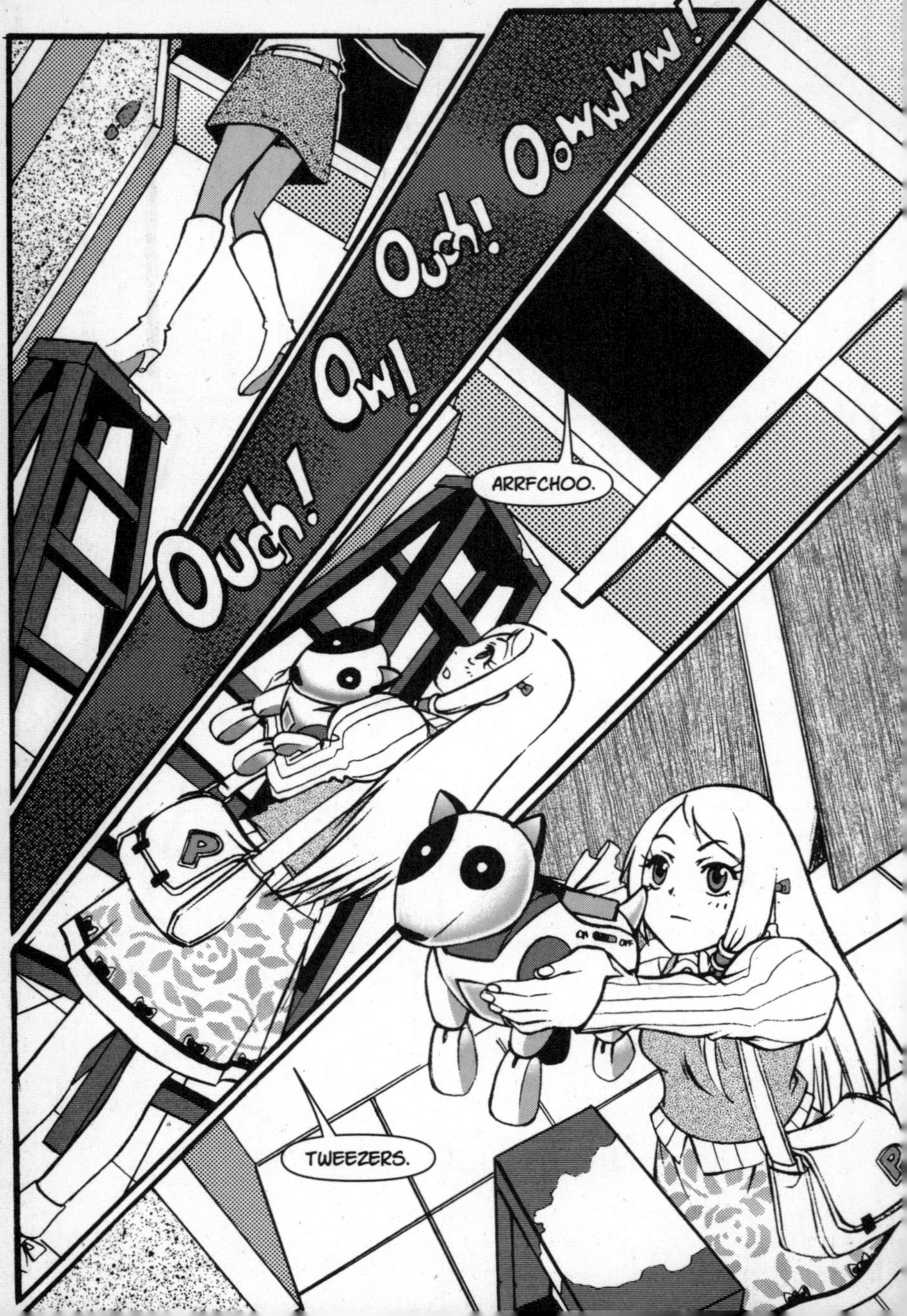
Ouch! Ow! Ouch! Oowwww!
ARRFCHOO.
TWEEZERS.

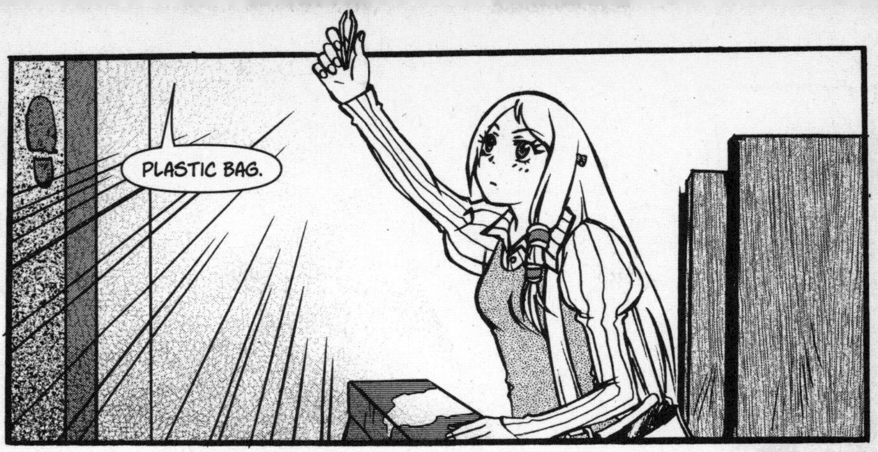
PLASTIC BAG.

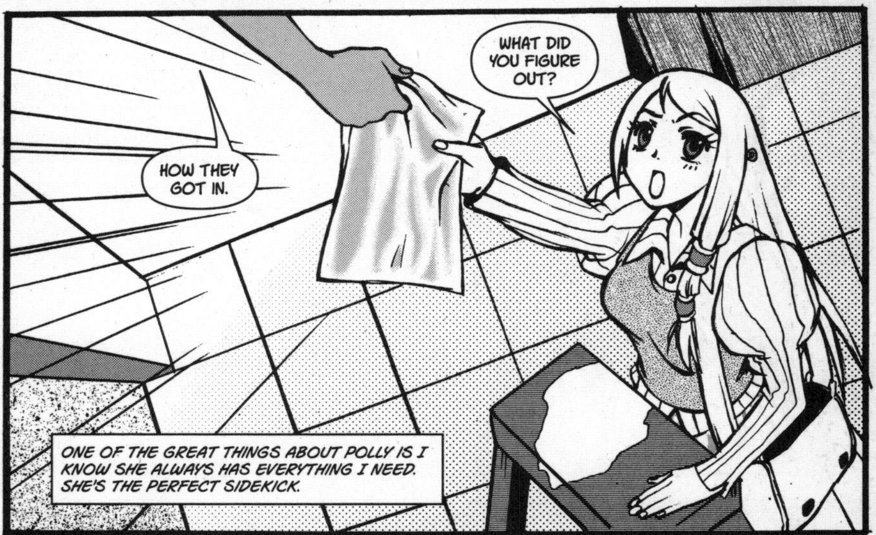
HOW THEY GOT IN.
WHAT DID YOU FIGURE OUT?
ONE OF THE GREAT THINGS ABOUT POLLY IS I KNOW SHE ALWAYS HAS EVERYTHING I NEED. SHE'S THE PERFECT SIDEKICK.

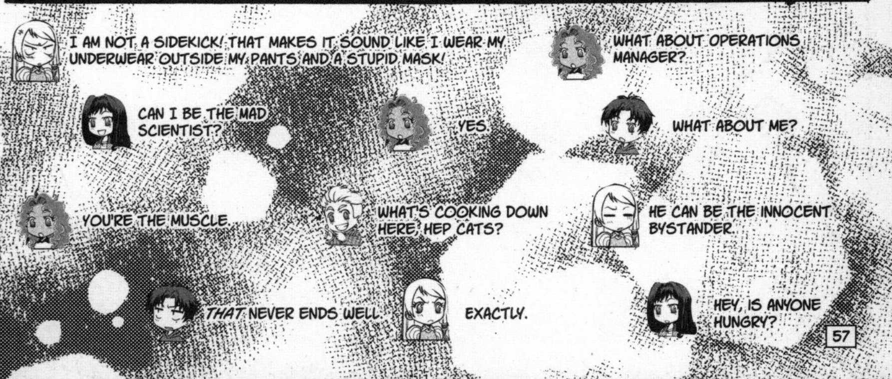
I AM NOT A SIDEKICK! THAT MAKES IT SOUND LIKE I WEAR MY UNDERWEAR OUTSIDE MY PANTS AND A STUPID MASK!
WHAT ABOUT OPERATIONS MANAGER?
CAN I BE THE MAD SCIENTIST?
YES.
WHAT ABOUT ME?
YOU'RE THE MUSCLE.
WHAT'S COOKING DOWN HERE, HEP CATS?
HE CAN BE THE INNOCENT BYSTANDER.
THAT NEVER ENDS WELL.
EXACTLY.
HEY, IS ANYONE HUNGRY?

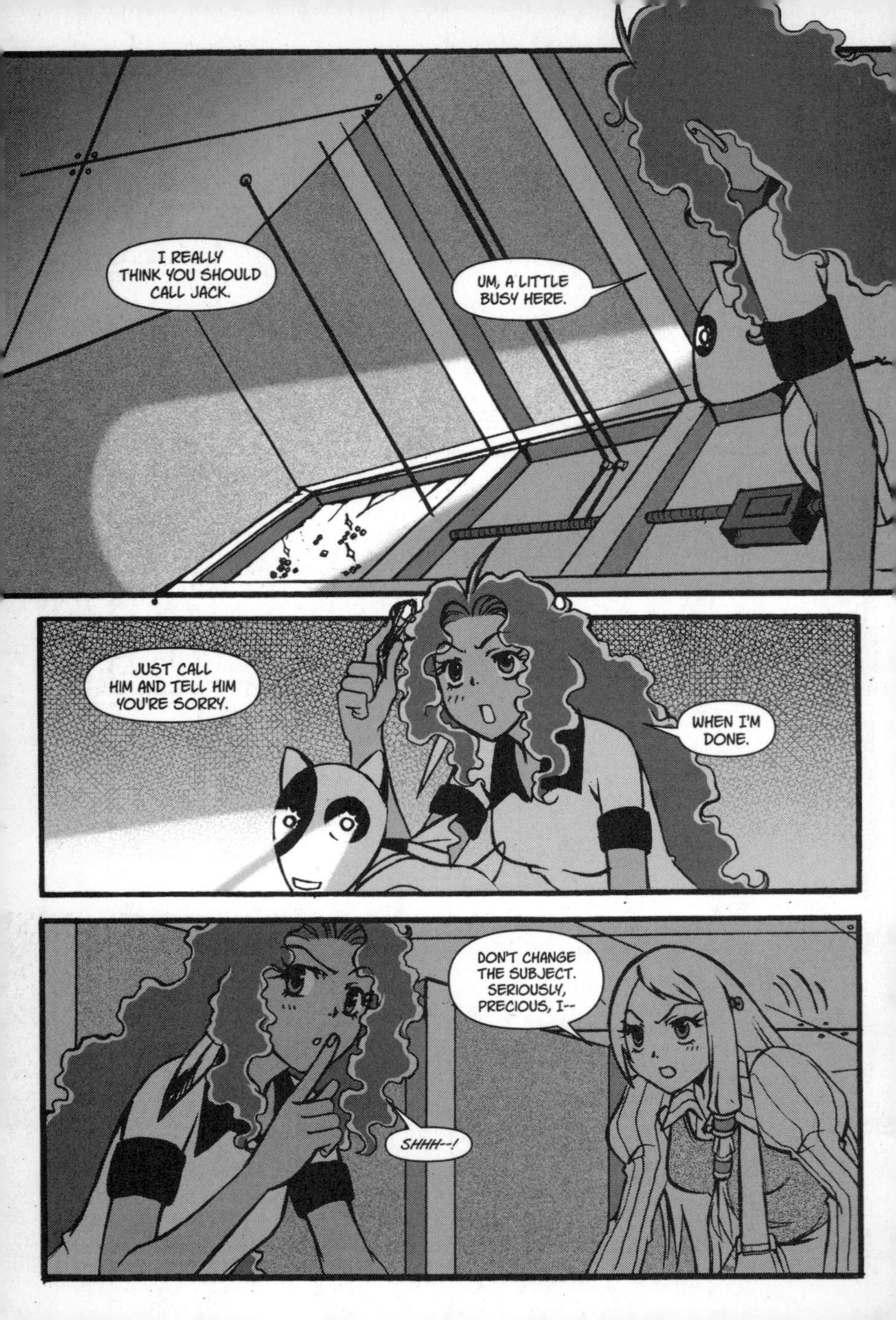
I REALLY THINK YOU SHOULD CALL JACK.
UM, A LITTLE BUSY HERE.
JUST CALL HIM AND TELL HIM YOU'RE SORRY.
WHEN I'M DONE.
DON'T CHANGE THE SUBJECT. SERIOUSLY, PRECIOUS, I--
SHHH--!

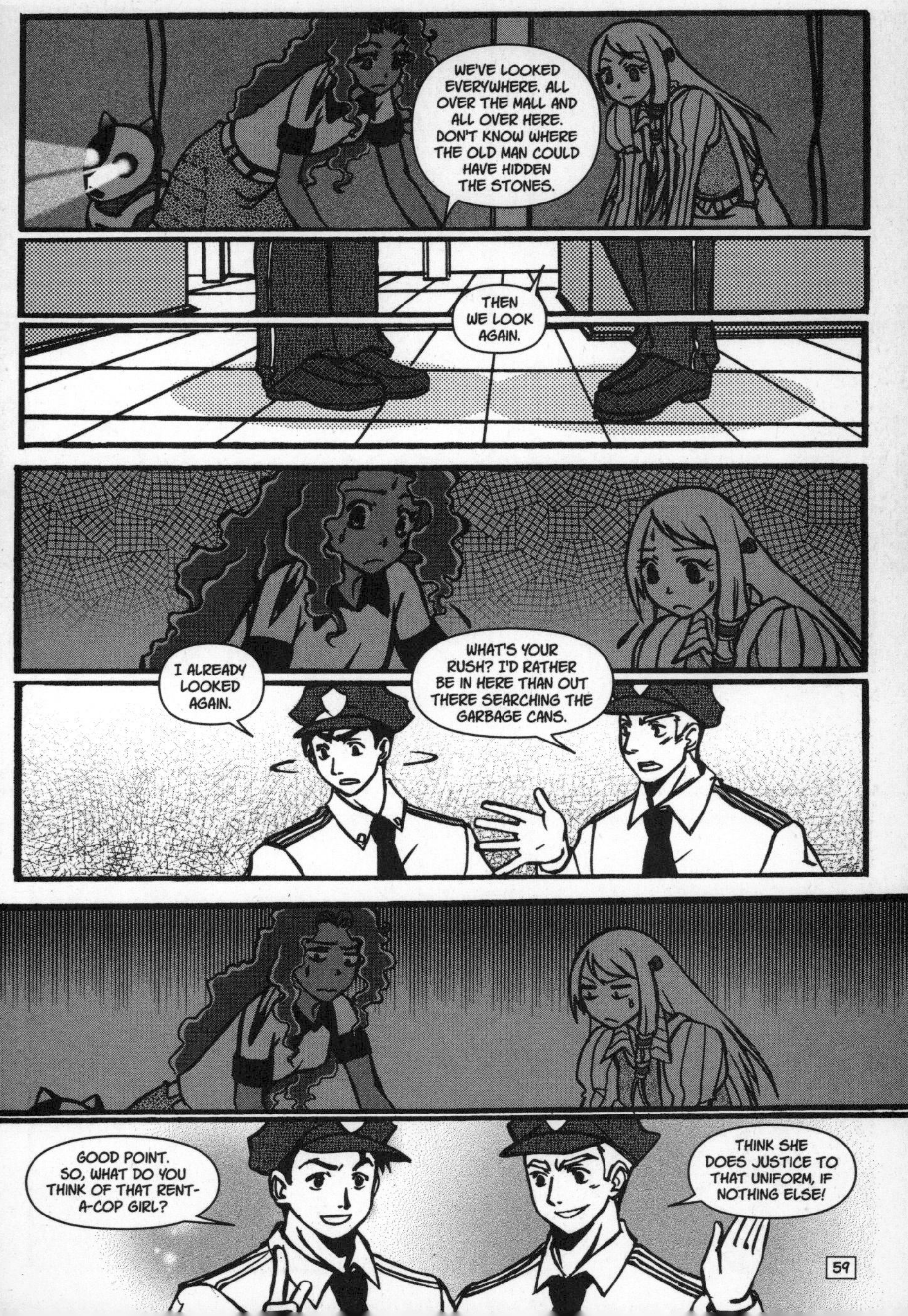
WE'VE LOOKED EVERYWHERE. ALL OVER THE MALL AND ALL OVER HERE. DON'T KNOW WHERE THE OLD MAN COULD HAVE HIDDEN THE STONES.
THEN WE LOOK AGAIN.
I ALREADY LOOKED AGAIN.
WHAT'S YOUR RUSH? I'D RATHER BE IN HERE THAN OUT THERE SEARCHING THE GARBAGE CANS.
GOOD POINT. SO, WHAT DO YOU THINK OF THAT RENT-A-COP GIRL?
THINK SHE DOES JUSTICE TO THAT UNIFORM, IF NOTHING ELSE!

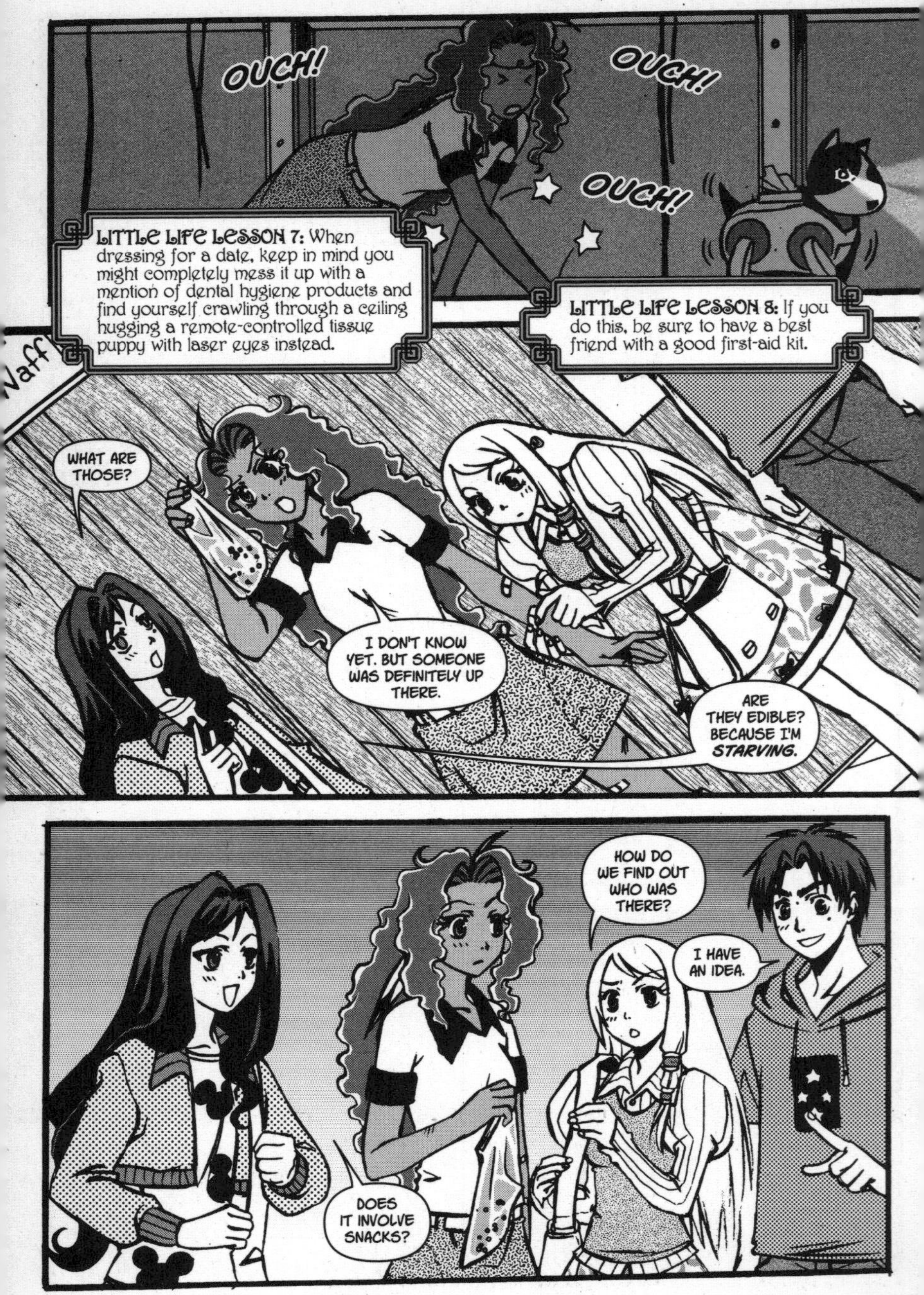
OUCH!
OUCH!
OUCH!
LITTLE LIFE LESSON 7: When dressing for a date, keep in mind you might completely mess it up with a mention of dental hygiene products and find yourself crawling through a ceiling hugging a remote-controlled tissue puppy with laser eyes instead.
LITTLE LIFE LESSON 8: If you do this, be sure to have a best friend with a good first-aid kit.
WHAT ARE THOSE?
I DON'T KNOW YET. BUT SOMEONE WAS DEFINITELY UP THERE.
ARE THEY EDIBLE? BECAUSE I'M STARVING.
HOW DO WE FIND OUT WHO WAS THERE?
I HAVE AN IDEA.
DOES IT INVOLVE SNACKS?

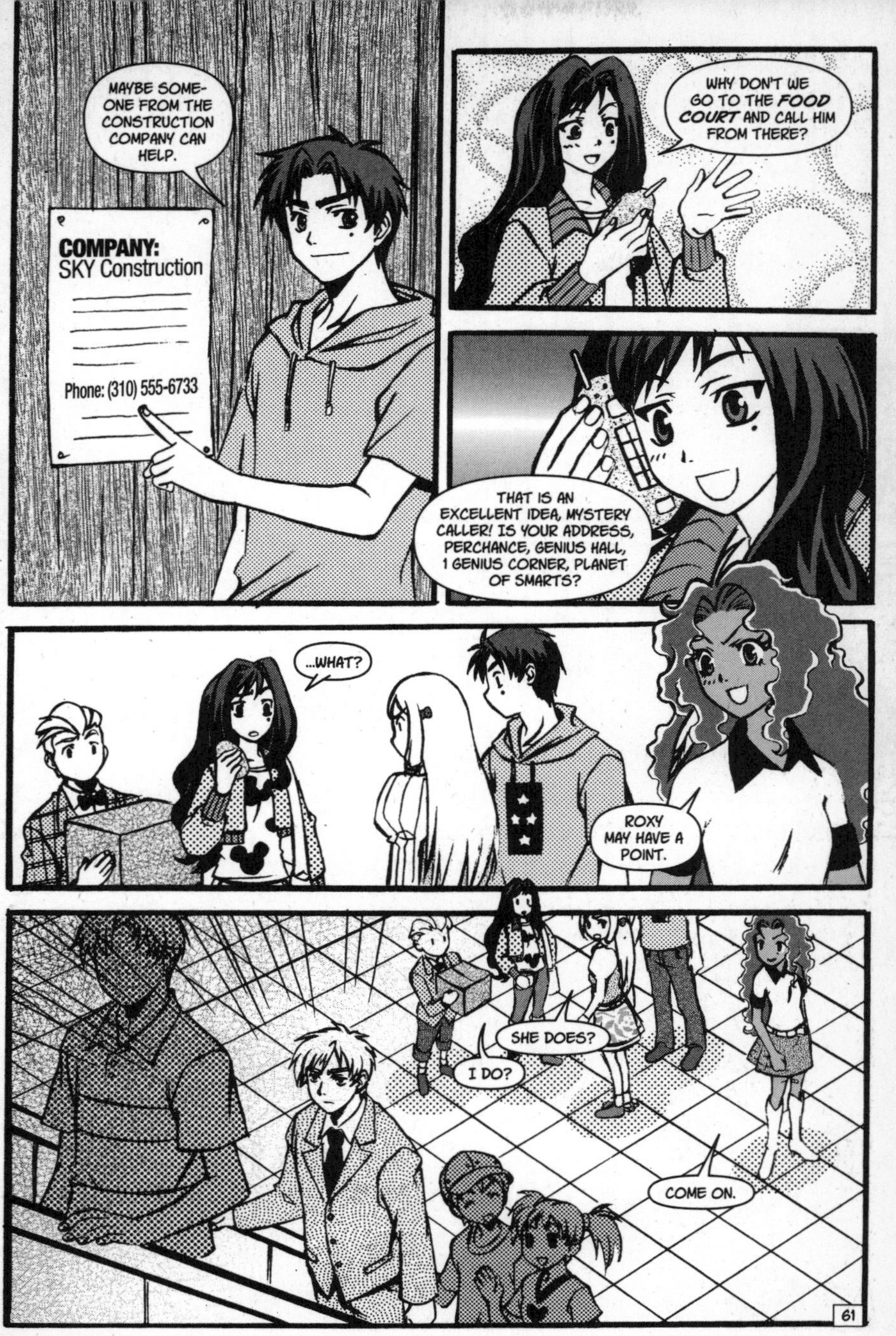
MAYBE SOME-ONE FROM THE CONSTRUCTION COMPANY CAN HELP.
COMPANY: SKY Construction
Phone: (310) 555-6733
WHY DON'T WE GO TO THE FOOD COURT AND CALL HIM FROM THERE?
THAT IS AN EXCELLENT IDEA, MYSTERY CALLER! IS YOUR ADDRESS, PERCHANCE, GENIUS HALL, 1 GENIUS CORNER, PLANET OF SMARTS?
...WHAT?
ROXY MAY HAVE A POINT.
SHE DOES?
I DO?
COME ON.

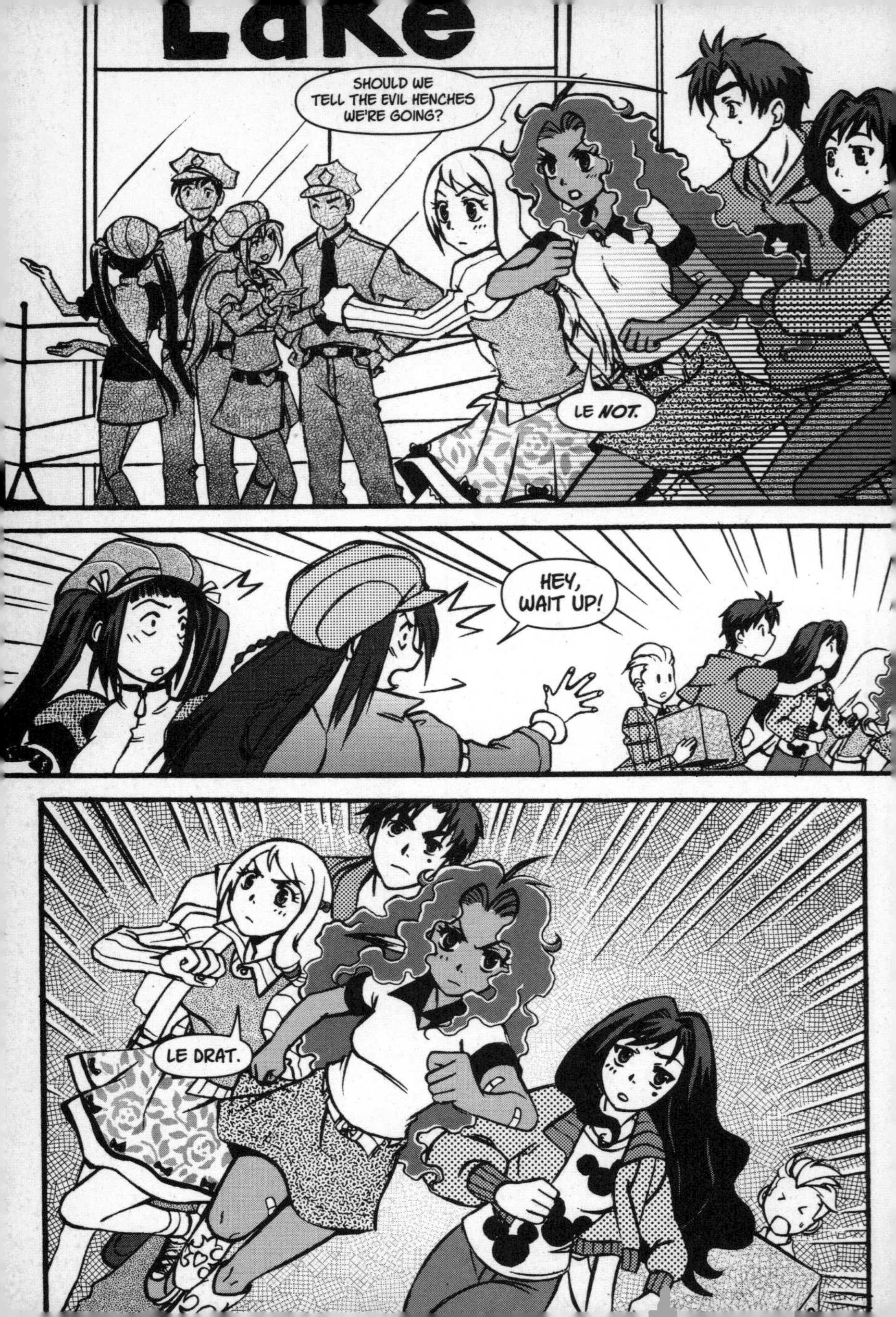
Lake
SHOULD WE TELL THE EVIL HENCHES WE'RE GOING?
LE *NOT.*
HEY, WAIT UP!
LE DRAT.

Chapter Three

Jasmine Callihan

HAIR:	On the Prowl for Danger (also Snacks!)
PORES:	Dusty
HEART:	LOW

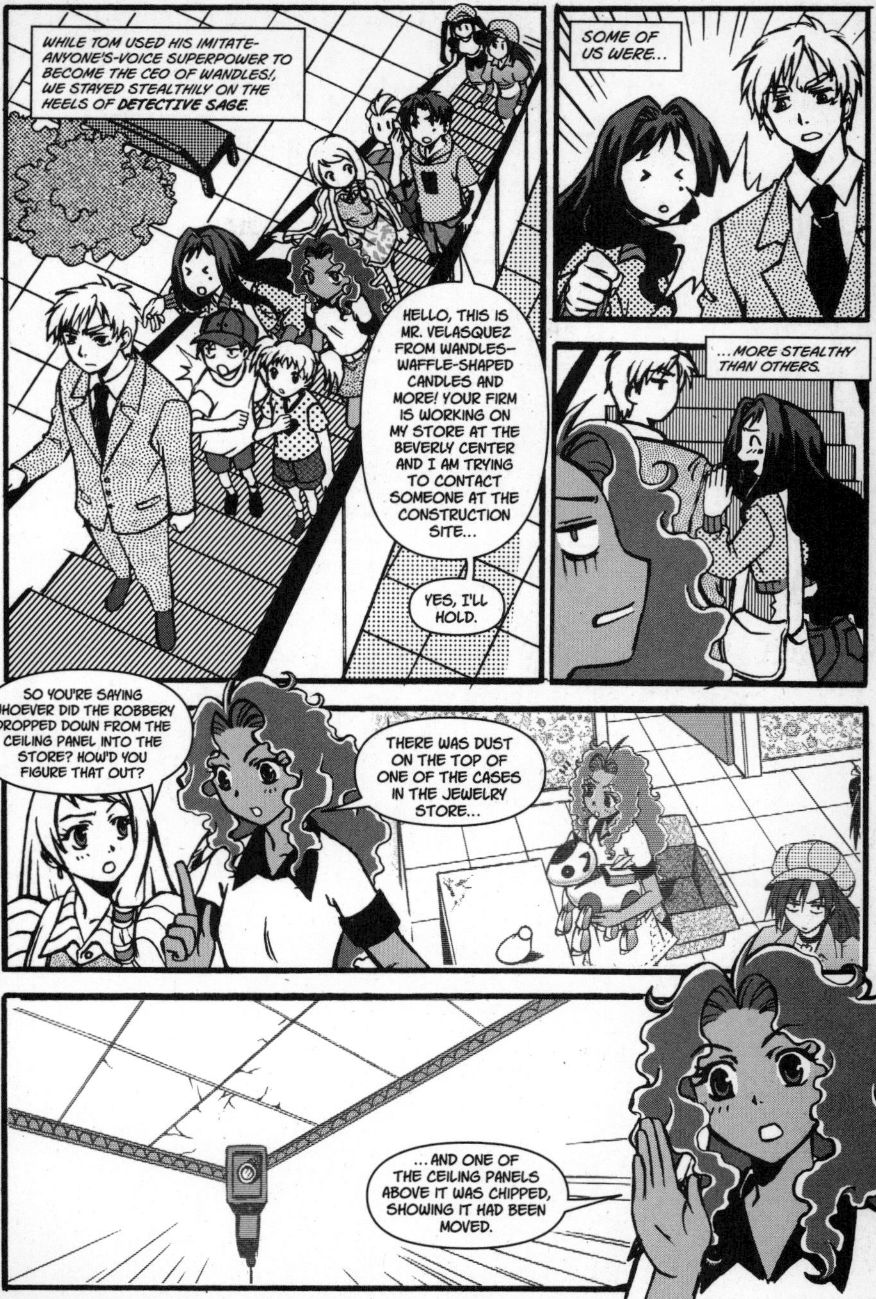
WHILE TOM USED HIS IMITATE-ANYONE'S-VOICE SUPERPOWER TO BECOME THE CEO OF WANDLES!, WE STAYED STEALTHILY ON THE HEELS OF **DETECTIVE SAGE**.
HELLO, THIS IS MR. VELASQUEZ FROM WANDLES-WAFFLE-SHAPED CANDLES AND MORE! YOUR FIRM IS WORKING ON MY STORE AT THE BEVERLY CENTER AND I AM TRYING TO CONTACT SOMEONE AT THE CONSTRUCTION SITE...
YES, I'LL HOLD.
SOME OF US WERE...
...MORE STEALTHY THAN OTHERS.
SO YOU'RE SAYING WHOEVER DID THE ROBBERY DROPPED DOWN FROM THE CEILING PANEL INTO THE STORE? HOW'D YOU FIGURE THAT OUT?
THERE WAS DUST ON THE TOP OF ONE OF THE CASES IN THE JEWELRY STORE...
...AND ONE OF THE CEILING PANELS ABOVE IT WAS CHIPPED, SHOWING IT HAD BEEN MOVED.

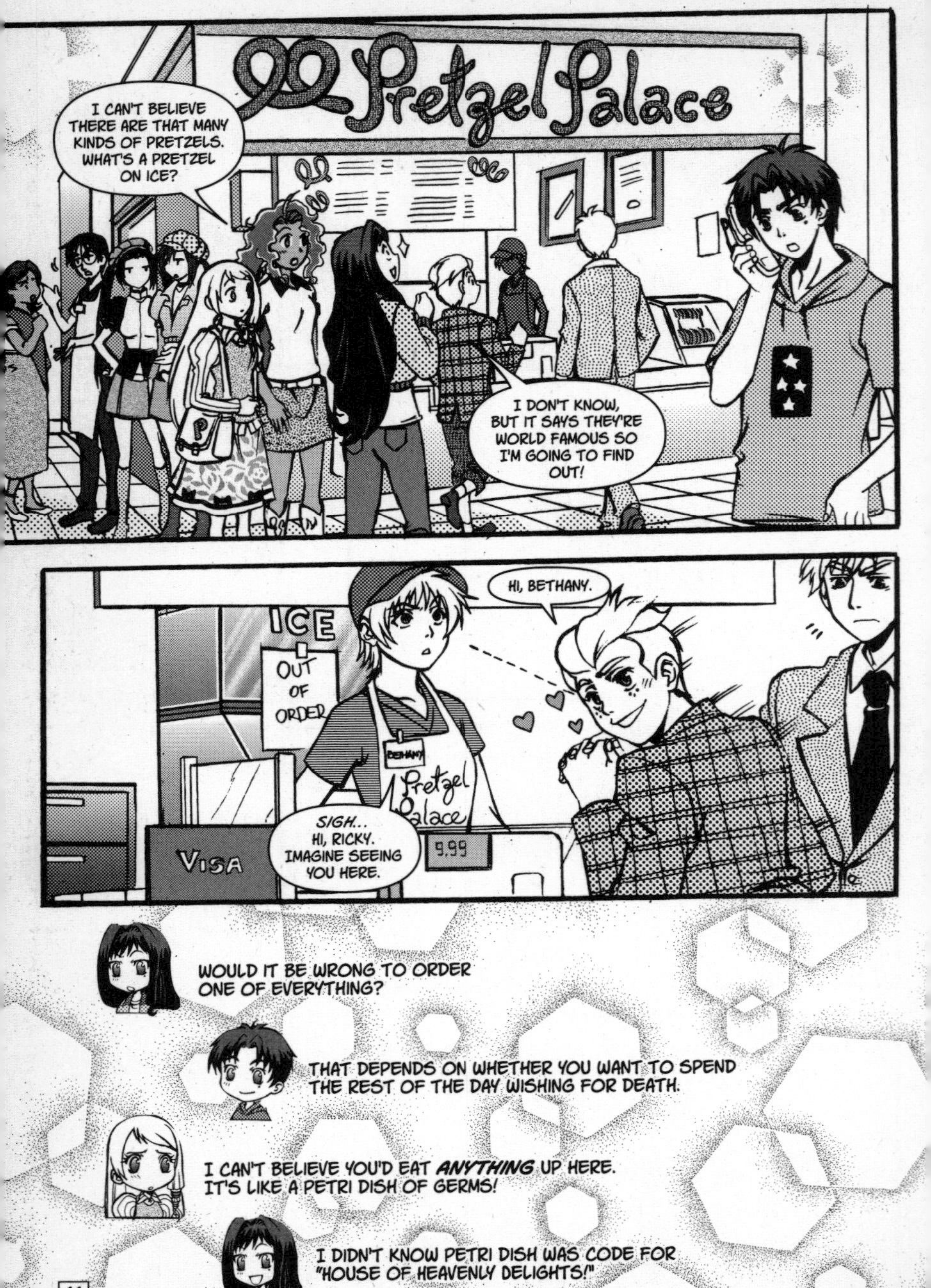
Pretzel Palace
I CAN'T BELIEVE THERE ARE THAT MANY KINDS OF PRETZELS. WHAT'S A PRETZEL ON ICE?
I DON'T KNOW, BUT IT SAYS THEY'RE WORLD FAMOUS SO I'M GOING TO FIND OUT!
ICE
OUT OF ORDER
HI, BETHANY.
BETHANY
Pretzel Palace
SIGH... HI, RICKY. IMAGINE SEEING YOU HERE.
9.99
VISA
WOULD IT BE WRONG TO ORDER ONE OF EVERYTHING?
THAT DEPENDS ON WHETHER YOU WANT TO SPEND THE REST OF THE DAY WISHING FOR DEATH.
I CAN'T BELIEVE YOU'D EAT *ANYTHING* UP HERE. IT'S LIKE A PETRI DISH OF GERMS!
I DIDN'T KNOW PETRI DISH WAS CODE FOR "HOUSE OF HEAVENLY DELIGHTS!"

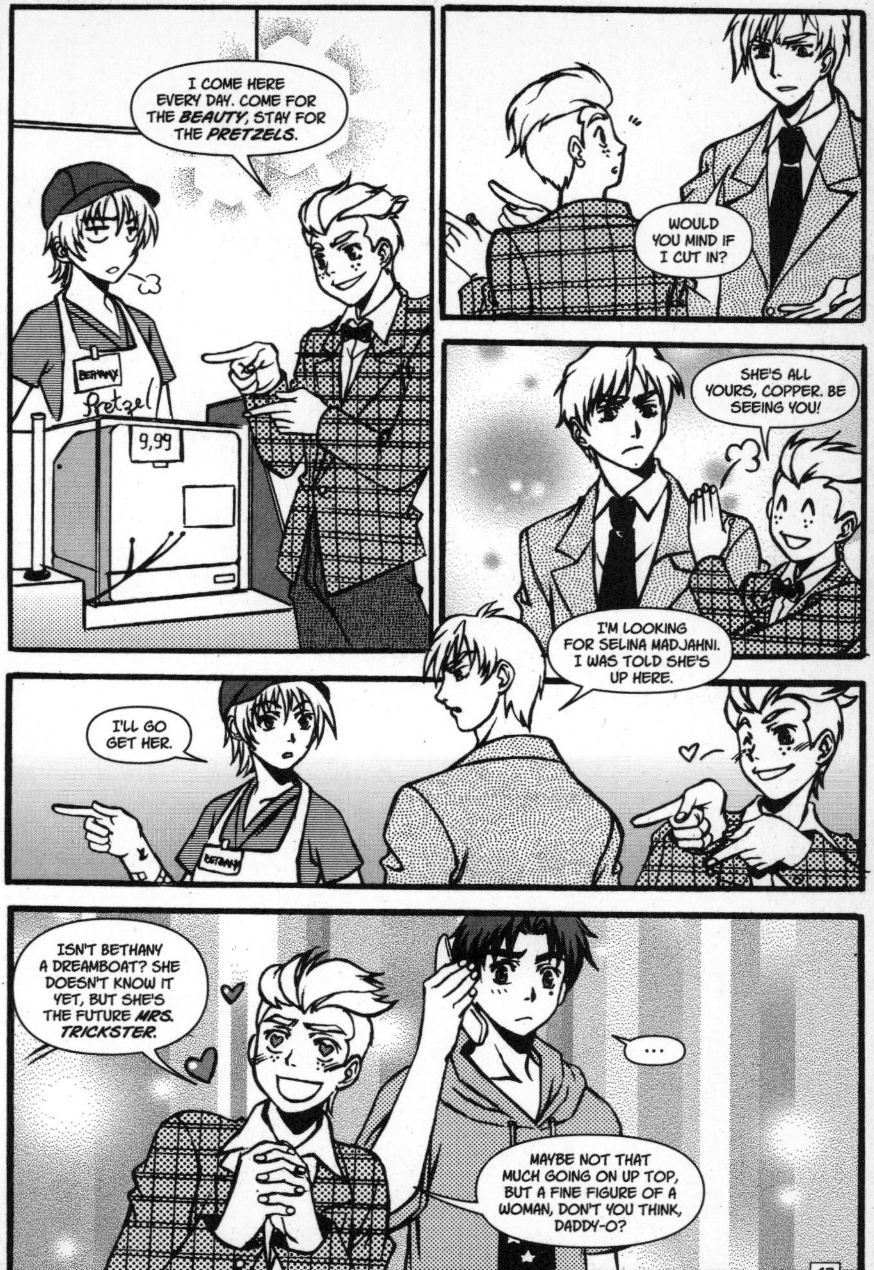
I COME HERE EVERY DAY. COME FOR THE *BEAUTY*, STAY FOR THE *PRETZELS*.
BETHANY
Pretzel
9,99
WOULD YOU MIND IF I CUT IN?
SHE'S ALL YOURS, COPPER. BE SEEING YOU!
I'M LOOKING FOR SELINA MADJAHNI. I WAS TOLD SHE'S UP HERE.
I'LL GO GET HER.
BETHANY
ISN'T BETHANY A DREAMBOAT? SHE DOESN'T KNOW IT YET, BUT SHE'S THE FUTURE *MRS. TRICKSTER*.
...
MAYBE NOT THAT MUCH GOING ON UP TOP, BUT A FINE FIGURE OF A WOMAN, DON'T YOU THINK, DADDY-O?

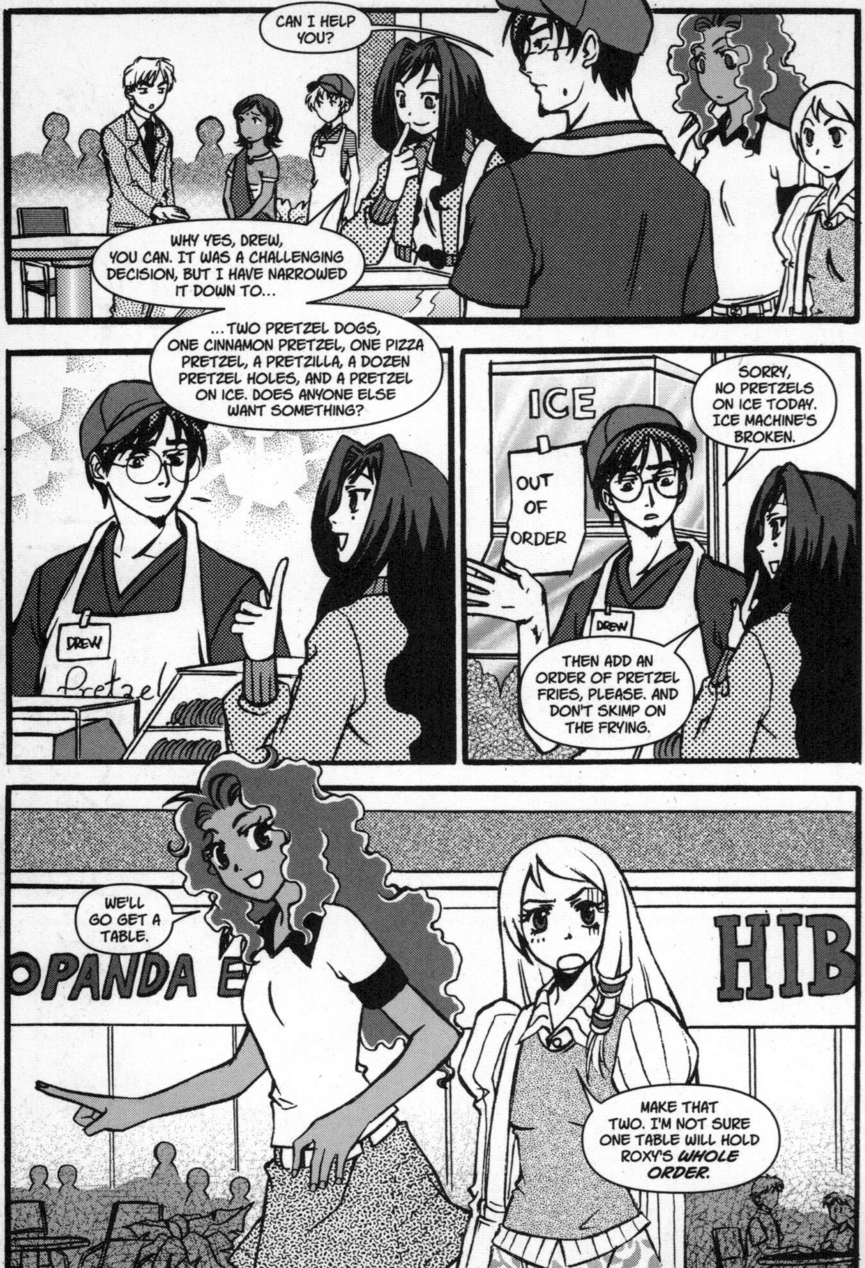
CAN I HELP YOU?
WHY YES, DREW, YOU CAN. IT WAS A CHALLENGING DECISION, BUT I HAVE NARROWED IT DOWN TO...
...TWO PRETZEL DOGS, ONE CINNAMON PRETZEL, ONE PIZZA PRETZEL, A PRETZILLA, A DOZEN PRETZEL HOLES, AND A PRETZEL ON ICE. DOES ANYONE ELSE WANT SOMETHING?
DREW
Pretzel
ICE
OUT OF ORDER
SORRY, NO PRETZELS ON ICE TODAY. ICE MACHINE'S BROKEN.
DREW
THEN ADD AN ORDER OF PRETZEL FRIES, PLEASE. AND DON'T SKIMP ON THE FRYING.
WE'LL GO GET A TABLE.
OPANDA E
HIB
MAKE THAT TWO. I'M NOT SURE ONE TABLE WILL HOLD ROXY'S ***WHOLE ORDER.***

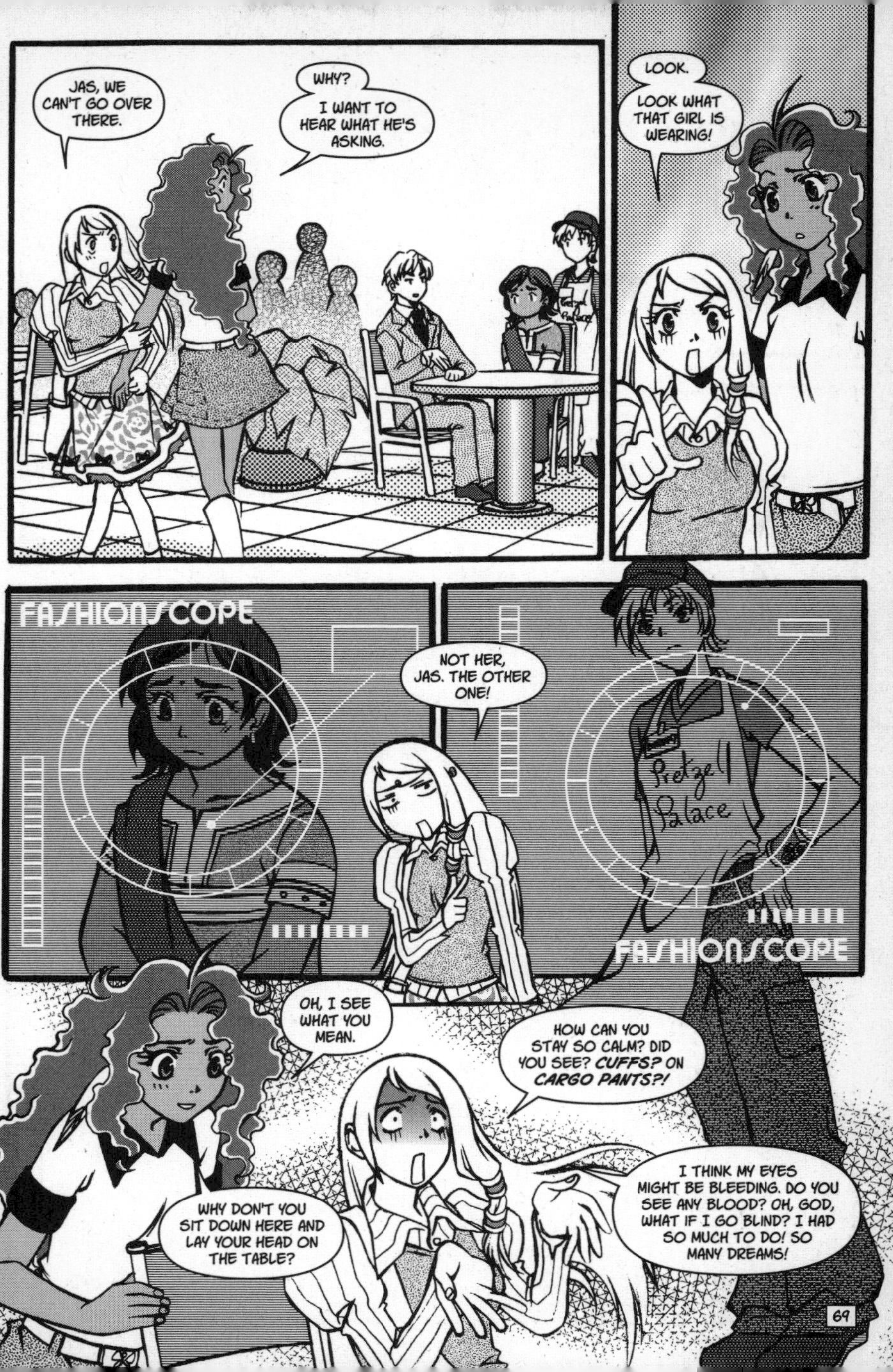

JAS, WE CAN'T GO OVER THERE.
WHY?
I WANT TO HEAR WHAT HE'S ASKING.
LOOK.
LOOK WHAT THAT GIRL IS WEARING!
FASHIONSCOPE
NOT HER, JAS. THE OTHER ONE!
Pretzel Palace
FASHIONSCOPE
OH, I SEE WHAT YOU MEAN.
HOW CAN YOU STAY SO CALM? DID YOU SEE? *CUFFS?* ON *CARGO PANTS?!*
WHY DON'T YOU SIT DOWN HERE AND LAY YOUR HEAD ON THE TABLE?
I THINK MY EYES MIGHT BE BLEEDING. DO YOU SEE ANY BLOOD? OH, GOD, WHAT IF I GO BLIND? I HAD SO MUCH TO DO! SO MANY DREAMS!

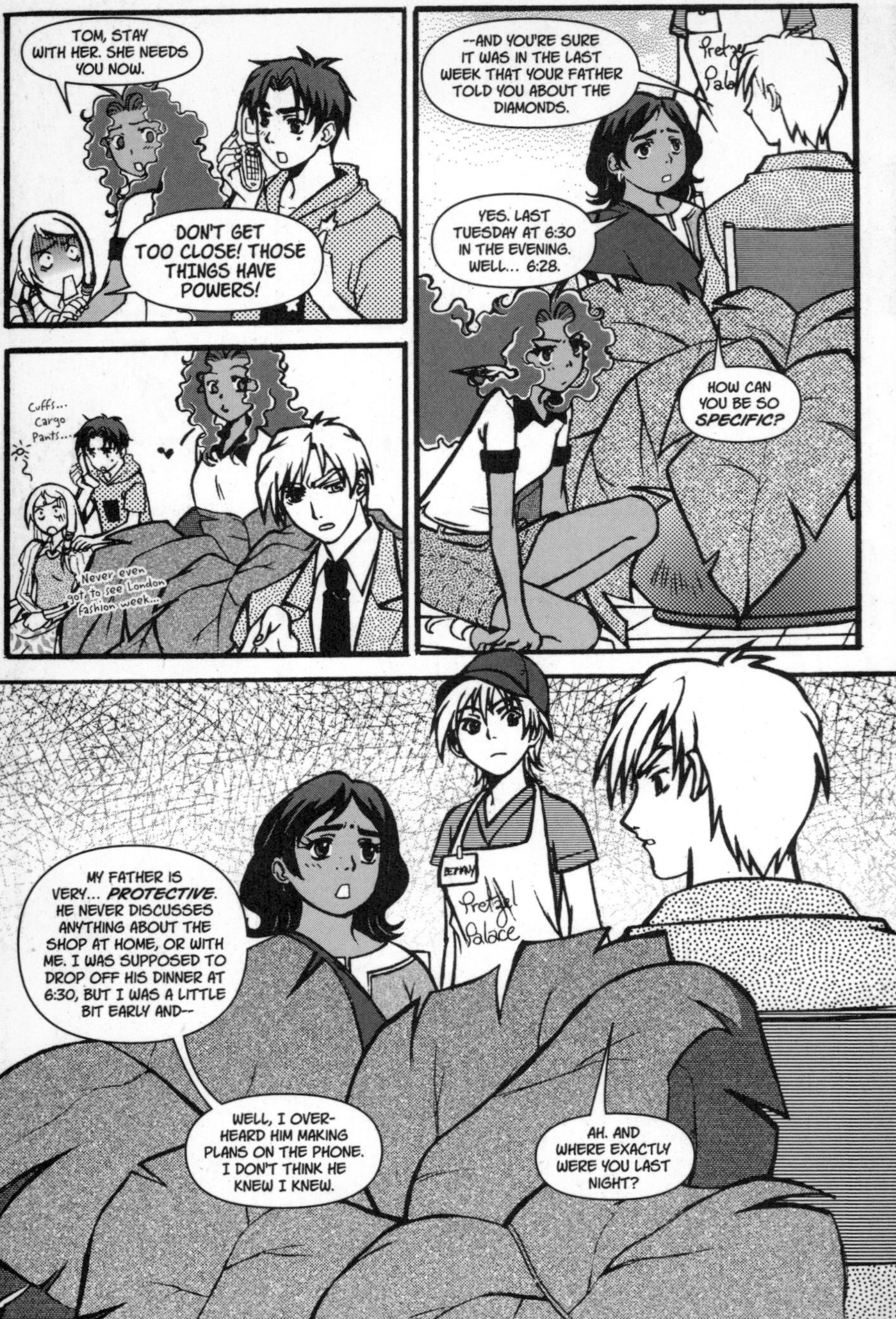
TOM, STAY WITH HER. SHE NEEDS YOU NOW.
DON'T GET TOO CLOSE! THOSE THINGS HAVE POWERS!
Cuffs... Cargo Pants...
Never even got to see London Fashion week...
--AND YOU'RE SURE IT WAS IN THE LAST WEEK THAT YOUR FATHER TOLD YOU ABOUT THE DIAMONDS.
YES. LAST TUESDAY AT 6:30 IN THE EVENING. WELL... 6:28.
HOW CAN YOU BE SO *SPECIFIC?*
MY FATHER IS VERY... ***PROTECTIVE***. HE NEVER DISCUSSES ANYTHING ABOUT THE SHOP AT HOME, OR WITH ME. I WAS SUPPOSED TO DROP OFF HIS DINNER AT 6:30, BUT I WAS A LITTLE BIT EARLY AND--
Pretzel Palace
WELL, I OVER-HEARD HIM MAKING PLANS ON THE PHONE. I DON'T THINK HE KNEW I KNEW.
AH. AND WHERE EXACTLY WERE YOU LAST NIGHT?

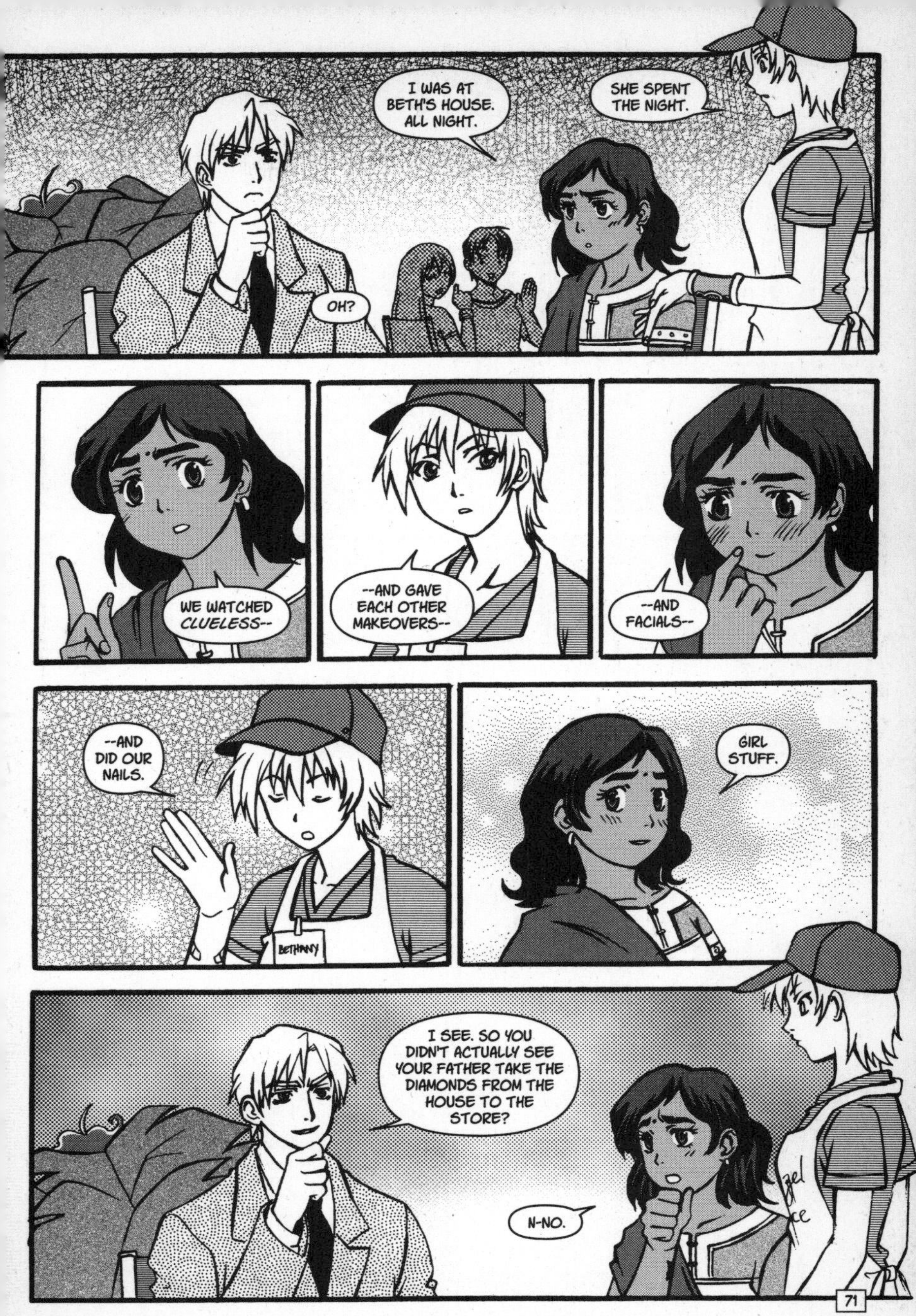
I WAS AT BETH'S HOUSE. ALL NIGHT.
SHE SPENT THE NIGHT.
OH?
WE WATCHED *CLUELESS*--
--AND GAVE EACH OTHER MAKEOVERS--
--AND FACIALS--
--AND DID OUR NAILS.
BETHANY
GIRL STUFF.
I SEE. SO YOU DIDN'T ACTUALLY SEE YOUR FATHER TAKE THE DIAMONDS FROM THE HOUSE TO THE STORE?
N-NO.

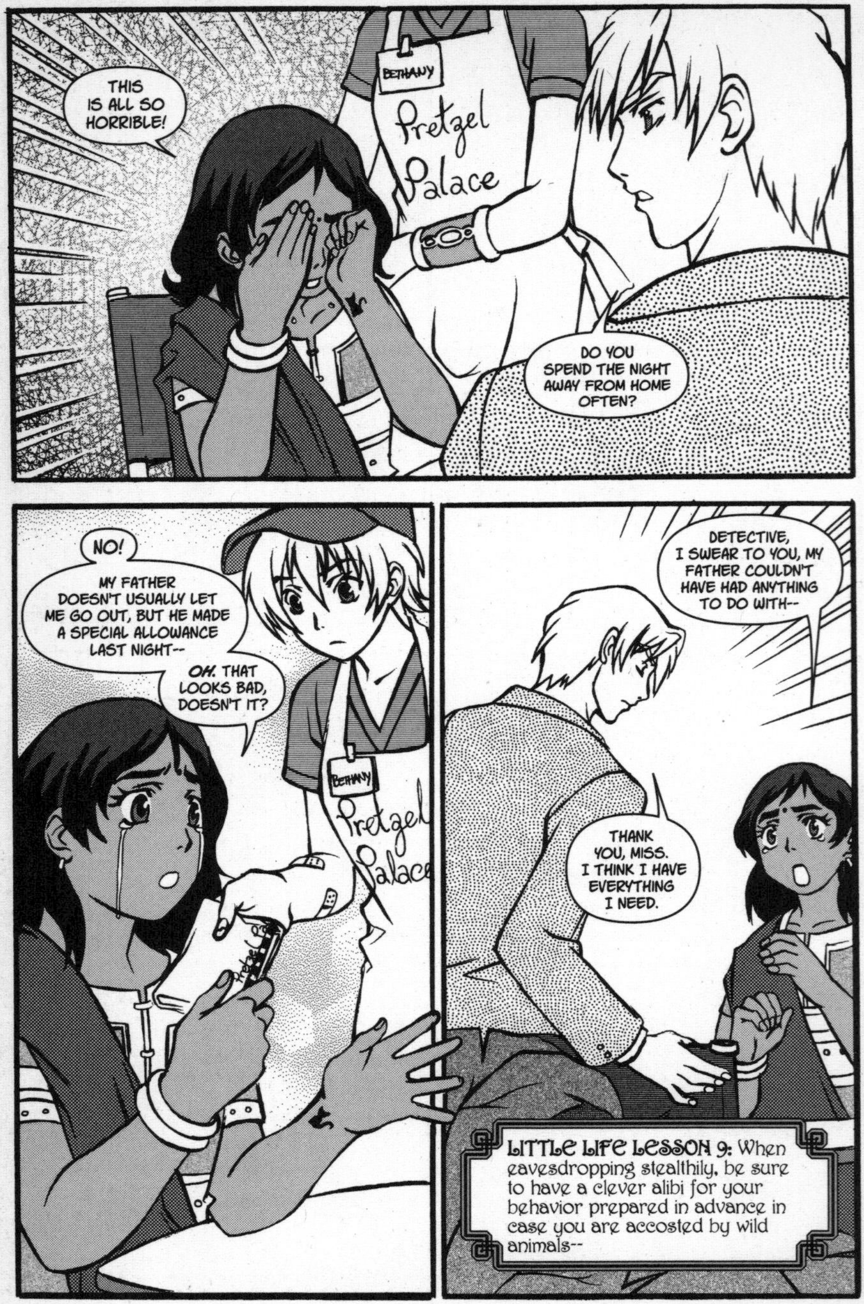
BETHANY
Pretzel Palace
THIS IS ALL SO HORRIBLE!
DO YOU SPEND THE NIGHT AWAY FROM HOME OFTEN?
NO!
MY FATHER DOESN'T USUALLY LET ME GO OUT, BUT HE MADE A SPECIAL ALLOWANCE LAST NIGHT--
OH. THAT LOOKS BAD, DOESN'T IT?
BETHANY
Pretzel Palace
DETECTIVE, I SWEAR TO YOU, MY FATHER COULDN'T HAVE HAD ANYTHING TO DO WITH--
THANK YOU, MISS. I THINK I HAVE EVERYTHING I NEED.
LITTLE LIFE LESSON 9: When eavesdropping stealthily, be sure to have a clever alibi for your behavior prepared in advance in case you are accosted by wild animals--

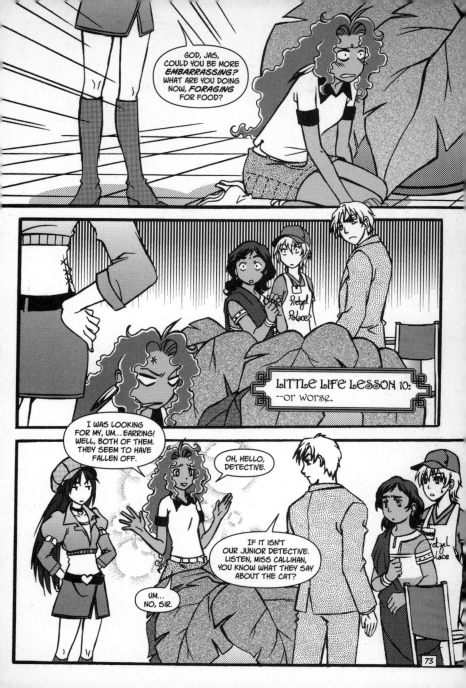

GOD, JAS, COULD YOU BE MORE *EMBARRASSING?* WHAT ARE YOU DOING NOW, *FORAGING* FOR FOOD?

LITTLE LIFE LESSON 10: --or worse.

I WAS LOOKING FOR MY, UM... EARRING! WELL, BOTH OF THEM. THEY SEEM TO HAVE FALLEN OFF.

OH, HELLO, DETECTIVE.

IF IT ISN'T OUR JUNIOR DETECTIVE. LISTEN, MISS CALLIHAN, YOU KNOW WHAT THEY SAY ABOUT THE CAT?

UM... NO, SIR.

73

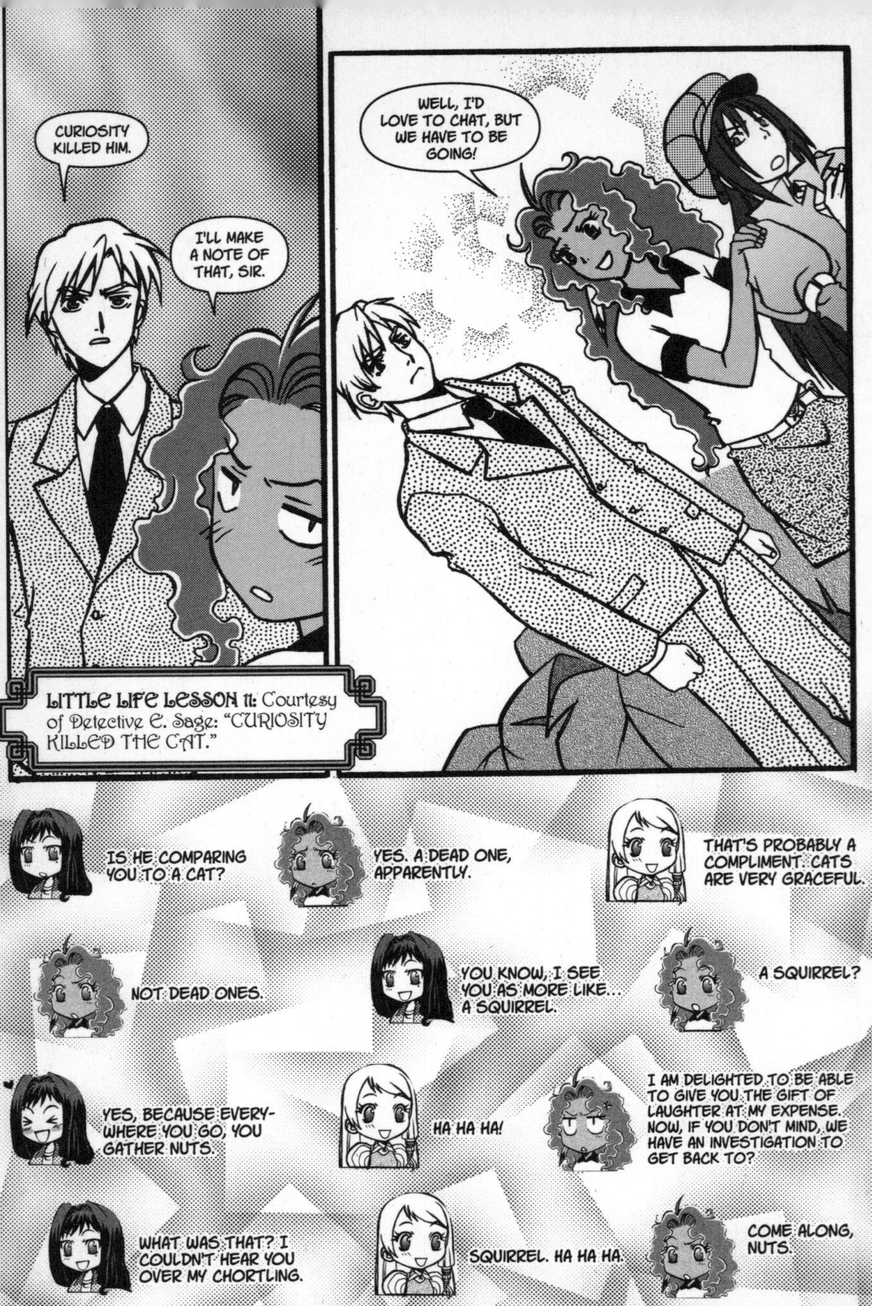
CURIOSITY KILLED HIM.
I'LL MAKE A NOTE OF THAT, SIR.
LITTLE LIFE LESSON 11: Courtesy of Detective E. Sage: "CURIOSITY KILLED THE CAT."
WELL, I'D LOVE TO CHAT, BUT WE HAVE TO BE GOING!
IS HE COMPARING YOU TO A CAT?
YES. A DEAD ONE, APPARENTLY.
THAT'S PROBABLY A COMPLIMENT. CATS ARE VERY GRACEFUL.
NOT DEAD ONES.
YOU KNOW, I SEE YOU AS MORE LIKE... A SQUIRREL.
A SQUIRREL?
YES, BECAUSE EVERY-WHERE YOU GO, YOU GATHER NUTS.
HA HA HA!
I AM DELIGHTED TO BE ABLE TO GIVE YOU THE GIFT OF LAUGHTER AT MY EXPENSE. NOW, IF YOU DON'T MIND, WE HAVE AN INVESTIGATION TO GET BACK TO?
WHAT WAS THAT? I COULDN'T HEAR YOU OVER MY CHORTLING.
SQUIRREL. HA HA HA.
COME ALONG, NUTS.

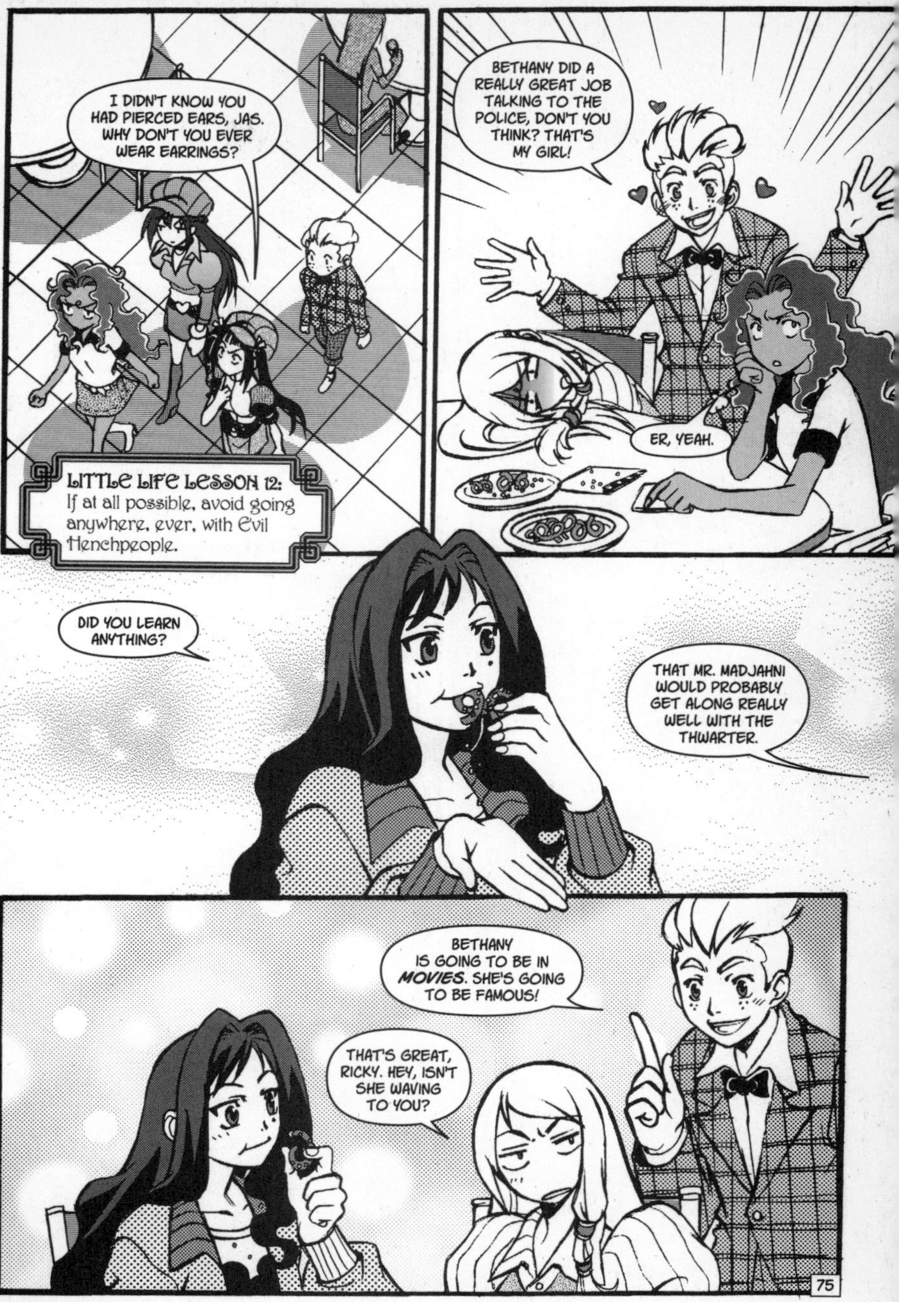
I DIDN'T KNOW YOU HAD PIERCED EARS, JAS. WHY DON'T YOU EVER WEAR EARRINGS?
LITTLE LIFE LESSON 12:
If at all possible, avoid going anywhere, ever, with Evil Henchpeople.
BETHANY DID A REALLY GREAT JOB TALKING TO THE POLICE, DON'T YOU THINK? THAT'S MY GIRL!
ER, YEAH.
DID YOU LEARN ANYTHING?
THAT MR. MADJAHNI WOULD PROBABLY GET ALONG REALLY WELL WITH THE THWARTER.
BETHANY IS GOING TO BE IN MOVIES. SHE'S GOING TO BE FAMOUS!
THAT'S GREAT, RICKY. HEY, ISN'T SHE WAVING TO YOU?

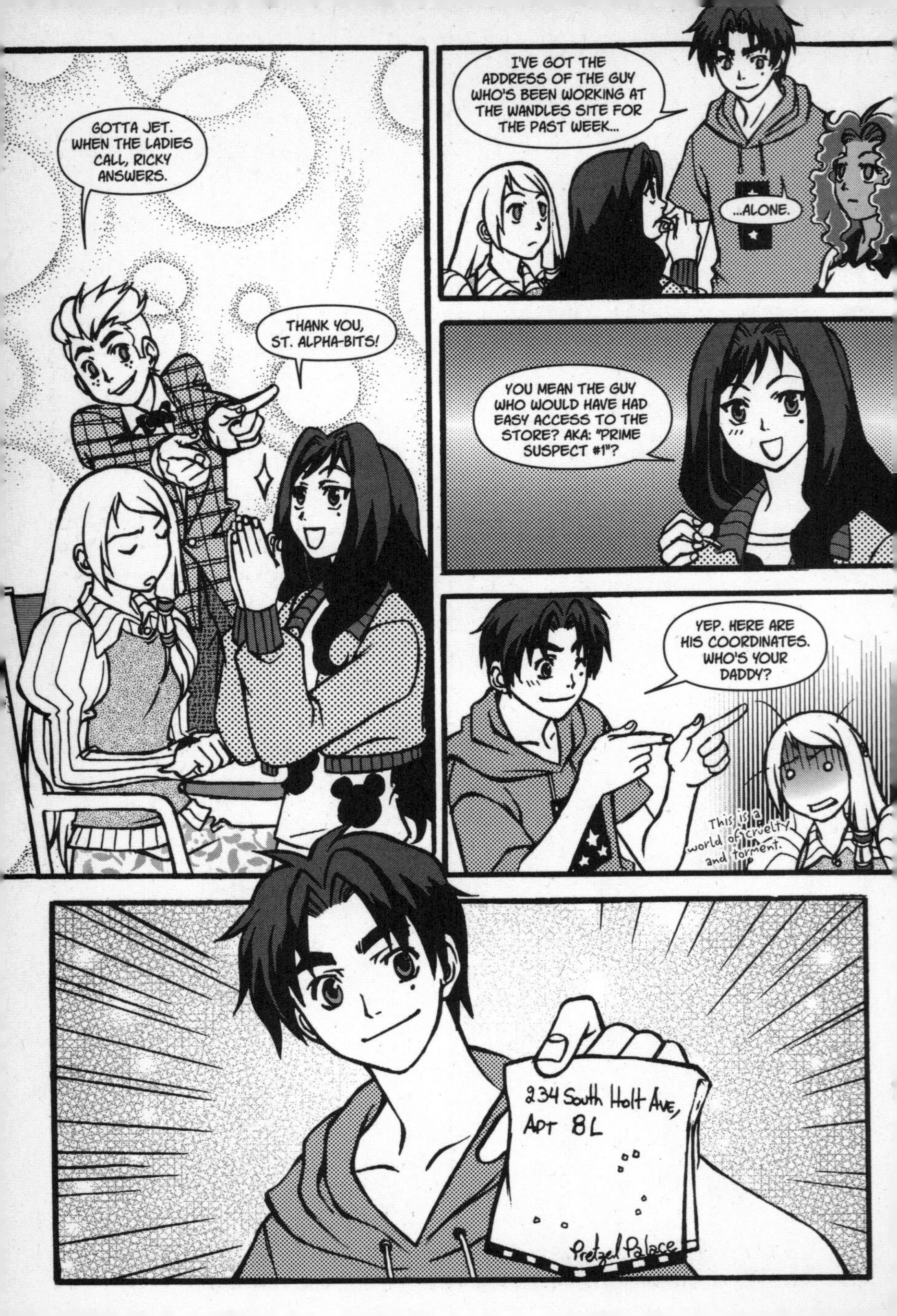
GOTTA JET. WHEN THE LADIES CALL, RICKY ANSWERS.
THANK YOU, ST. ALPHA-BITS!
I'VE GOT THE ADDRESS OF THE GUY WHO'S BEEN WORKING AT THE WANDLES SITE FOR THE PAST WEEK...
...ALONE.
YOU MEAN THE GUY WHO WOULD HAVE HAD EASY ACCESS TO THE STORE? AKA: "PRIME SUSPECT #1"?
YEP. HERE ARE HIS COORDINATES. WHO'S YOUR DADDY?
This is a world of cruelty and torment.
234 South Holt Ave, Apt 8L
Pretzel Palace

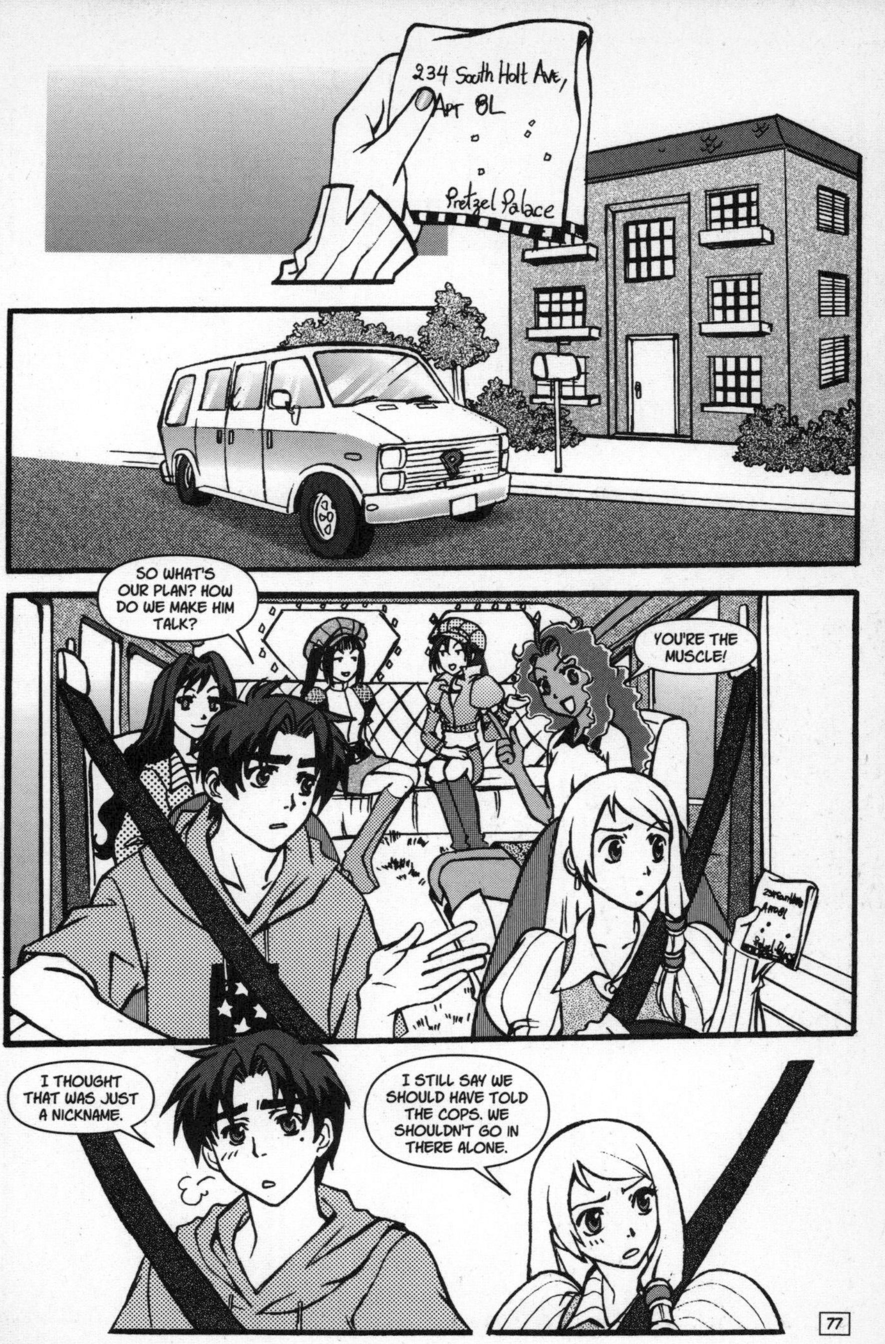
234 South Holt Ave,
Apt 8L
Pretzel Palace
SO WHAT'S OUR PLAN? HOW DO WE MAKE HIM TALK?
YOU'RE THE MUSCLE!
I THOUGHT THAT WAS JUST A NICKNAME.
I STILL SAY WE SHOULD HAVE TOLD THE COPS. WE SHOULDN'T GO IN THERE ALONE.

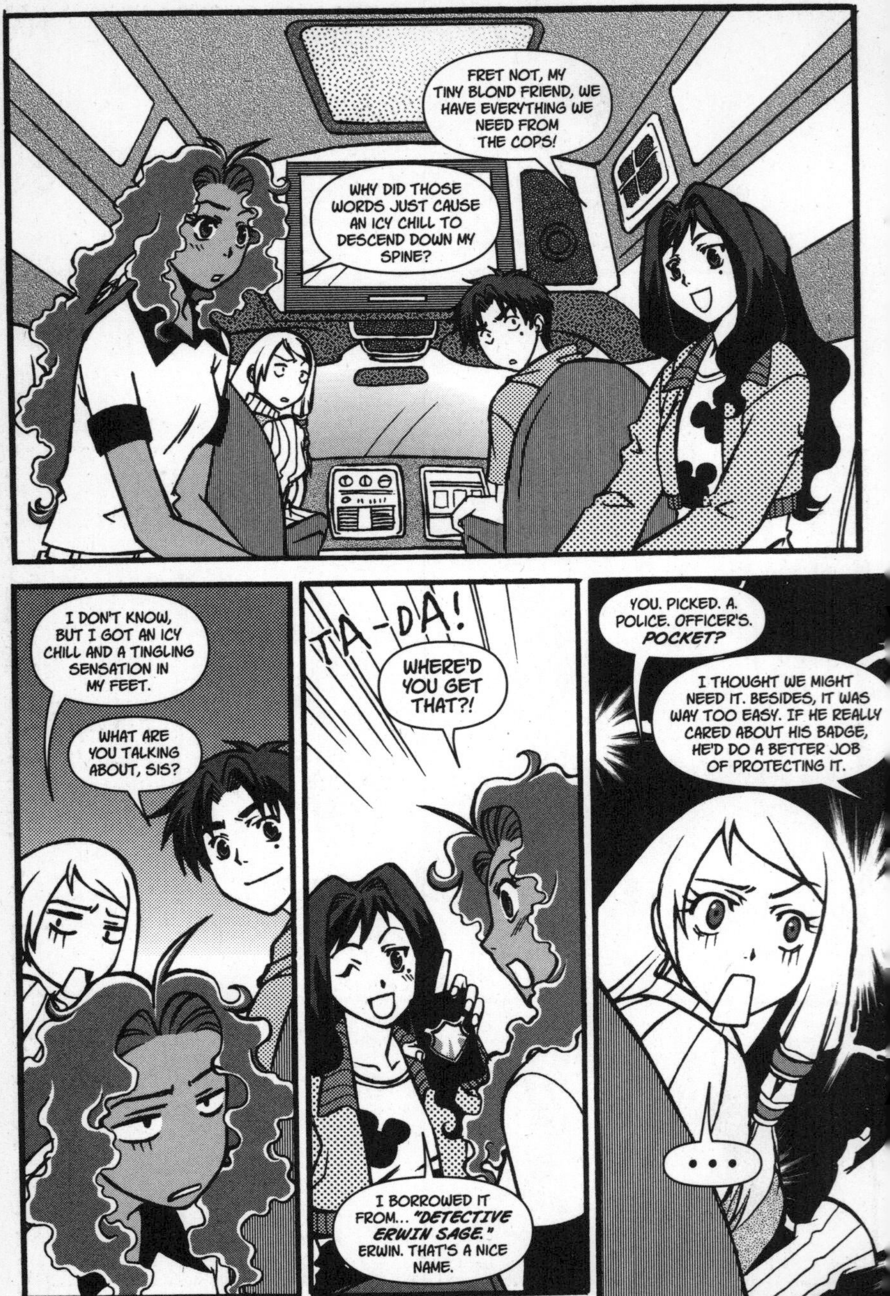
FRET NOT, MY TINY BLOND FRIEND, WE HAVE EVERYTHING WE NEED FROM THE COPS!
WHY DID THOSE WORDS JUST CAUSE AN ICY CHILL TO DESCEND DOWN MY SPINE?
I DON'T KNOW, BUT I GOT AN ICY CHILL AND A TINGLING SENSATION IN MY FEET.
WHAT ARE YOU TALKING ABOUT, SIS?
TA-DA!
WHERE'D YOU GET THAT?!
I BORROWED IT FROM... "DETECTIVE ERWIN SAGE." ERWIN. THAT'S A NICE NAME.
YOU. PICKED. A. POLICE. OFFICER'S. POCKET?
I THOUGHT WE MIGHT NEED IT. BESIDES, IT WAS WAY TOO EASY. IF HE REALLY CARED ABOUT HIS BADGE, HE'D DO A BETTER JOB OF PROTECTING IT.
...

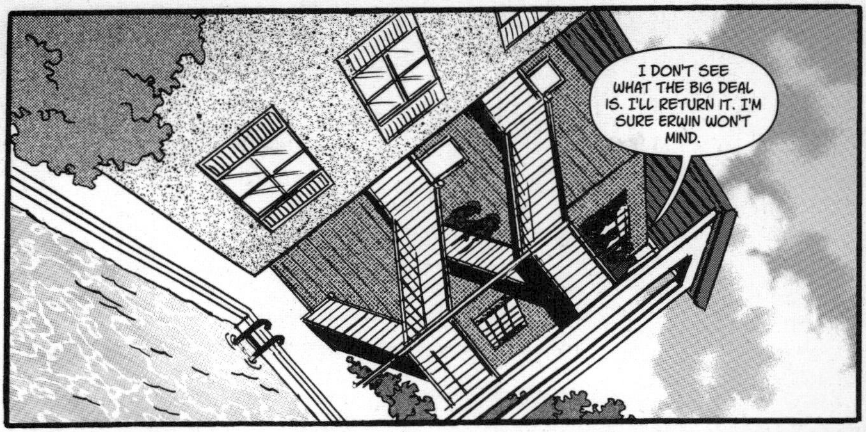
I DON'T SEE WHAT THE BIG DEAL IS. I'LL RETURN IT. I'M SURE ERWIN WON'T MIND.

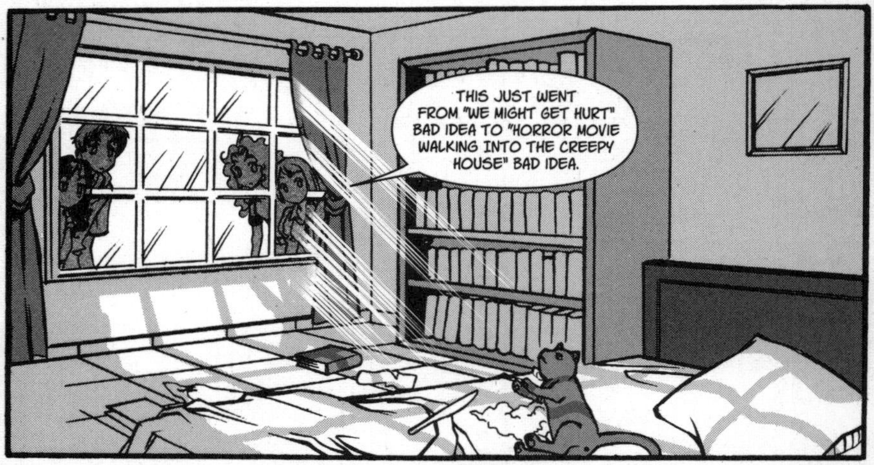
THIS JUST WENT FROM "WE MIGHT GET HURT" BAD IDEA TO "HORROR MOVIE WALKING INTO THE CREEPY HOUSE" BAD IDEA.

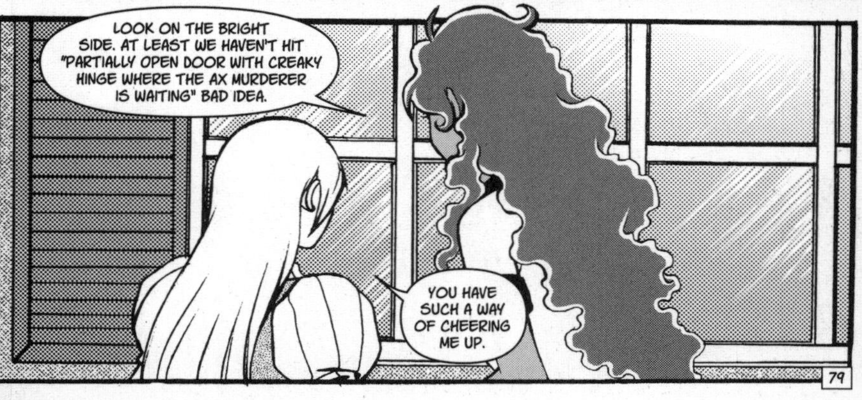
LOOK ON THE BRIGHT SIDE. AT LEAST WE HAVEN'T HIT "PARTIALLY OPEN DOOR WITH CREAKY HINGE WHERE THE AX MURDERER IS WAITING" BAD IDEA.
YOU HAVE SUCH A WAY OF CHEERING ME UP.

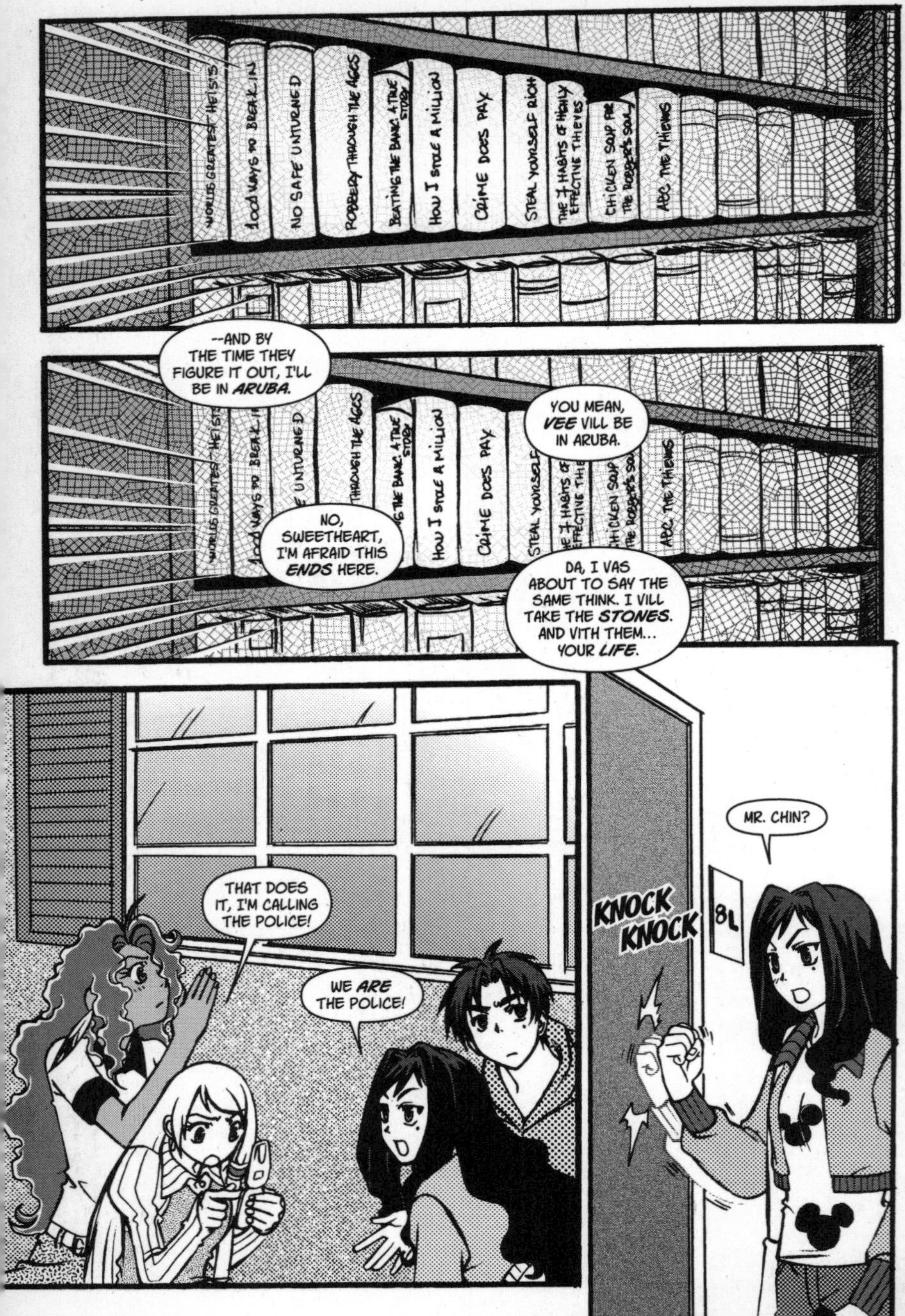
WORLD'S GREATEST HEISTS
100 WAYS TO BREAK IN
NO SAFE UNTURNED
ROBBERY THROUGH THE AGES
BEATING THE BANK: A TRUE STORY
HOW I STOLE A MILLION
CRIME DOES PAY
STEAL YOURSELF RICH
THE 7 HABITS OF HIGHLY EFFECTIVE THIEVES
CHICKEN SOUP FOR THE ROBBER'S SOUL
ABC THE THIEVES
--AND BY THE TIME THEY FIGURE IT OUT, I'LL BE IN ARUBA.
YOU MEAN, VEE VILL BE IN ARUBA.
NO, SWEETHEART, I'M AFRAID THIS ENDS HERE.
DA, I VAS ABOUT TO SAY THE SAME THINK. I VILL TAKE THE STONES. AND VITH THEM... YOUR LIFE.
THAT DOES IT, I'M CALLING THE POLICE!
WE ARE THE POLICE!
KNOCK KNOCK
8L
MR. CHIN?

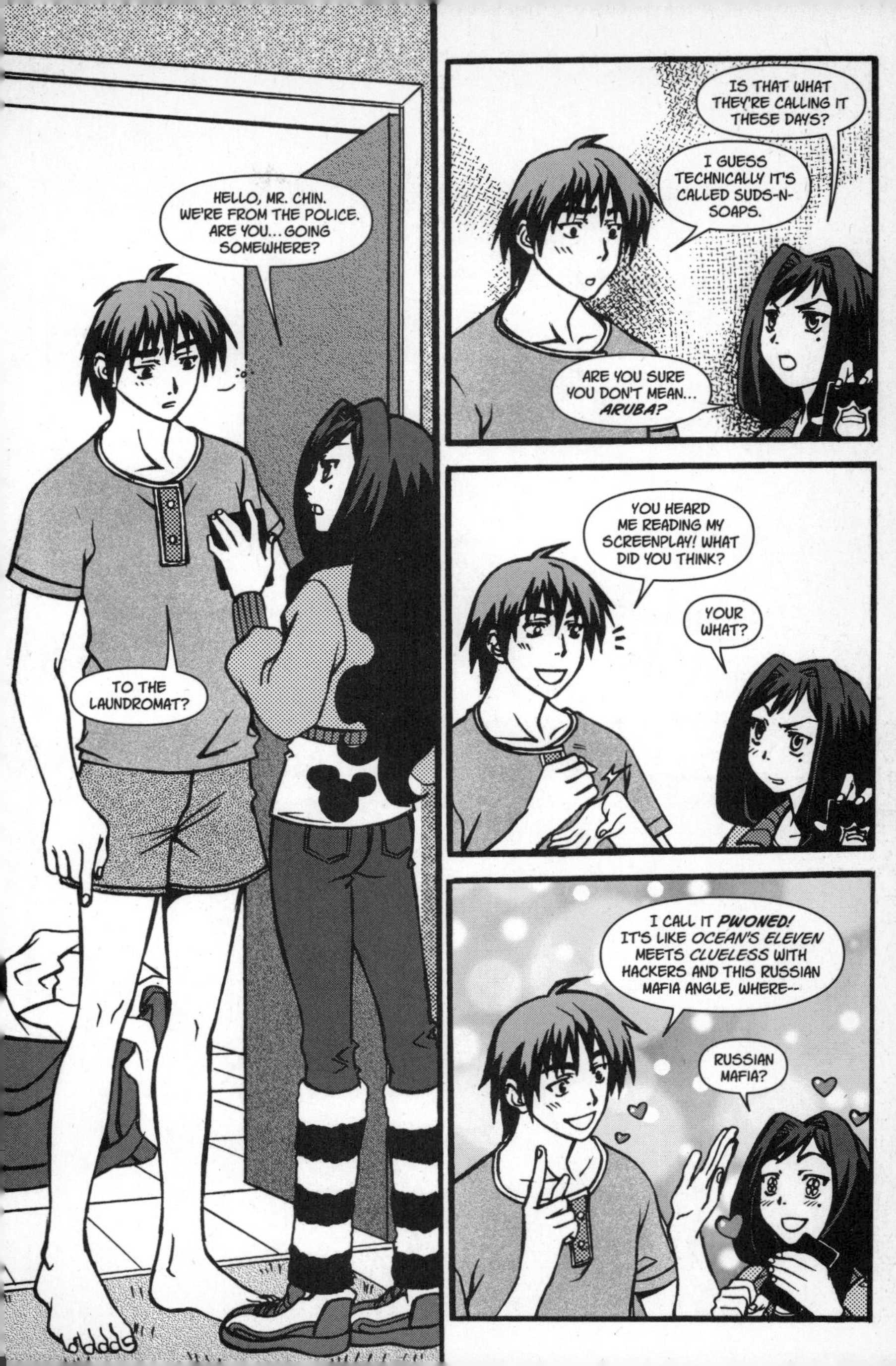
HELLO, MR. CHIN. WE'RE FROM THE POLICE. ARE YOU... GOING SOMEWHERE?
TO THE LAUNDROMAT?
IS THAT WHAT THEY'RE CALLING IT THESE DAYS?
I GUESS TECHNICALLY IT'S CALLED SUDS-N-SOAPS.
ARE YOU SURE YOU DON'T MEAN... *ARUBA?*
YOU HEARD ME READING MY SCREENPLAY! WHAT DID YOU THINK?
YOUR WHAT?
I CALL IT ***PWONED!*** IT'S LIKE *OCEAN'S ELEVEN* MEETS *CLUELESS* WITH HACKERS AND THIS RUSSIAN MAFIA ANGLE, WHERE--
RUSSIAN MAFIA?

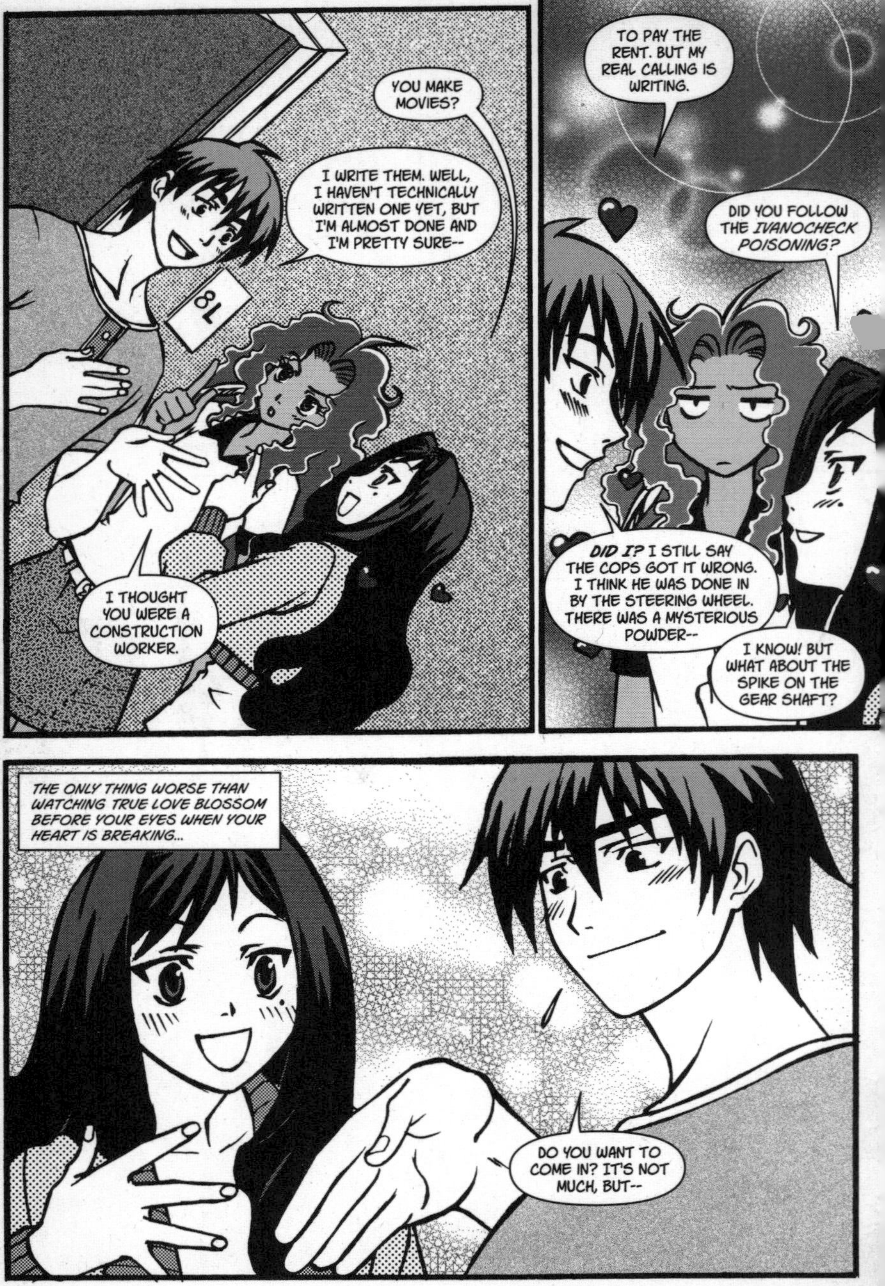
YOU MAKE MOVIES?
I WRITE THEM. WELL, I HAVEN'T TECHNICALLY WRITTEN ONE YET, BUT I'M ALMOST DONE AND I'M PRETTY SURE--
18
I THOUGHT YOU WERE A CONSTRUCTION WORKER.
TO PAY THE RENT. BUT MY REAL CALLING IS WRITING.
DID YOU FOLLOW THE *IVANOCHECK POISONING?*
DID I? I STILL SAY THE COPS GOT IT WRONG. I THINK HE WAS DONE IN BY THE STEERING WHEEL. THERE WAS A MYSTERIOUS POWDER--
I KNOW! BUT WHAT ABOUT THE SPIKE ON THE GEAR SHAFT?
THE ONLY THING WORSE THAN WATCHING TRUE LOVE BLOSSOM BEFORE YOUR EYES WHEN YOUR HEART IS BREAKING...
DO YOU WANT TO COME IN? IT'S NOT MUCH, BUT--

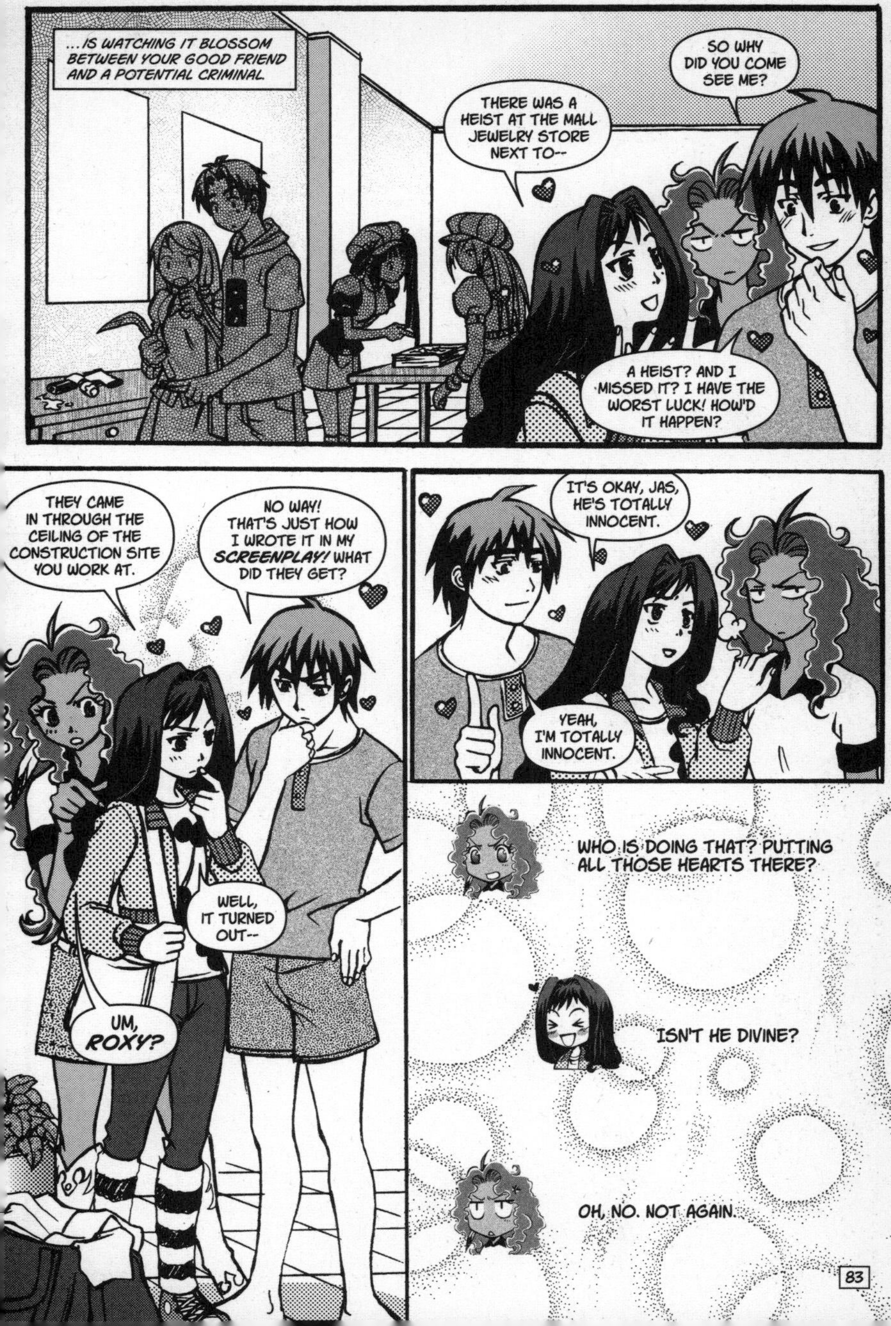
...IS WATCHING IT BLOSSOM BETWEEN YOUR GOOD FRIEND AND A POTENTIAL CRIMINAL.
THERE WAS A HEIST AT THE MALL JEWELRY STORE NEXT TO--
SO WHY DID YOU COME SEE ME?
A HEIST? AND I MISSED IT? I HAVE THE WORST LUCK! HOW'D IT HAPPEN?
THEY CAME IN THROUGH THE CEILING OF THE CONSTRUCTION SITE YOU WORK AT.
NO WAY! THAT'S JUST HOW I WROTE IT IN MY SCREENPLAY! WHAT DID THEY GET?
WELL, IT TURNED OUT--
UM, ROXY?
IT'S OKAY, JAS, HE'S TOTALLY INNOCENT.
YEAH, I'M TOTALLY INNOCENT.
WHO IS DOING THAT? PUTTING ALL THOSE HEARTS THERE?
ISN'T HE DIVINE?
OH, NO. NOT AGAIN.

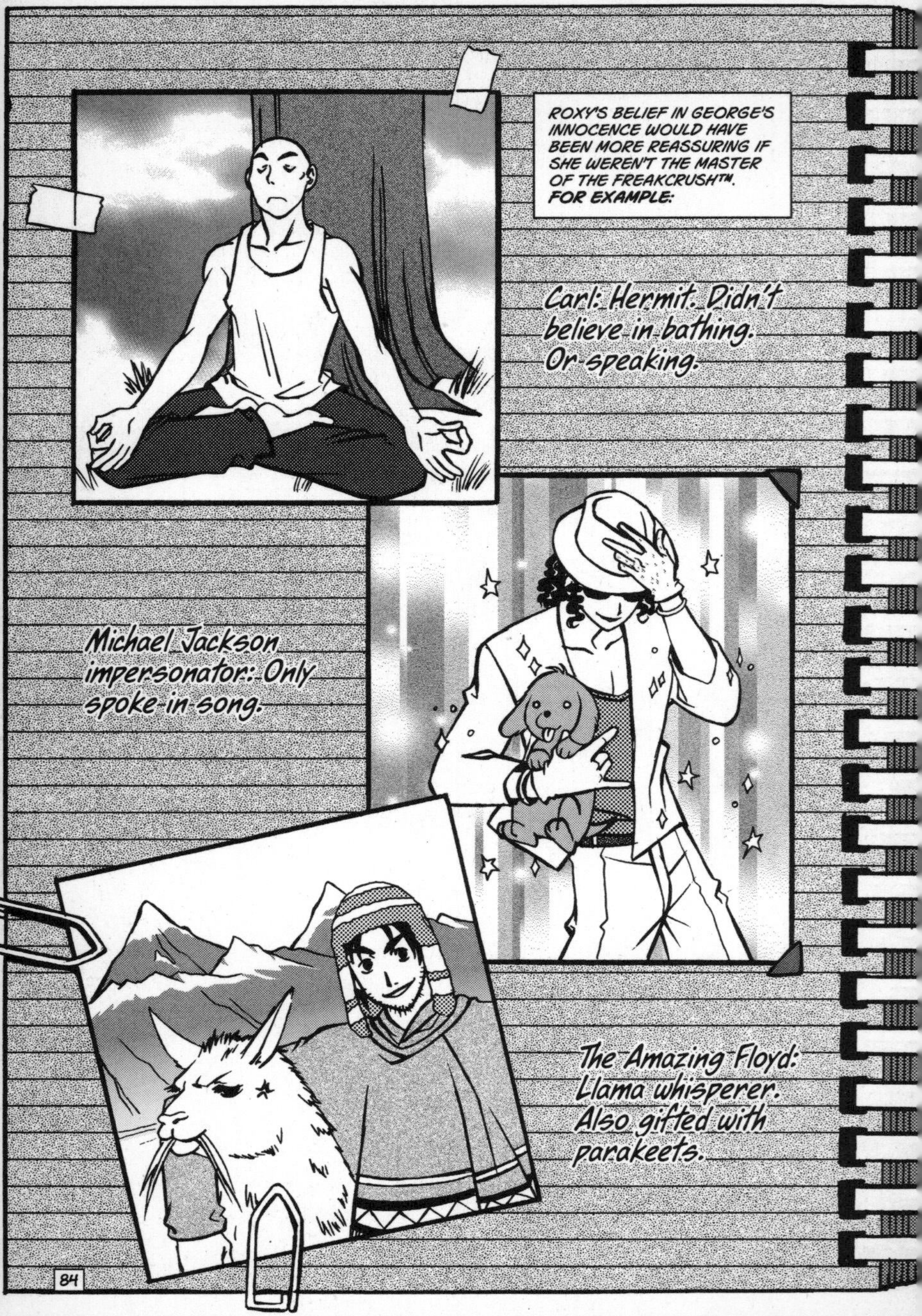
ROXY'S BELIEF IN GEORGE'S INNOCENCE WOULD HAVE BEEN MORE REASSURING IF SHE WEREN'T THE MASTER OF THE FREAKCRUSH™. FOR EXAMPLE:
Carl: Hermit. Didn't believe in bathing. Or speaking.
Michael Jackson impersonator: Only spoke in song.
The Amazing Floyd: Llama whisperer. Also gifted with parakeets.

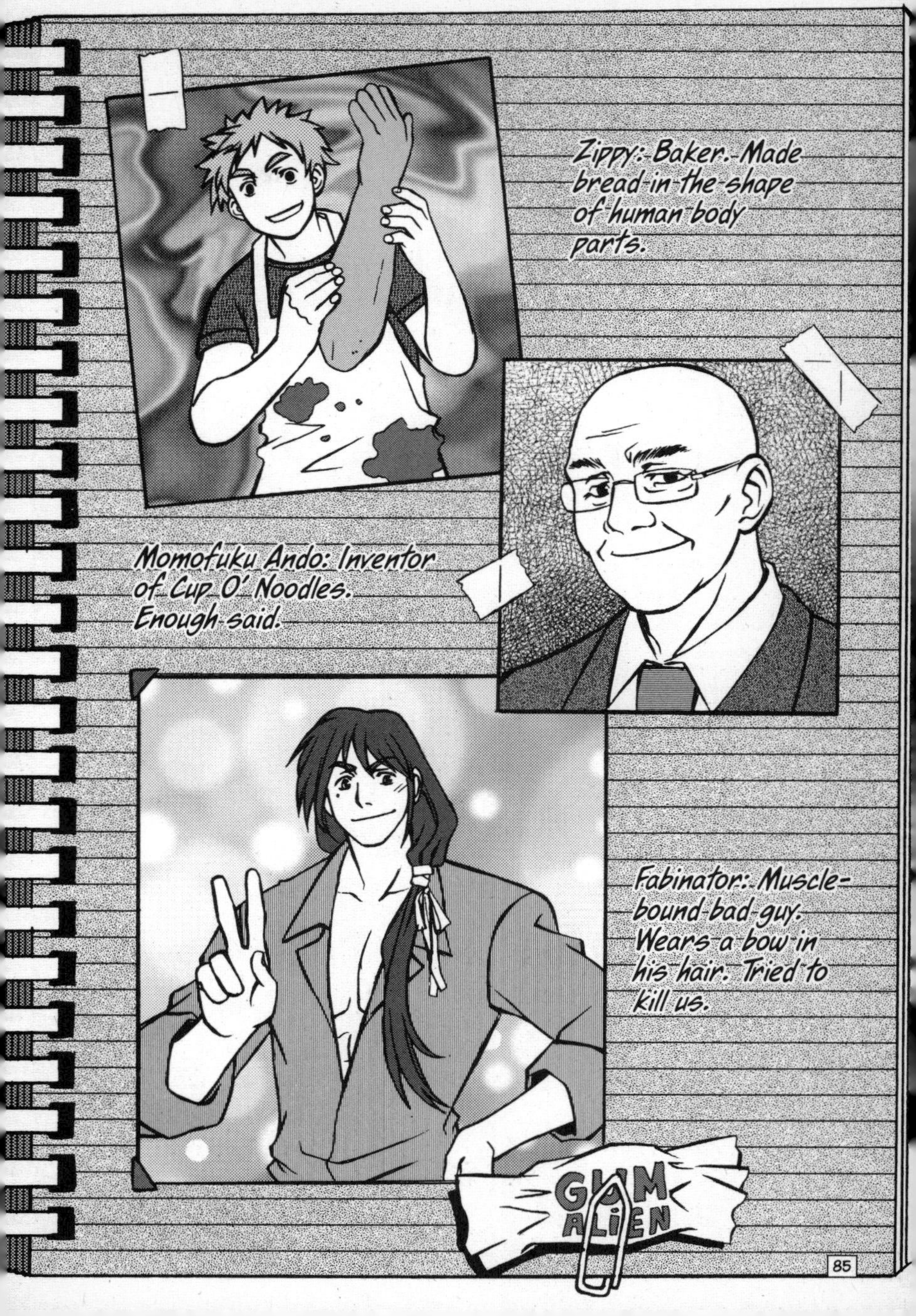
Zippy: Baker. Made bread in the shape of human body parts.
Momofuku Ando: Inventor of Cup O' Noodles. Enough said.
Fabinator: Muscle-bound bad guy. Wears a bow in his hair. Tried to kill us.
GUM ALIEN

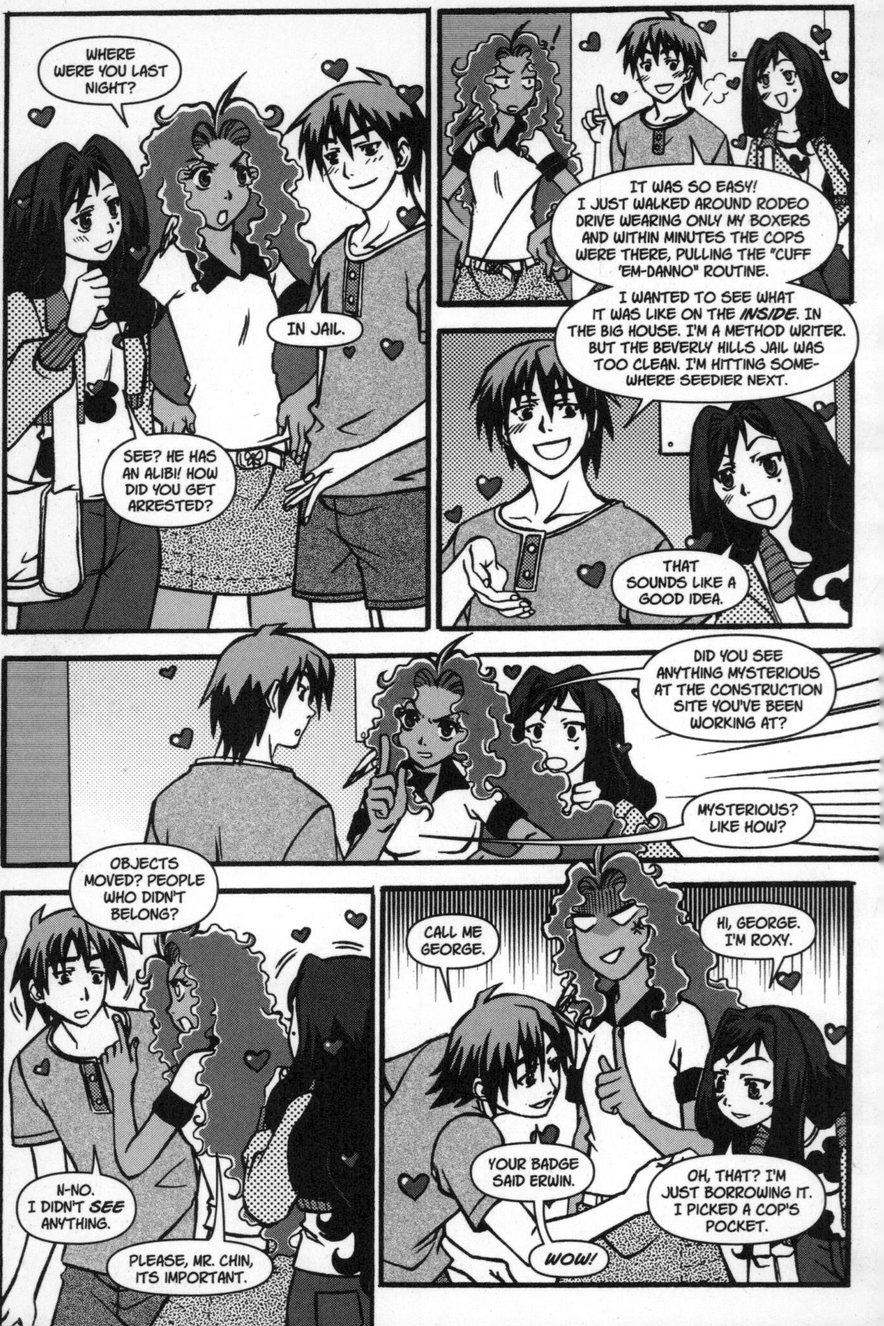
WHERE WERE YOU LAST NIGHT?
IN JAIL.
SEE? HE HAS AN ALIBI! HOW DID YOU GET ARRESTED?
IT WAS SO EASY! I JUST WALKED AROUND RODEO DRIVE WEARING ONLY MY BOXERS AND WITHIN MINUTES THE COPS WERE THERE, PULLING THE "CUFF 'EM-DANNO" ROUTINE.
I WANTED TO SEE WHAT IT WAS LIKE ON THE *INSIDE*. IN THE BIG HOUSE. I'M A METHOD WRITER. BUT THE BEVERLY HILLS JAIL WAS TOO CLEAN. I'M HITTING SOMEWHERE SEEDIER NEXT.
THAT SOUNDS LIKE A GOOD IDEA.
DID YOU SEE ANYTHING MYSTERIOUS AT THE CONSTRUCTION SITE YOU'VE BEEN WORKING AT?
MYSTERIOUS? LIKE HOW?
OBJECTS MOVED? PEOPLE WHO DIDN'T BELONG?
N-NO. I DIDN'T *SEE* ANYTHING.
PLEASE, MR. CHIN, ITS IMPORTANT.
CALL ME GEORGE.
HI, GEORGE. I'M ROXY.
YOUR BADGE SAID ERWIN.
OH, THAT? I'M JUST BORROWING IT. I PICKED A COP'S POCKET.
WOW!

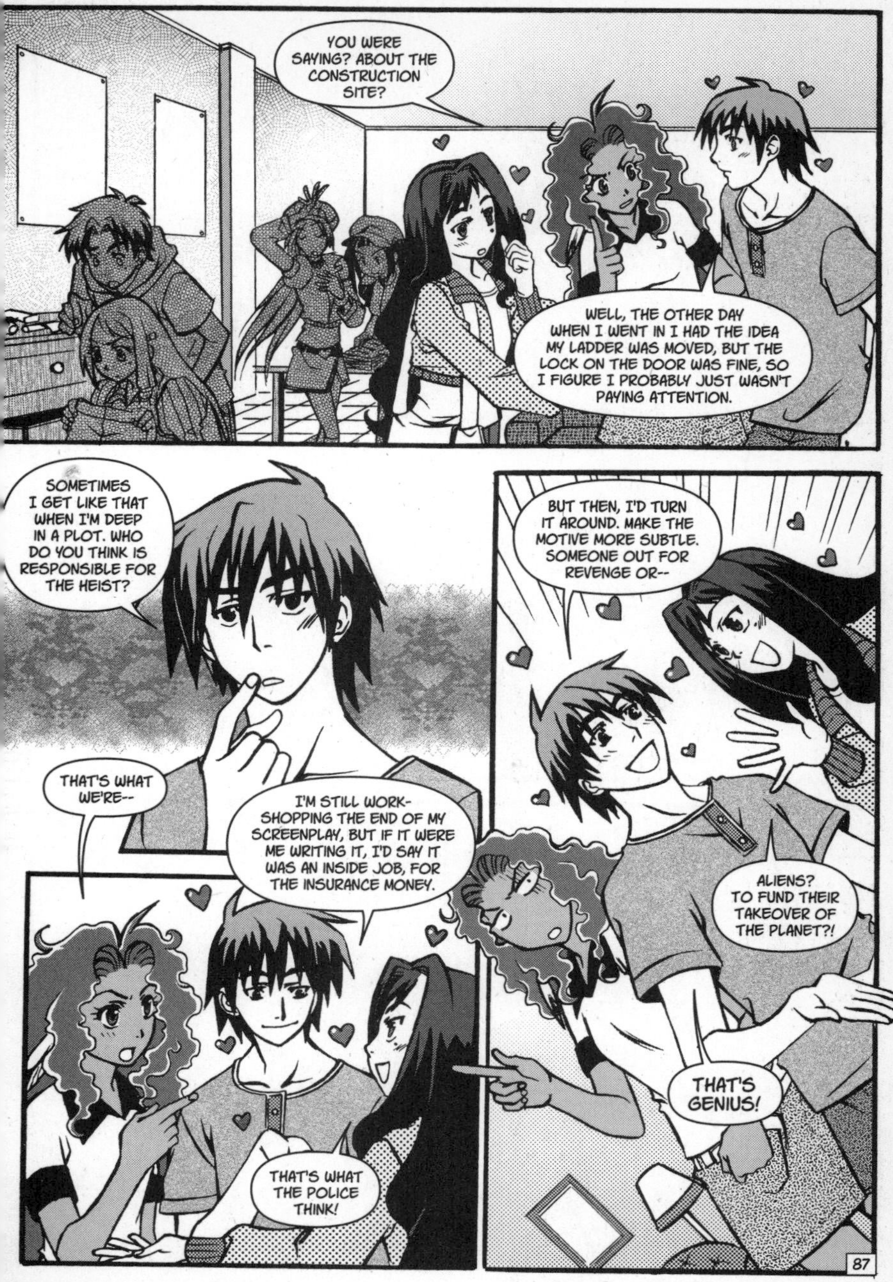
YOU WERE SAYING? ABOUT THE CONSTRUCTION SITE?
WELL, THE OTHER DAY WHEN I WENT IN I HAD THE IDEA MY LADDER WAS MOVED, BUT THE LOCK ON THE DOOR WAS FINE, SO I FIGURE I PROBABLY JUST WASN'T PAYING ATTENTION.
SOMETIMES I GET LIKE THAT WHEN I'M DEEP IN A PLOT. WHO DO YOU THINK IS RESPONSIBLE FOR THE HEIST?
THAT'S WHAT WE'RE--
I'M STILL WORK-SHOPPING THE END OF MY SCREENPLAY, BUT IF IT WERE ME WRITING IT, I'D SAY IT WAS AN INSIDE JOB, FOR THE INSURANCE MONEY.
THAT'S WHAT THE POLICE THINK!
BUT THEN, I'D TURN IT AROUND. MAKE THE MOTIVE MORE SUBTLE. SOMEONE OUT FOR REVENGE OR--
ALIENS? TO FUND THEIR TAKEOVER OF THE PLANET?!
THAT'S GENIUS!

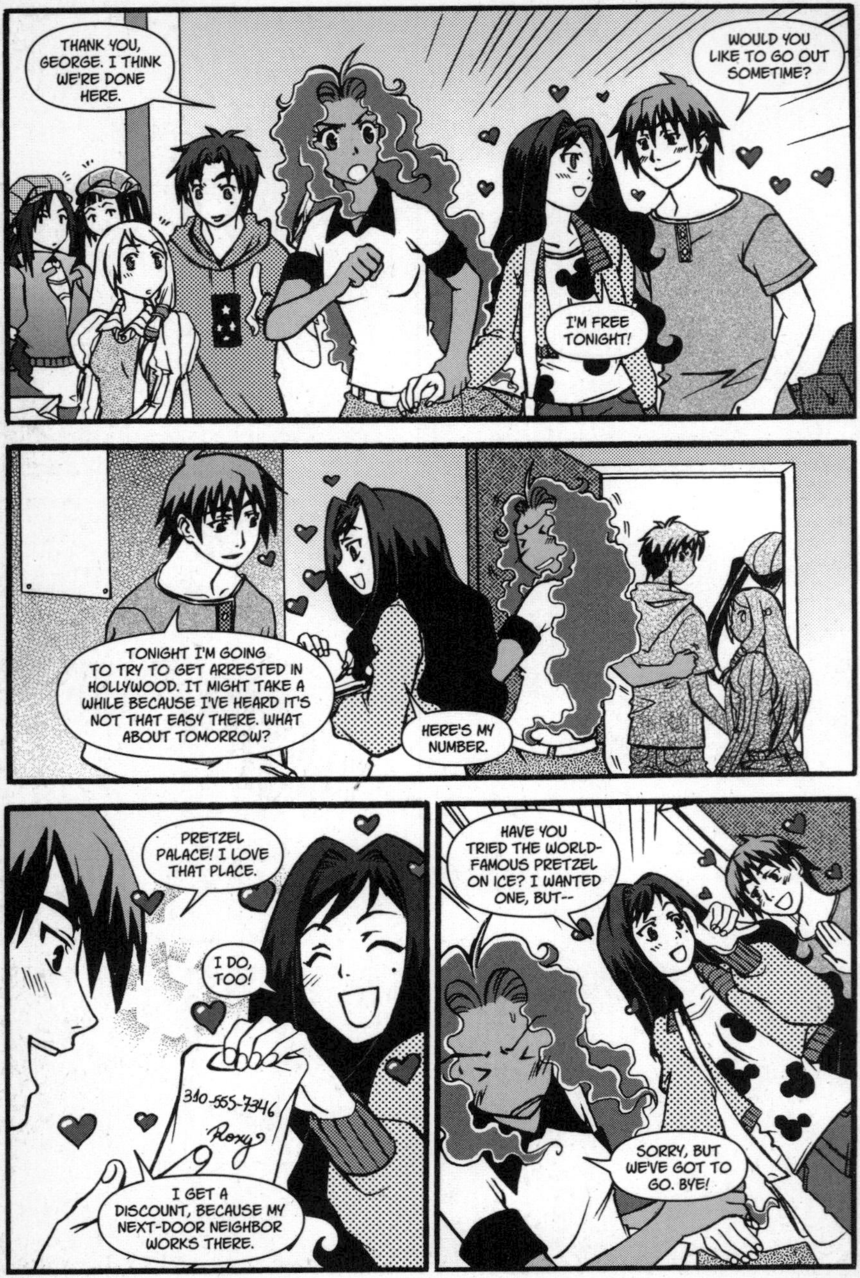
THANK YOU, GEORGE. I THINK WE'RE DONE HERE.
WOULD YOU LIKE TO GO OUT SOMETIME?
I'M FREE TONIGHT!
TONIGHT I'M GOING TO TRY TO GET ARRESTED IN HOLLYWOOD. IT MIGHT TAKE A WHILE BECAUSE I'VE HEARD IT'S NOT THAT EASY THERE. WHAT ABOUT TOMORROW?
HERE'S MY NUMBER.
PRETZEL PALACE! I LOVE THAT PLACE.
I DO, TOO!
310-555-7346
Roxy
I GET A DISCOUNT, BECAUSE MY NEXT-DOOR NEIGHBOR WORKS THERE.
HAVE YOU TRIED THE WORLD-FAMOUS PRETZEL ON ICE? I WANTED ONE, BUT--
SORRY, BUT WE'VE GOT TO GO. BYE!

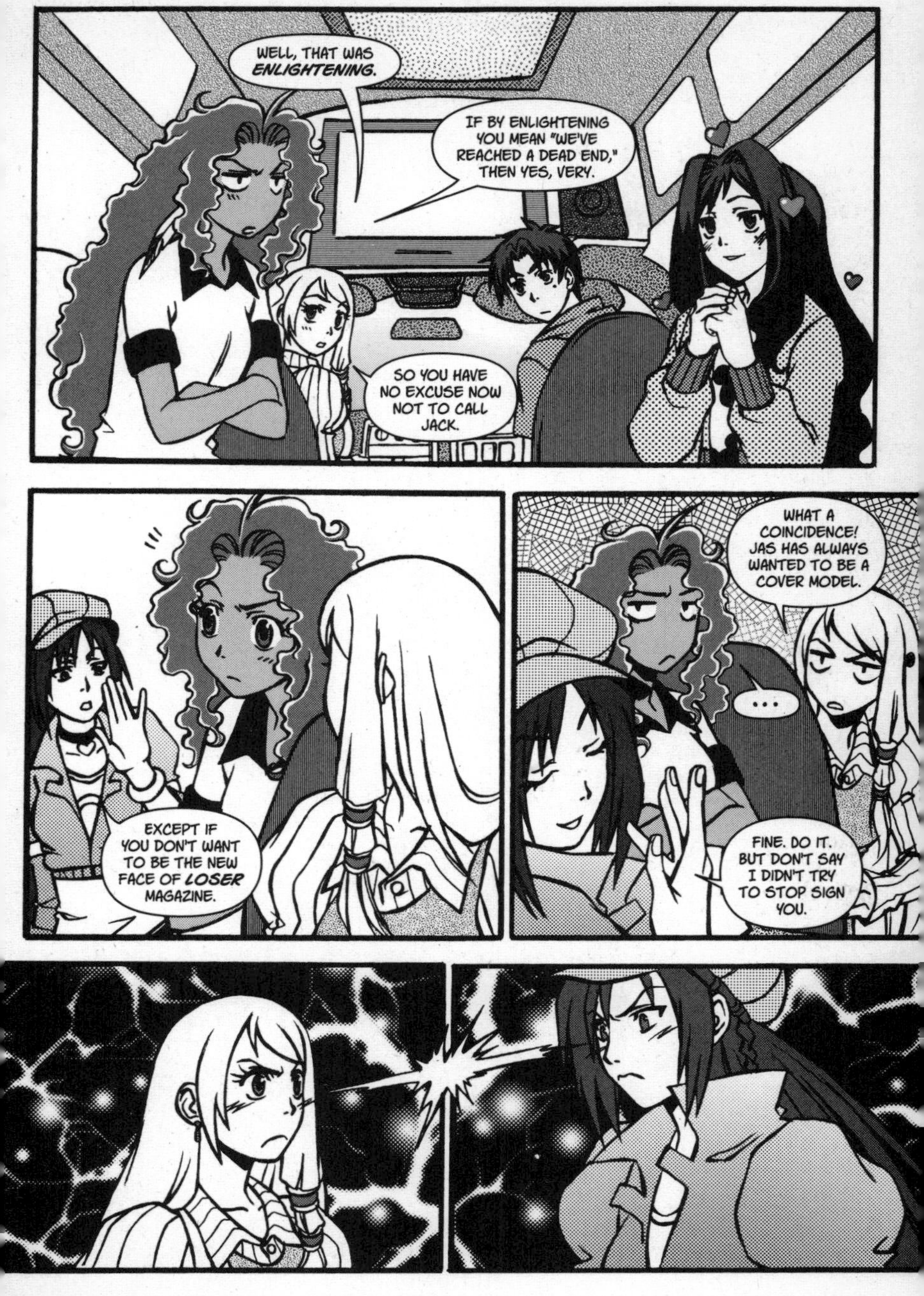
WELL, THAT WAS *ENLIGHTENING*.
IF BY ENLIGHTENING YOU MEAN "WE'VE REACHED A DEAD END," THEN YES, VERY.
SO YOU HAVE NO EXCUSE NOW NOT TO CALL JACK.
EXCEPT IF YOU DON'T WANT TO BE THE NEW FACE OF *LOSER* MAGAZINE.
WHAT A COINCIDENCE! JAS HAS ALWAYS WANTED TO BE A COVER MODEL.
...
FINE. DO IT. BUT DON'T SAY I DIDN'T TRY TO STOP SIGN YOU.

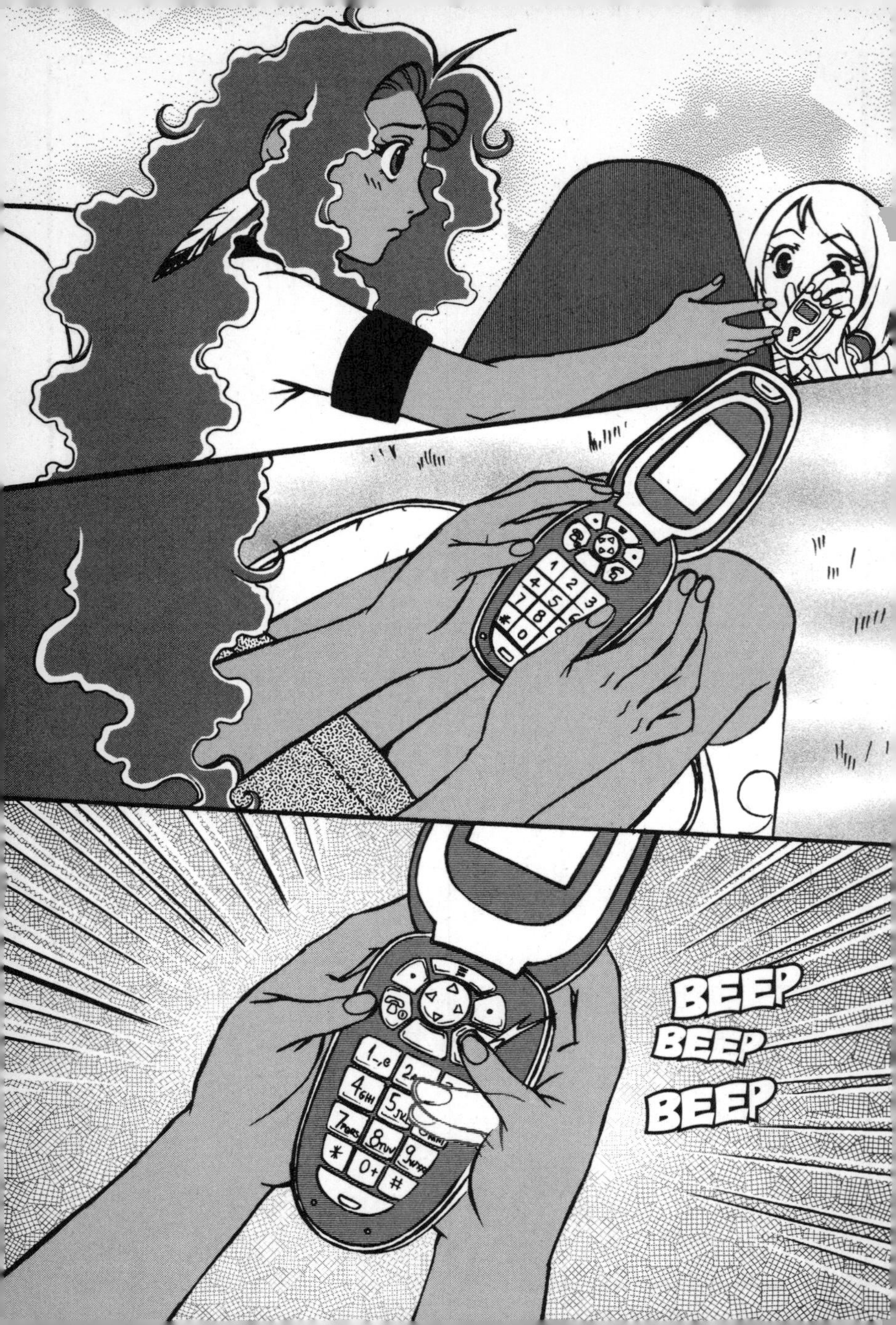
BEEP
BEEP
BEEP

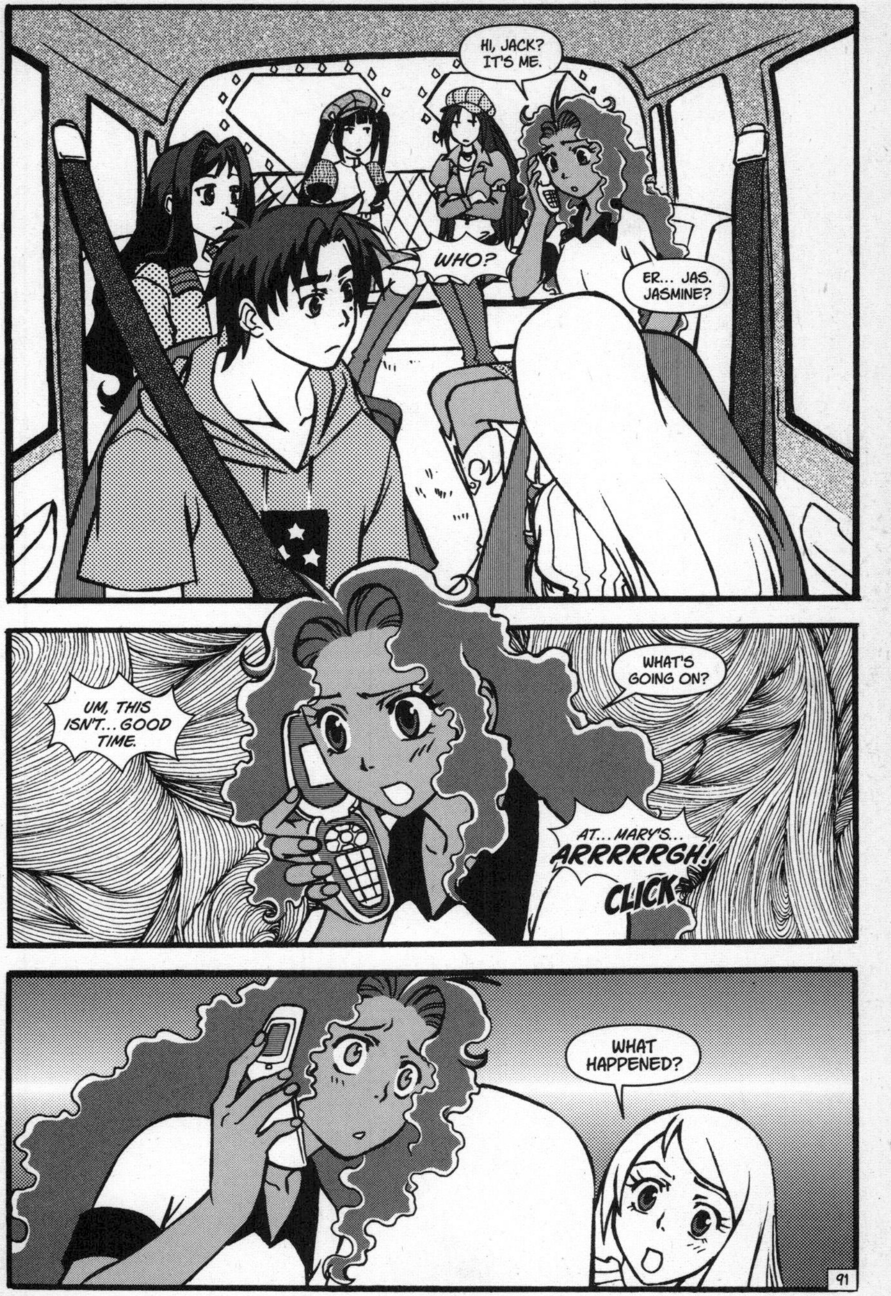
HI, JACK? IT'S ME.
WHO?
ER... JAS. JASMINE?
UM, THIS ISN'T... GOOD TIME.
WHAT'S GOING ON?
AT... MARY'S... ARRRRRGH!
CLICK
WHAT HAPPENED?

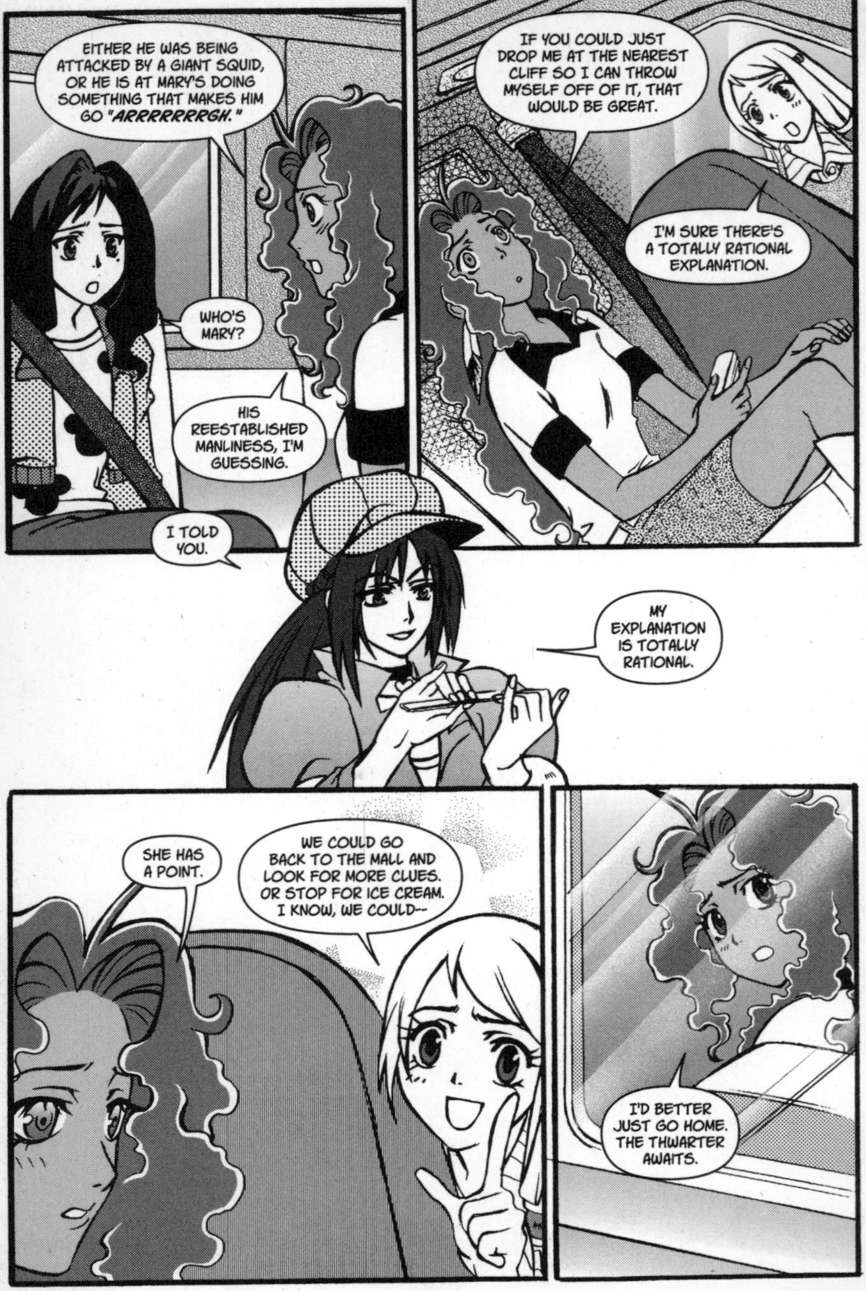

EITHER HE WAS BEING ATTACKED BY A GIANT SQUID, OR HE IS AT MARY'S DOING SOMETHING THAT MAKES HIM GO "ARRRRRRRGH."
WHO'S MARY?
HIS REESTABLISHED MANLINESS, I'M GUESSING.
IF YOU COULD JUST DROP ME AT THE NEAREST CLIFF SO I CAN THROW MYSELF OFF OF IT, THAT WOULD BE GREAT.
I'M SURE THERE'S A TOTALLY RATIONAL EXPLANATION.
I TOLD YOU.
MY EXPLANATION IS TOTALLY RATIONAL.
SHE HAS A POINT.
WE COULD GO BACK TO THE MALL AND LOOK FOR MORE CLUES. OR STOP FOR ICE CREAM. I KNOW, WE COULD--
I'D BETTER JUST GO HOME. THE THWARTER AWAITS.

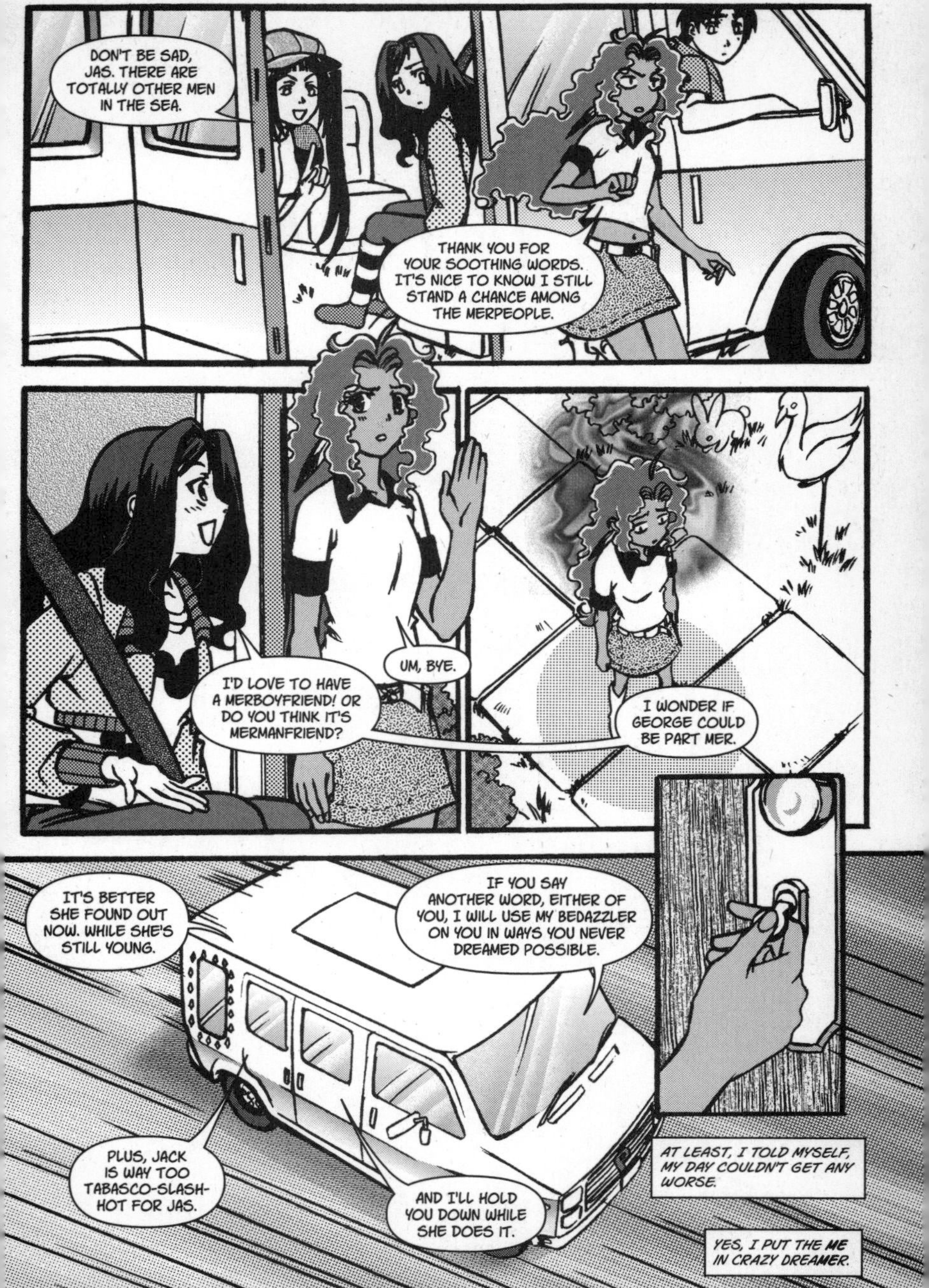
DON'T BE SAD, JAS. THERE ARE TOTALLY OTHER MEN IN THE SEA.
THANK YOU FOR YOUR SOOTHING WORDS. IT'S NICE TO KNOW I STILL STAND A CHANCE AMONG THE MERPEOPLE.
I'D LOVE TO HAVE A MERBOYFRIEND! OR DO YOU THINK IT'S MERMANFRIEND?
UM, BYE.
I WONDER IF GEORGE COULD BE PART MER.
IT'S BETTER SHE FOUND OUT NOW. WHILE SHE'S STILL YOUNG.
IF YOU SAY ANOTHER WORD, EITHER OF YOU, I WILL USE MY BEDAZZLER ON YOU IN WAYS YOU NEVER DREAMED POSSIBLE.
PLUS, JACK IS WAY TOO TABASCO-SLASH-HOT FOR JAS.
AND I'LL HOLD YOU DOWN WHILE SHE DOES IT.
AT LEAST, I TOLD MYSELF, MY DAY COULDN'T GET ANY WORSE.
YES, I PUT THE ME IN CRAZY DREAMER.

Chapter Four

Jasmine Callihan

HAIR: Too Depressed for Mischief

PORES: Small. When it doesn't matter.

HEART: EMPTY

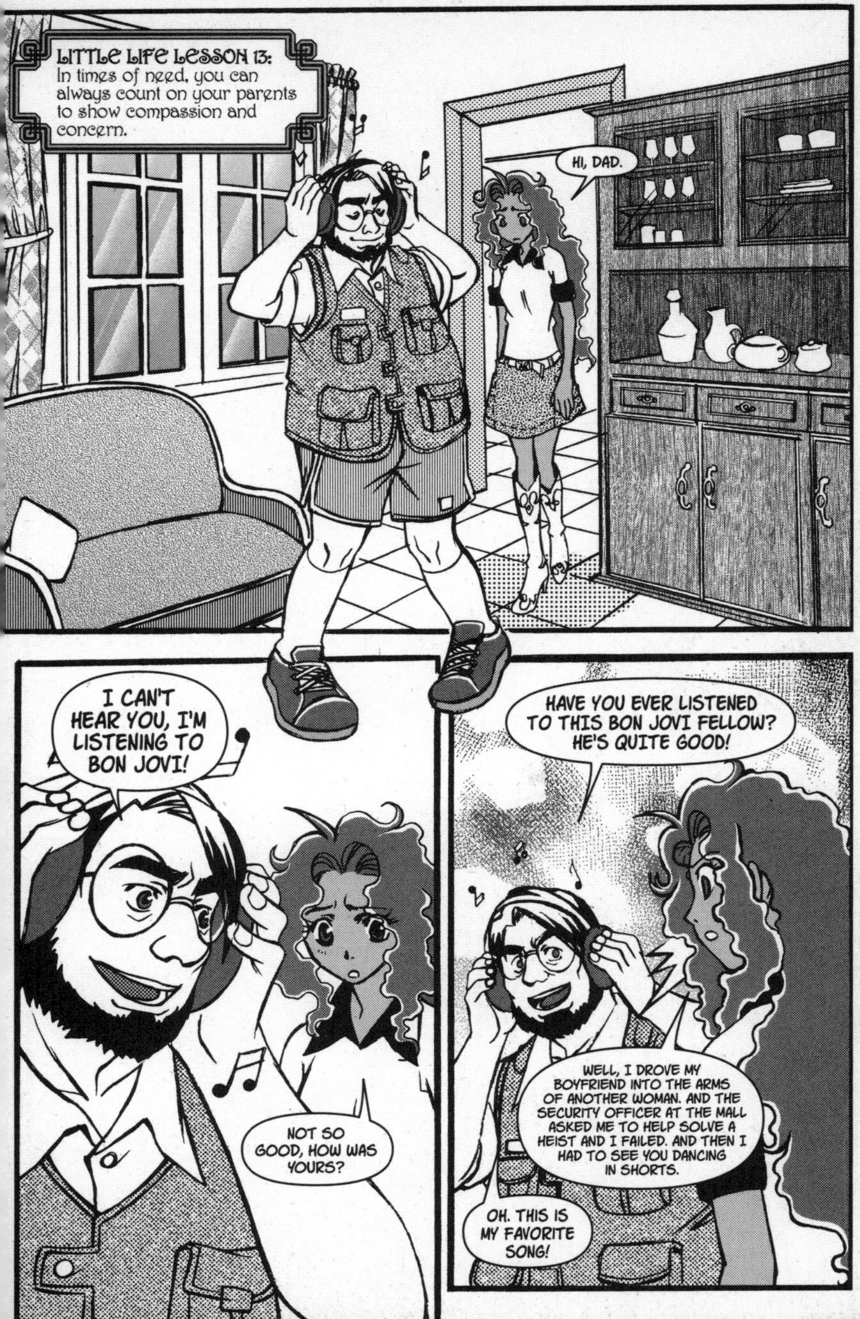
LITTLE LIFE LESSON 13:
In times of need, you can always count on your parents to show compassion and concern.
HI, DAD.
I CAN'T HEAR YOU, I'M LISTENING TO BON JOVI!
NOT SO GOOD, HOW WAS YOURS?
HAVE YOU EVER LISTENED TO THIS BON JOVI FELLOW? HE'S QUITE GOOD!
WELL, I DROVE MY BOYFRIEND INTO THE ARMS OF ANOTHER WOMAN. AND THE SECURITY OFFICER AT THE MALL ASKED ME TO HELP SOLVE A HEIST AND I FAILED. AND THEN I HAD TO SEE YOU DANCING IN SHORTS.
OH. THIS IS MY FAVORITE SONG!

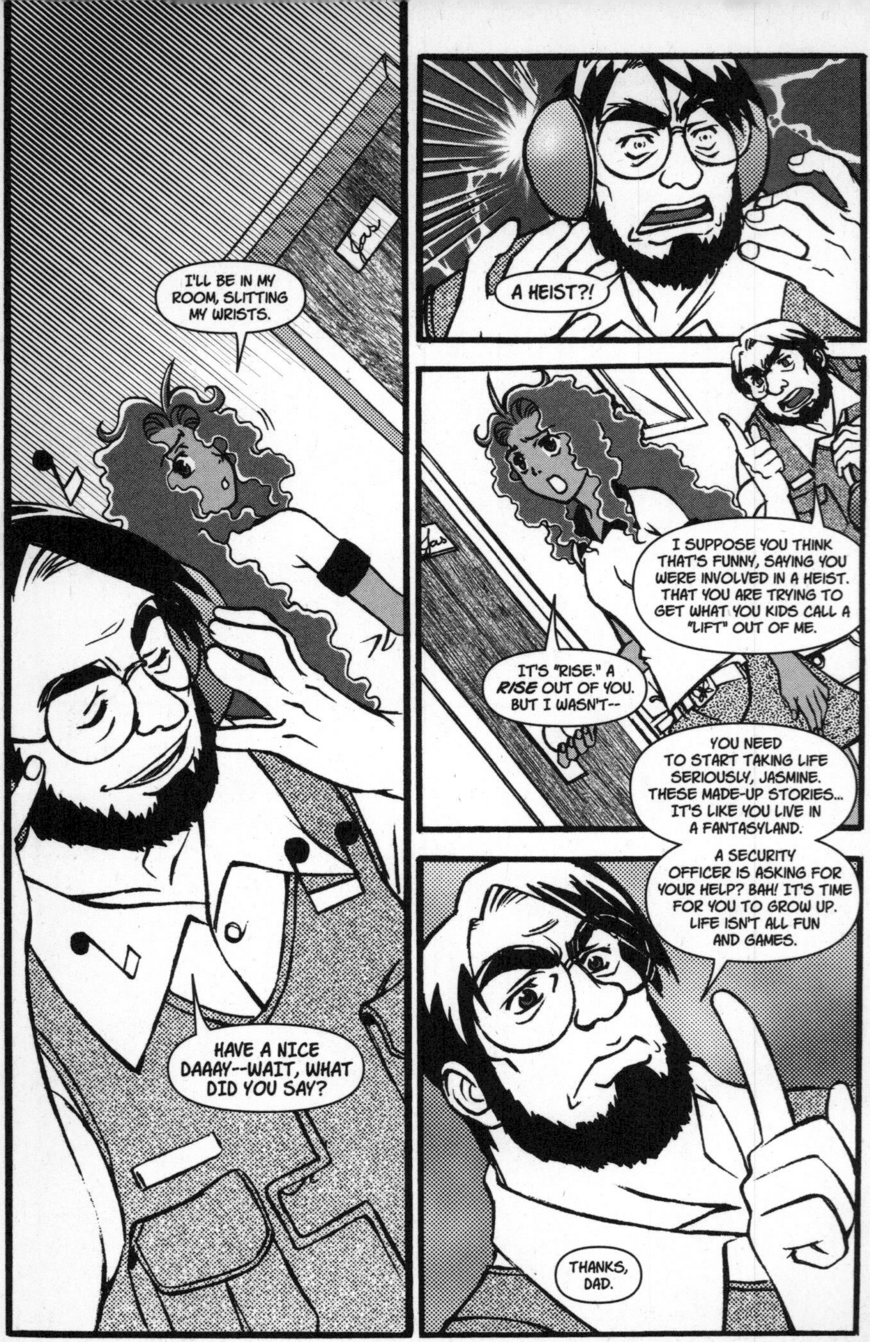
I'LL BE IN MY ROOM, SLITTING MY WRISTS.
HAVE A NICE DAAAY--WAIT, WHAT DID YOU SAY?
A HEIST?!
I SUPPOSE YOU THINK THAT'S FUNNY, SAYING YOU WERE INVOLVED IN A HEIST. THAT YOU ARE TRYING TO GET WHAT YOU KIDS CALL A "LIFT" OUT OF ME.
IT'S "RISE." A *RISE* OUT OF YOU. BUT I WASN'T--
YOU NEED TO START TAKING LIFE SERIOUSLY, JASMINE. THESE MADE-UP STORIES... IT'S LIKE YOU LIVE IN A FANTASYLAND.
A SECURITY OFFICER IS ASKING FOR YOUR HELP? BAH! IT'S TIME FOR YOU TO GROW UP. LIFE ISN'T ALL FUN AND GAMES.
THANKS, DAD.

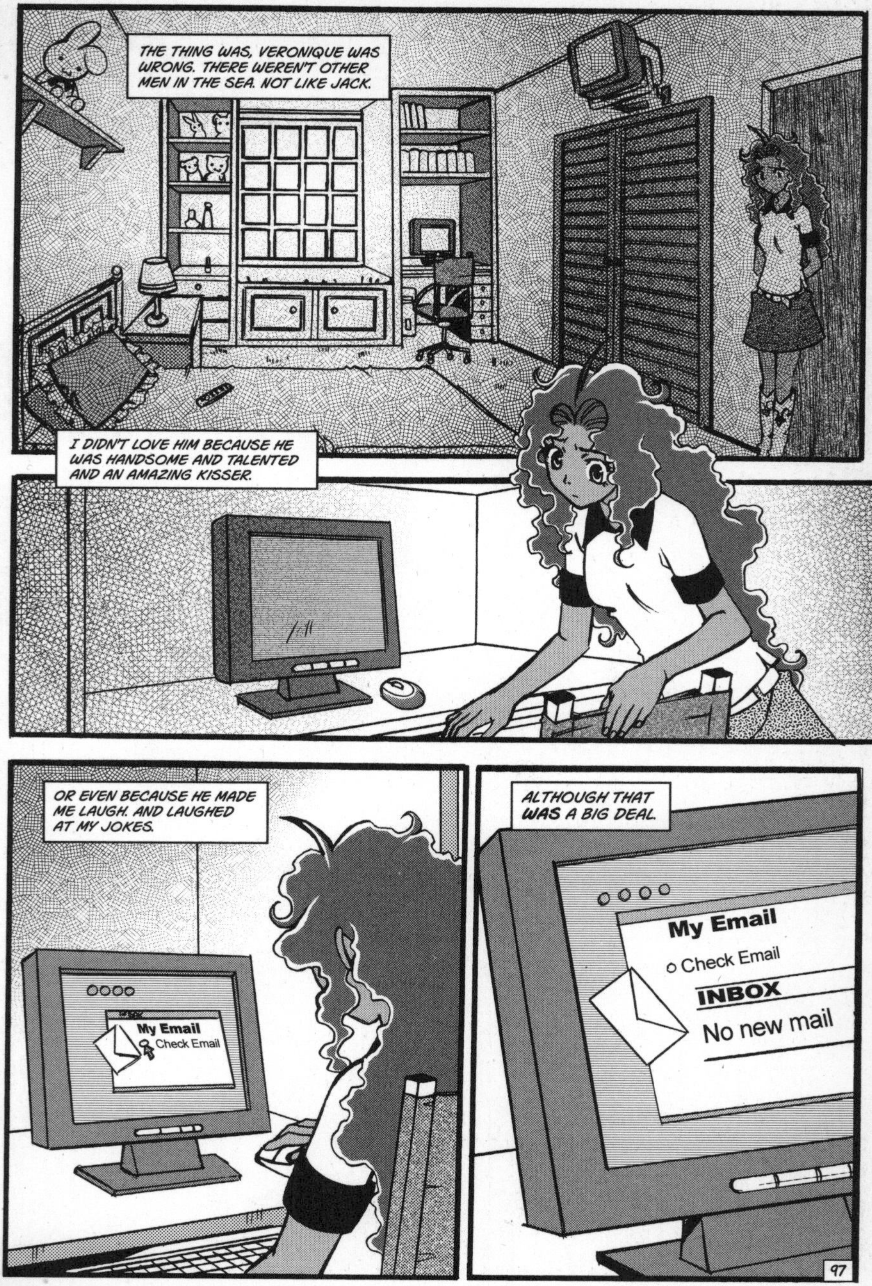
THE THING WAS, VERONIQUE WAS WRONG. THERE WEREN'T OTHER MEN IN THE SEA. NOT LIKE JACK.
I DIDN'T LOVE HIM BECAUSE HE WAS HANDSOME AND TALENTED AND AN AMAZING KISSER.
OR EVEN BECAUSE HE MADE ME LAUGH. AND LAUGHED AT MY JOKES.
My Email
Check Email
ALTHOUGH THAT WAS A BIG DEAL.
My Email
Check Email
INBOX
No new mail

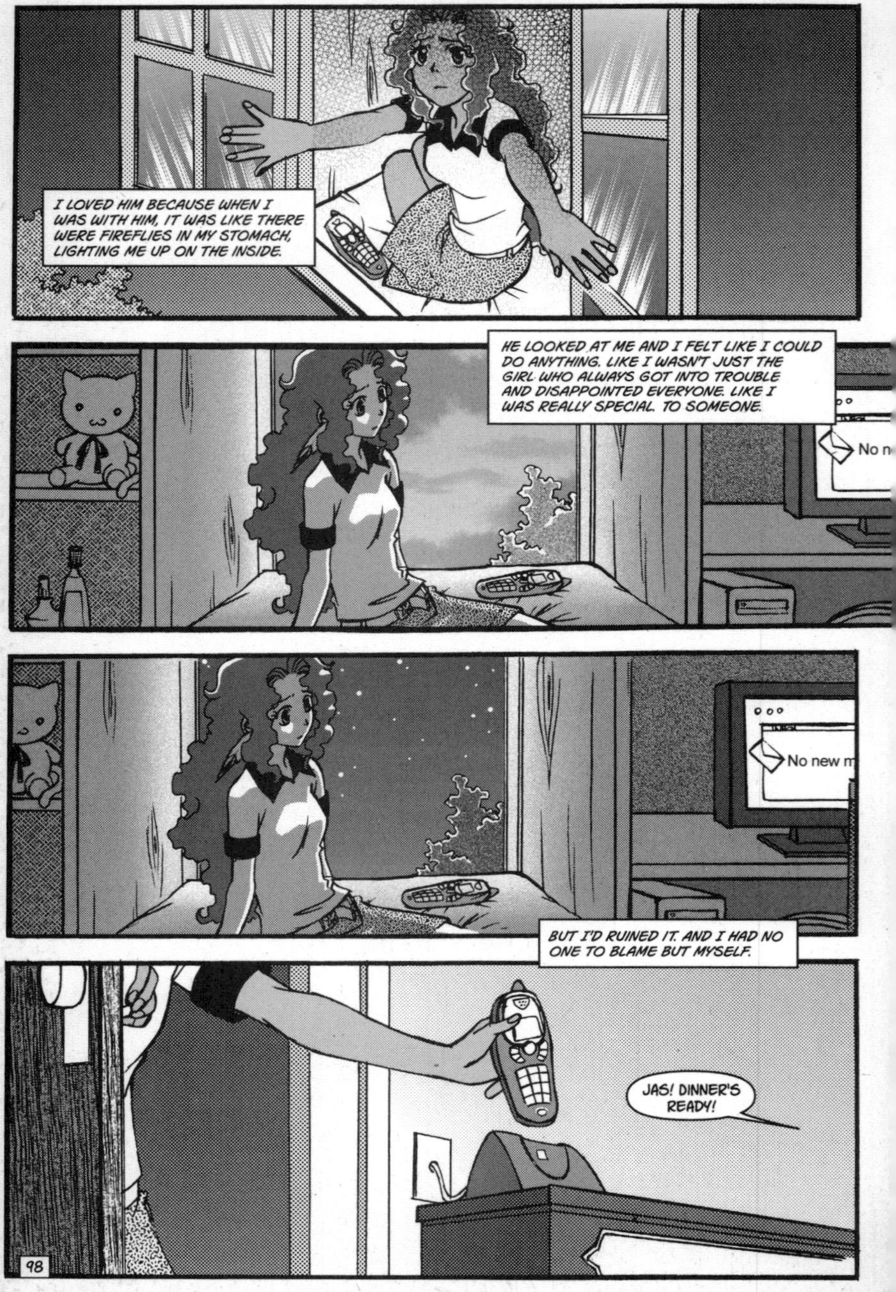
I LOVED HIM BECAUSE WHEN I WAS WITH HIM, IT WAS LIKE THERE WERE FIREFLIES IN MY STOMACH, LIGHTING ME UP ON THE INSIDE.
HE LOOKED AT ME AND I FELT LIKE I COULD DO ANYTHING. LIKE I WASN'T JUST THE GIRL WHO ALWAYS GOT INTO TROUBLE AND DISAPPOINTED EVERYONE. LIKE I WAS REALLY SPECIAL. TO SOMEONE.
No new m
BUT I'D RUINED IT. AND I HAD NO ONE TO BLAME BUT MYSELF.
JAS! DINNER'S READY!

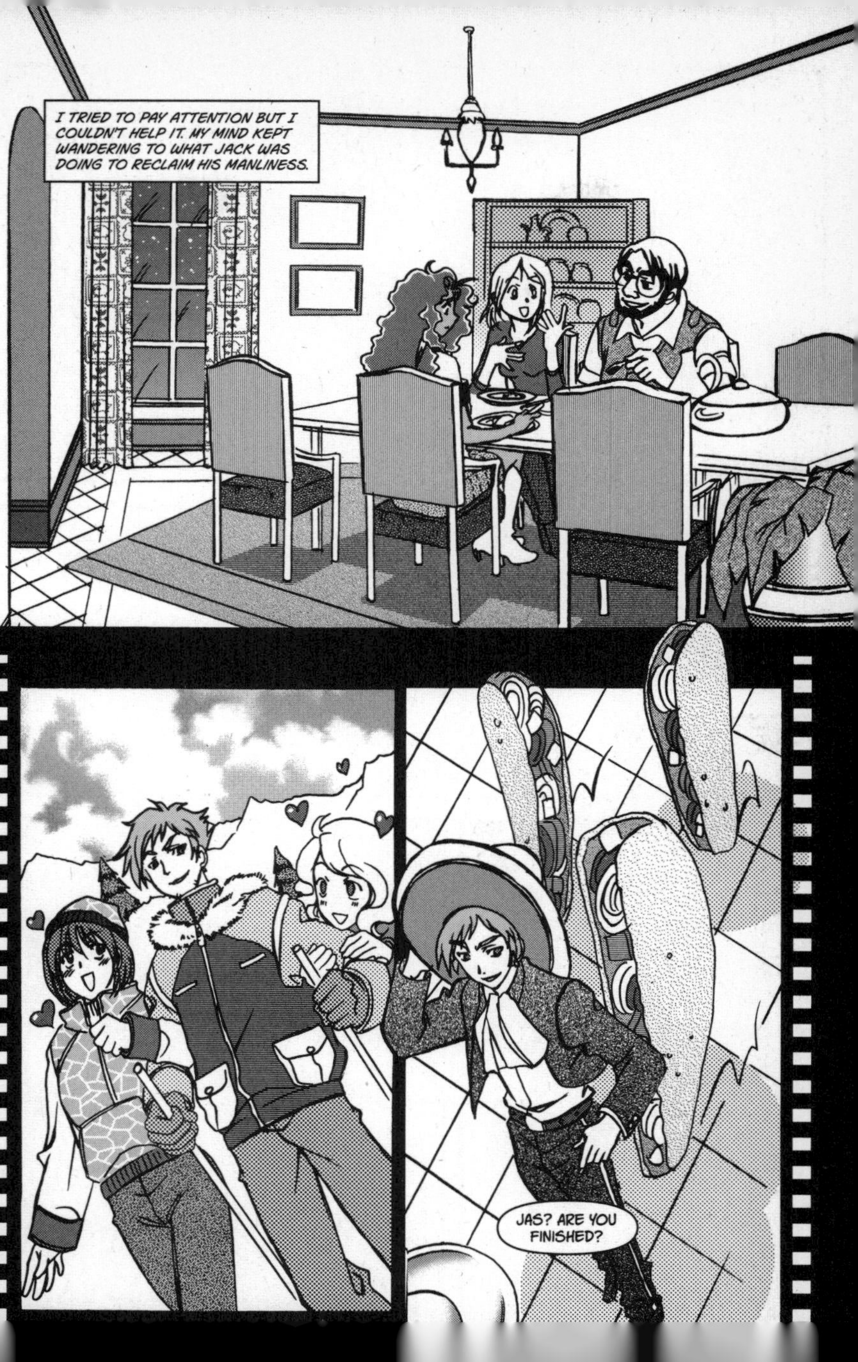
I TRIED TO PAY ATTENTION BUT I COULDN'T HELP IT. MY MIND KEPT WANDERING TO WHAT JACK WAS DOING TO RECLAIM HIS MANLINESS.
JAS? ARE YOU FINISHED?

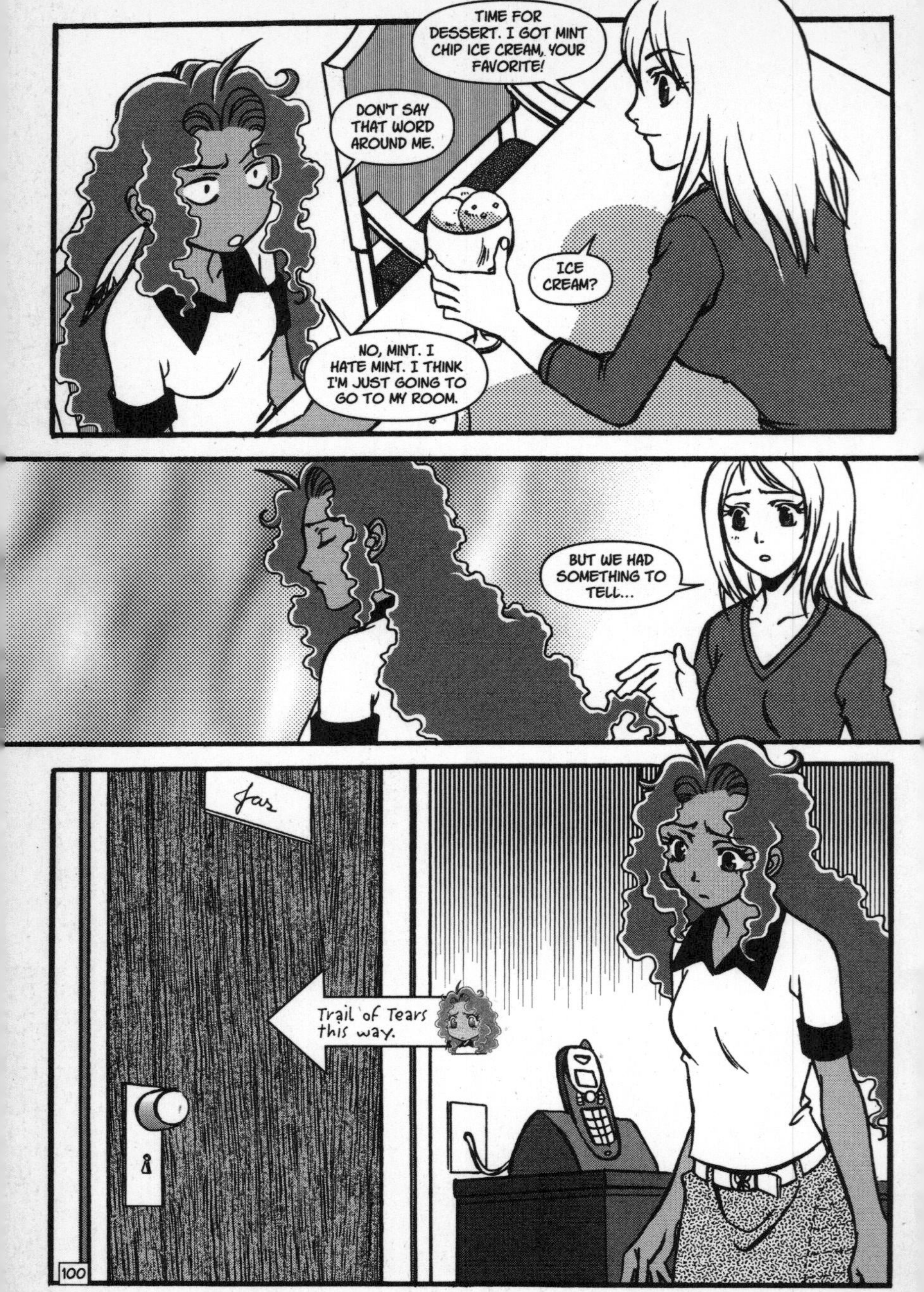
TIME FOR DESSERT. I GOT MINT CHIP ICE CREAM, YOUR FAVORITE!
DON'T SAY THAT WORD AROUND ME.
ICE CREAM?
NO, MINT. I HATE MINT. I THINK I'M JUST GOING TO GO TO MY ROOM.
BUT WE HAD SOMETHING TO TELL...
Jaz
Trail of Tears this way.

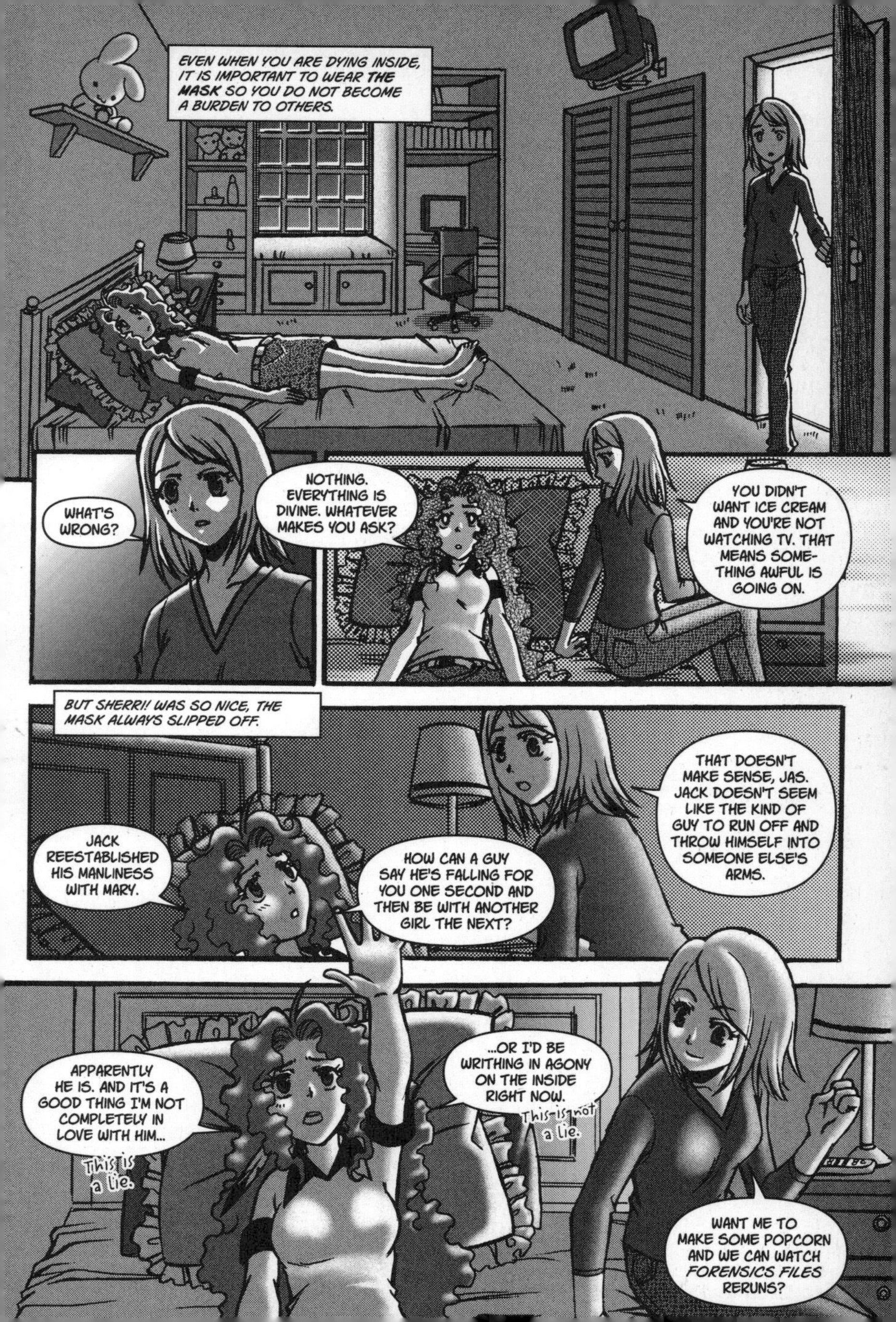
EVEN WHEN YOU ARE DYING INSIDE, IT IS IMPORTANT TO WEAR THE MASK SO YOU DO NOT BECOME A BURDEN TO OTHERS.
WHAT'S WRONG?
NOTHING. EVERYTHING IS DIVINE. WHATEVER MAKES YOU ASK?
YOU DIDN'T WANT ICE CREAM AND YOU'RE NOT WATCHING TV. THAT MEANS SOME-THING AWFUL IS GOING ON.
BUT SHERRI! WAS SO NICE, THE MASK ALWAYS SLIPPED OFF.
JACK REESTABLISHED HIS MANLINESS WITH MARY.
HOW CAN A GUY SAY HE'S FALLING FOR YOU ONE SECOND AND THEN BE WITH ANOTHER GIRL THE NEXT?
THAT DOESN'T MAKE SENSE, JAS. JACK DOESN'T SEEM LIKE THE KIND OF GUY TO RUN OFF AND THROW HIMSELF INTO SOMEONE ELSE'S ARMS.
APPARENTLY HE IS. AND IT'S A GOOD THING I'M NOT COMPLETELY IN LOVE WITH HIM...
This is a lie.
...OR I'D BE WRITHING IN AGONY ON THE INSIDE RIGHT NOW.
This is not a lie.
WANT ME TO MAKE SOME POPCORN AND WE CAN WATCH FORENSICS FILES RERUNS?

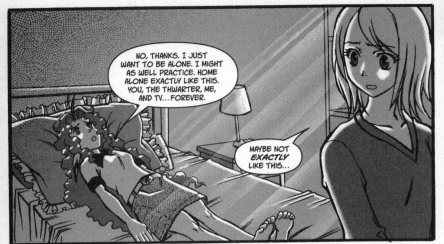

NO, THANKS. I JUST WANT TO BE ALONE. I MIGHT AS WELL PRACTICE. HOME ALONE EXACTLY LIKE THIS. YOU, THE THWARTER, ME, AND TV...FOREVER.

MAYBE NOT *EXACTLY* LIKE THIS...

AND IT'S A SIGN OF MY IMMENSE, INTENSE DEPRESSION THAT I DIDN'T EVEN SAY, "WHAT DO YOU MEAN?" OR THINK, "WHAT DO YOU MEAN?" OR NOTICE HOW SHERRI!'S EYES SPARKLED. INSTEAD I WENT, "SURE, OKAY," AND RESUMED MY PREVIOUS OCCUPATION.

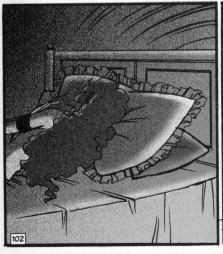

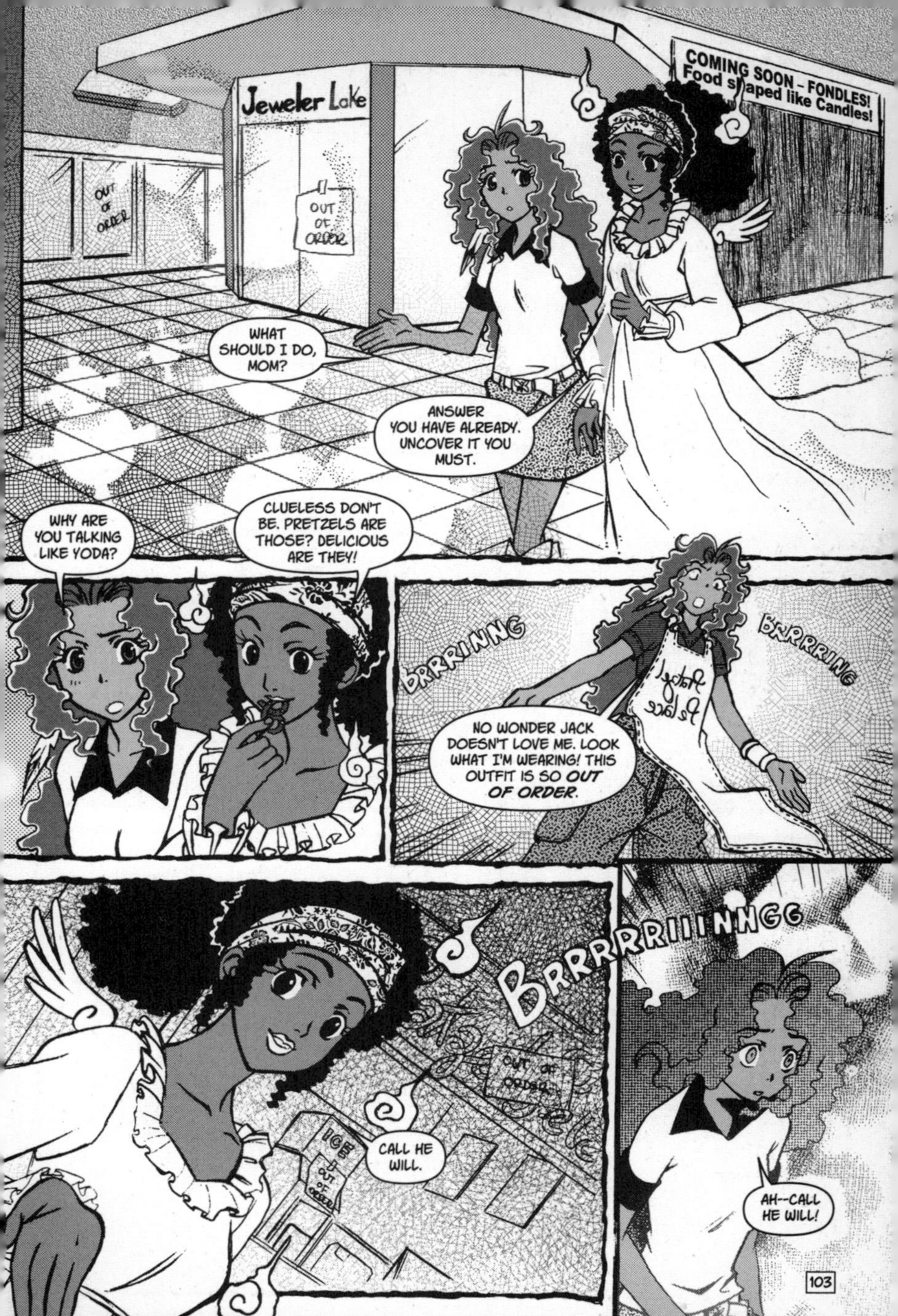
COMING SOON - FONDLES! Food shaped like Candles!
Jeweler Lake
OUT OF ORDER
OUT OF ORDER
WHAT SHOULD I DO, MOM?
ANSWER YOU HAVE ALREADY. UNCOVER IT YOU MUST.
WHY ARE YOU TALKING LIKE YODA?
CLUELESS DON'T BE. PRETZELS ARE THOSE? DELICIOUS ARE THEY!
BRRRINNG
BRRRRING
NO WONDER JACK DOESN'T LOVE ME. LOOK WHAT I'M WEARING! THIS OUTFIT IS SO ***OUT OF ORDER***.
BRRRRRIIINNGG
OUT OF ORDER
CALL HE WILL.
AH--CALL HE WILL!

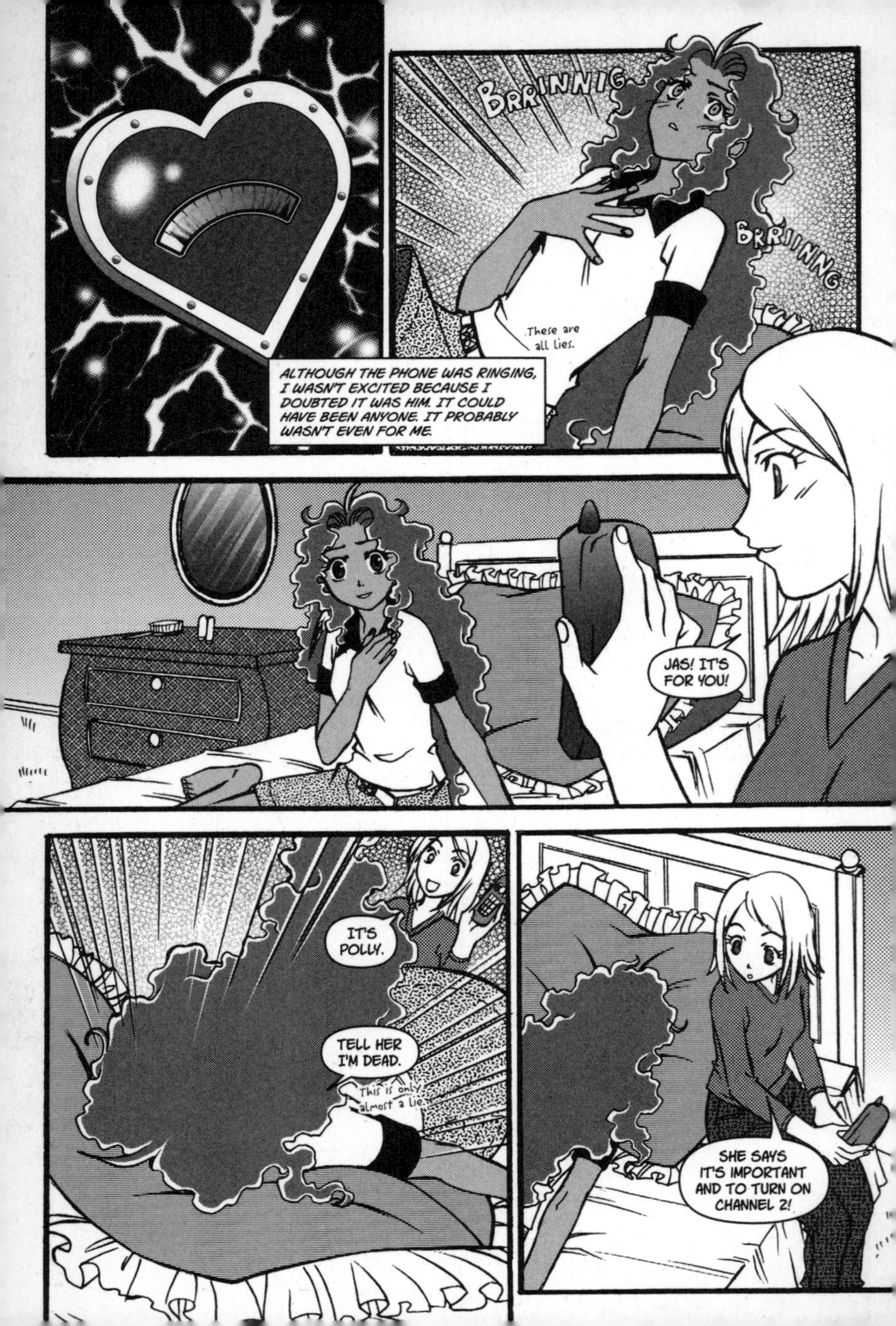
BRRINNIG
BRRJINNG
These are all lies.
ALTHOUGH THE PHONE WAS RINGING, I WASN'T EXCITED BECAUSE I DOUBTED IT WAS HIM. IT COULD HAVE BEEN ANYONE. IT PROBABLY WASN'T EVEN FOR ME.
JAS! IT'S FOR YOU!
IT'S POLLY.
TELL HER I'M DEAD.
This is only almost a lie.
SHE SAYS IT'S IMPORTANT AND TO TURN ON CHANNEL 2!

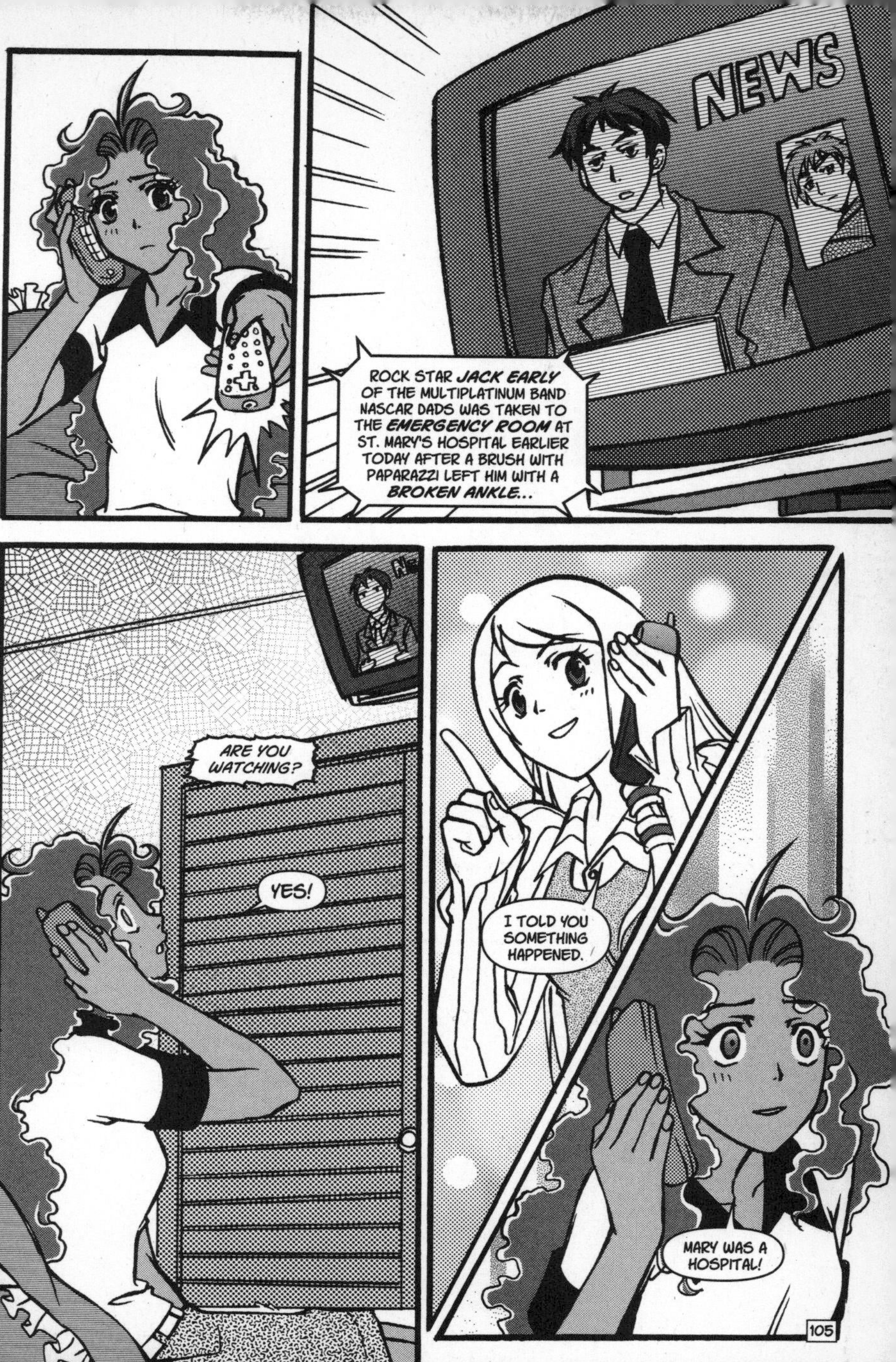
NEWS
ROCK STAR JACK EARLY OF THE MULTIPLATINUM BAND NASCAR DADS WAS TAKEN TO THE EMERGENCY ROOM AT ST. MARY'S HOSPITAL EARLIER TODAY AFTER A BRUSH WITH PAPARAZZI LEFT HIM WITH A BROKEN ANKLE...
ARE YOU WATCHING?
YES!
I TOLD YOU SOMETHING HAPPENED.
MARY WAS A HOSPITAL!

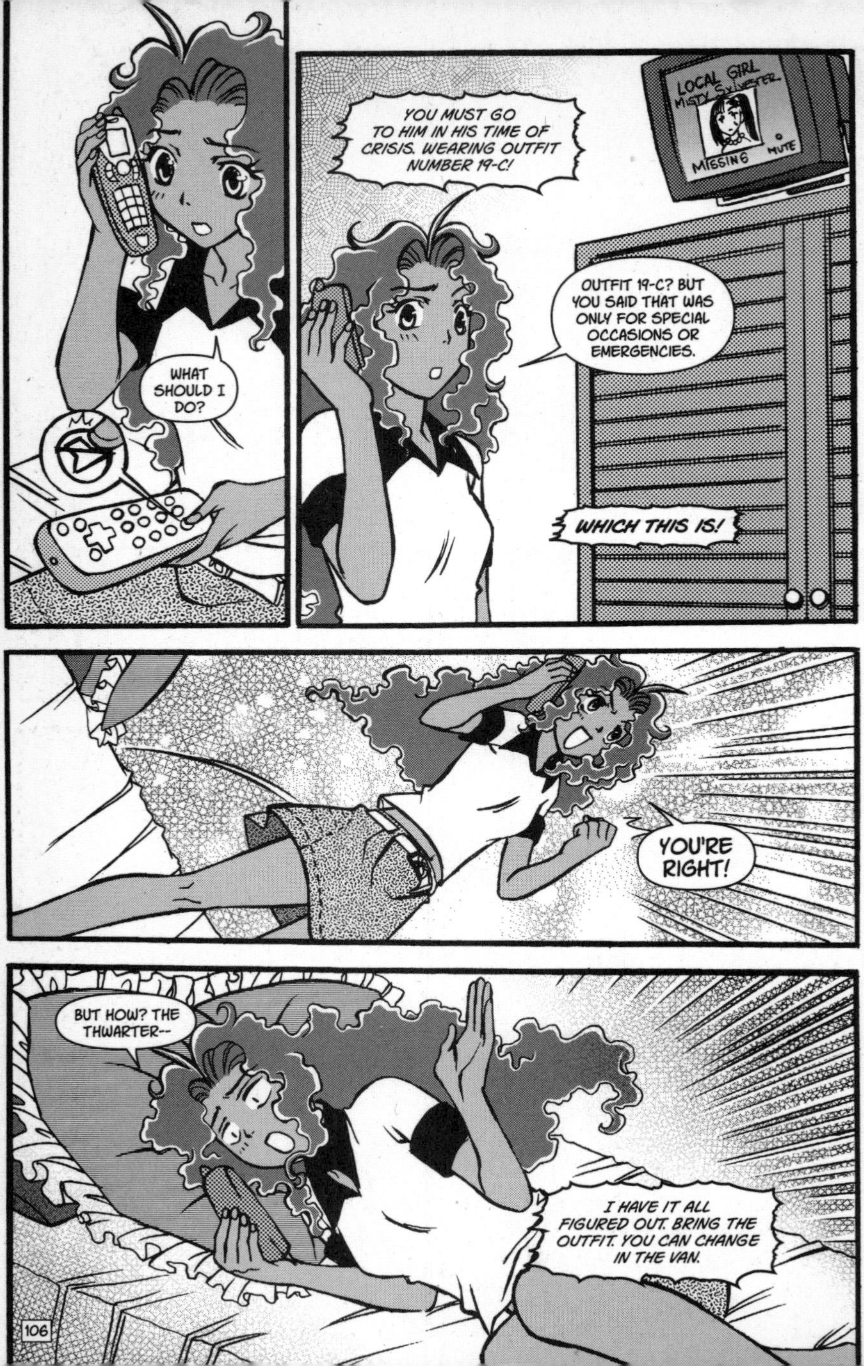
WHAT SHOULD I DO?
YOU MUST GO TO HIM IN HIS TIME OF CRISIS. WEARING OUTFIT NUMBER 19-C!
LOCAL GIRL
MISTY SYLVESTER
MISSING
MUTE
OUTFIT 19-C? BUT YOU SAID THAT WAS ONLY FOR SPECIAL OCCASIONS OR EMERGENCIES.
WHICH THIS IS!
YOU'RE RIGHT!
BUT HOW? THE THWARTER--
I HAVE IT ALL FIGURED OUT. BRING THE OUTFIT. YOU CAN CHANGE IN THE VAN.

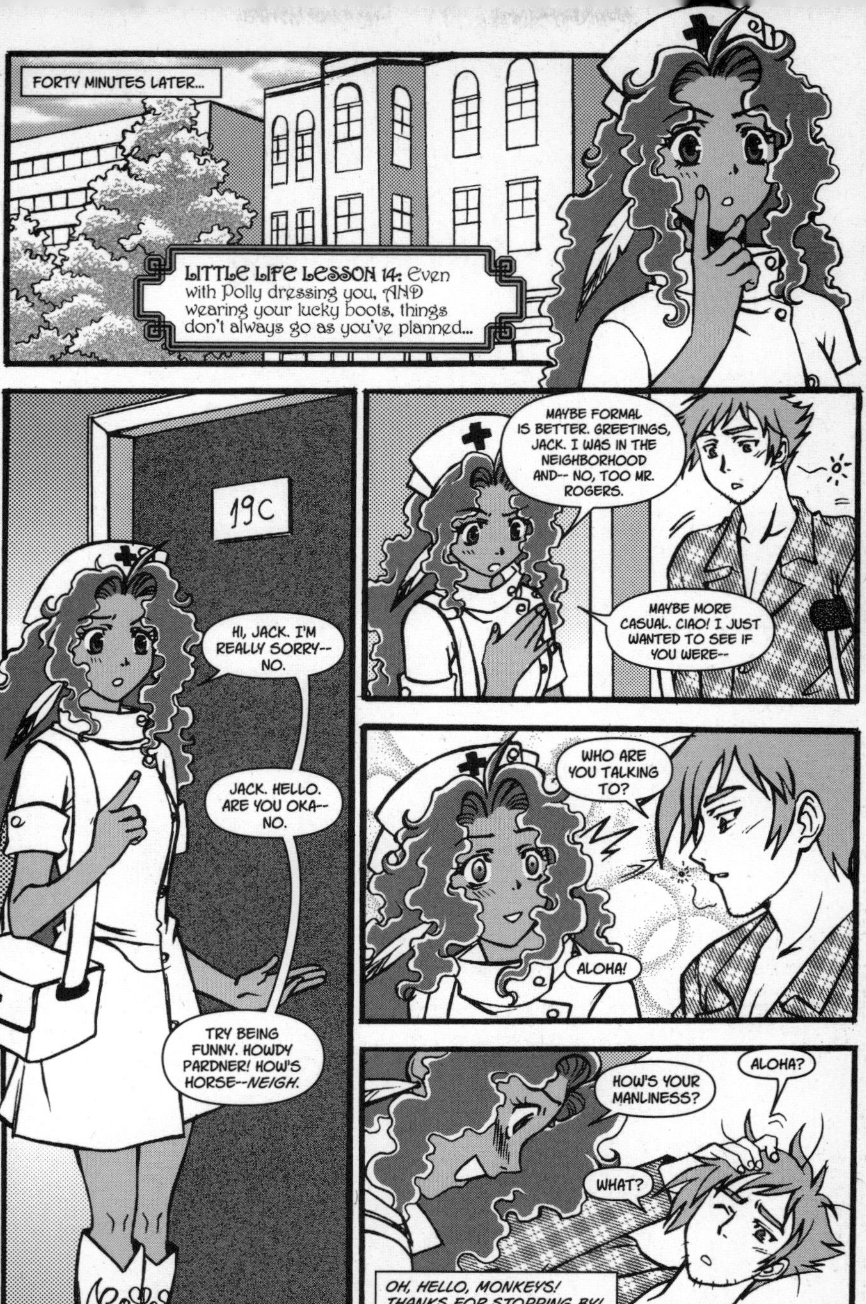
FORTY MINUTES LATER...
LITTLE LIFE LESSON 14: Even with Polly dressing you, AND wearing your lucky boots, things don't always go as you've planned...
19C
HI, JACK. I'M REALLY SORRY-- NO.
JACK. HELLO. ARE YOU OKA-- NO.
TRY BEING FUNNY. HOWDY PARDNER! HOW'S HORSE--*NEIGH*.
MAYBE FORMAL IS BETTER. GREETINGS, JACK. I WAS IN THE NEIGHBORHOOD AND-- NO, TOO MR. ROGERS.
MAYBE MORE CASUAL. CIAO! I JUST WANTED TO SEE IF YOU WERE--
WHO ARE YOU TALKING TO?
ALOHA!
HOW'S YOUR MANLINESS?
ALOHA?
WHAT?
OH, HELLO, MONKEYS! THANKS FOR STOPPING BY!

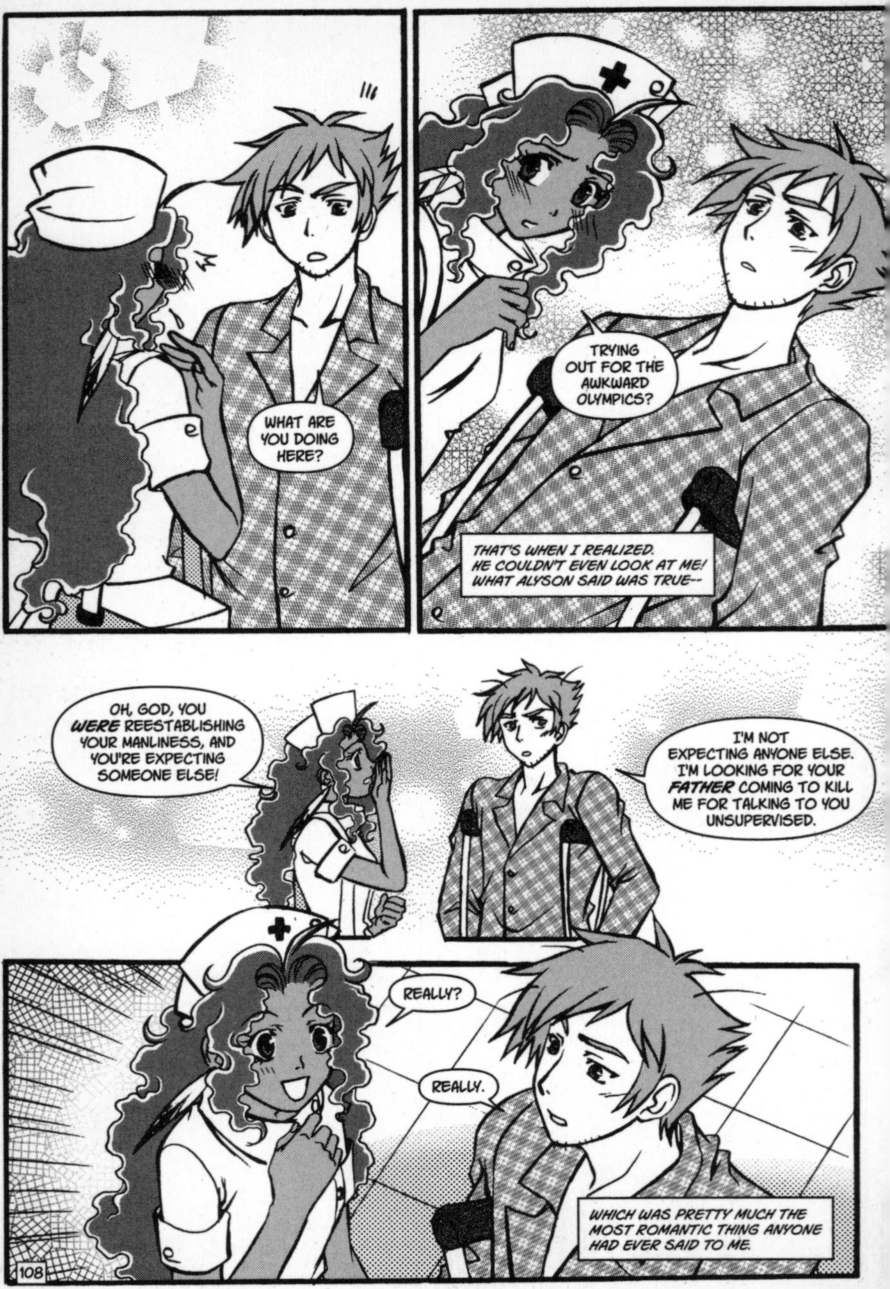
WHAT ARE YOU DOING HERE?
TRYING OUT FOR THE AWKWARD OLYMPICS?
THAT'S WHEN I REALIZED. HE COULDN'T EVEN LOOK AT ME! WHAT ALYSON SAID WAS TRUE--
OH, GOD, YOU WERE REESTABLISHING YOUR MANLINESS, AND YOU'RE EXPECTING SOMEONE ELSE!
I'M NOT EXPECTING ANYONE ELSE. I'M LOOKING FOR YOUR FATHER COMING TO KILL ME FOR TALKING TO YOU UNSUPERVISED.
REALLY?
REALLY.
WHICH WAS PRETTY MUCH THE MOST ROMANTIC THING ANYONE HAD EVER SAID TO ME.

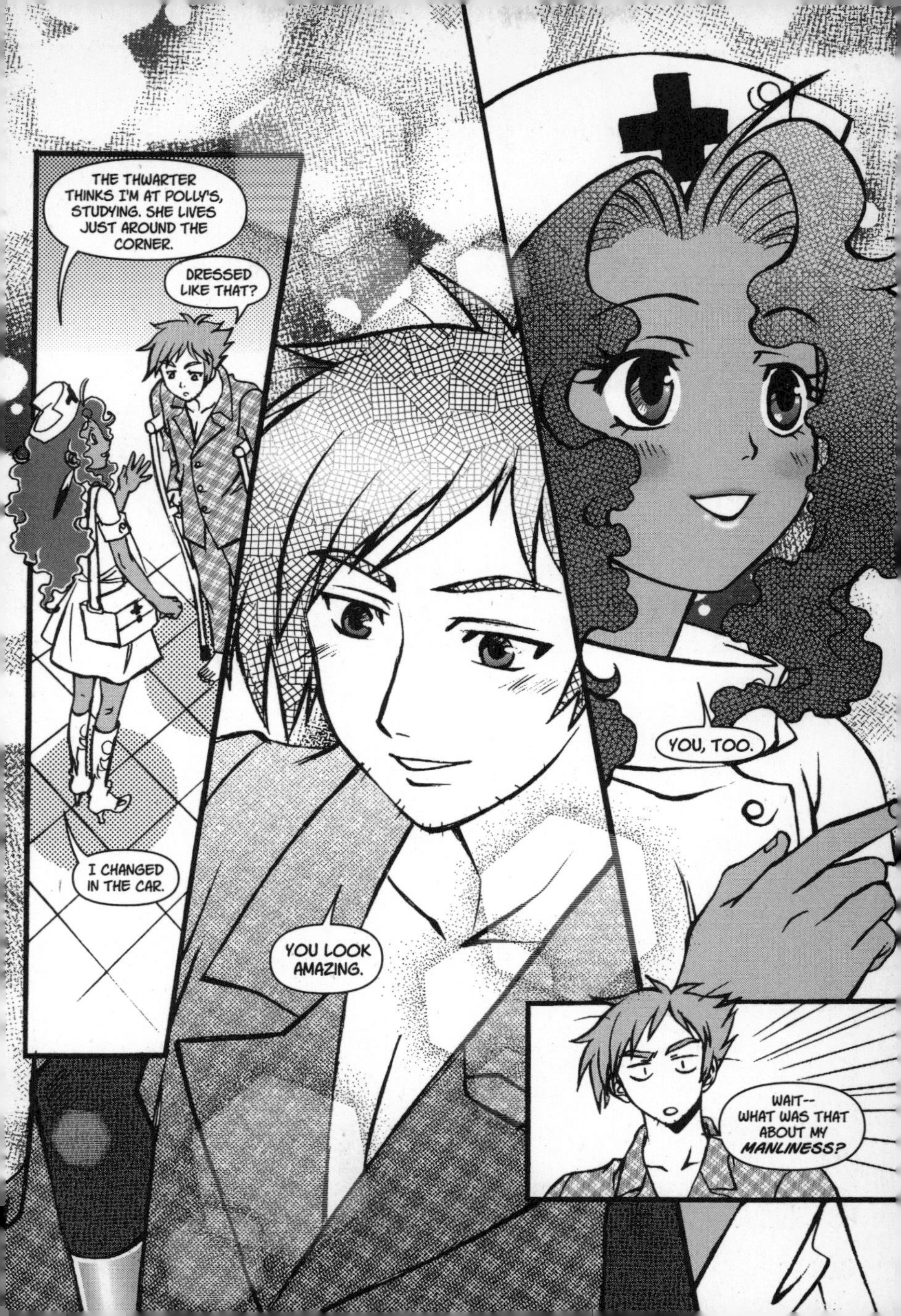
THE THWARTER THINKS I'M AT POLLY'S, STUDYING. SHE LIVES JUST AROUND THE CORNER.
DRESSED LIKE THAT?
I CHANGED IN THE CAR.
YOU LOOK AMAZING.
YOU, TOO.
WAIT-- WHAT WAS THAT ABOUT MY *MANLINESS?*

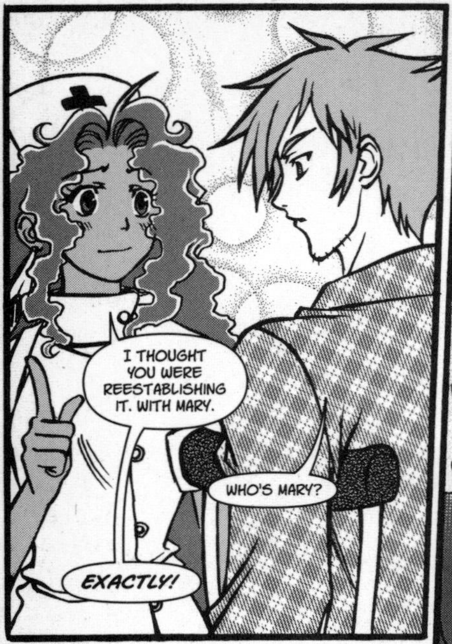
I THOUGHT YOU WERE REESTABLISHING IT. WITH MARY.
WHO'S MARY?
EXACTLY!

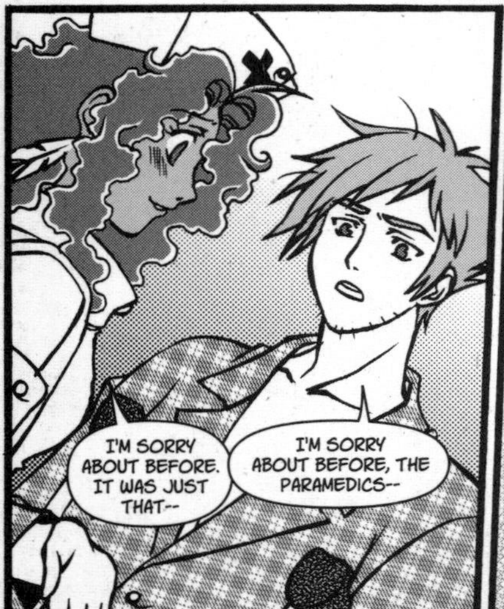
I'M SORRY ABOUT BEFORE. IT WAS JUST THAT--
I'M SORRY ABOUT BEFORE, THE PARAMEDICS--

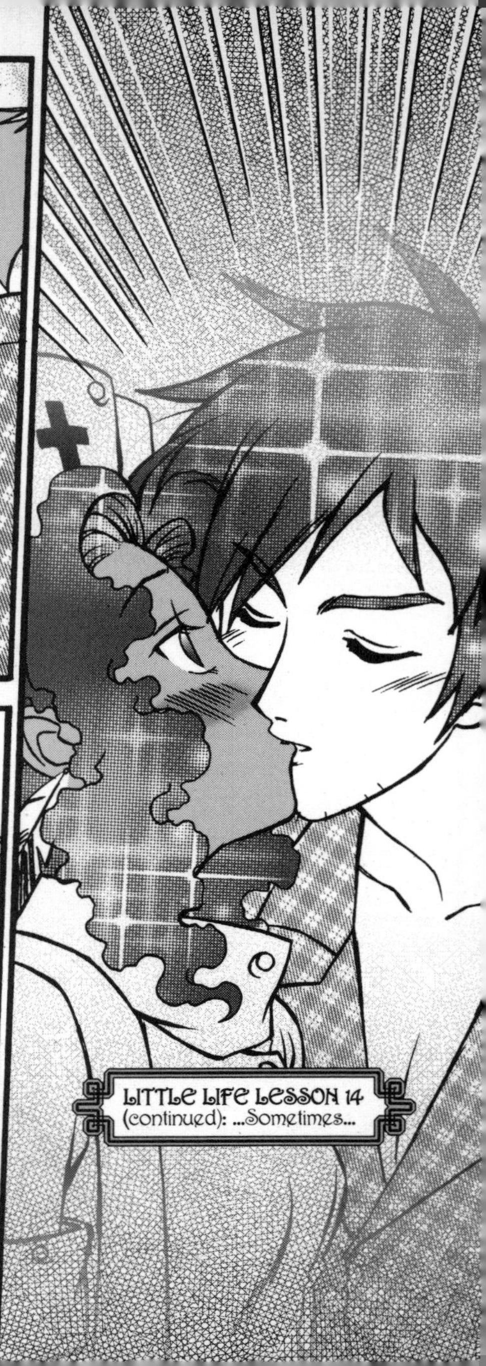
LITTLE LIFE LESSON 14
(continued): ...Sometimes...

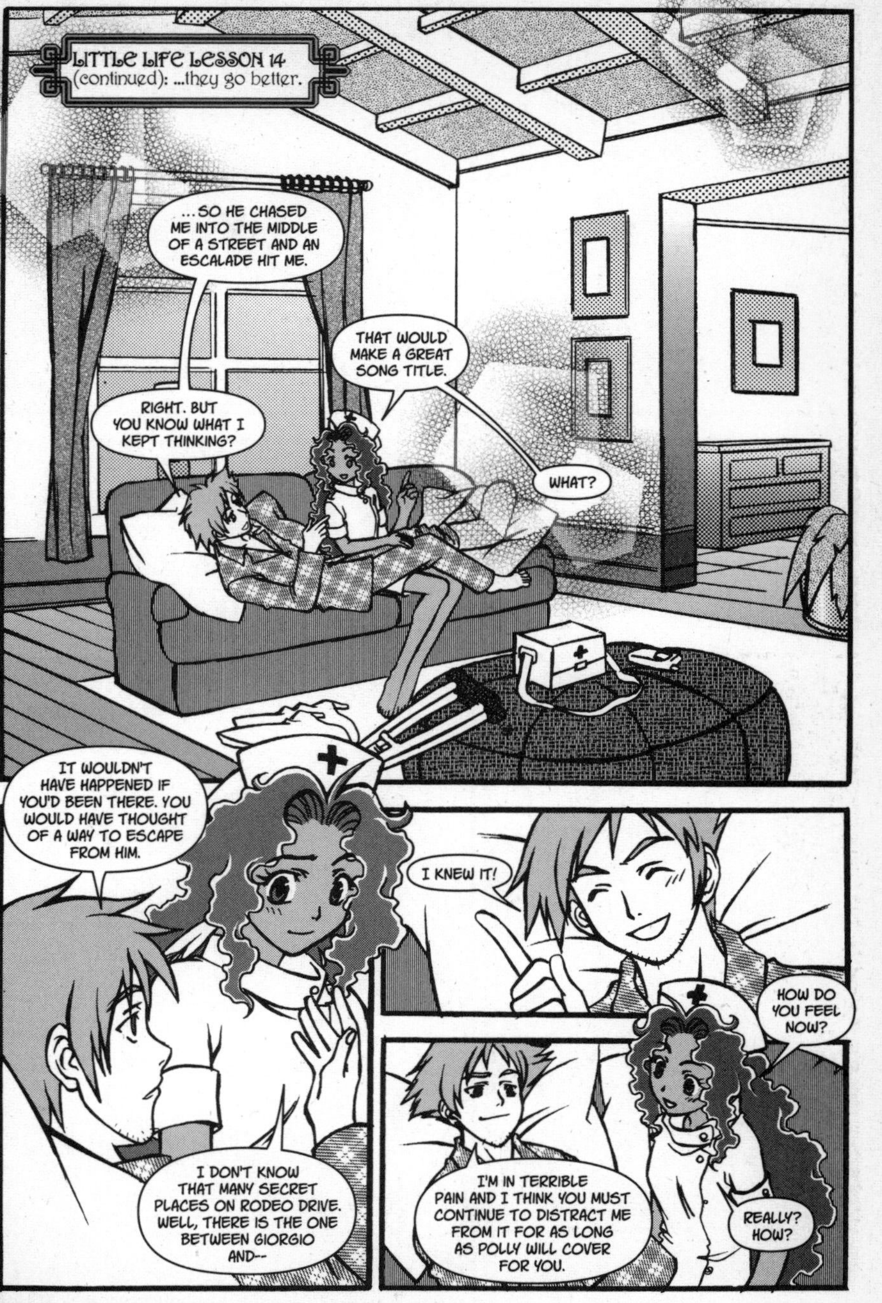
LITTLE LIFE LESSON 14
(continued): ...they go better.
...SO HE CHASED ME INTO THE MIDDLE OF A STREET AND AN ESCALADE HIT ME.
THAT WOULD MAKE A GREAT SONG TITLE.
RIGHT. BUT YOU KNOW WHAT I KEPT THINKING?
WHAT?
IT WOULDN'T HAVE HAPPENED IF YOU'D BEEN THERE. YOU WOULD HAVE THOUGHT OF A WAY TO ESCAPE FROM HIM.
I DON'T KNOW THAT MANY SECRET PLACES ON RODEO DRIVE. WELL, THERE IS THE ONE BETWEEN GIORGIO AND--
I KNEW IT!
HOW DO YOU FEEL NOW?
I'M IN TERRIBLE PAIN AND I THINK YOU MUST CONTINUE TO DISTRACT ME FROM IT FOR AS LONG AS POLLY WILL COVER FOR YOU.
REALLY? HOW?

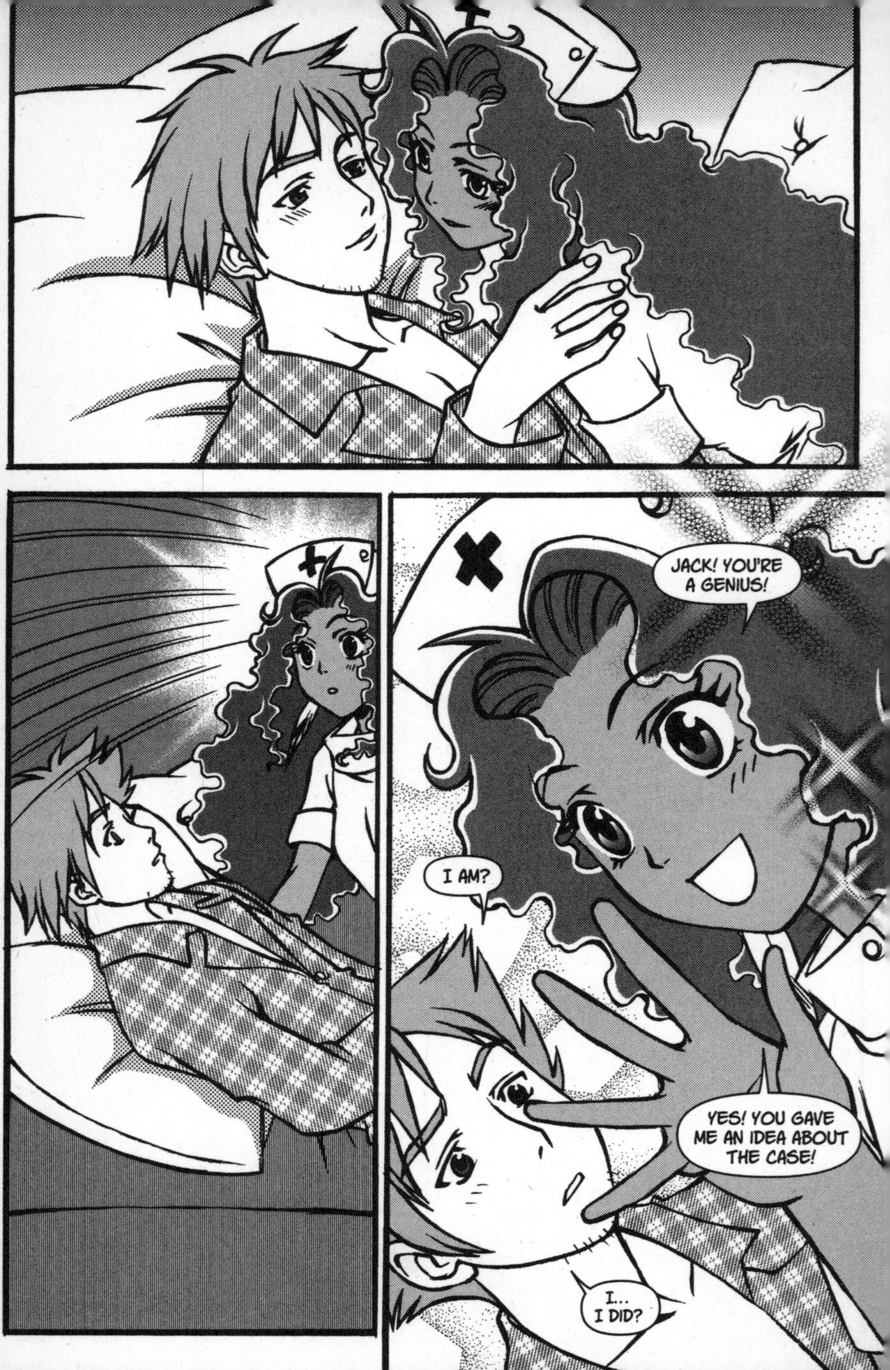
JACK! YOU'RE A GENIUS!
I AM?
YES! YOU GAVE ME AN IDEA ABOUT THE CASE!
I... I DID?

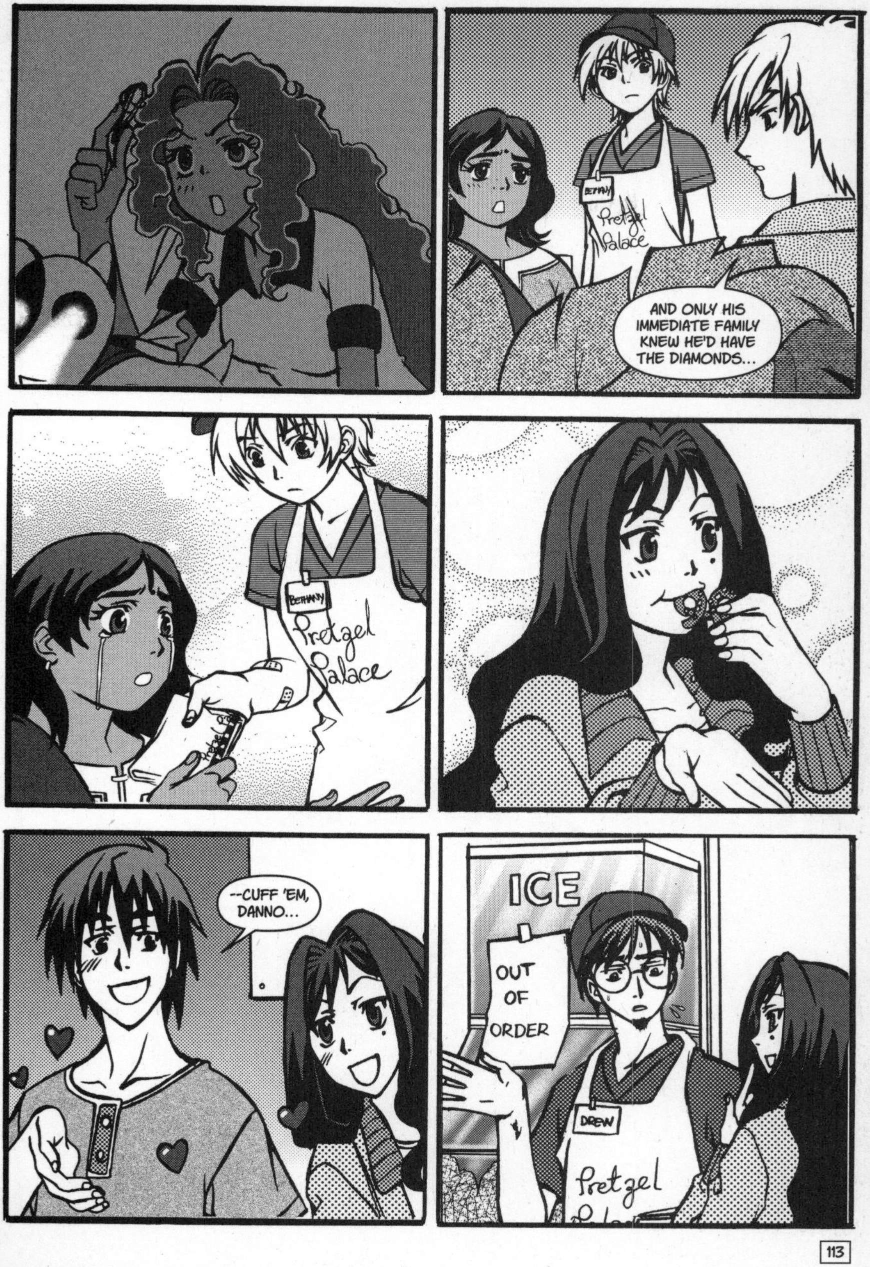
BETHANY
Pretzel Palace
AND ONLY HIS IMMEDIATE FAMILY KNEW HE'D HAVE THE DIAMONDS...
BETHANY
Pretzel Palace
--CUFF 'EM, DANNO...
ICE
OUT OF ORDER
DREW
Pretzel

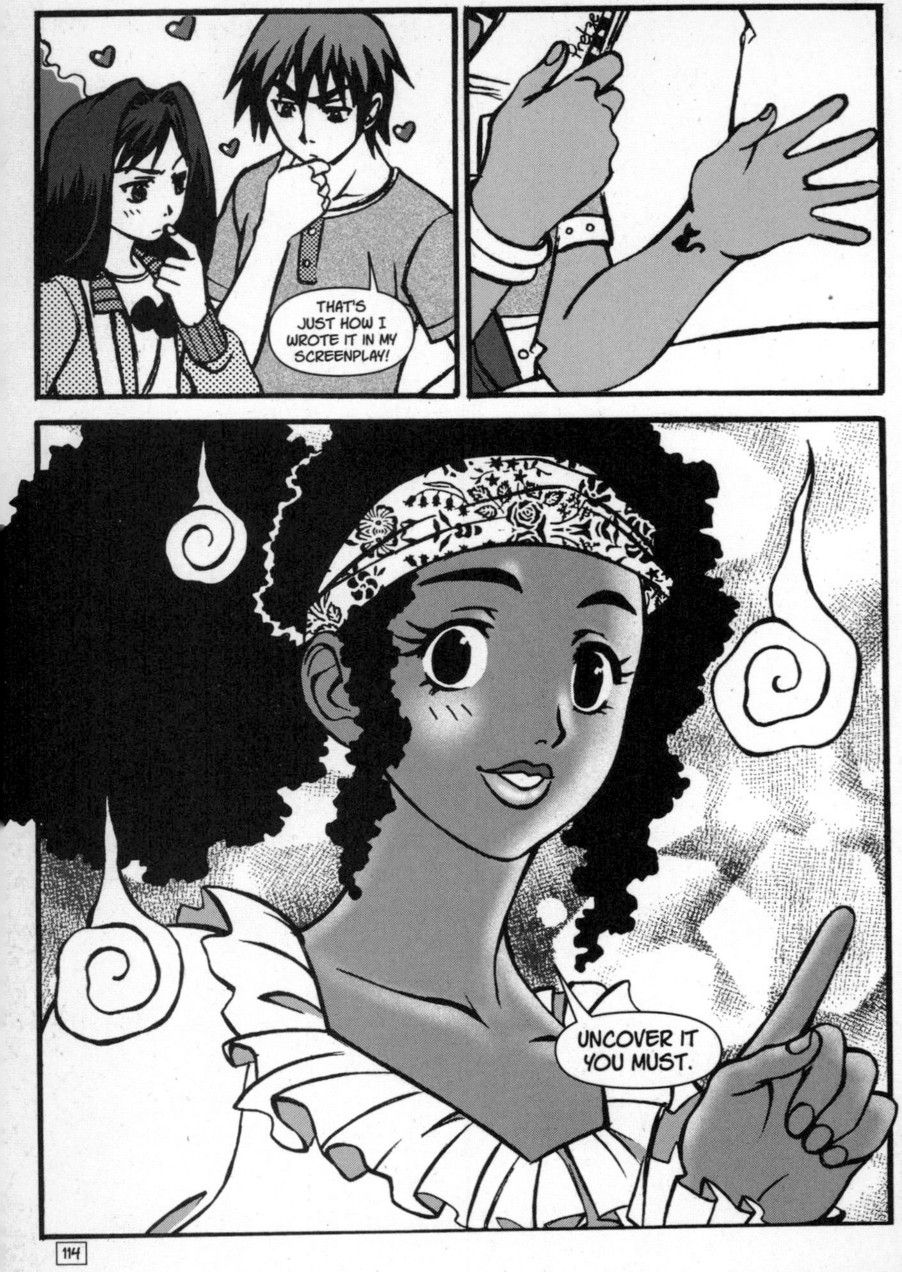
THAT'S JUST HOW I WROTE IT IN MY SCREENPLAY!
UNCOVER IT YOU MUST.

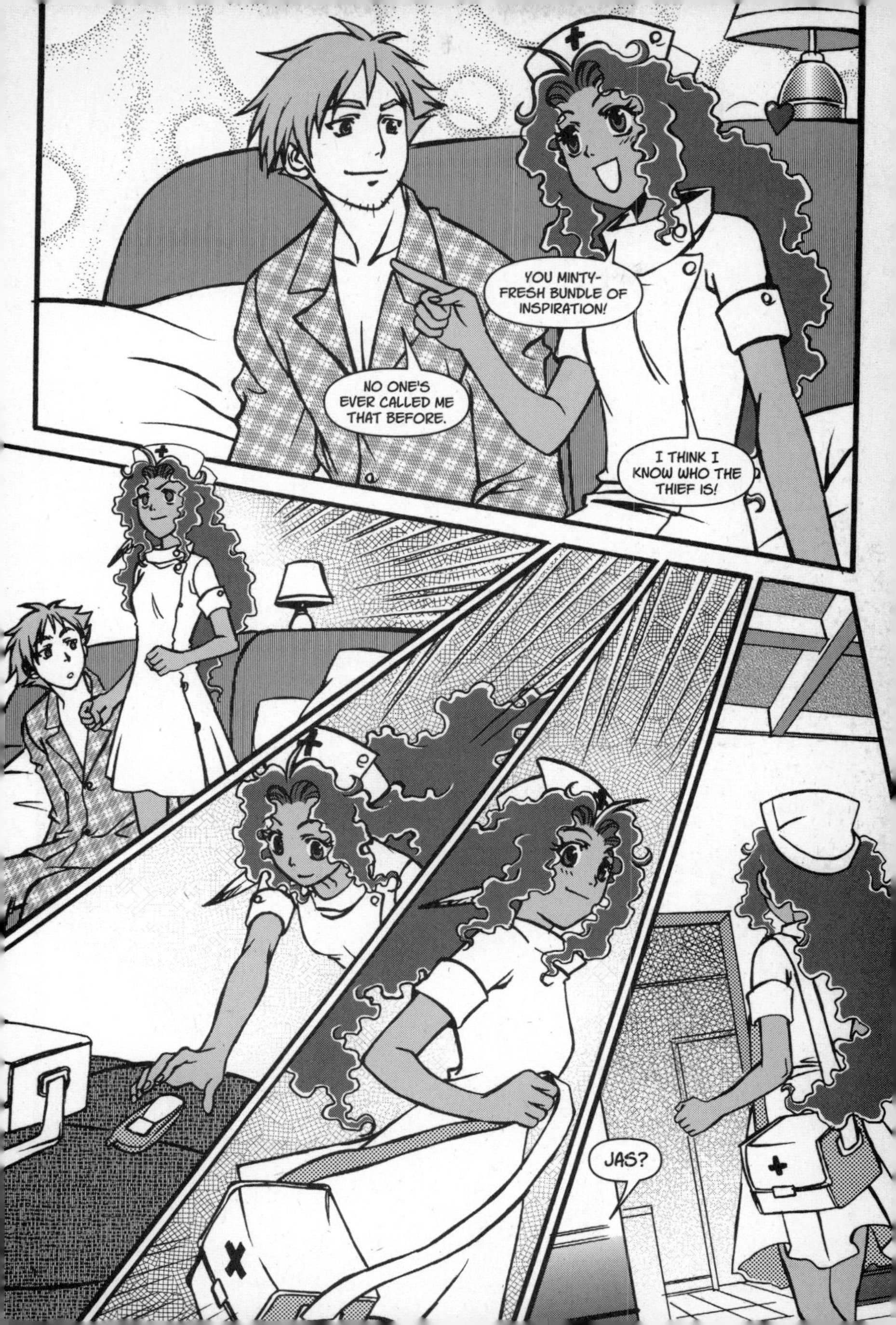
YOU MINTY-FRESH BUNDLE OF INSPIRATION!
NO ONE'S EVER CALLED ME THAT BEFORE.
I THINK I KNOW WHO THE THIEF IS!
JAS?

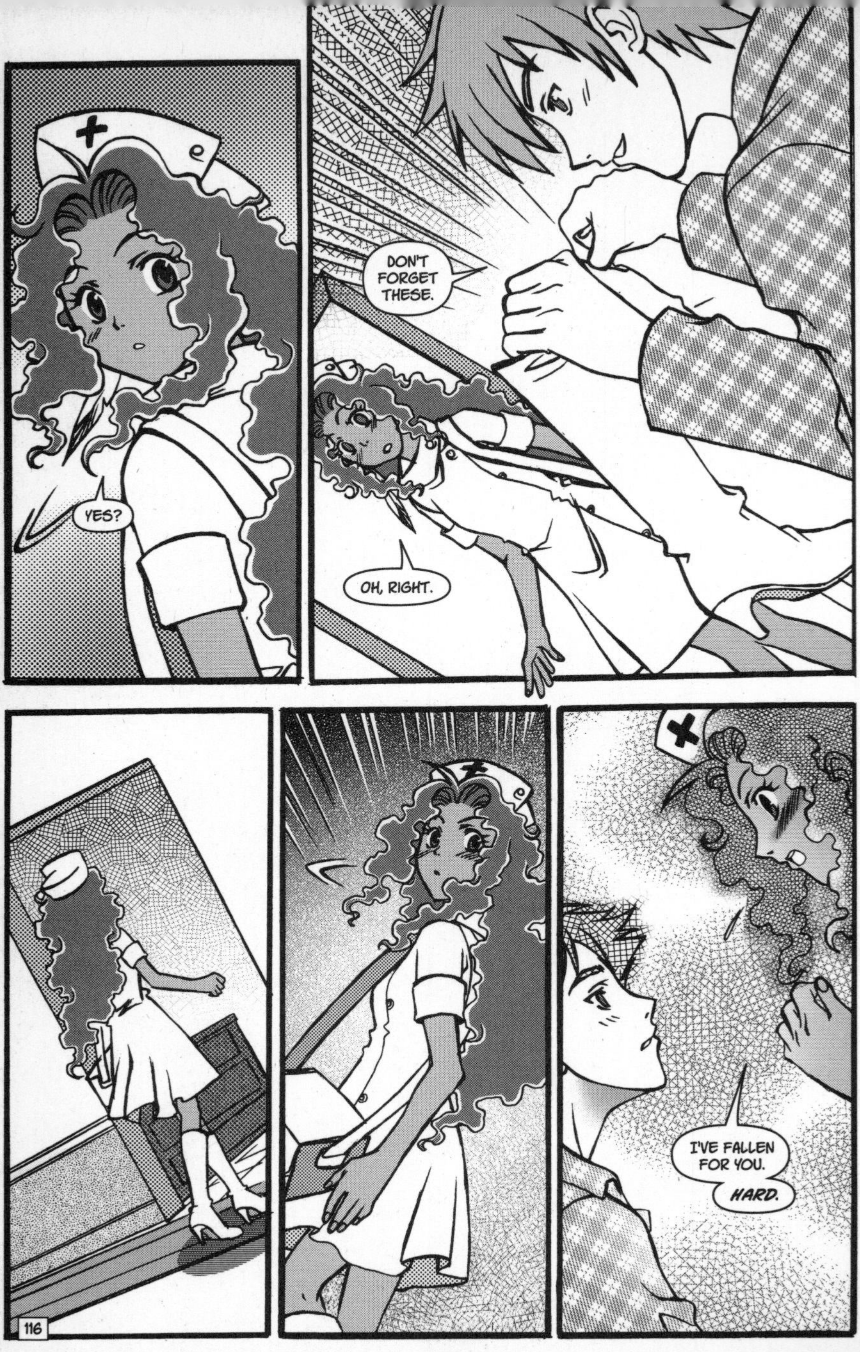
YES?
DON'T FORGET THESE.
OH, RIGHT.
I'VE FALLEN FOR YOU.
HARD.

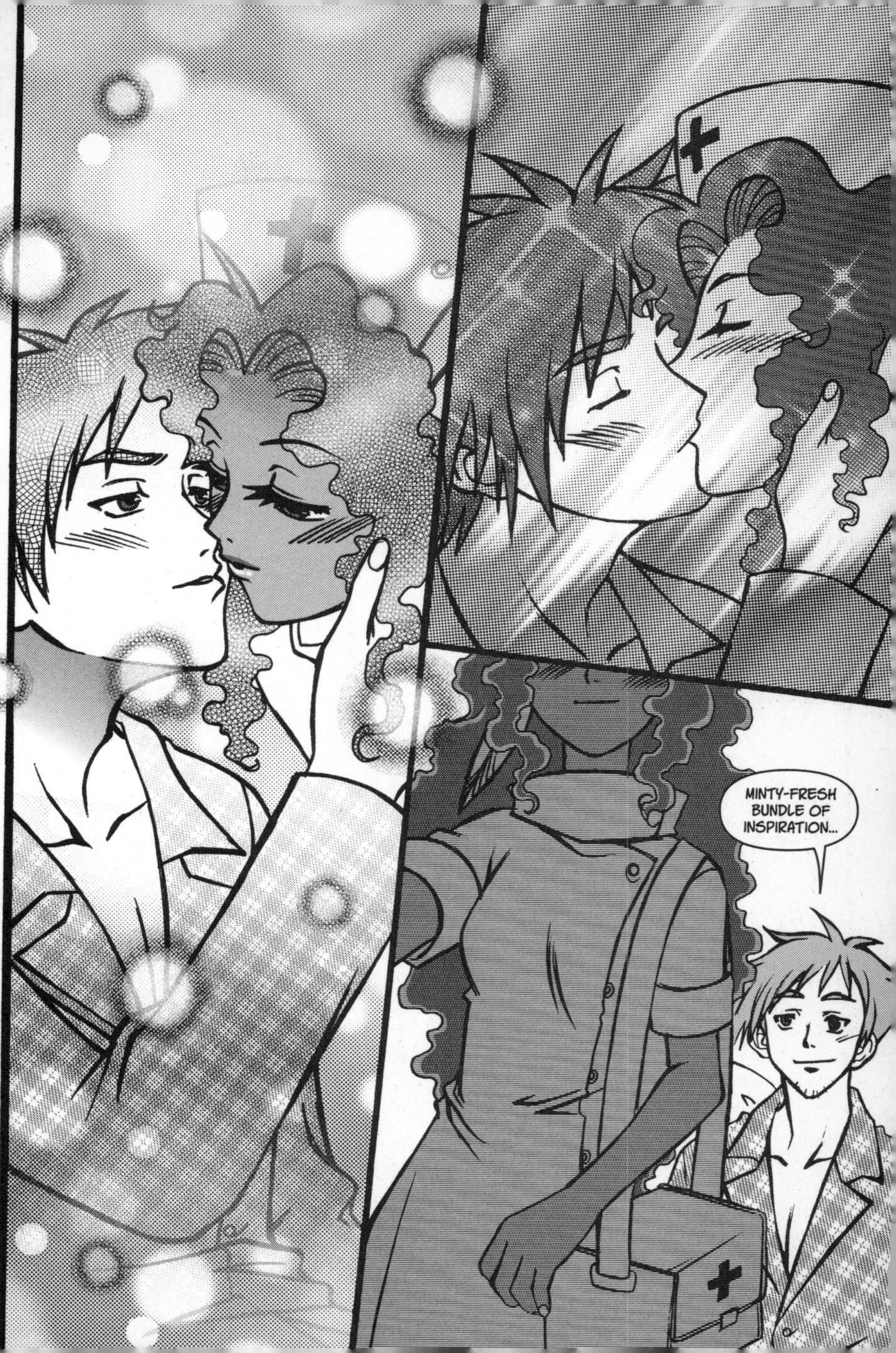
MINTY-FRESH BUNDLE OF INSPIRATION...

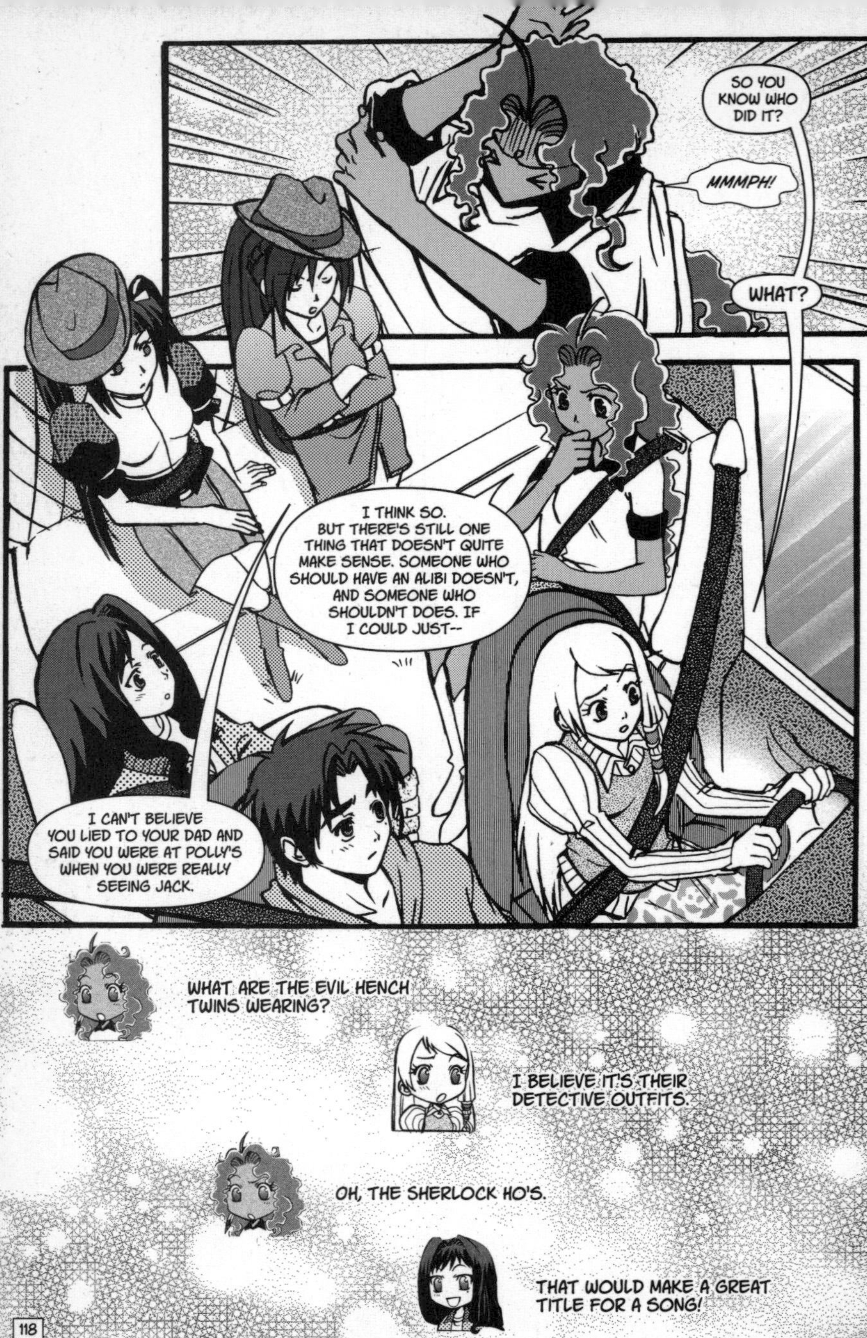
SO YOU KNOW WHO DID IT?
MMMPH!
WHAT?
I THINK SO. BUT THERE'S STILL ONE THING THAT DOESN'T QUITE MAKE SENSE. SOMEONE WHO SHOULD HAVE AN ALIBI DOESN'T, AND SOMEONE WHO SHOULDN'T DOES. IF I COULD JUST--
I CAN'T BELIEVE YOU LIED TO YOUR DAD AND SAID YOU WERE AT POLLY'S WHEN YOU WERE REALLY SEEING JACK.
WHAT ARE THE EVIL HENCH TWINS WEARING?
I BELIEVE IT'S THEIR DETECTIVE OUTFITS.
OH, THE SHERLOCK HO'S.
THAT WOULD MAKE A GREAT TITLE FOR A SONG!

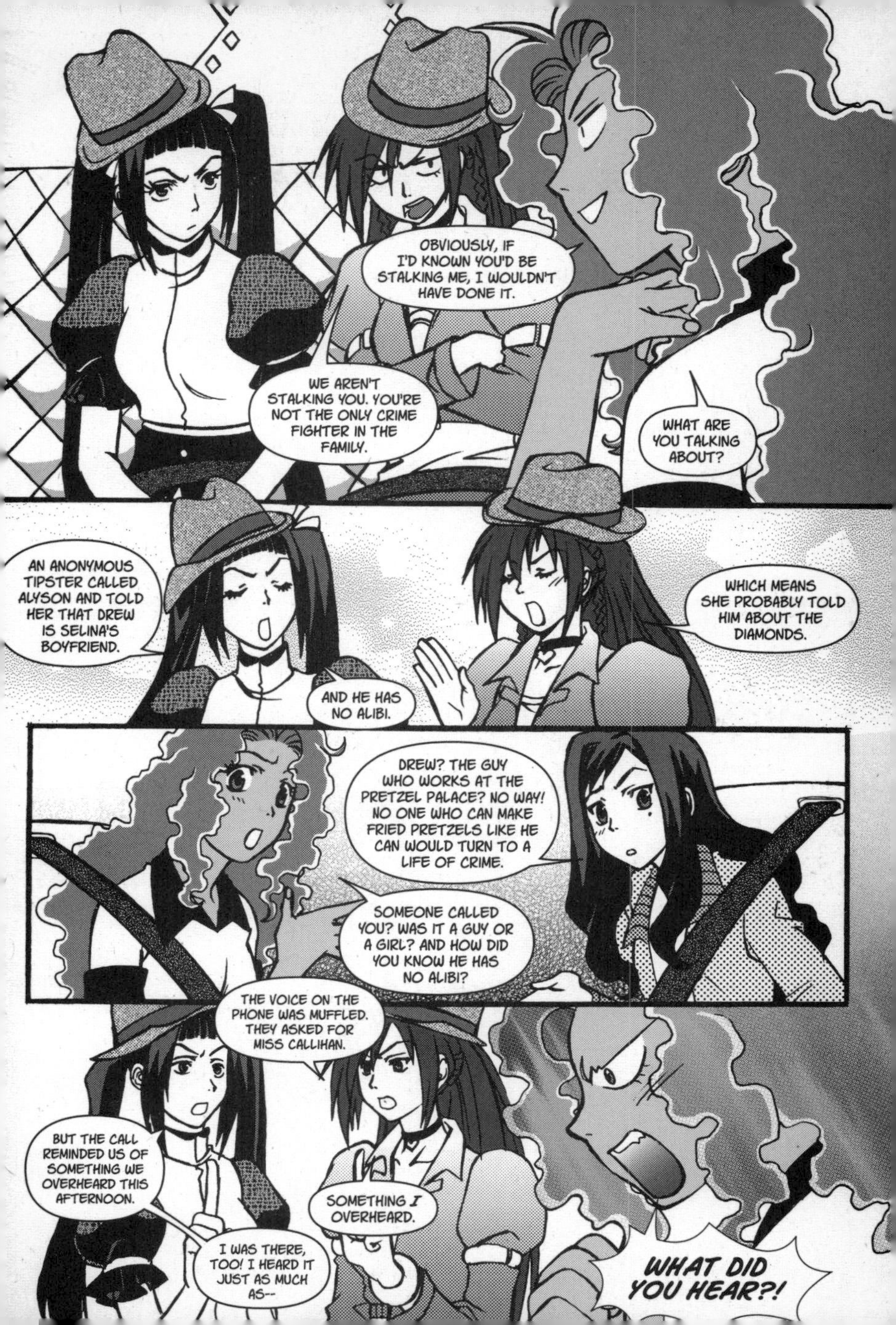
OBVIOUSLY, IF I'D KNOWN YOU'D BE STALKING ME, I WOULDN'T HAVE DONE IT.
WE AREN'T STALKING YOU. YOU'RE NOT THE ONLY CRIME FIGHTER IN THE FAMILY.
WHAT ARE YOU TALKING ABOUT?
AN ANONYMOUS TIPSTER CALLED ALYSON AND TOLD HER THAT DREW IS SELINA'S BOYFRIEND.
AND HE HAS NO ALIBI.
WHICH MEANS SHE PROBABLY TOLD HIM ABOUT THE DIAMONDS.
DREW? THE GUY WHO WORKS AT THE PRETZEL PALACE? NO WAY! NO ONE WHO CAN MAKE FRIED PRETZELS LIKE HE CAN WOULD TURN TO A LIFE OF CRIME.
SOMEONE CALLED YOU? WAS IT A GUY OR A GIRL? AND HOW DID YOU KNOW HE HAS NO ALIBI?
THE VOICE ON THE PHONE WAS MUFFLED. THEY ASKED FOR MISS CALLIHAN.
BUT THE CALL REMINDED US OF SOMETHING WE OVERHEARD THIS AFTERNOON.
SOMETHING *I* OVERHEARD.
I WAS THERE, TOO! I HEARD IT JUST AS MUCH AS--
WHAT DID YOU HEAR?!

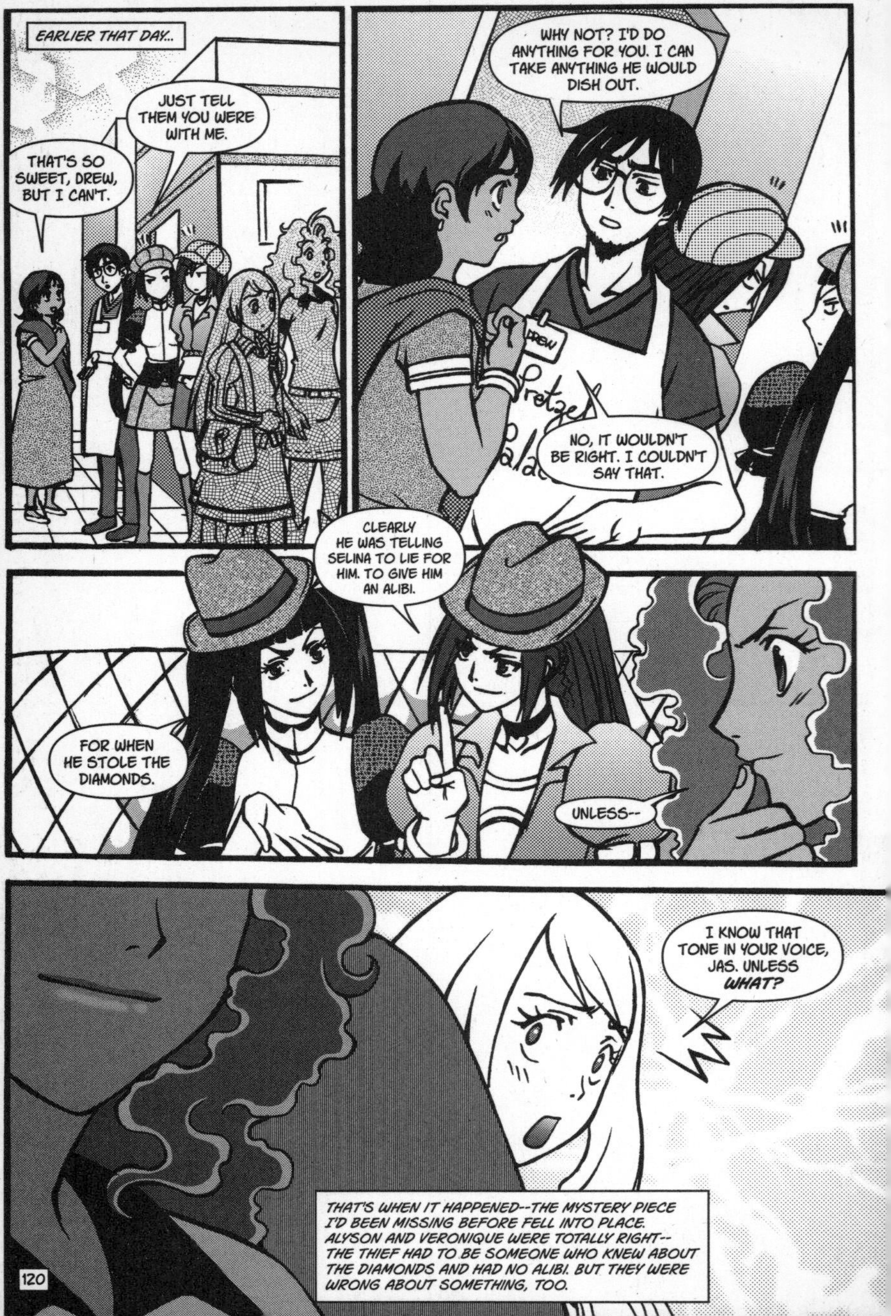
EARLIER THAT DAY...
JUST TELL THEM YOU WERE WITH ME.
THAT'S SO SWEET, DREW, BUT I CAN'T.
WHY NOT? I'D DO ANYTHING FOR YOU. I CAN TAKE ANYTHING HE WOULD DISH OUT.
DREW
NO, IT WOULDN'T BE RIGHT. I COULDN'T SAY THAT.
CLEARLY HE WAS TELLING SELINA TO LIE FOR HIM. TO GIVE HIM AN ALIBI.
FOR WHEN HE STOLE THE DIAMONDS.
UNLESS--
I KNOW THAT TONE IN YOUR VOICE, JAS. UNLESS ***WHAT?***
THAT'S WHEN IT HAPPENED--THE MYSTERY PIECE I'D BEEN MISSING BEFORE FELL INTO PLACE. ALYSON AND VERONIQUE WERE TOTALLY RIGHT-- THE THIEF HAD TO BE SOMEONE WHO KNEW ABOUT THE DIAMONDS AND HAD NO ALIBI. BUT THEY WERE WRONG ABOUT SOMETHING, TOO.

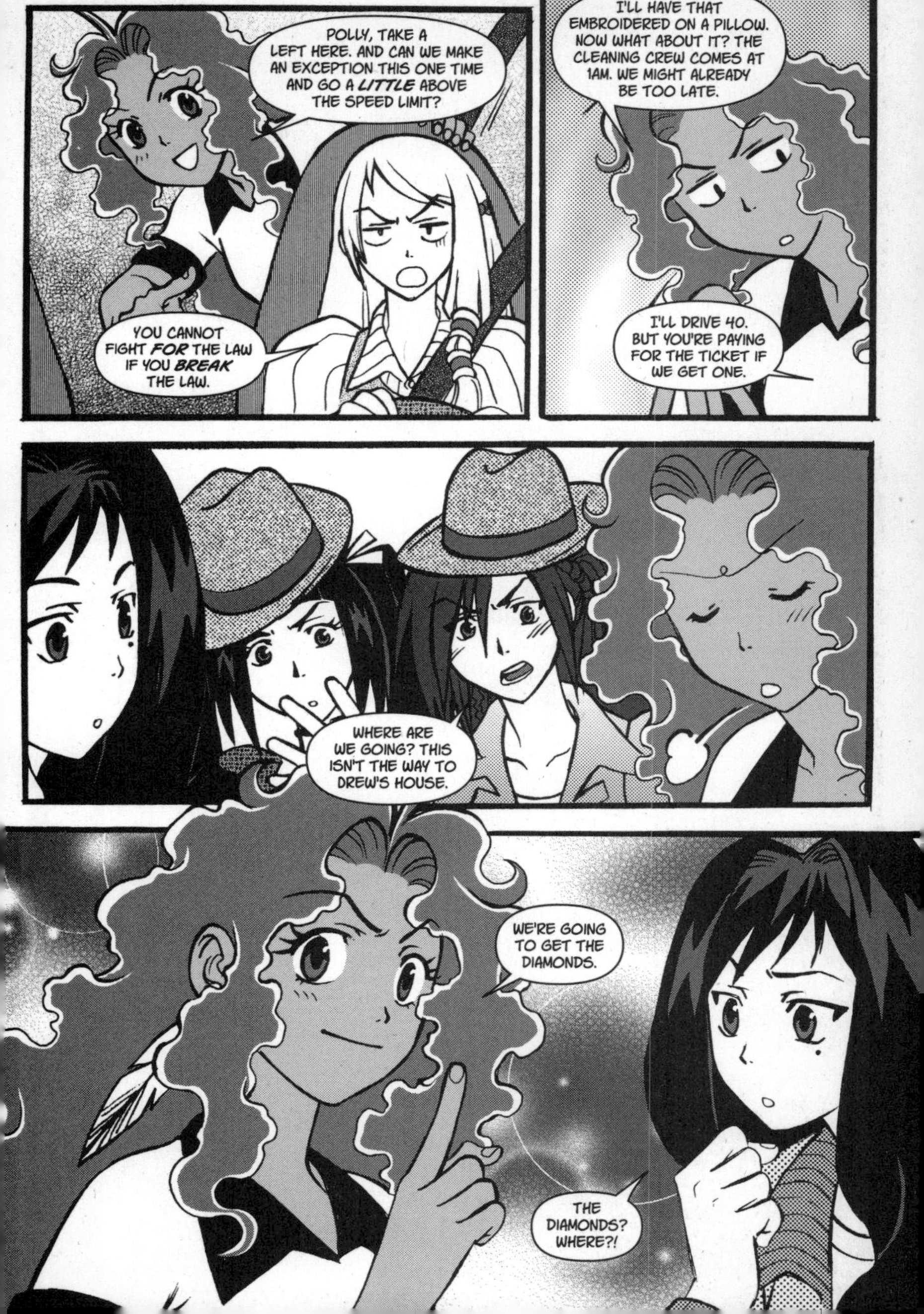
POLLY, TAKE A LEFT HERE. AND CAN WE MAKE AN EXCEPTION THIS ONE TIME AND GO A *LITTLE* ABOVE THE SPEED LIMIT?
YOU CANNOT FIGHT *FOR* THE LAW IF YOU *BREAK* THE LAW.
I'LL HAVE THAT EMBROIDERED ON A PILLOW. NOW WHAT ABOUT IT? THE CLEANING CREW COMES AT 1AM. WE MIGHT ALREADY BE TOO LATE.
I'LL DRIVE 40. BUT YOU'RE PAYING FOR THE TICKET IF WE GET ONE.
WHERE ARE WE GOING? THIS ISN'T THE WAY TO DREW'S HOUSE.
WE'RE GOING TO GET THE DIAMONDS.
THE DIAMONDS? WHERE?!

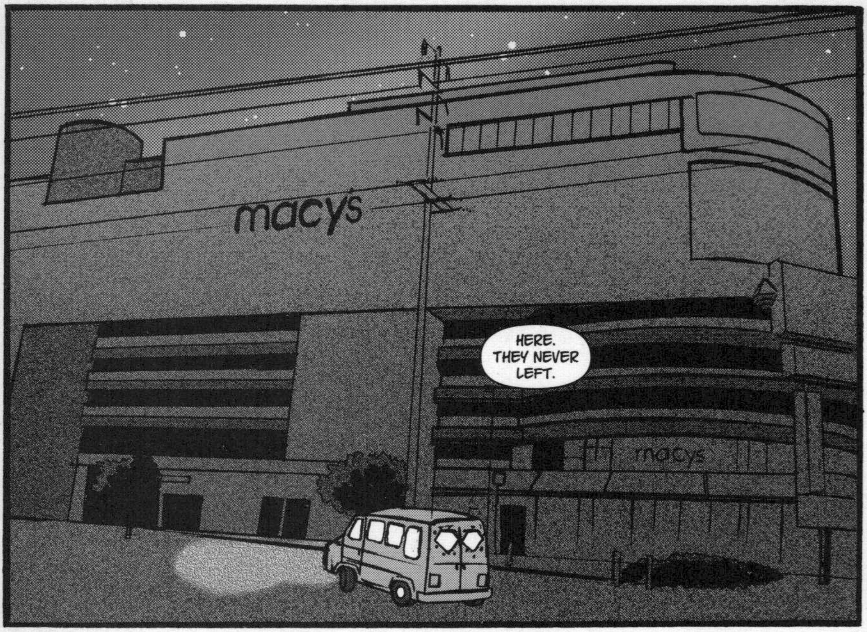
macy's
HERE. THEY NEVER LEFT.
macy's

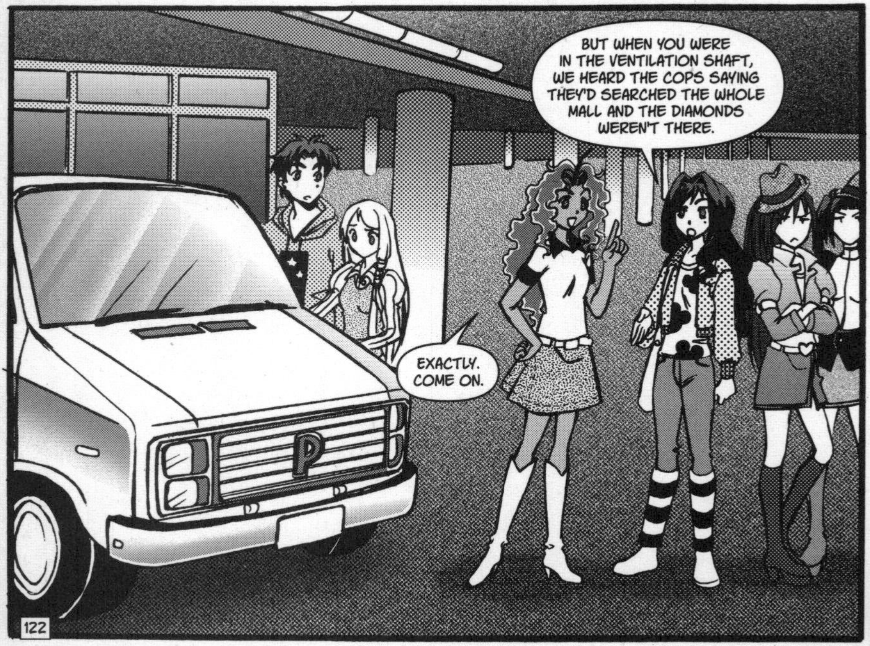
BUT WHEN YOU WERE IN THE VENTILATION SHAFT, WE HEARD THE COPS SAYING THEY'D SEARCHED THE WHOLE MALL AND THE DIAMONDS WEREN'T THERE.
EXACTLY. COME ON.

Chapter Five

Jasmine Callihan

HAIR:	Malicious
PORES:	Medium

HEART: FULL!

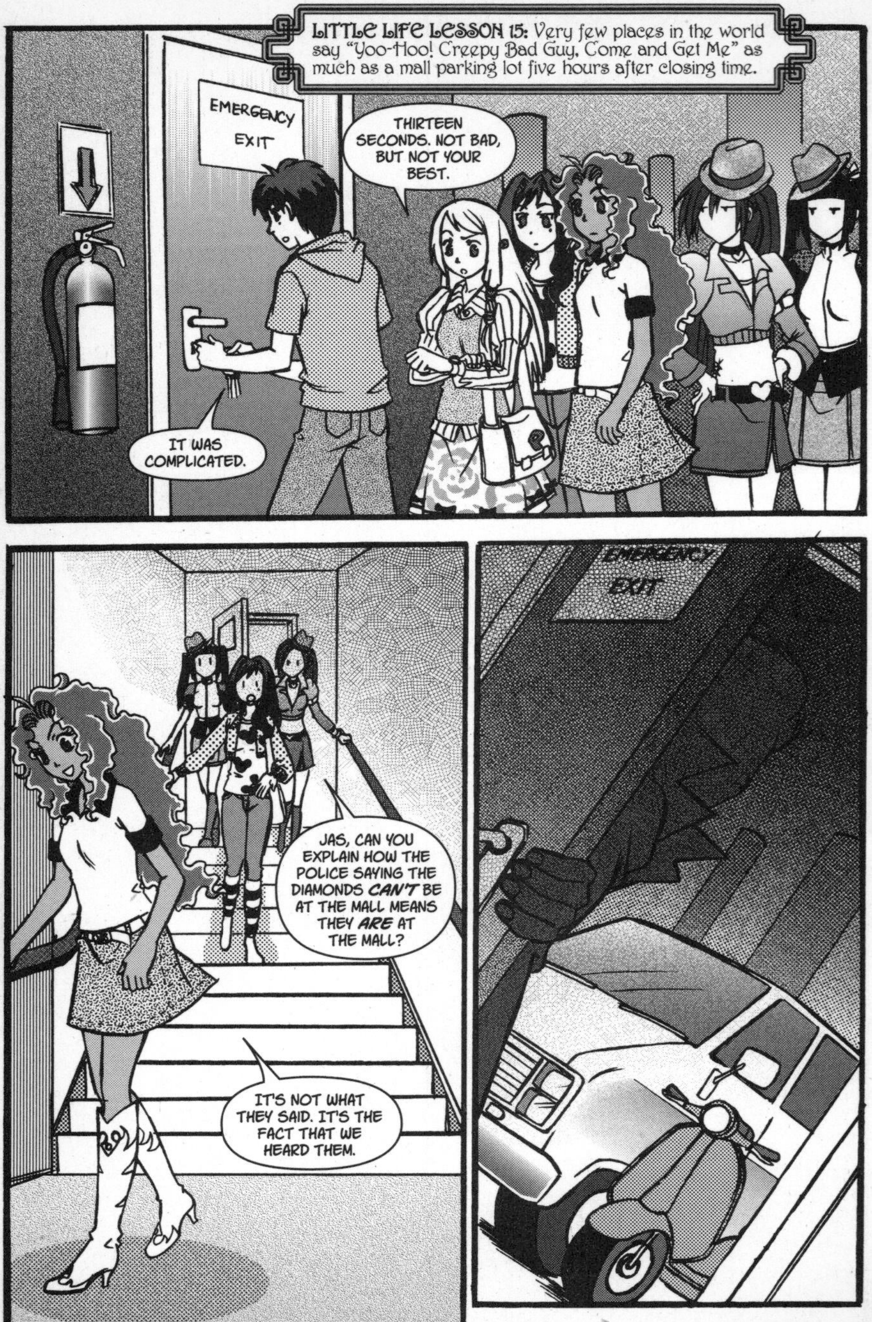
LITTLE LIFE LESSON 15: Very few places in the world say "Yoo-Hoo! Creepy Bad Guy, Come and Get Me" as much as a mall parking lot five hours after closing time.
EMERGENCY EXIT
THIRTEEN SECONDS. NOT BAD, BUT NOT YOUR BEST.
IT WAS COMPLICATED.
JAS, CAN YOU EXPLAIN HOW THE POLICE SAYING THE DIAMONDS *CAN'T* BE AT THE MALL MEANS THEY *ARE* AT THE MALL?
IT'S NOT WHAT THEY SAID. IT'S THE FACT THAT WE HEARD THEM.
EMERGENCY EXIT

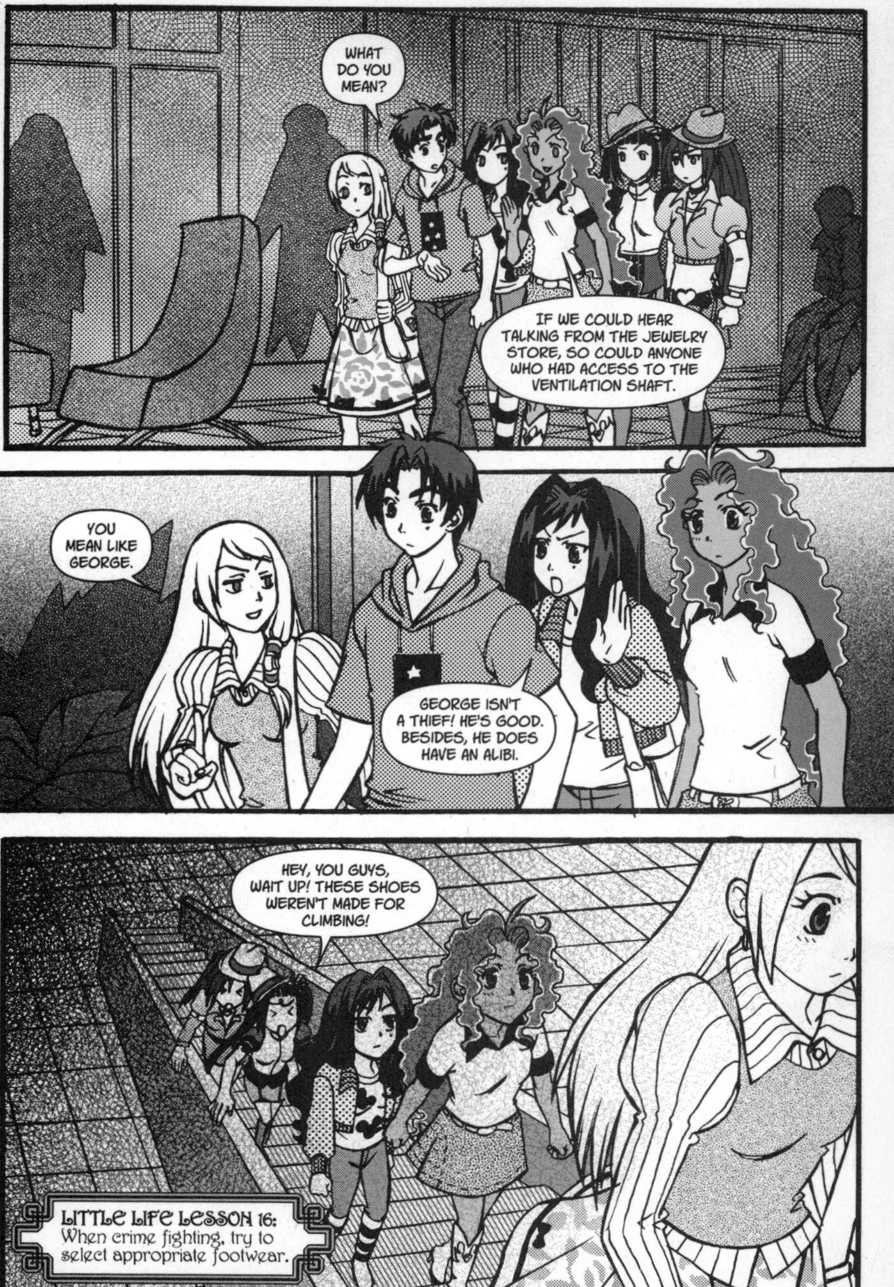
WHAT DO YOU MEAN?
IF WE COULD HEAR TALKING FROM THE JEWELRY STORE, SO COULD ANYONE WHO HAD ACCESS TO THE VENTILATION SHAFT.
YOU MEAN LIKE GEORGE.
GEORGE ISN'T A THIEF! HE'S GOOD. BESIDES, HE DOES HAVE AN ALIBI.
HEY, YOU GUYS, WAIT UP! THESE SHOES WEREN'T MADE FOR CLIMBING!
LITTLE LIFE LESSON 16:
When crime fighting, try to select appropriate footwear.

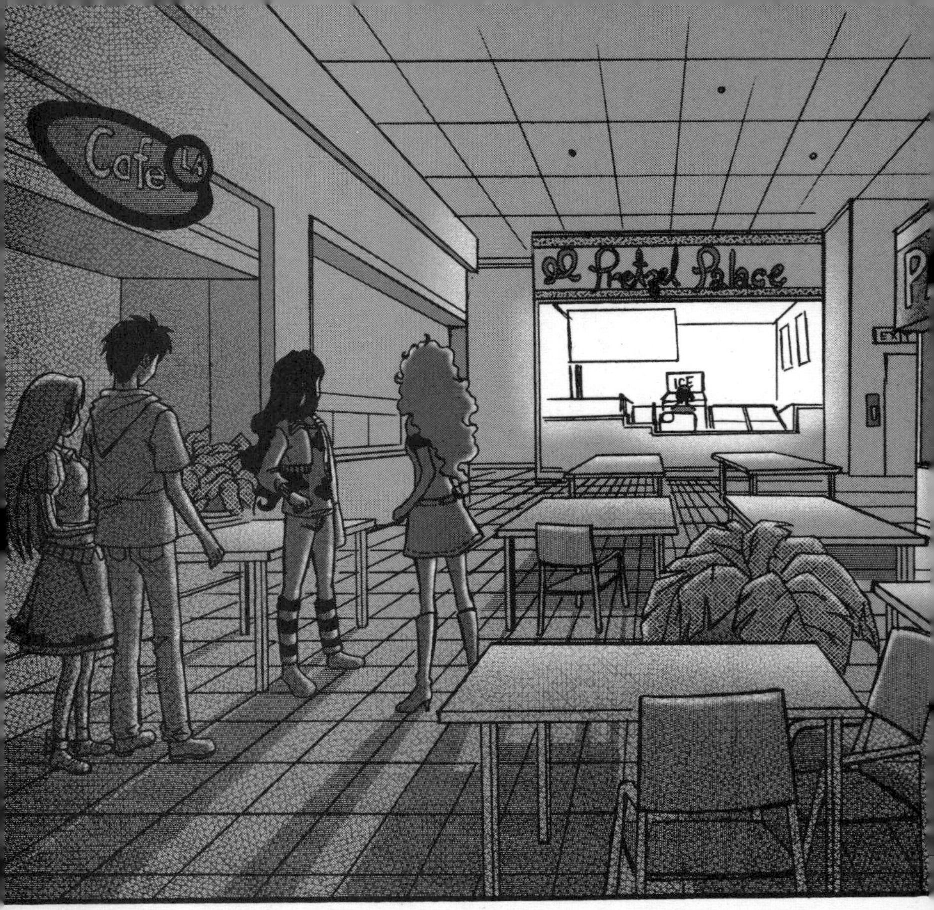
Cafe
Pretzel Palace
ICE

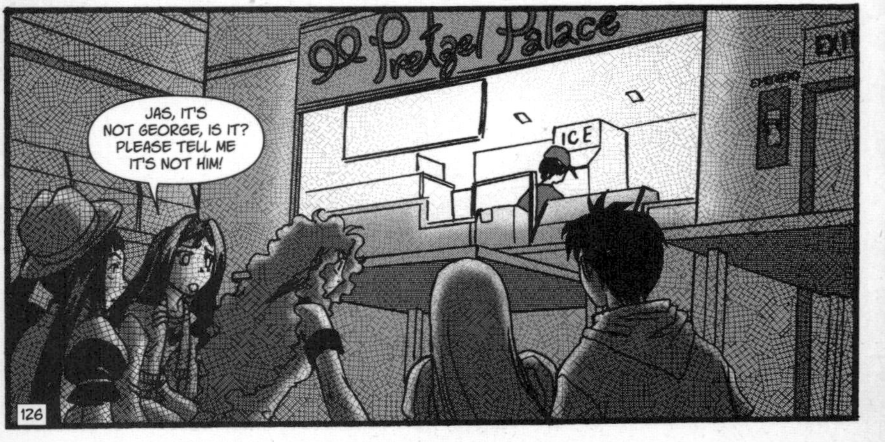
Pretzel Palace
ICE
JAS, IT'S NOT GEORGE, IS IT? PLEASE TELL ME IT'S NOT HIM!

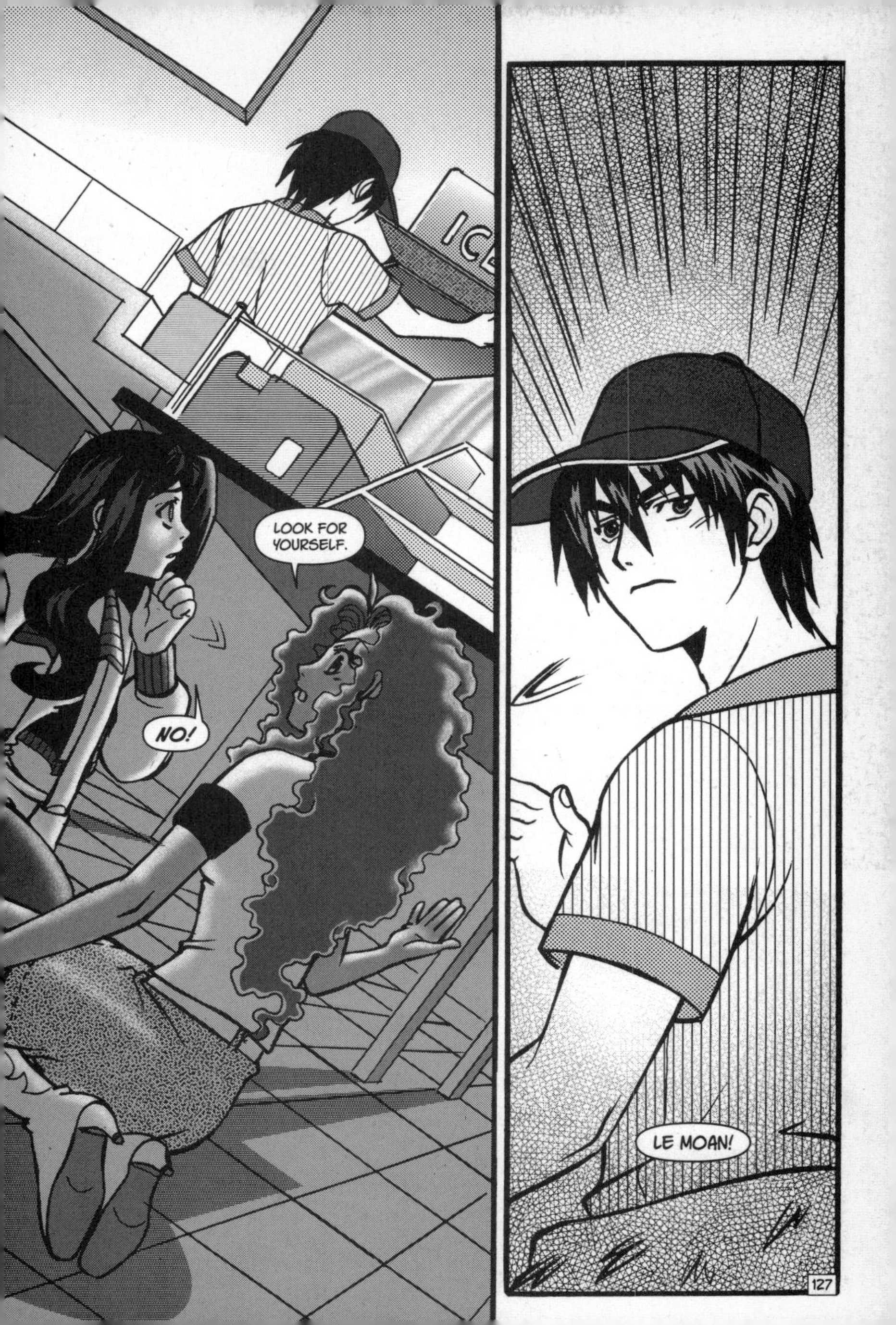
ICE
LOOK FOR YOURSELF.
NO!
LE MOAN!

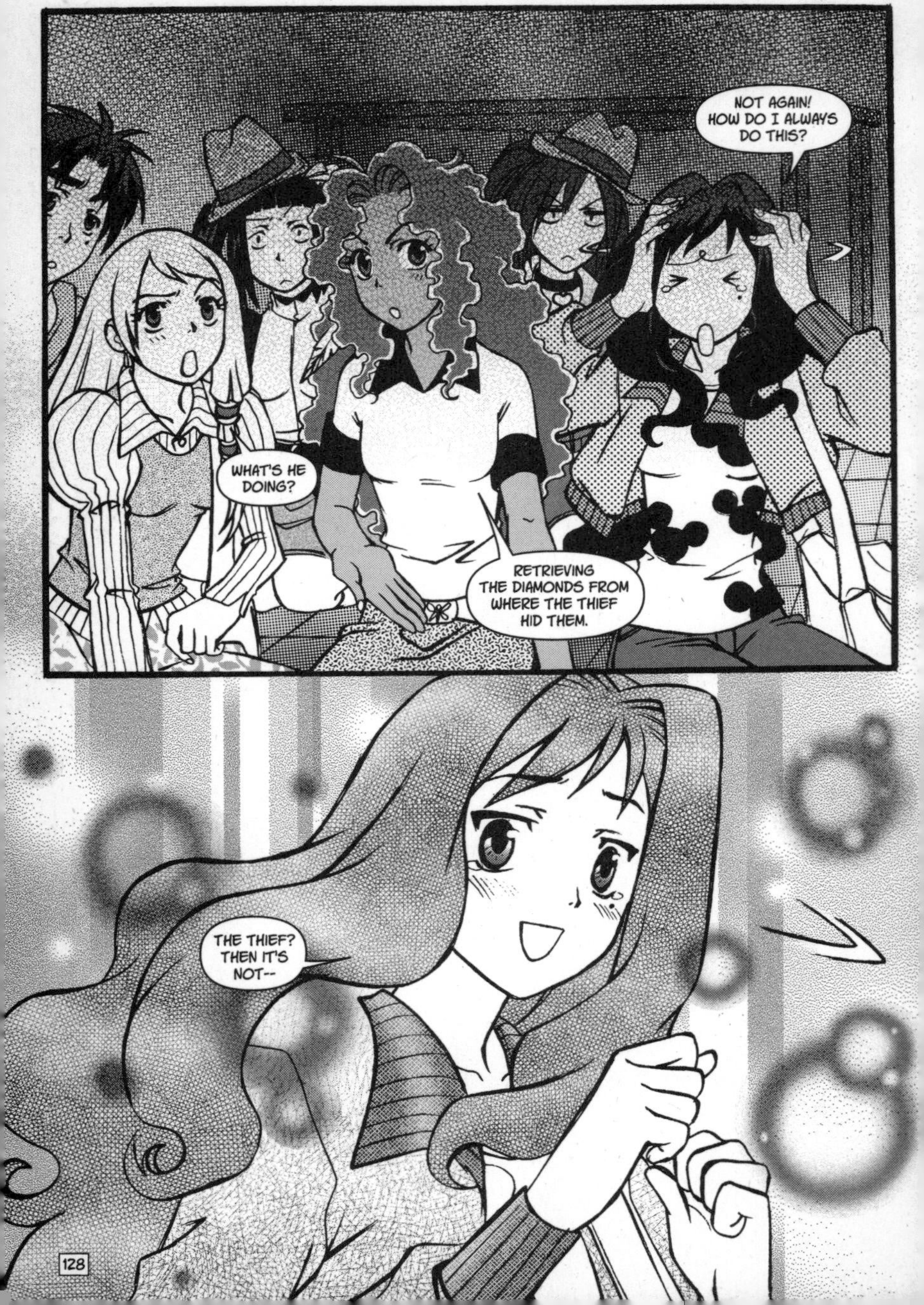
WHAT'S HE DOING?
NOT AGAIN! HOW DO I ALWAYS DO THIS?
RETRIEVING THE DIAMONDS FROM WHERE THE THIEF HID THEM.
THE THIEF? THEN IT'S NOT--

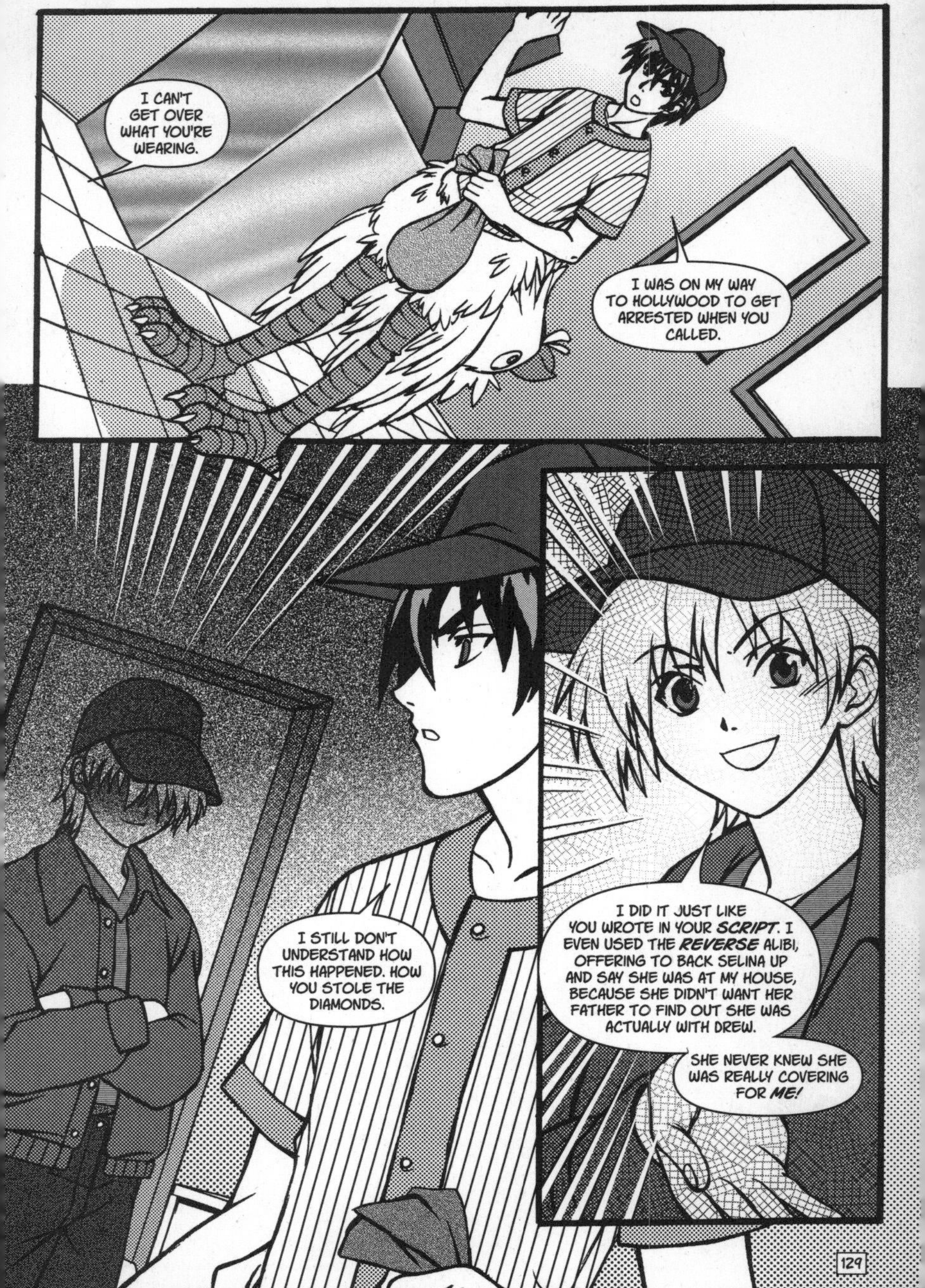
I CAN'T GET OVER WHAT YOU'RE WEARING.
I WAS ON MY WAY TO HOLLYWOOD TO GET ARRESTED WHEN YOU CALLED.
I STILL DON'T UNDERSTAND HOW THIS HAPPENED. HOW YOU STOLE THE DIAMONDS.
I DID IT JUST LIKE YOU WROTE IN YOUR ***SCRIPT***. I EVEN USED THE ***REVERSE*** ALIBI, OFFERING TO BACK SELINA UP AND SAY SHE WAS AT MY HOUSE, BECAUSE SHE DIDN'T WANT HER FATHER TO FIND OUT SHE WAS ACTUALLY WITH DREW.
SHE NEVER KNEW SHE WAS REALLY COVERING FOR ***ME!***

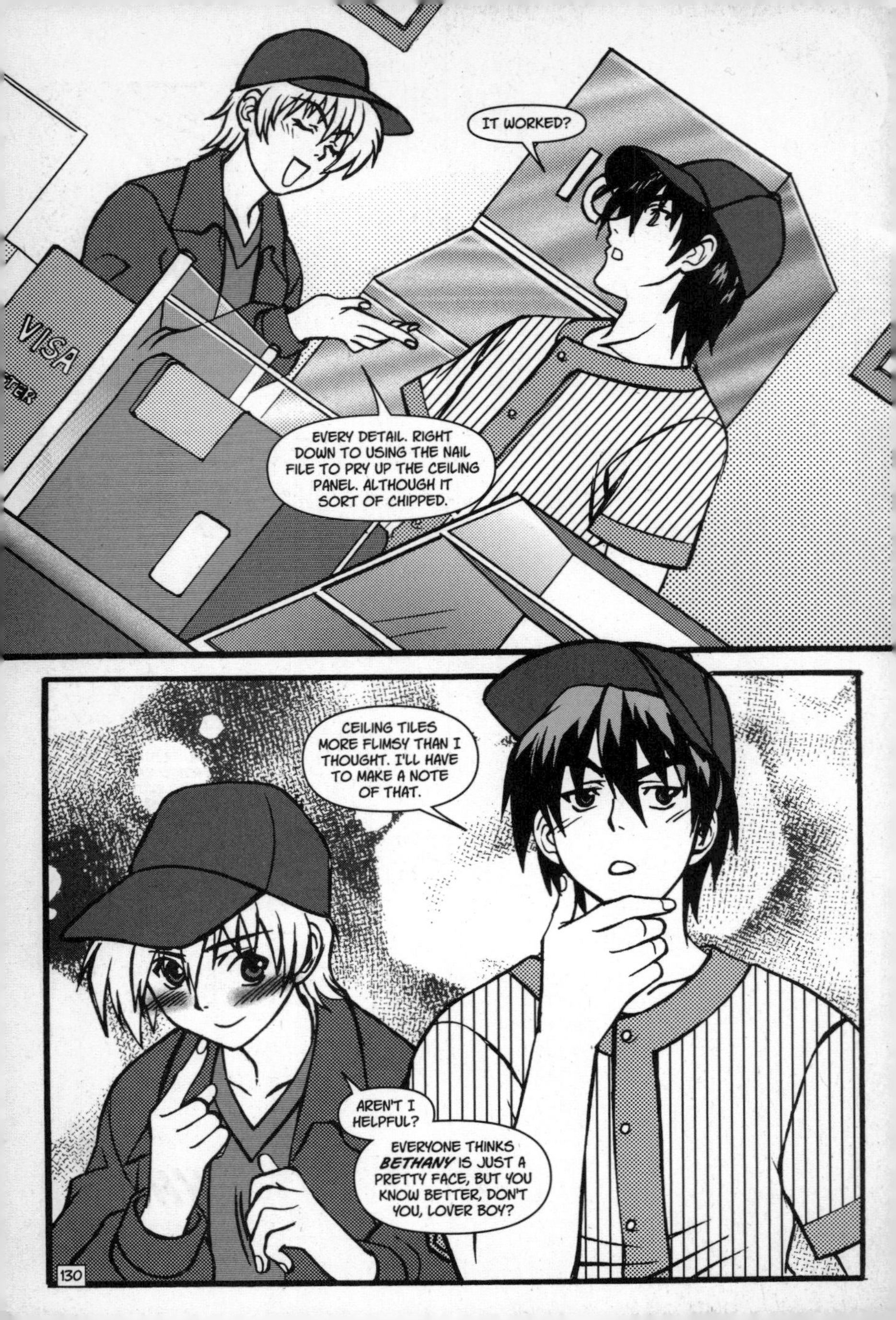
IT WORKED?
VISA
EVERY DETAIL. RIGHT DOWN TO USING THE NAIL FILE TO PRY UP THE CEILING PANEL. ALTHOUGH IT SORT OF CHIPPED.
CEILING TILES MORE FLIMSY THAN I THOUGHT. I'LL HAVE TO MAKE A NOTE OF THAT.
AREN'T I HELPFUL?
EVERYONE THINKS ***BETHANY*** IS JUST A PRETTY FACE, BUT YOU KNOW BETTER, DON'T YOU, LOVER BOY?

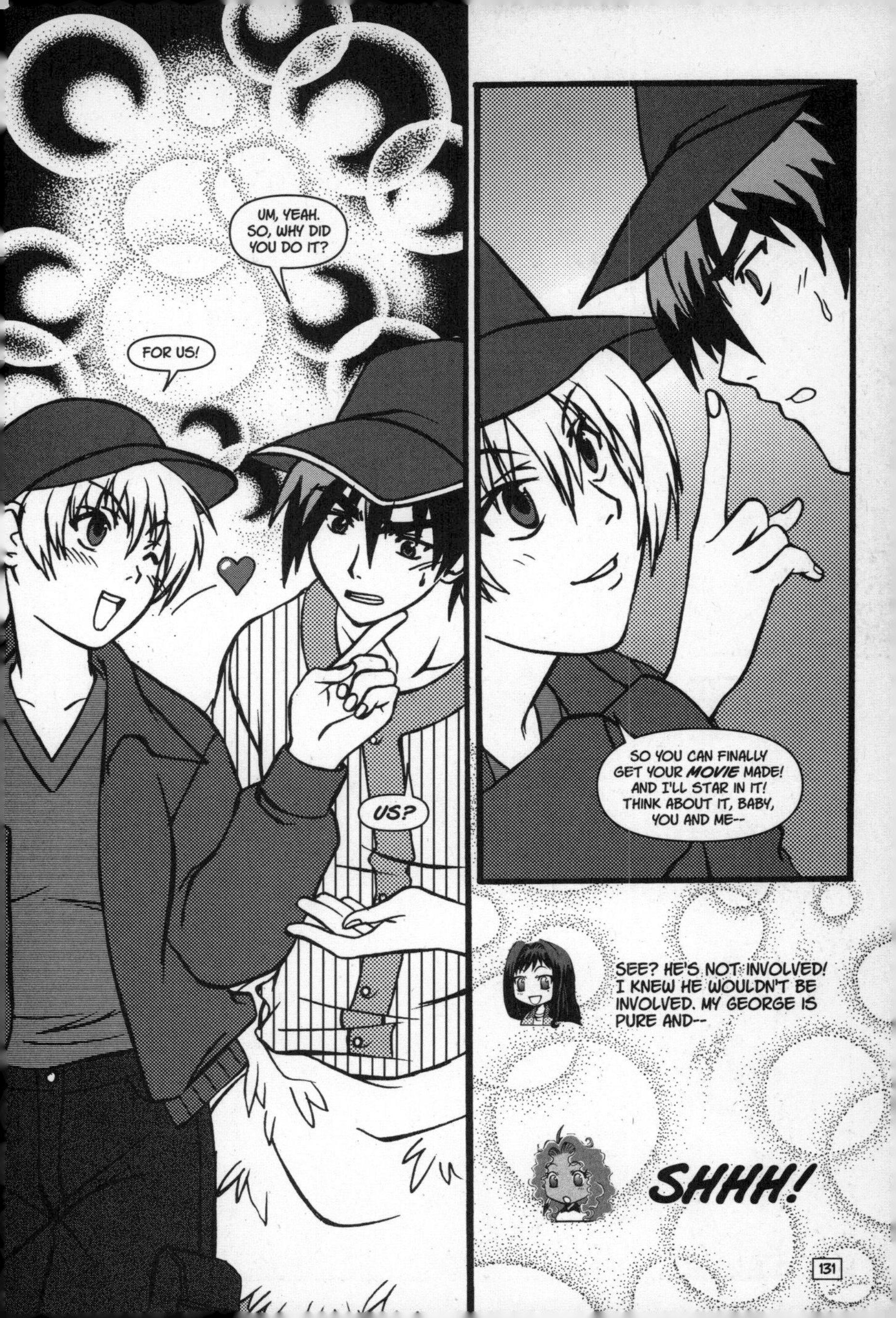
UM, YEAH. SO, WHY DID YOU DO IT?
FOR US!
US?
SO YOU CAN FINALLY GET YOUR MOVIE MADE! AND I'LL STAR IN IT! THINK ABOUT IT, BABY, YOU AND ME--
SEE? HE'S NOT INVOLVED! I KNEW HE WOULDN'T BE INVOLVED. MY GEORGE IS PURE AND--
SHHH!

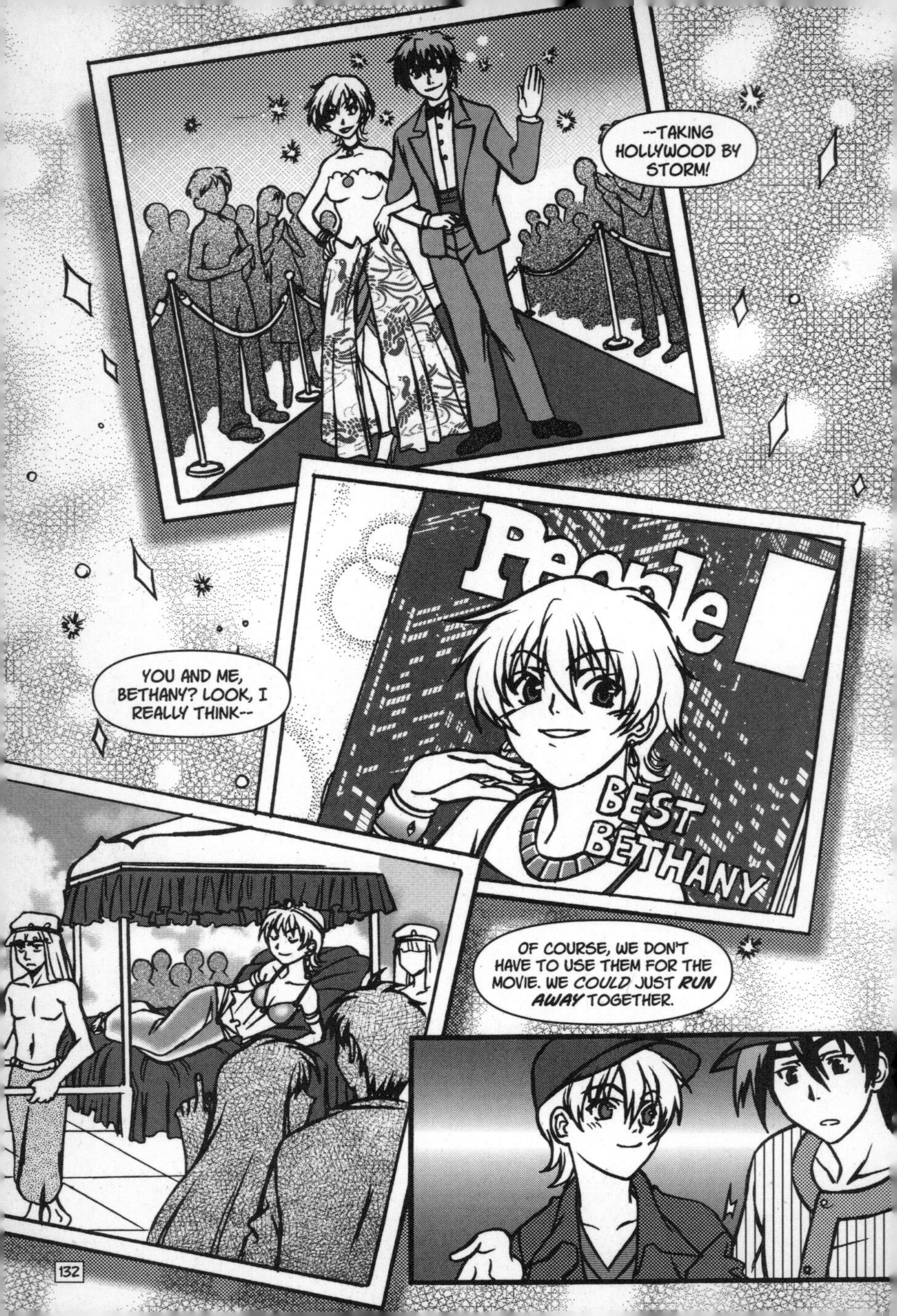
--TAKING HOLLYWOOD BY STORM!
People
YOU AND ME, BETHANY? LOOK, I REALLY THINK--
BEST BETHANY
OF COURSE, WE DON'T HAVE TO USE THEM FOR THE MOVIE. WE *COULD* JUST ***RUN AWAY*** TOGETHER.

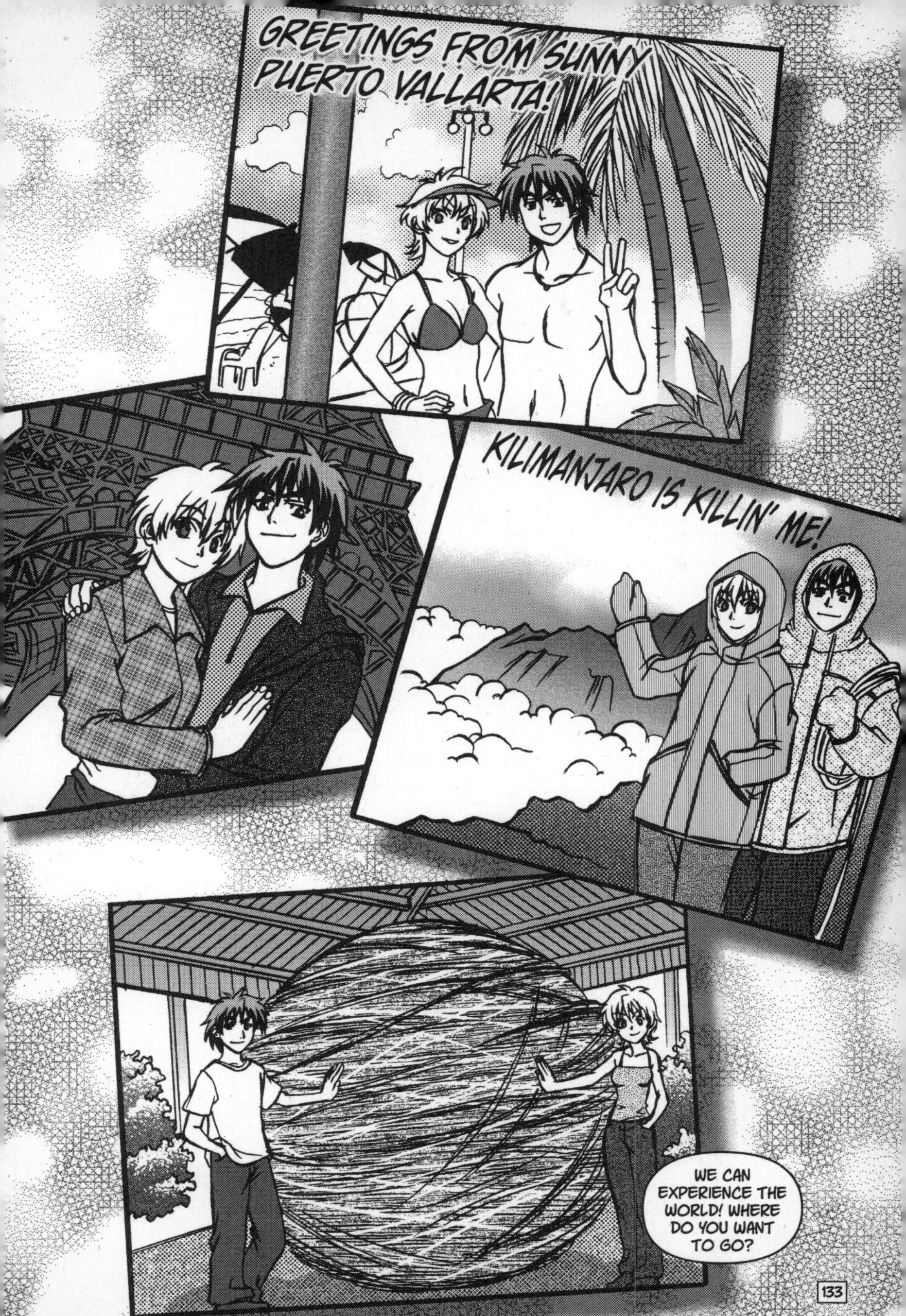
GREETINGS FROM SUNNY PUERTO VALLARTA!
KILIMANJARO IS KILLIN' ME!
WE CAN EXPERIENCE THE WORLD! WHERE DO YOU WANT TO GO?

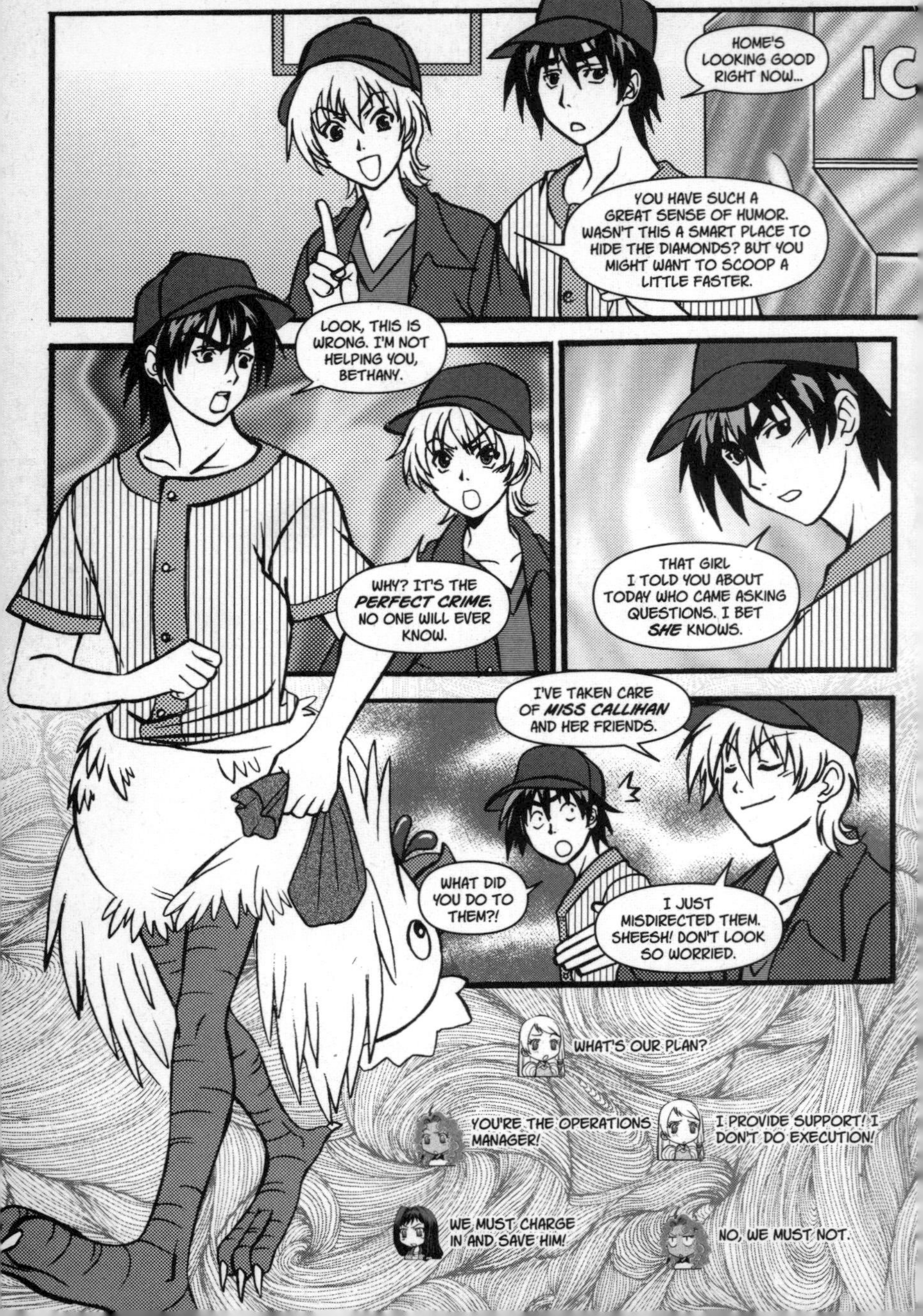
HOME'S LOOKING GOOD RIGHT NOW...
YOU HAVE SUCH A GREAT SENSE OF HUMOR. WASN'T THIS A SMART PLACE TO HIDE THE DIAMONDS? BUT YOU MIGHT WANT TO SCOOP A LITTLE FASTER.
LOOK, THIS IS WRONG. I'M NOT HELPING YOU, BETHANY.
WHY? IT'S THE *PERFECT CRIME.* NO ONE WILL EVER KNOW.
THAT GIRL I TOLD YOU ABOUT TODAY WHO CAME ASKING QUESTIONS. I BET *SHE* KNOWS.
I'VE TAKEN CARE OF *MISS CALLIHAN* AND HER FRIENDS.
WHAT DID YOU DO TO THEM?!
I JUST MISDIRECTED THEM. SHEESH! DON'T LOOK SO WORRIED.
WHAT'S OUR PLAN?
YOU'RE THE OPERATIONS MANAGER!
I PROVIDE SUPPORT! I DON'T DO EXECUTION!
WE MUST CHARGE IN AND SAVE HIM!
NO, WE MUST NOT.

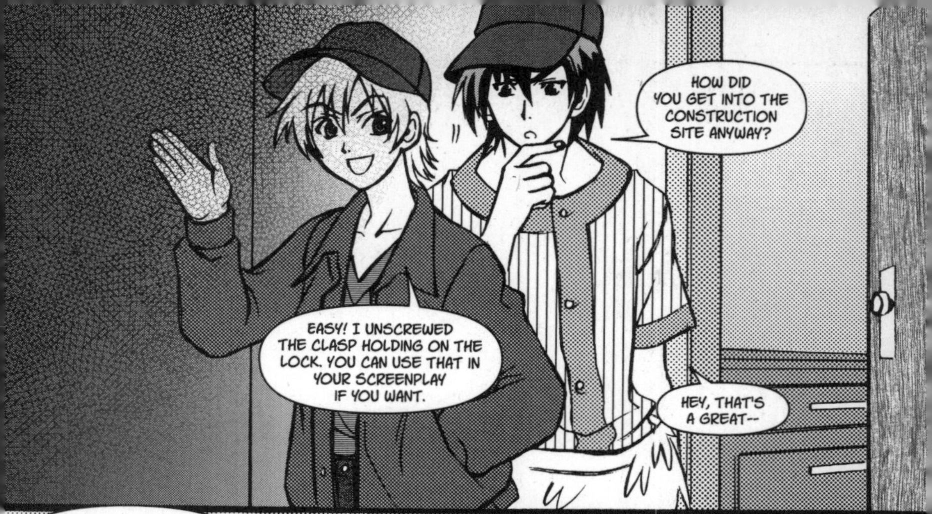
HOW DID YOU GET INTO THE CONSTRUCTION SITE ANYWAY?
EASY! I UNSCREWED THE CLASP HOLDING ON THE LOCK. YOU CAN USE THAT IN YOUR SCREENPLAY IF YOU WANT.
HEY, THAT'S A GREAT--

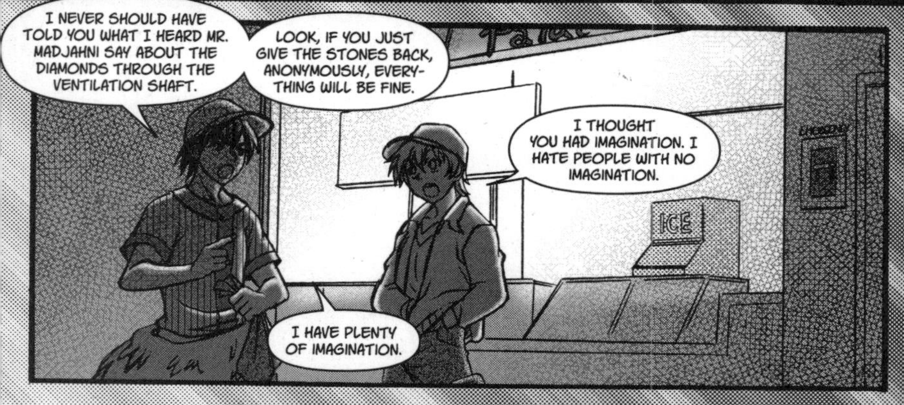
I NEVER SHOULD HAVE TOLD YOU WHAT I HEARD MR. MADJAHNI SAY ABOUT THE DIAMONDS THROUGH THE VENTILATION SHAFT.
LOOK, IF YOU JUST GIVE THE STONES BACK, ANONYMOUSLY, EVERY-THING WILL BE FINE.
I THOUGHT YOU HAD IMAGINATION. I HATE PEOPLE WITH NO IMAGINATION.
ICE
I HAVE PLENTY OF IMAGINATION.

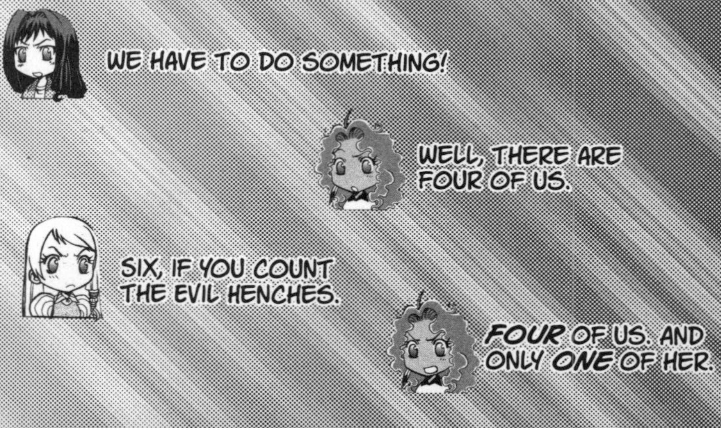
WE HAVE TO DO SOMETHING!
WELL, THERE ARE FOUR OF US.
SIX, IF YOU COUNT THE EVIL HENCHES.
FOUR OF US. AND ONLY ONE OF HER.

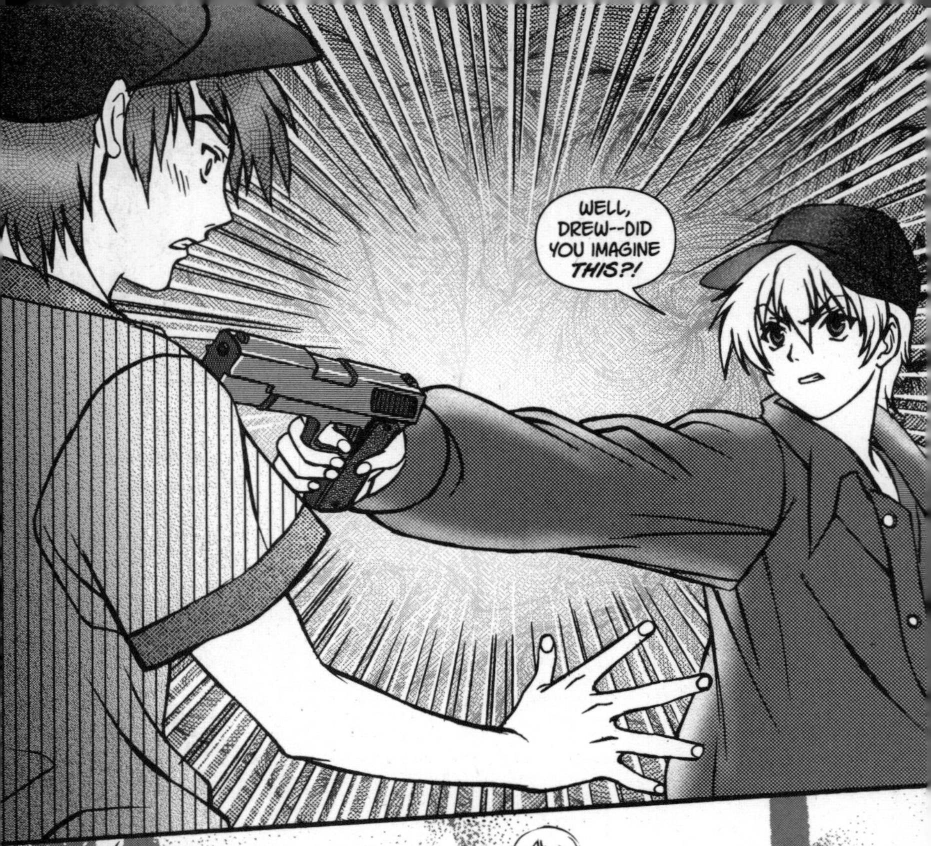
WELL, DREW--DID YOU IMAGINE ***THIS?!***

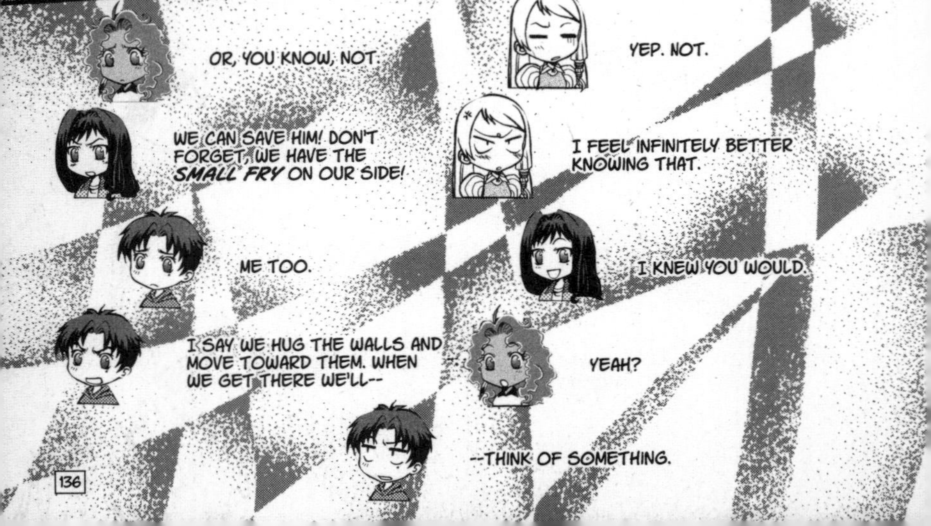
OR, YOU KNOW, NOT.
YEP. NOT.
WE CAN SAVE HIM! DON'T FORGET, WE HAVE THE ***SMALL FRY*** ON OUR SIDE!
I FEEL INFINITELY BETTER KNOWING THAT.
ME TOO.
I KNEW YOU WOULD.
I SAY WE HUG THE WALLS AND MOVE TOWARD THEM. WHEN WE GET THERE WE'LL--
YEAH?
--THINK OF SOMETHING.

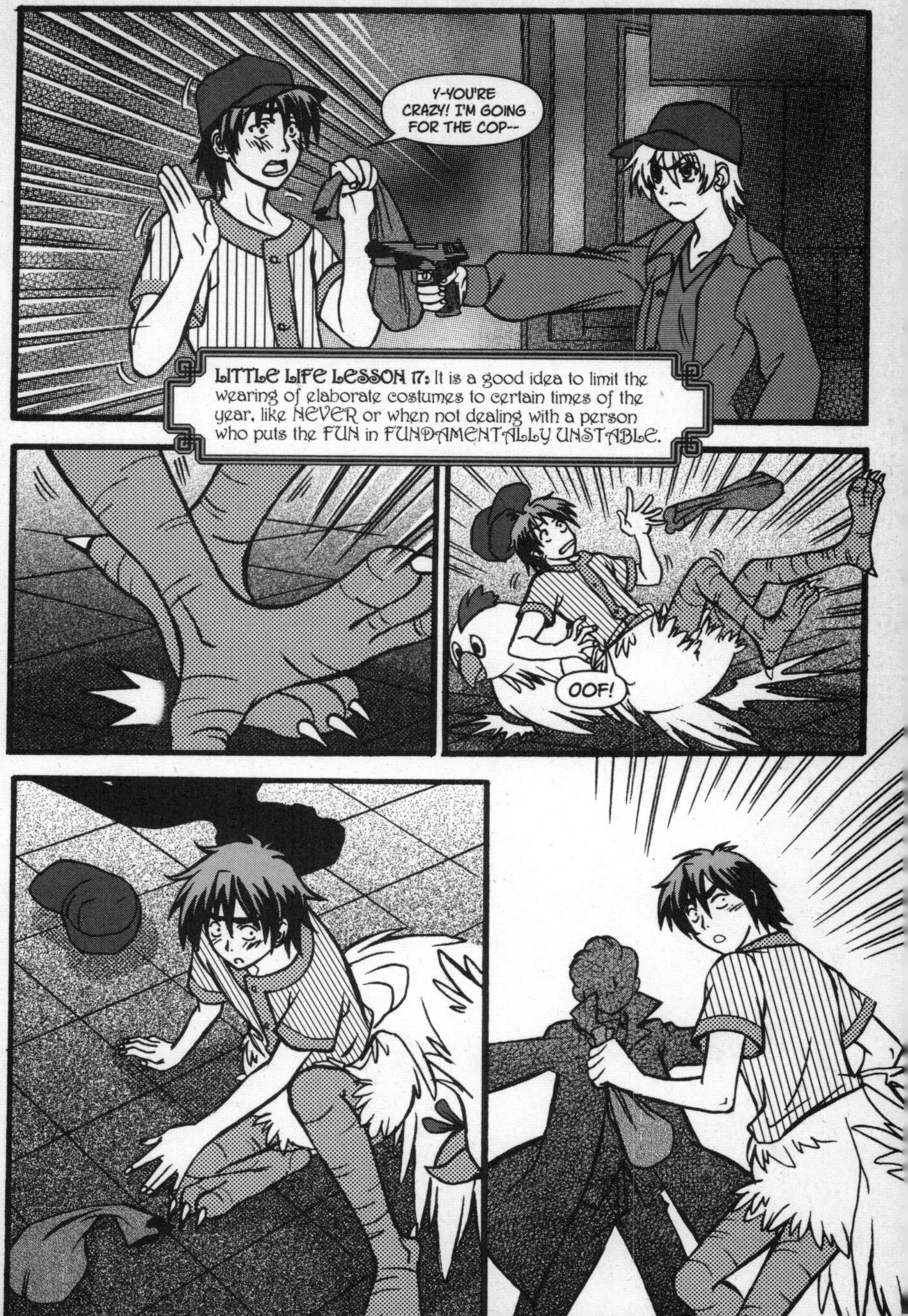
Y-YOU'RE CRAZY! I'M GOING FOR THE COP--
LITTLE LIFE LESSON 17: It is a good idea to limit the wearing of elaborate costumes to certain times of the year, like NEVER or when not dealing with a person who puts the FUN in FUNDAMENTALLY UNSTABLE.
OOF!

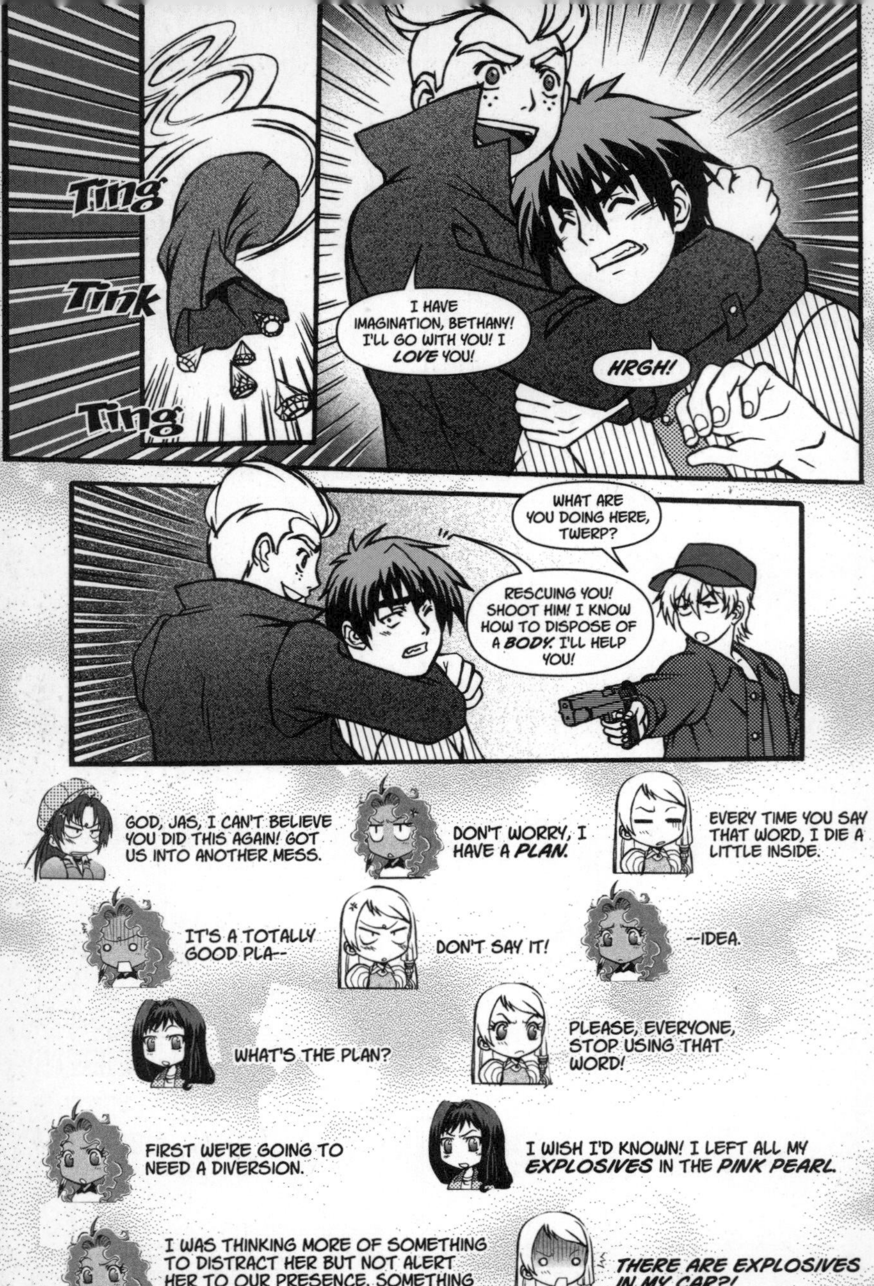
Ting
Tink
Ting
I HAVE IMAGINATION, BETHANY! I'LL GO WITH YOU! I *LOVE* YOU!
HRGH!
WHAT ARE YOU DOING HERE, TWERP?
RESCUING YOU! SHOOT HIM! I KNOW HOW TO DISPOSE OF A *BODY.* I'LL HELP YOU!
GOD, JAS, I CAN'T BELIEVE YOU DID THIS AGAIN! GOT US INTO ANOTHER MESS.
DON'T WORRY, I HAVE A *PLAN.*
EVERY TIME YOU SAY THAT WORD, I DIE A LITTLE INSIDE.
IT'S A TOTALLY GOOD PLA--
DON'T SAY IT!
--IDEA.
WHAT'S THE PLAN?
PLEASE, EVERYONE, STOP USING THAT WORD!
FIRST WE'RE GOING TO NEED A DIVERSION.
I WISH I'D KNOWN! I LEFT ALL MY *EXPLOSIVES* IN THE *PINK PEARL.*
I WAS THINKING MORE OF SOMETHING TO DISTRACT HER BUT NOT ALERT HER TO OUR PRESENCE. SOMETHING STEALTHY.
THERE ARE EXPLOSIVES IN MY CAR?!

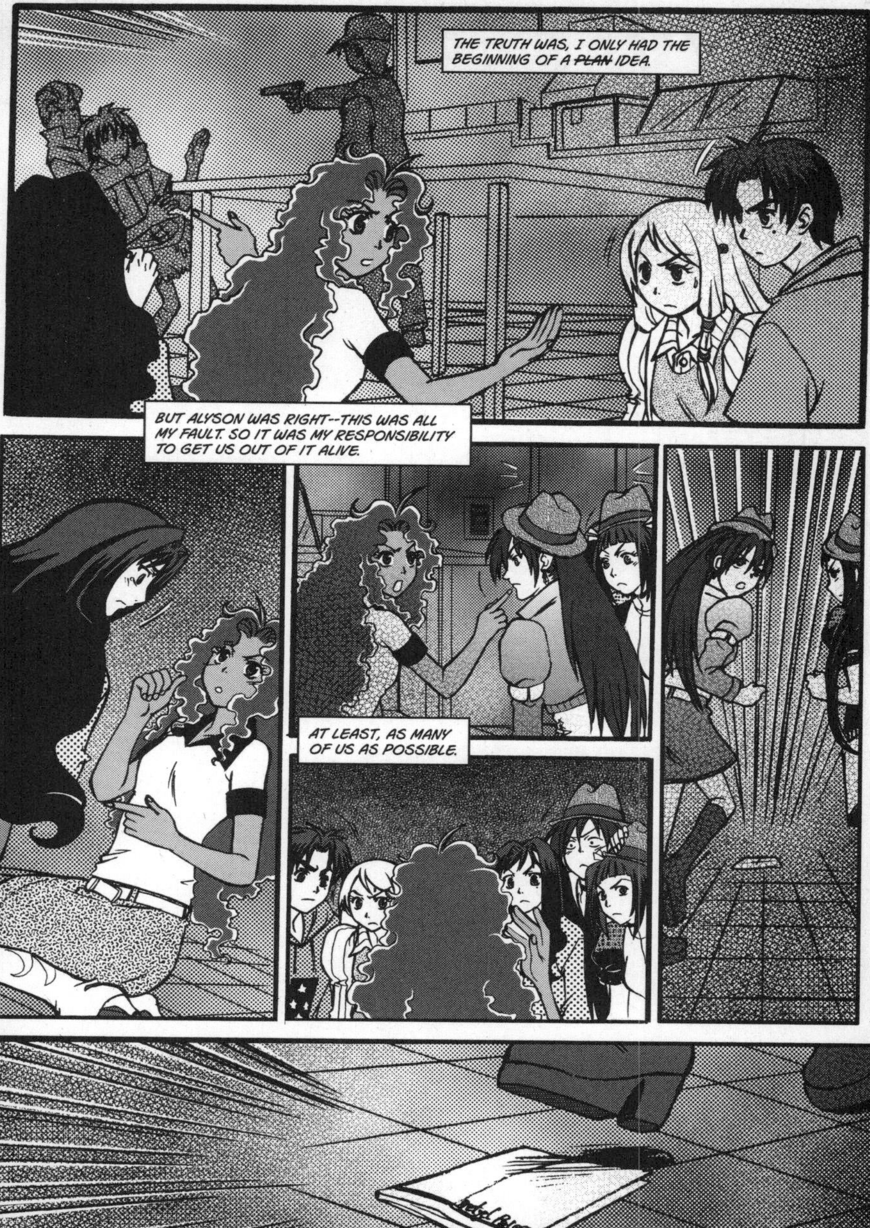
THE TRUTH WAS, I ONLY HAD THE BEGINNING OF A ~~PLAN~~ IDEA.
BUT ALYSON WAS RIGHT--THIS WAS ALL MY FAULT. SO IT WAS MY RESPONSIBILITY TO GET US OUT OF IT ALIVE.
AT LEAST, AS MANY OF US AS POSSIBLE.

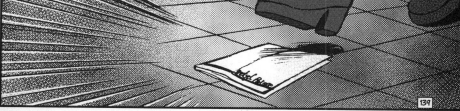

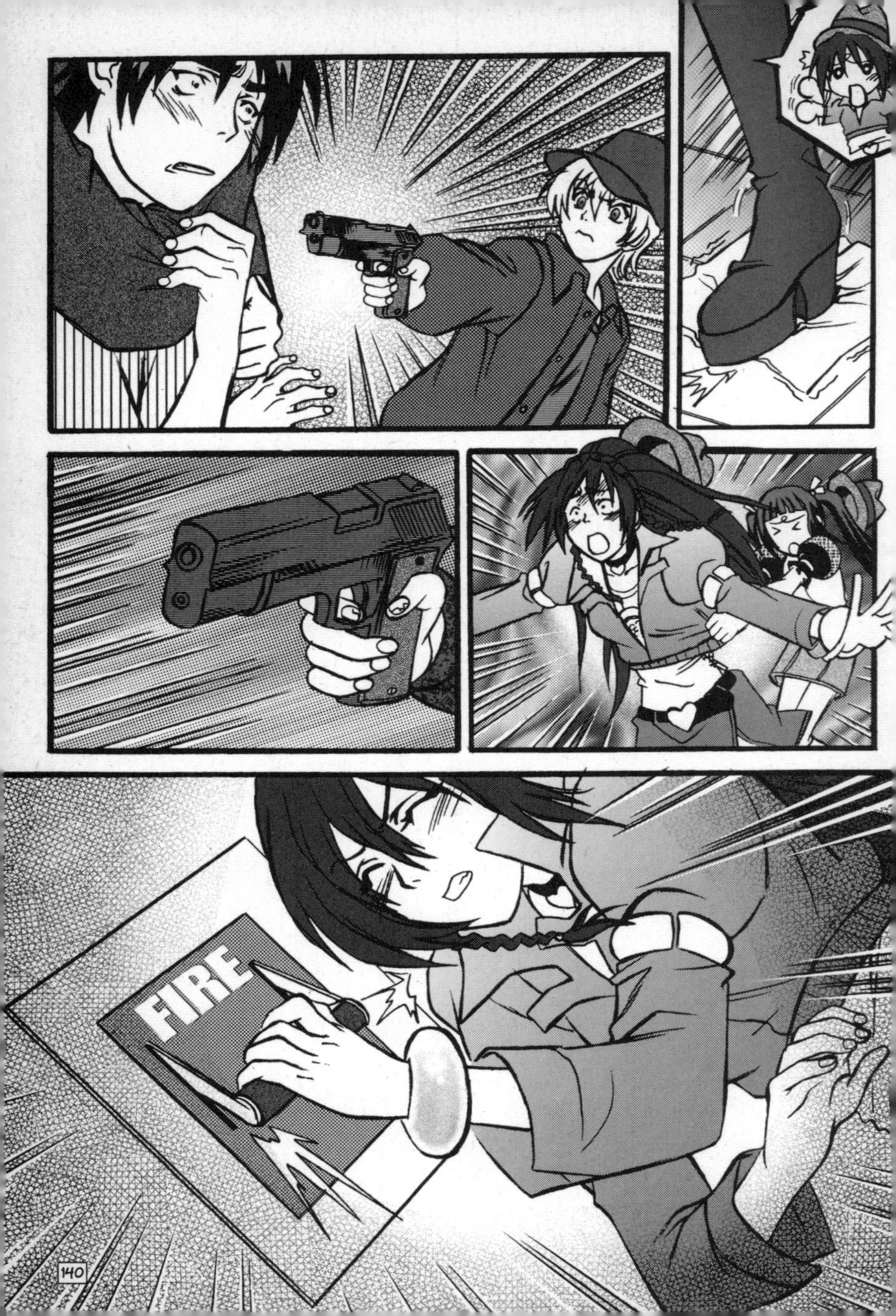
FIRE

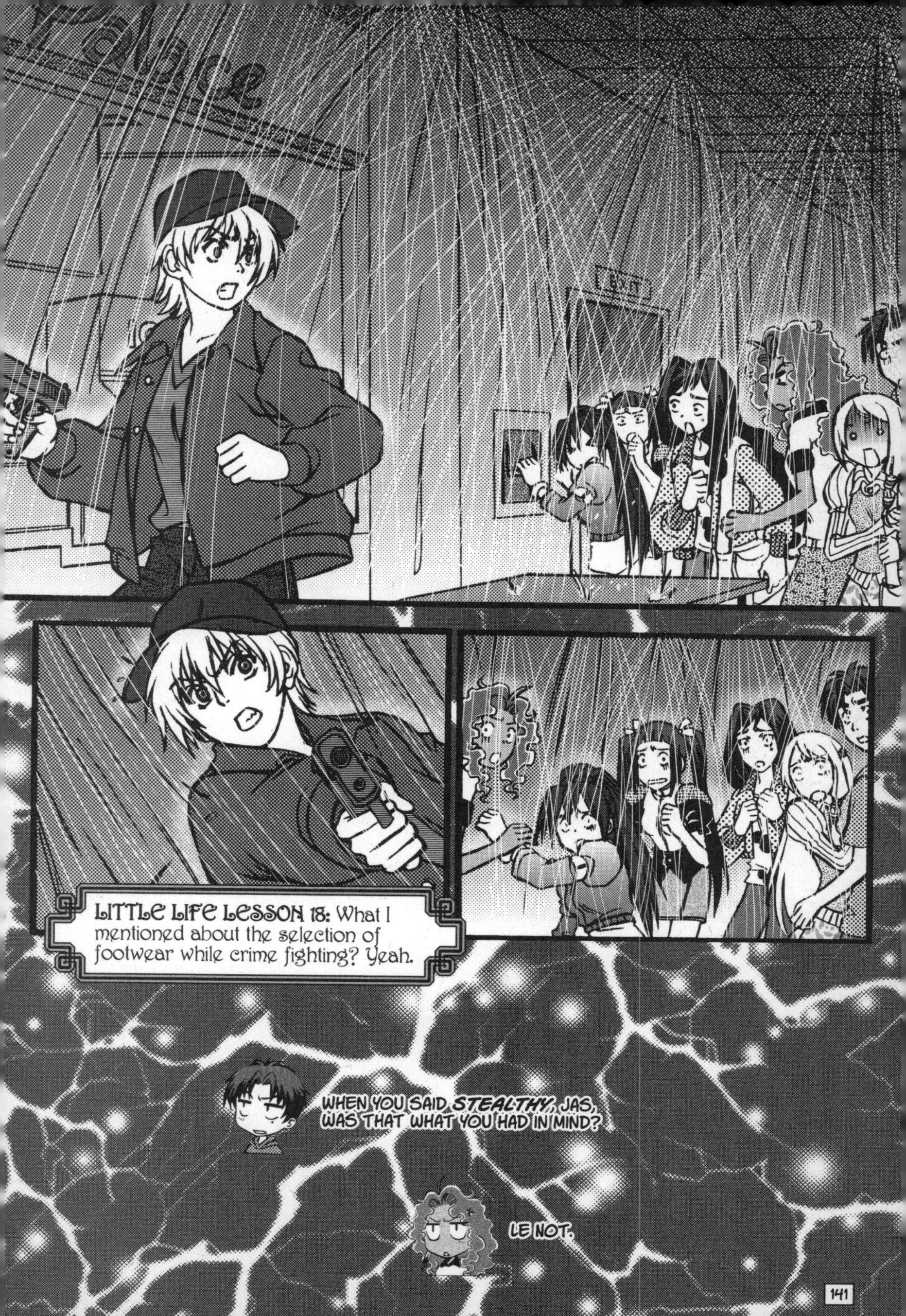
EXIT
LITTLE LIFE LESSON 18: What I mentioned about the selection of footwear while crime fighting? Yeah.
WHEN YOU SAID STEALTHY, JAS, WAS THAT WHAT YOU HAD IN MIND?
LE NOT.

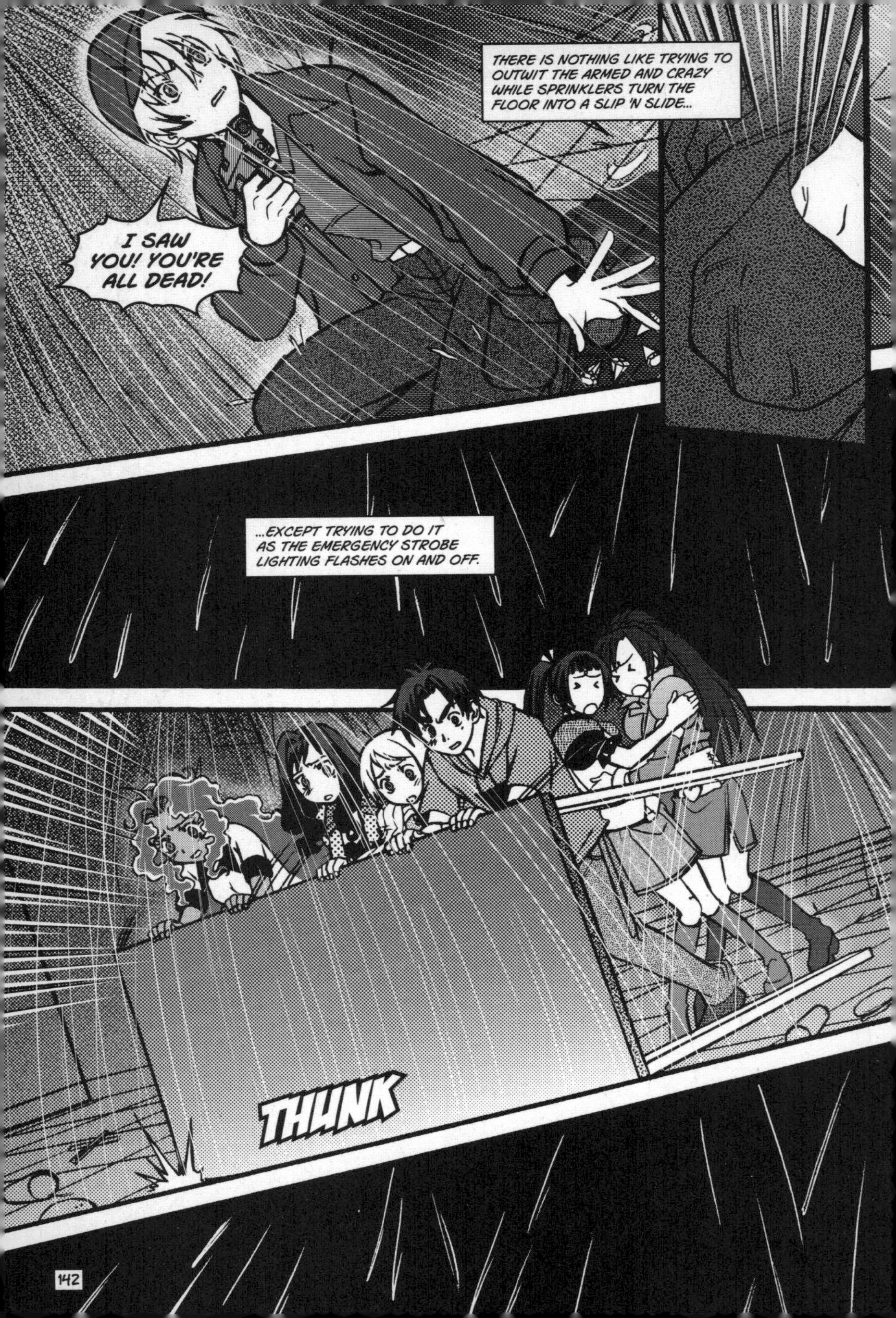
THERE IS NOTHING LIKE TRYING TO OUTWIT THE ARMED AND CRAZY WHILE SPRINKLERS TURN THE FLOOR INTO A SLIP 'N SLIDE...
I SAW YOU! YOU'RE ALL DEAD!
...EXCEPT TRYING TO DO IT AS THE EMERGENCY STROBE LIGHTING FLASHES ON AND OFF.
THUNK

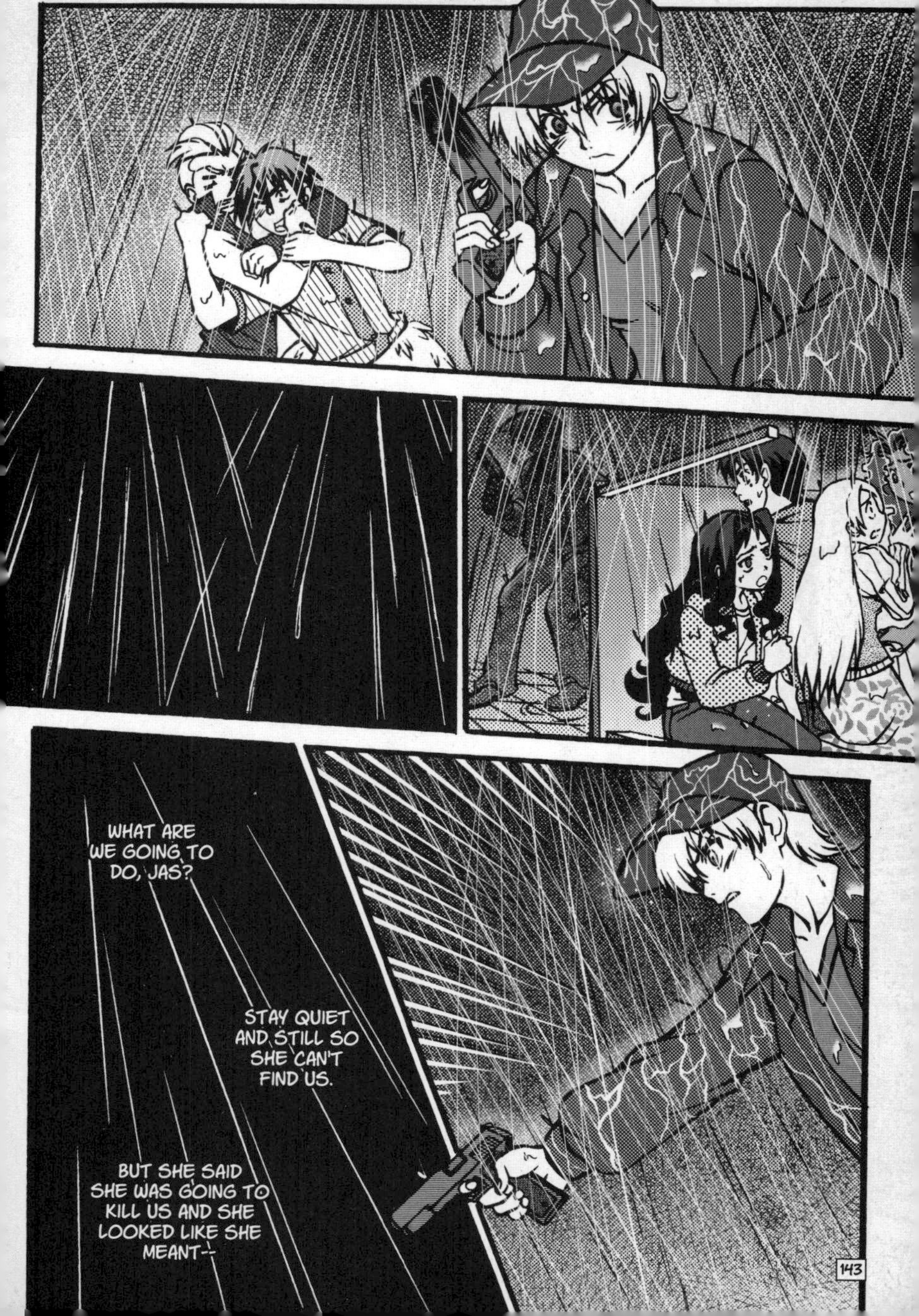
WHAT ARE WE GOING TO DO, JAS?
STAY QUIET AND STILL SO SHE CAN'T FIND US.
BUT SHE SAID SHE WAS GOING TO KILL US AND SHE LOOKED LIKE SHE MEANT--

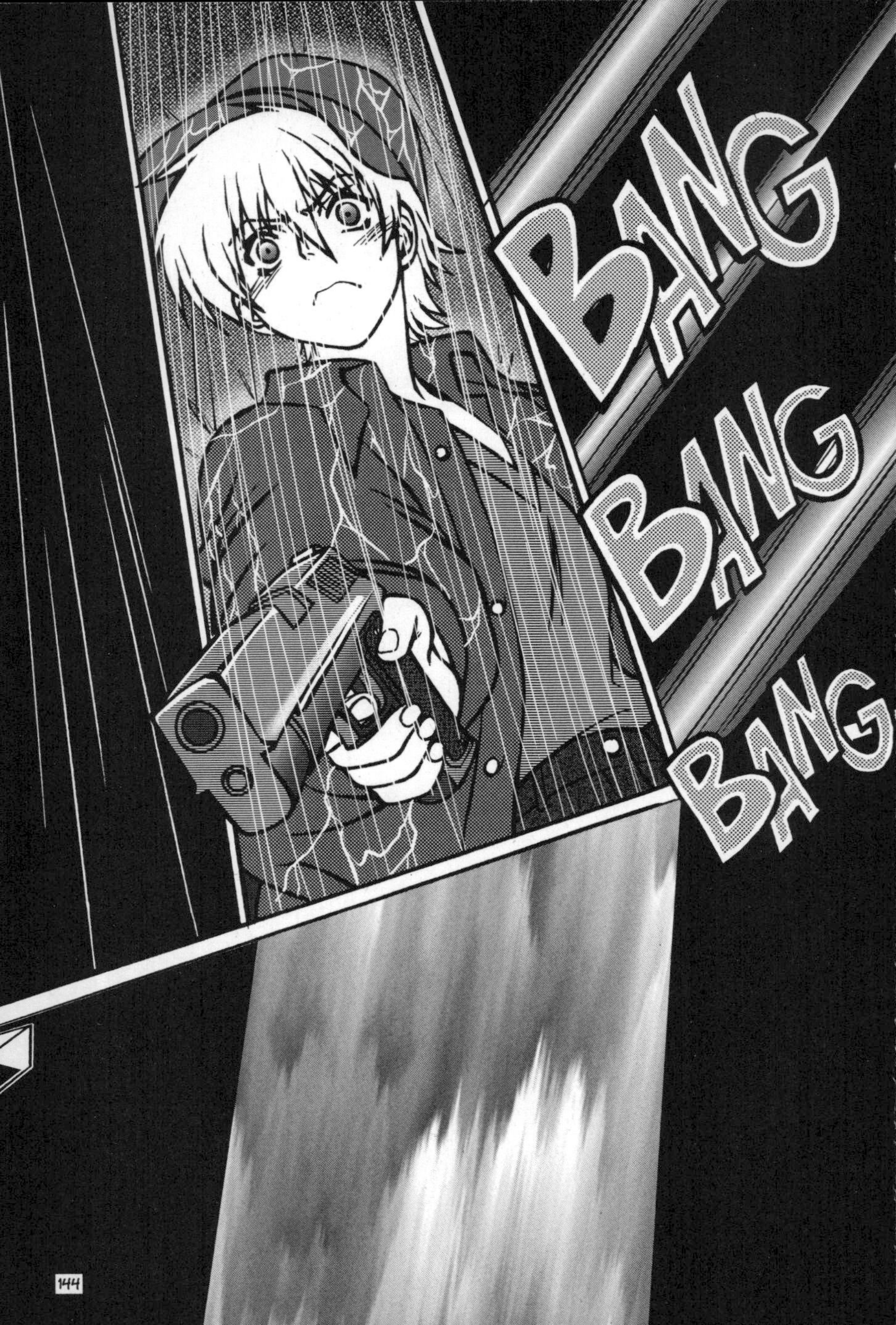
BANG
BANG
BANG

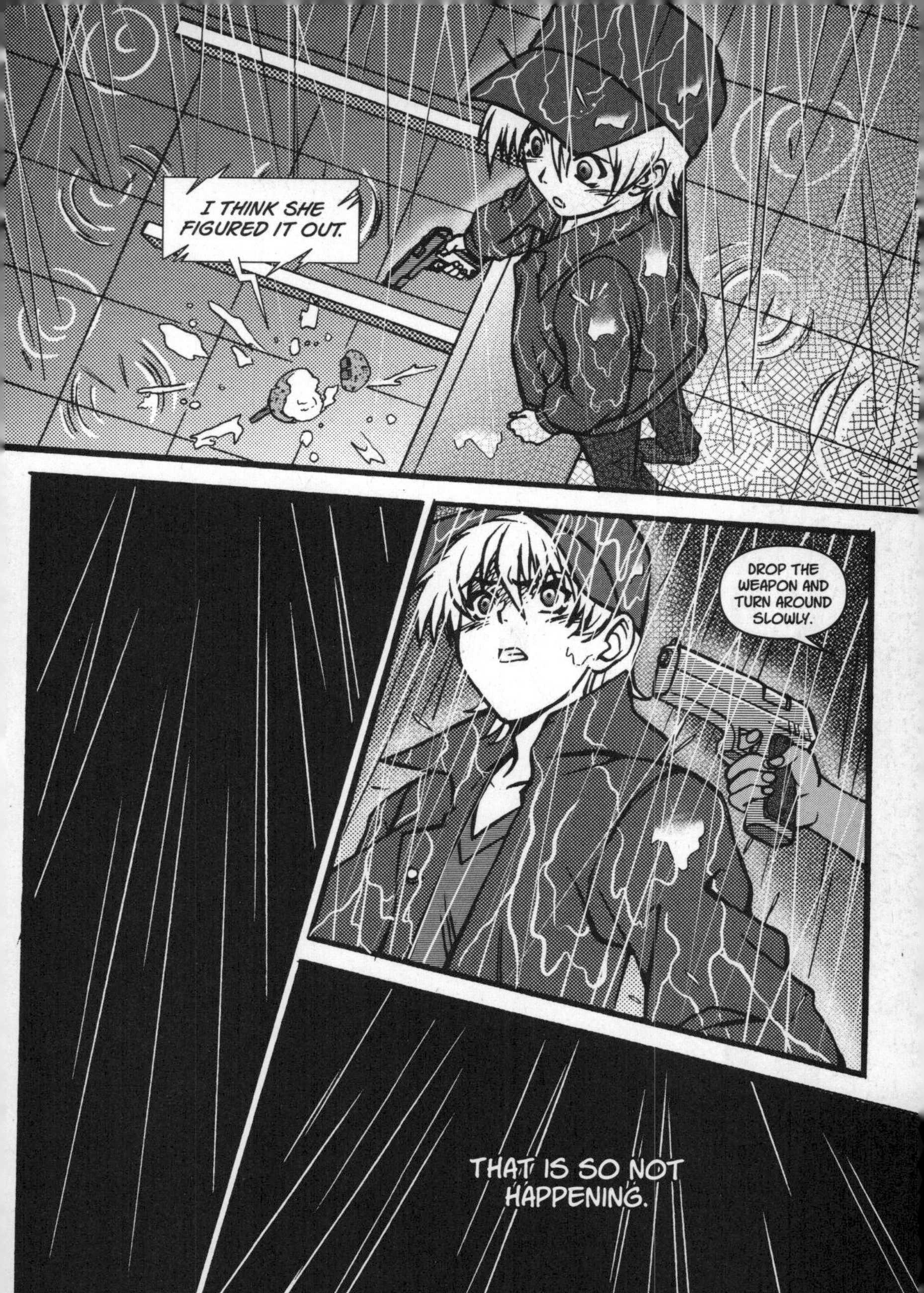
I THINK SHE FIGURED IT OUT.
DROP THE WEAPON AND TURN AROUND SLOWLY.
THAT IS SO NOT HAPPENING.

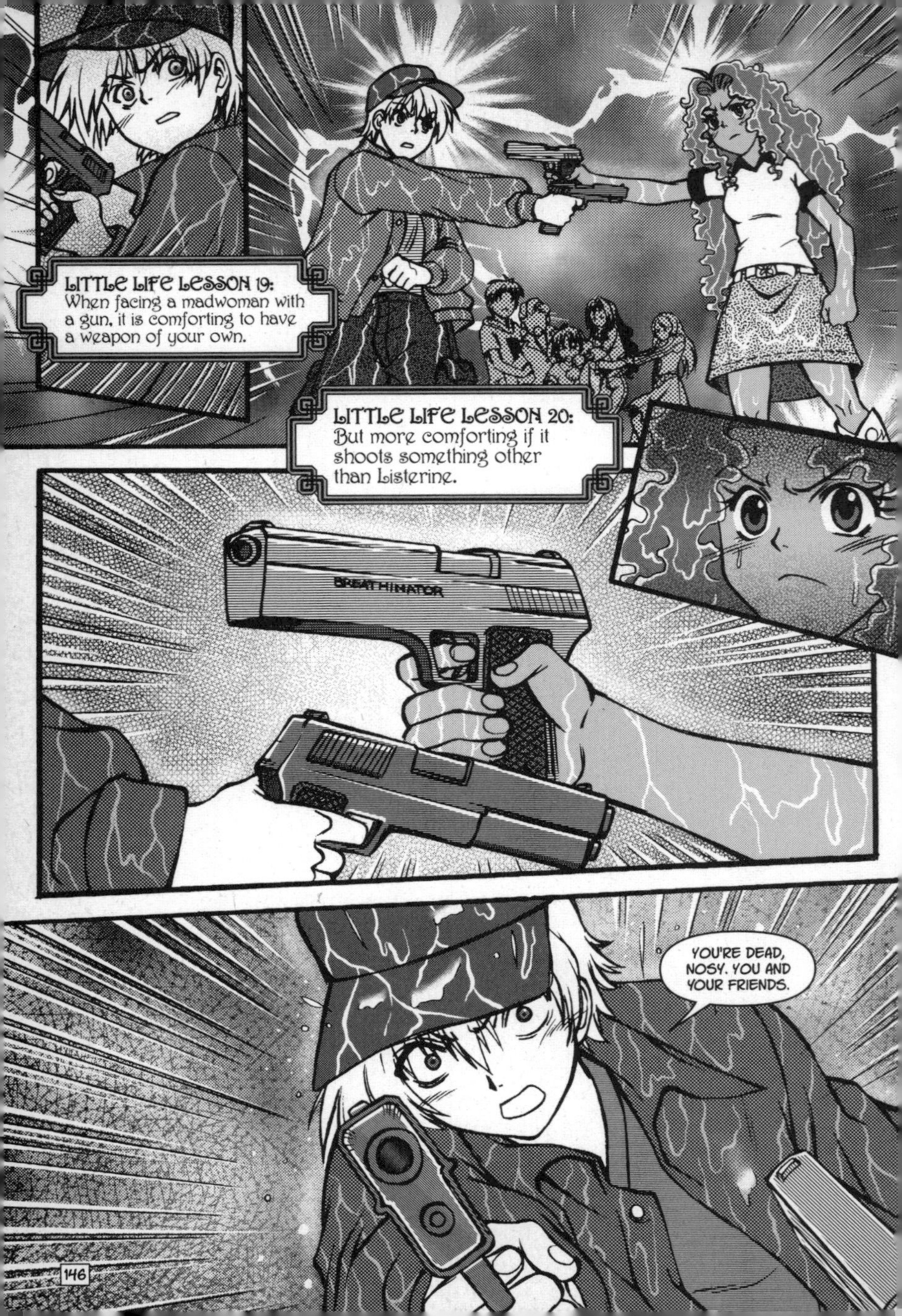
LITTLE LIFE LESSON 19:
When facing a madwoman with a gun, it is comforting to have a weapon of your own.
LITTLE LIFE LESSON 20:
But more comforting if it shoots something other than Listerine.
BREATHINATOR
YOU'RE DEAD, NOSY. YOU AND YOUR FRIENDS.

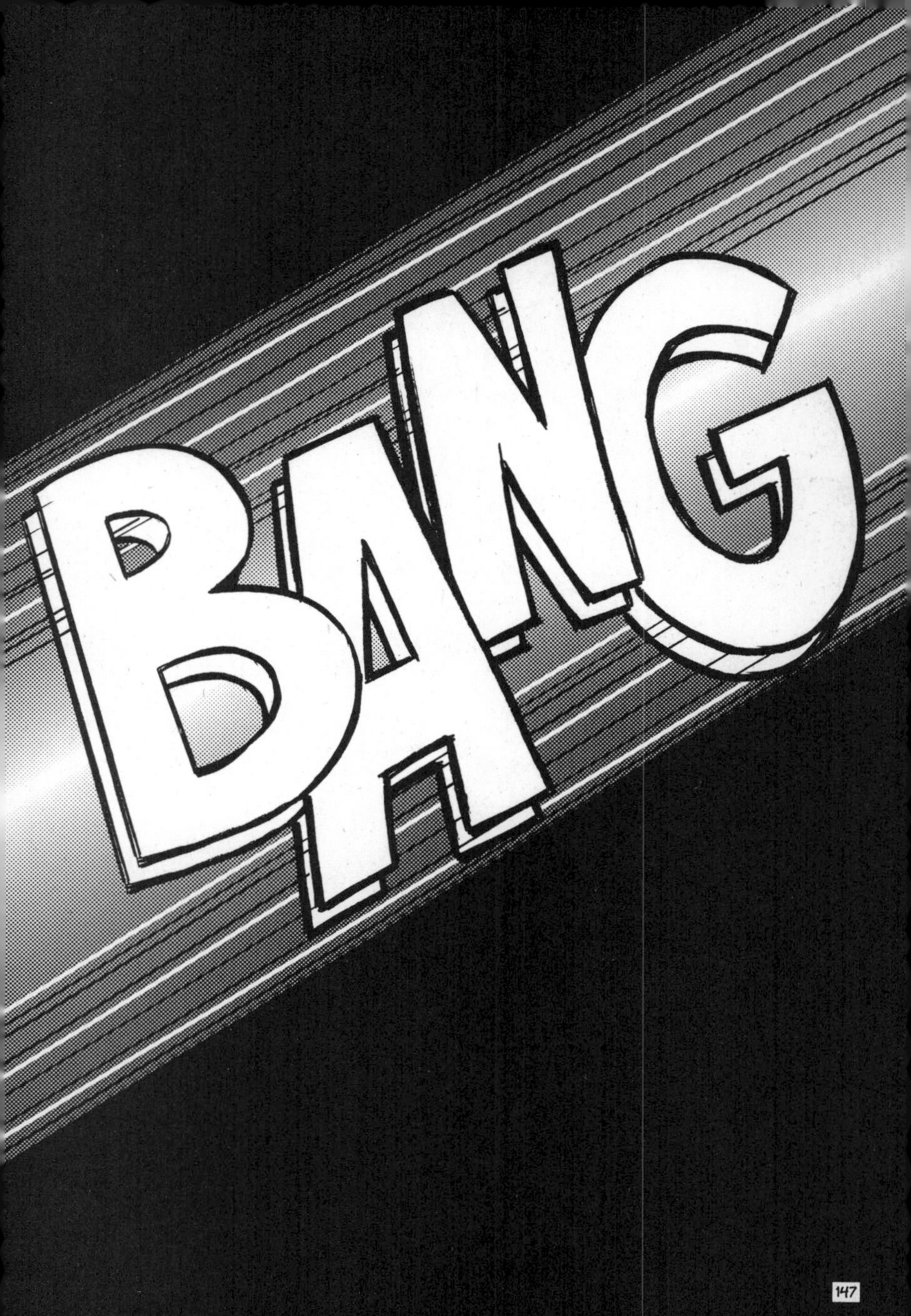
BANG

Chapter Six

Jasmine Callihan

HAIR: UNKNOWN

PORES: UNKNOWN

HEART: UNKNOWN

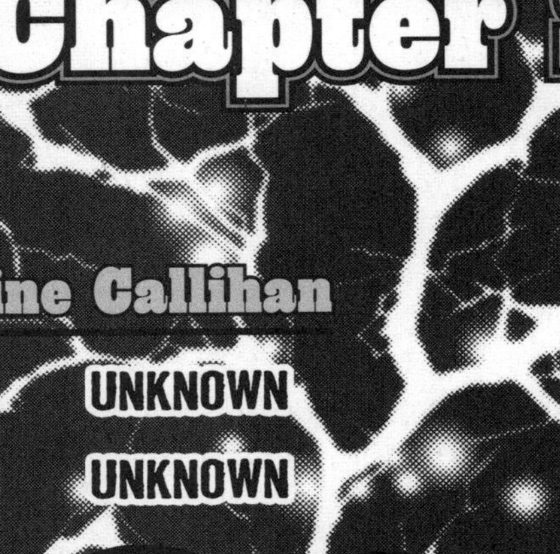

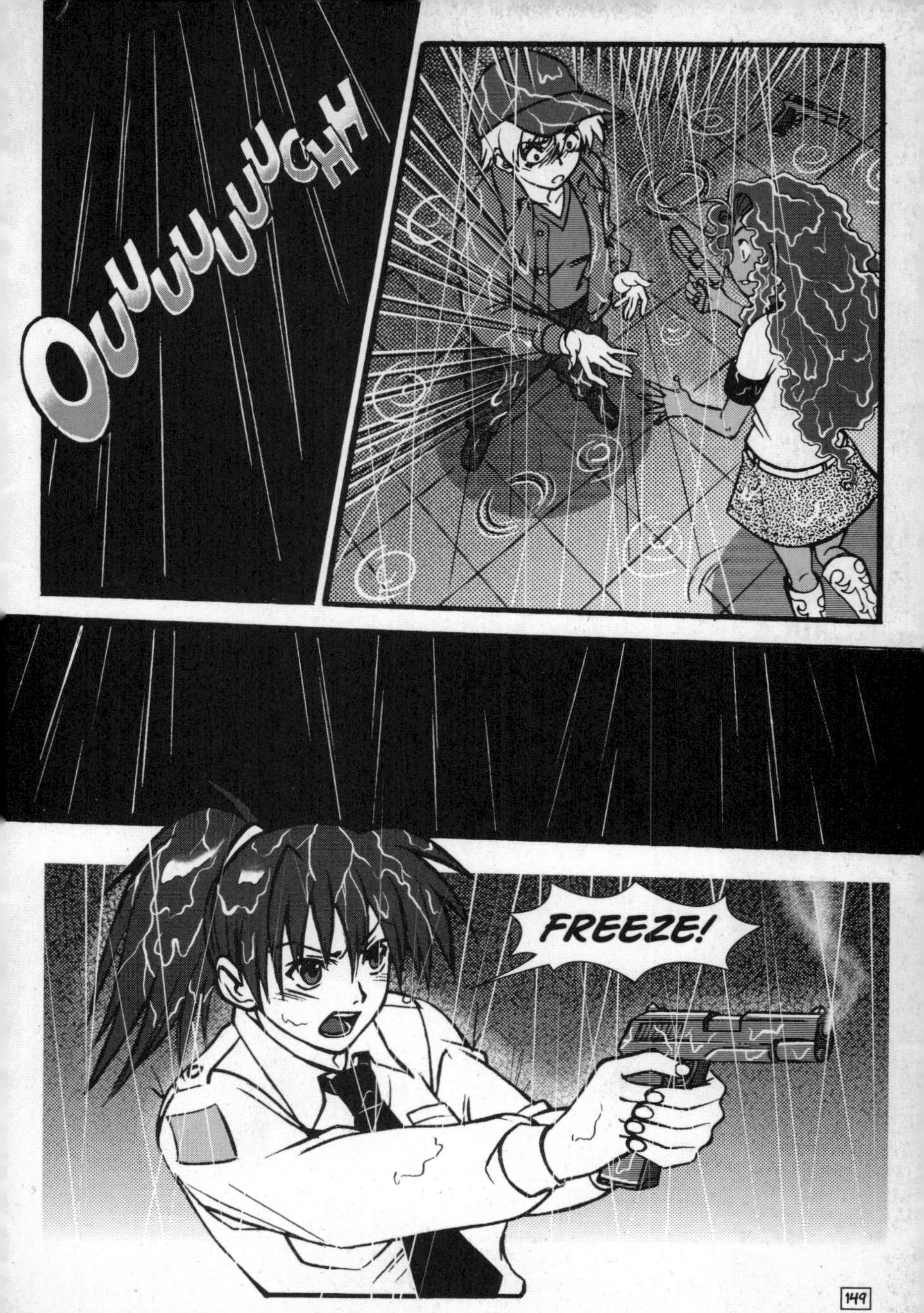
OUUUUUUCH
FREEZE!

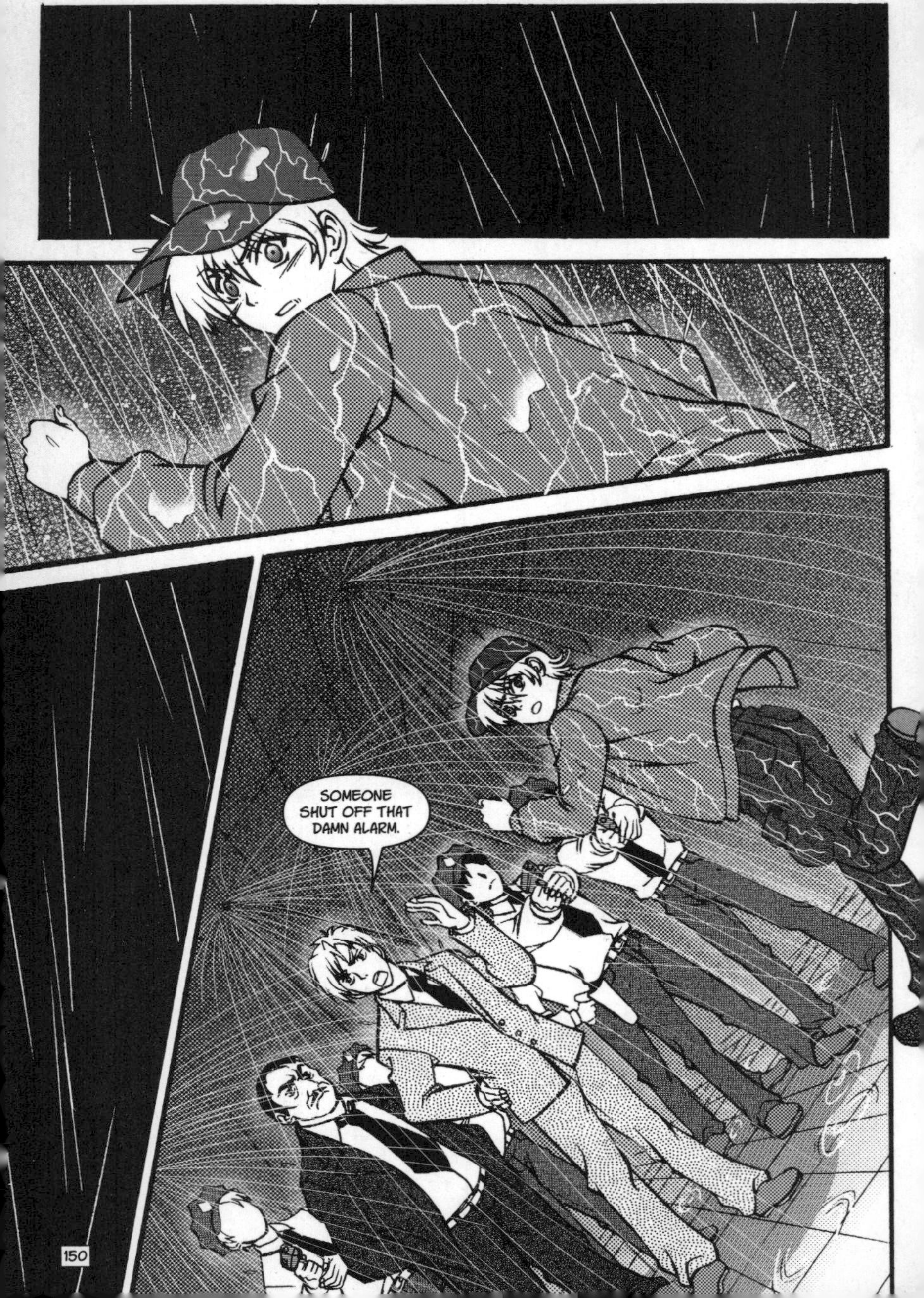
SOMEONE SHUT OFF THAT DAMN ALARM.

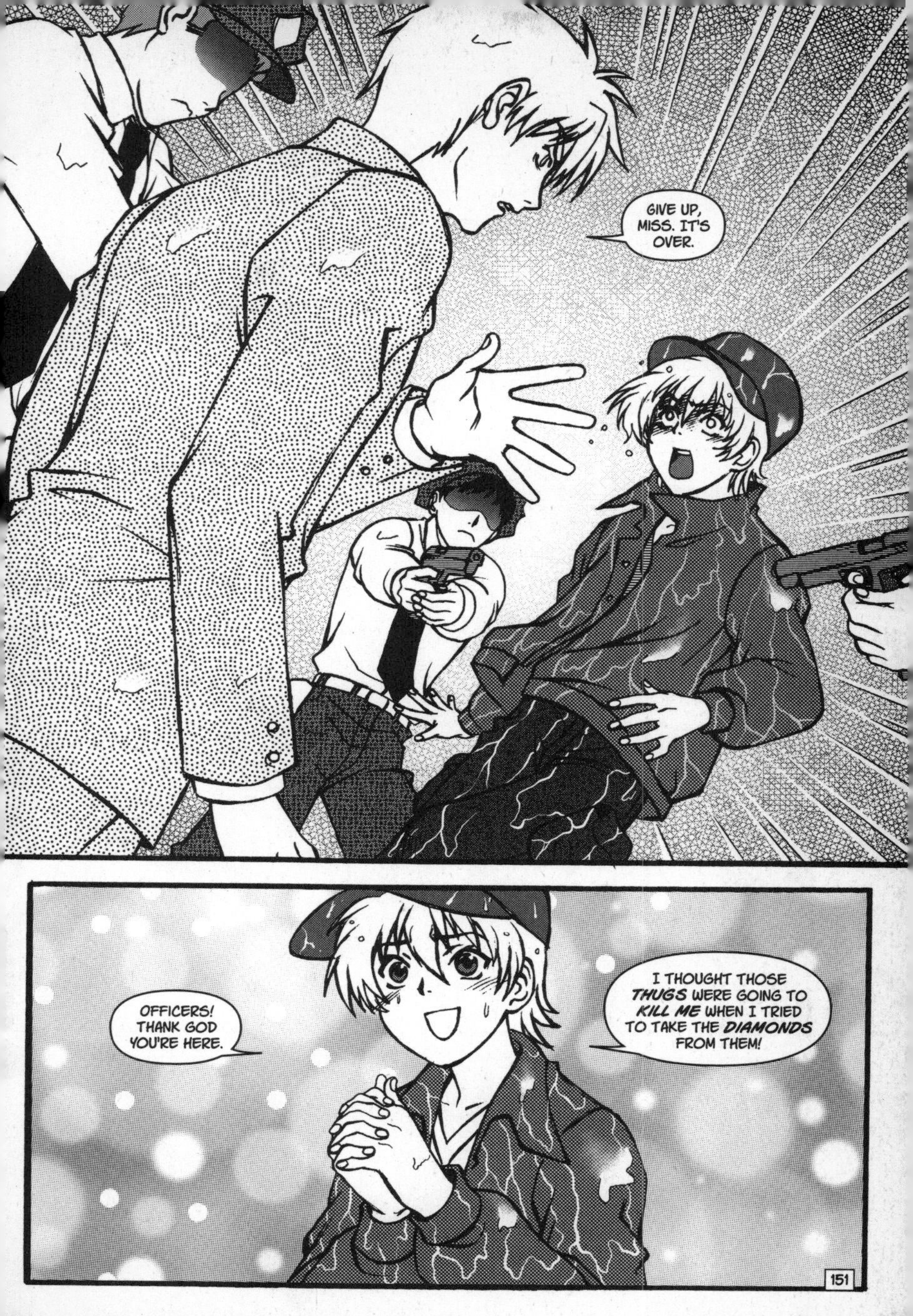
GIVE UP, MISS. IT'S OVER.
OFFICERS! THANK GOD YOU'RE HERE.
I THOUGHT THOSE THUGS WERE GOING TO KILL ME WHEN I TRIED TO TAKE THE DIAMONDS FROM THEM!

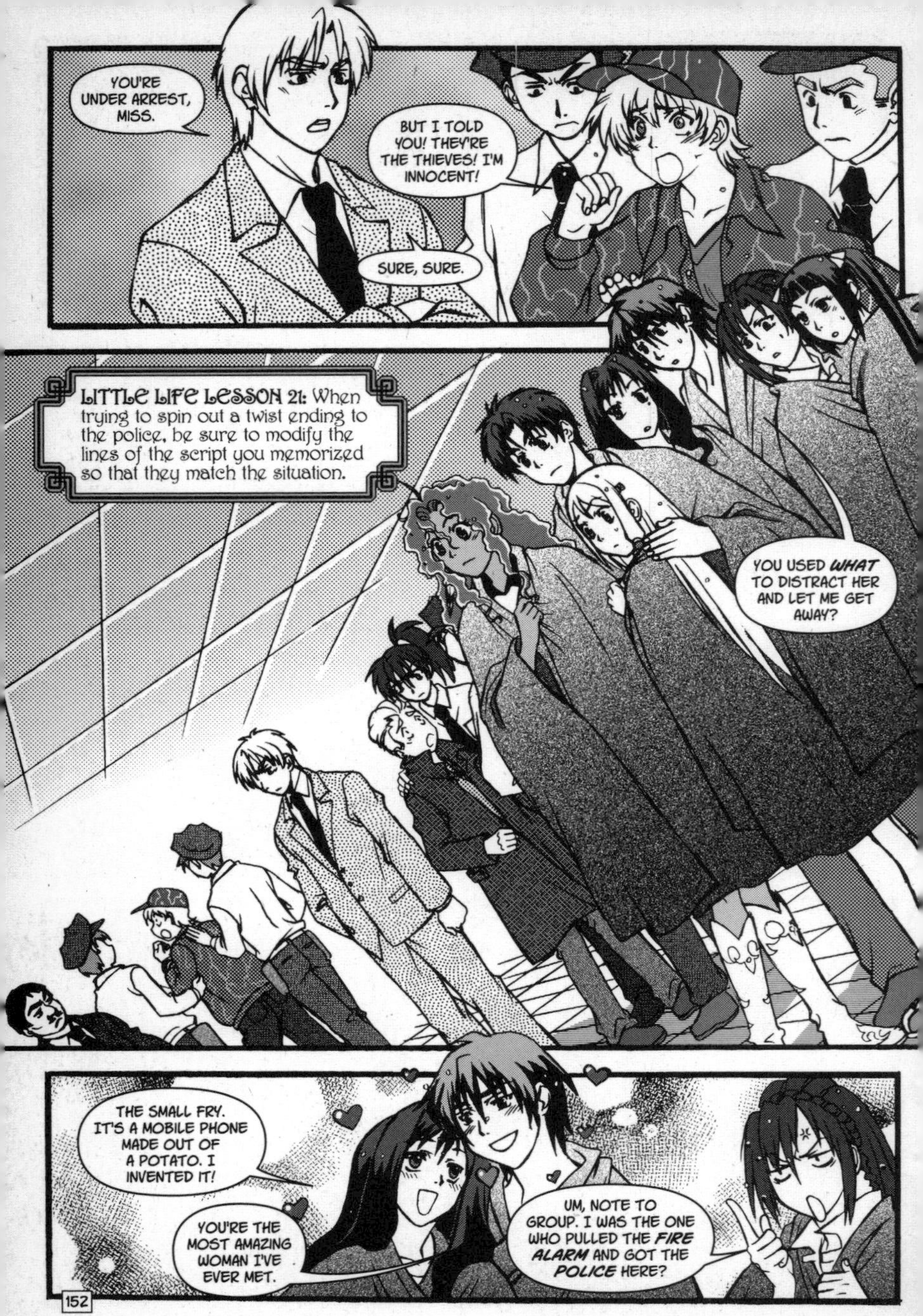

YOU'RE UNDER ARREST, MISS.
BUT I TOLD YOU! THEY'RE THE THIEVES! I'M INNOCENT!
SURE, SURE.
LITTLE LIFE LESSON 21: When trying to spin out a twist ending to the police, be sure to modify the lines of the script you memorized so that they match the situation.
YOU USED *WHAT* TO DISTRACT HER AND LET ME GET AWAY?
THE SMALL FRY. IT'S A MOBILE PHONE MADE OUT OF A POTATO. I INVENTED IT!
YOU'RE THE MOST AMAZING WOMAN I'VE EVER MET.
UM, NOTE TO GROUP. I WAS THE ONE WHO PULLED THE *FIRE ALARM* AND GOT THE *POLICE* HERE?

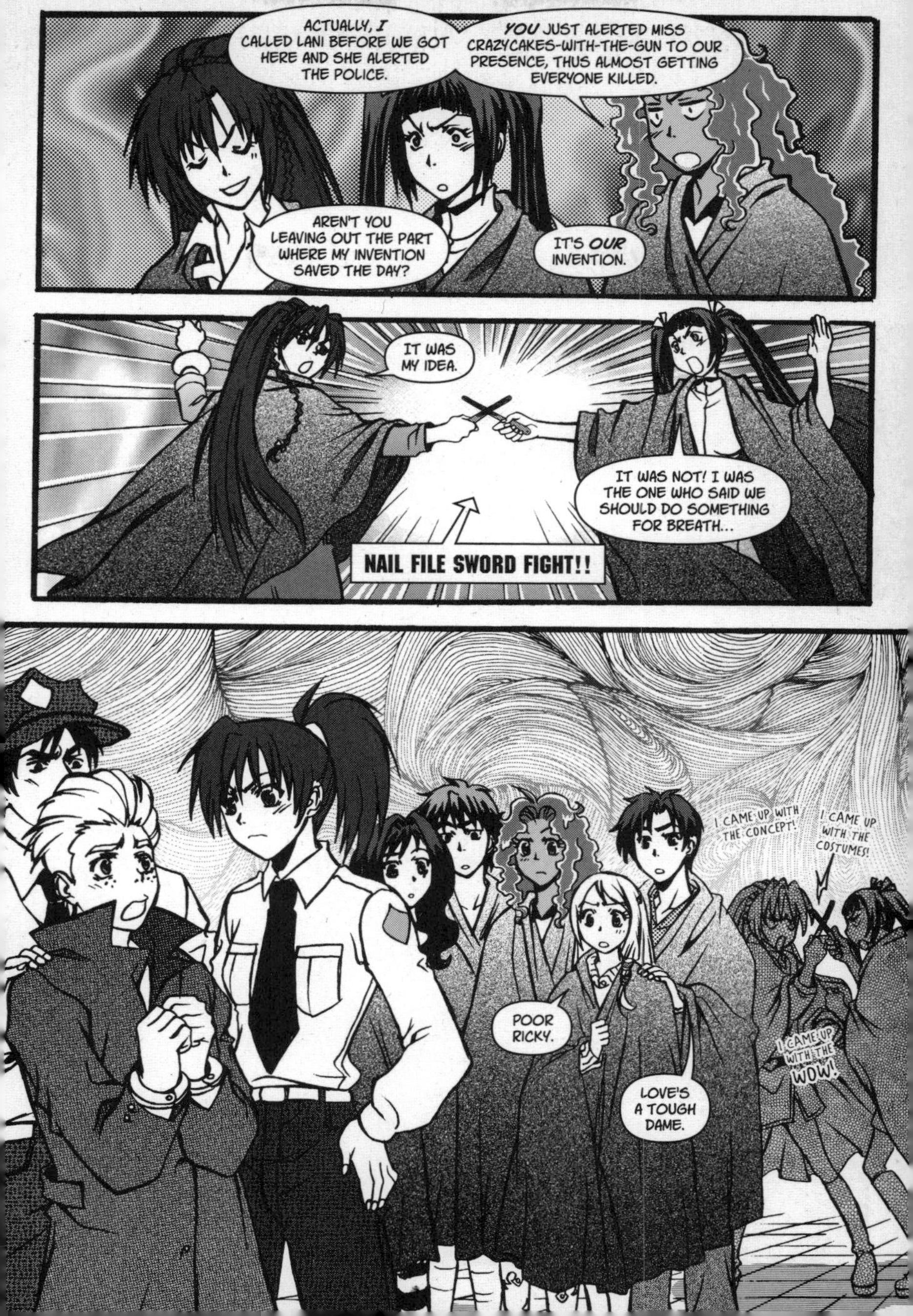
ACTUALLY, *I* CALLED LANI BEFORE WE GOT HERE AND SHE ALERTED THE POLICE.
YOU JUST ALERTED MISS CRAZYCAKES-WITH-THE-GUN TO OUR PRESENCE, THUS ALMOST GETTING EVERYONE KILLED.
AREN'T YOU LEAVING OUT THE PART WHERE MY INVENTION SAVED THE DAY?
IT'S *OUR* INVENTION.
IT WAS MY IDEA.
IT WAS NOT! I WAS THE ONE WHO SAID WE SHOULD DO SOMETHING FOR BREATH...
NAIL FILE SWORD FIGHT!!
I CAME UP WITH THE CONCEPT!
I CAME UP WITH THE COSTUMES!
POOR RICKY.
LOVE'S A TOUGH DAME.
I CAME UP WITH THE WOW!

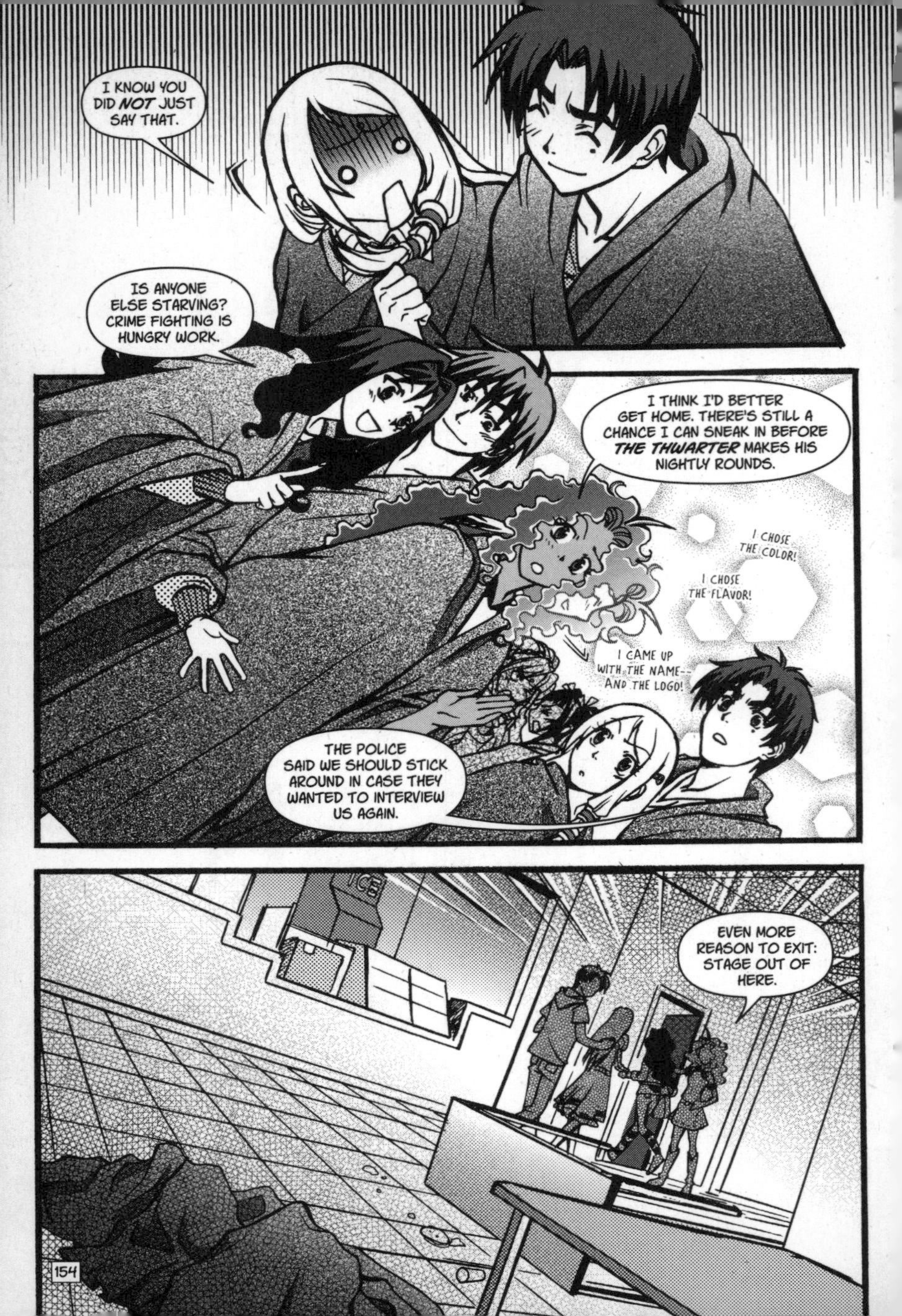
I KNOW YOU DID NOT JUST SAY THAT.
IS ANYONE ELSE STARVING? CRIME FIGHTING IS HUNGRY WORK.
I THINK I'D BETTER GET HOME. THERE'S STILL A CHANCE I CAN SNEAK IN BEFORE THE THWARTER MAKES HIS NIGHTLY ROUNDS.
I CHOSE THE COLOR!
I CHOSE THE FLAVOR!
I CAME UP WITH THE NAME-- AND THE LOGO!
THE POLICE SAID WE SHOULD STICK AROUND IN CASE THEY WANTED TO INTERVIEW US AGAIN.
EVEN MORE REASON TO EXIT: STAGE OUT OF HERE.

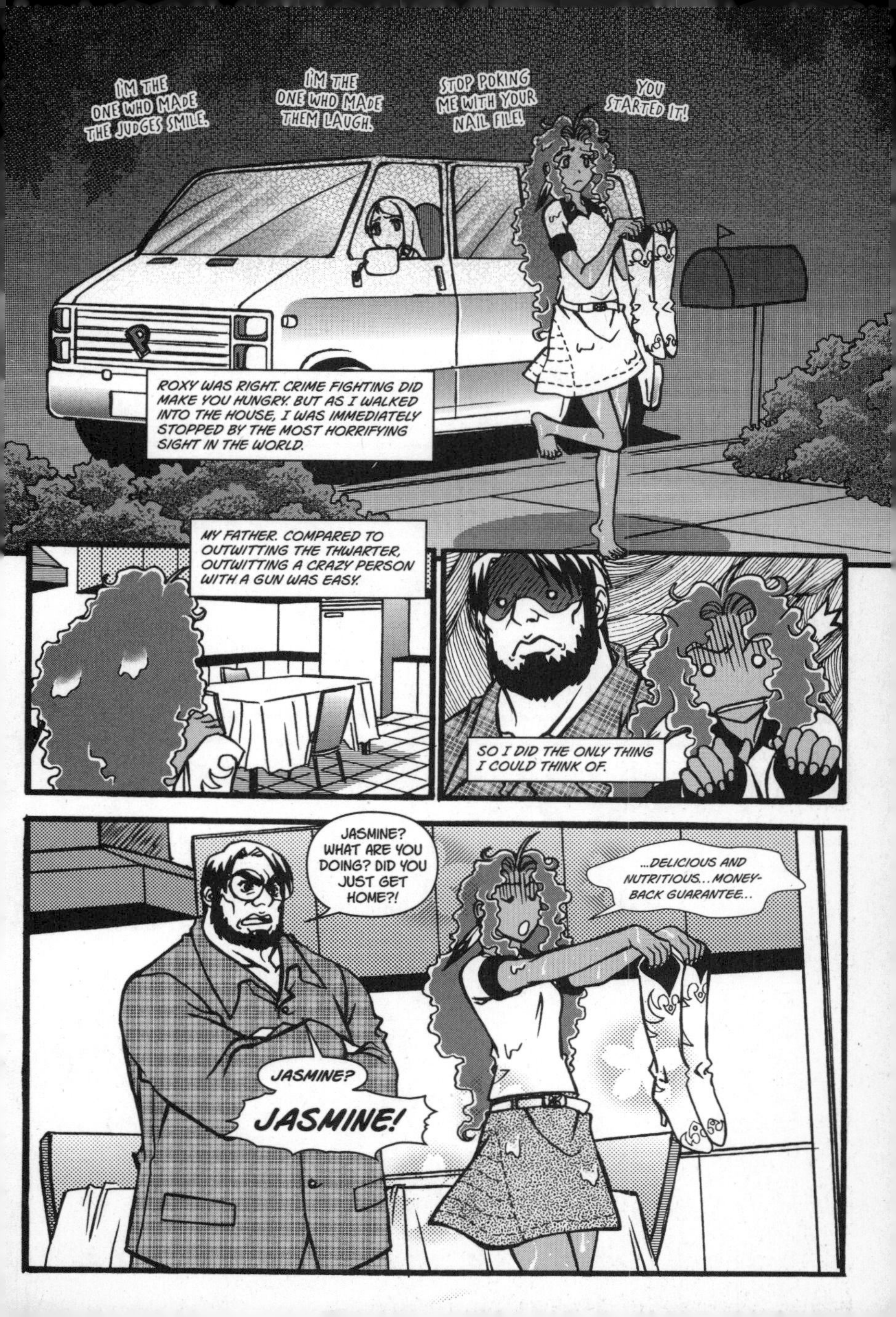
I'M THE ONE WHO MADE THE JUDGES SMILE.
I'M THE ONE WHO MADE THEM LAUGH.
STOP POKING ME WITH YOUR NAIL FILE!
YOU STARTED IT!
ROXY WAS RIGHT. CRIME FIGHTING DID MAKE YOU HUNGRY. BUT AS I WALKED INTO THE HOUSE, I WAS IMMEDIATELY STOPPED BY THE MOST HORRIFYING SIGHT IN THE WORLD.
MY FATHER. COMPARED TO OUTWITTING THE THWARTER, OUTWITTING A CRAZY PERSON WITH A GUN WAS EASY.
SO I DID THE ONLY THING I COULD THINK OF.
JASMINE? WHAT ARE YOU DOING? DID YOU JUST GET HOME?!
...DELICIOUS AND NUTRITIOUS... MONEY-BACK GUARANTEE...
JASMINE?
JASMINE!

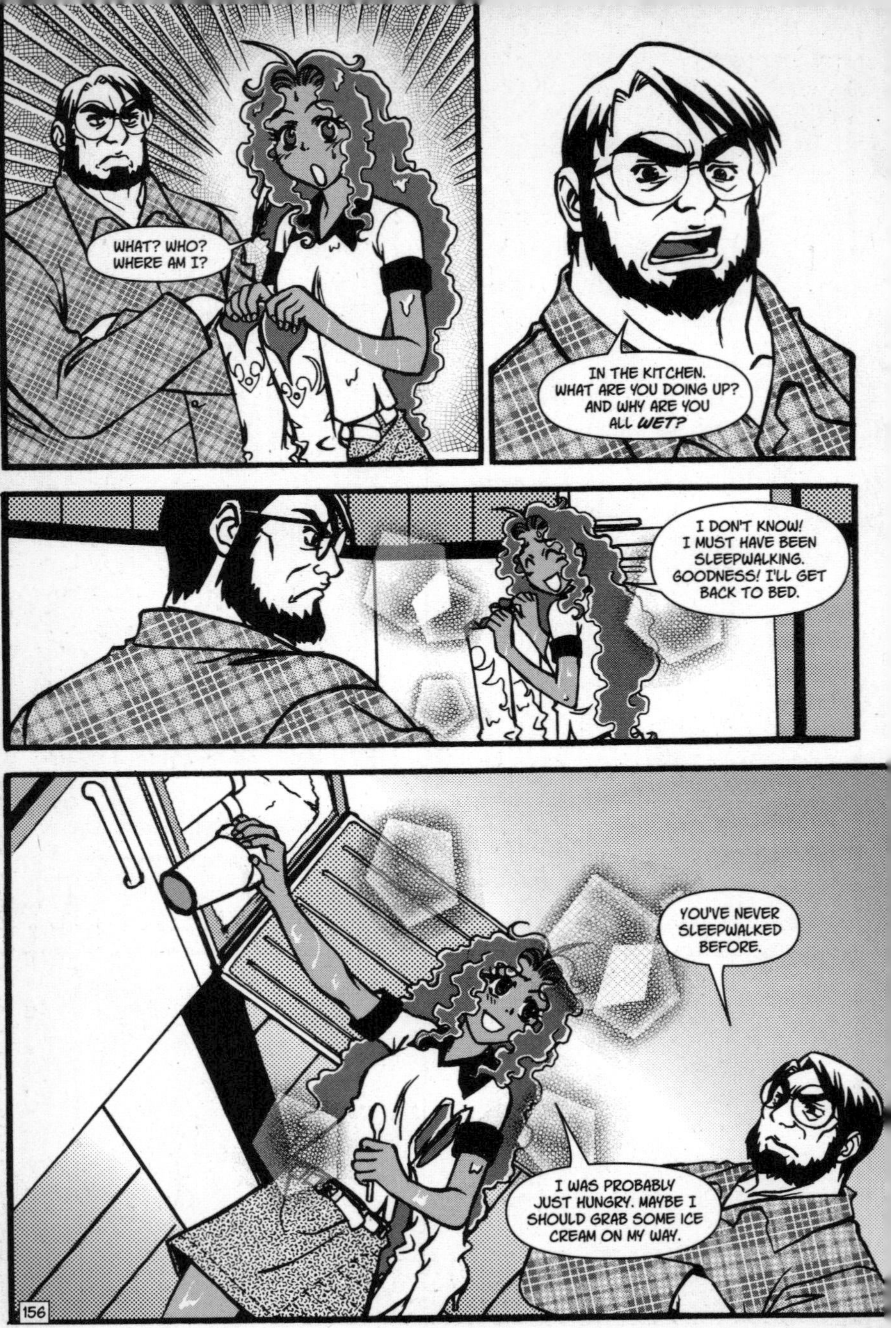
WHAT? WHO? WHERE AM I?
IN THE KITCHEN. WHAT ARE YOU DOING UP? AND WHY ARE YOU ALL *WET?*
I DON'T KNOW! I MUST HAVE BEEN SLEEPWALKING. GOODNESS! I'LL GET BACK TO BED.
YOU'VE NEVER SLEEPWALKED BEFORE.
I WAS PROBABLY JUST HUNGRY. MAYBE I SHOULD GRAB SOME ICE CREAM ON MY WAY.

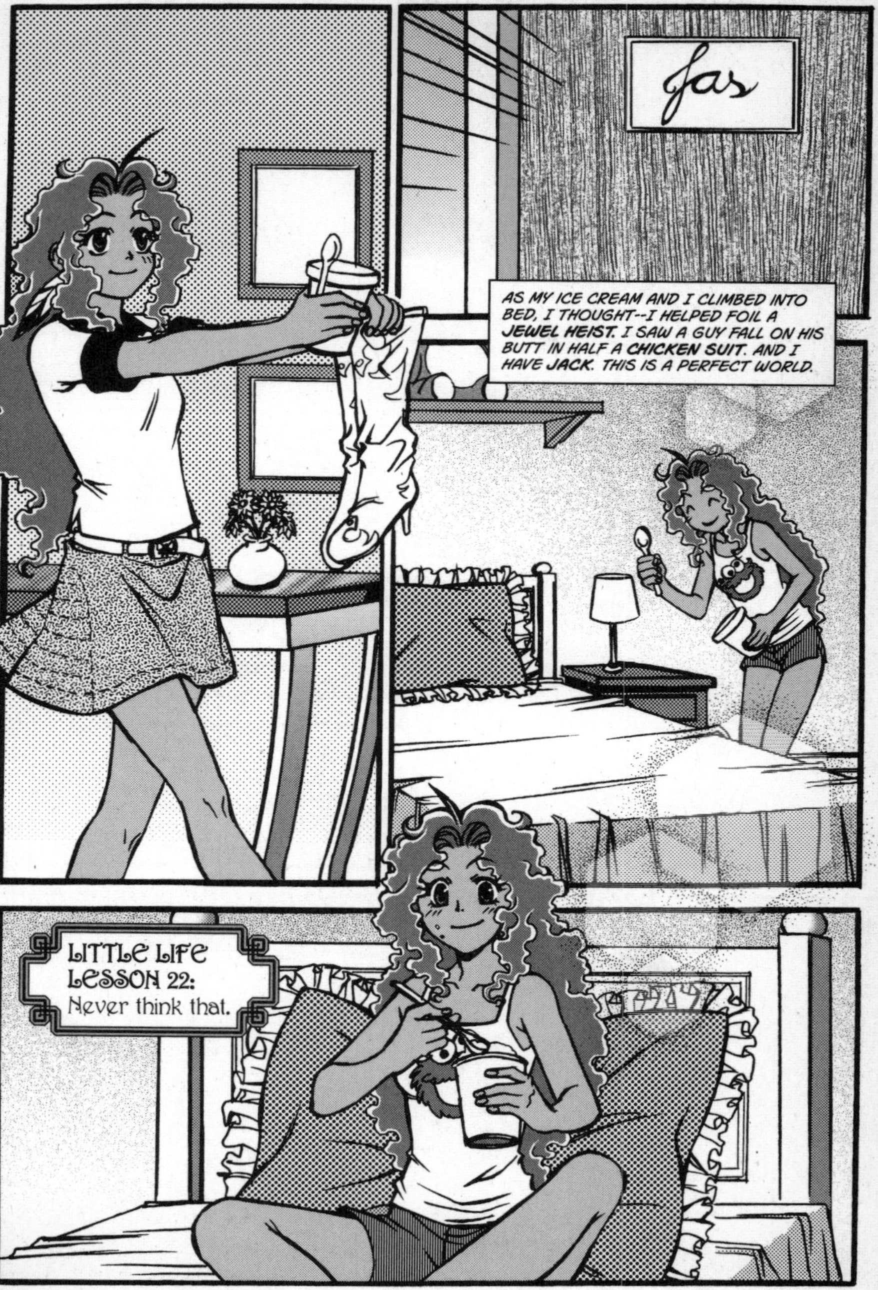
Jas
AS MY ICE CREAM AND I CLIMBED INTO BED, I THOUGHT--I HELPED FOIL A JEWEL HEIST. I SAW A GUY FALL ON HIS BUTT IN HALF A CHICKEN SUIT. AND I HAVE JACK. THIS IS A PERFECT WORLD.
LITTLE LIFE LESSON 22: Never think that.

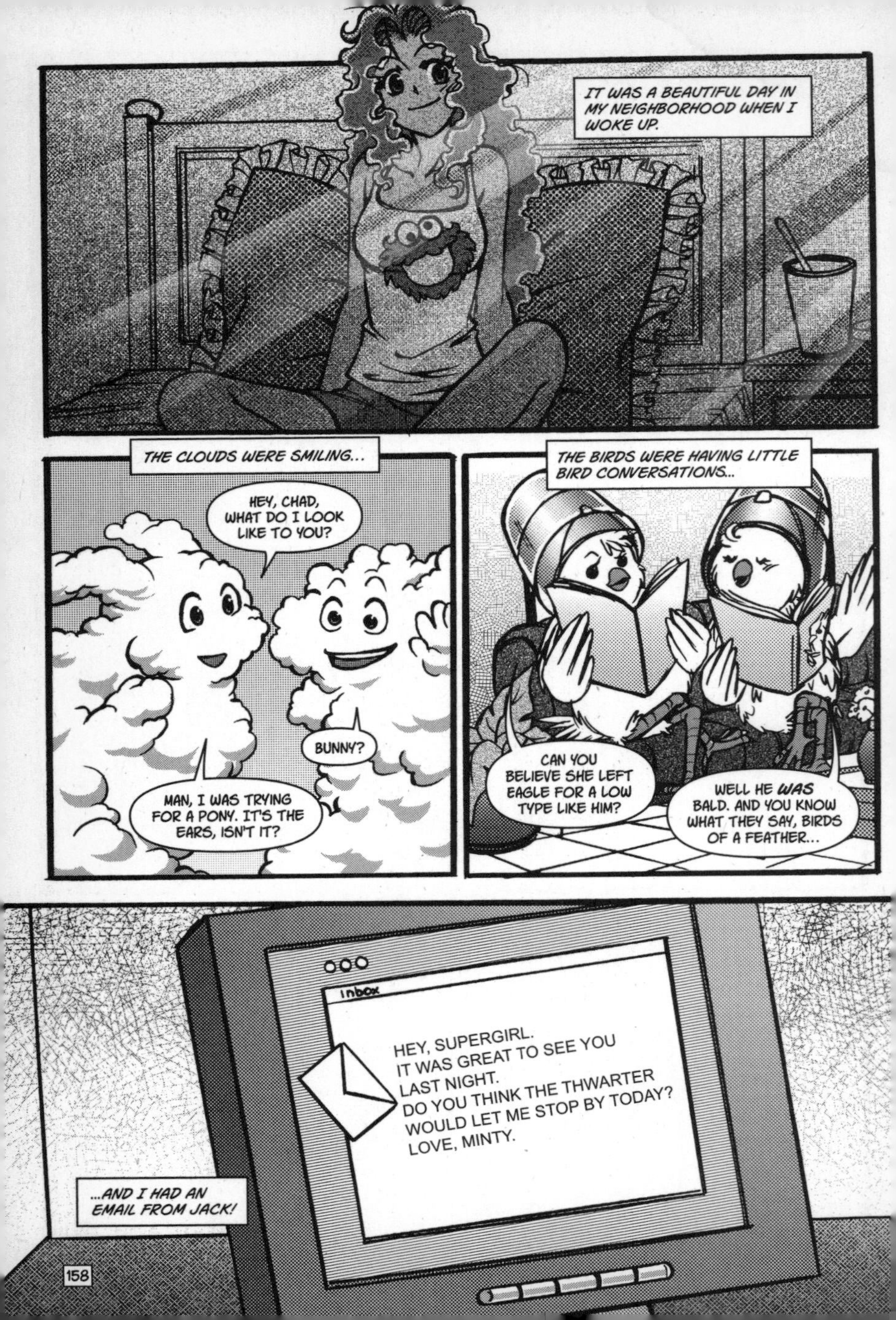

IT WAS A BEAUTIFUL DAY IN MY NEIGHBORHOOD WHEN I WOKE UP.
THE CLOUDS WERE SMILING...
HEY, CHAD, WHAT DO I LOOK LIKE TO YOU?
BUNNY?
MAN, I WAS TRYING FOR A PONY. IT'S THE EARS, ISN'T IT?
THE BIRDS WERE HAVING LITTLE BIRD CONVERSATIONS...
CAN YOU BELIEVE SHE LEFT EAGLE FOR A LOW TYPE LIKE HIM?
WELL HE *WAS* BALD. AND YOU KNOW WHAT THEY SAY, BIRDS OF A FEATHER...
...AND I HAD AN EMAIL FROM JACK!
inbox
HEY, SUPERGIRL.
IT WAS GREAT TO SEE YOU
LAST NIGHT.
DO YOU THINK THE THWARTER
WOULD LET ME STOP BY TODAY?
LOVE, MINTY.

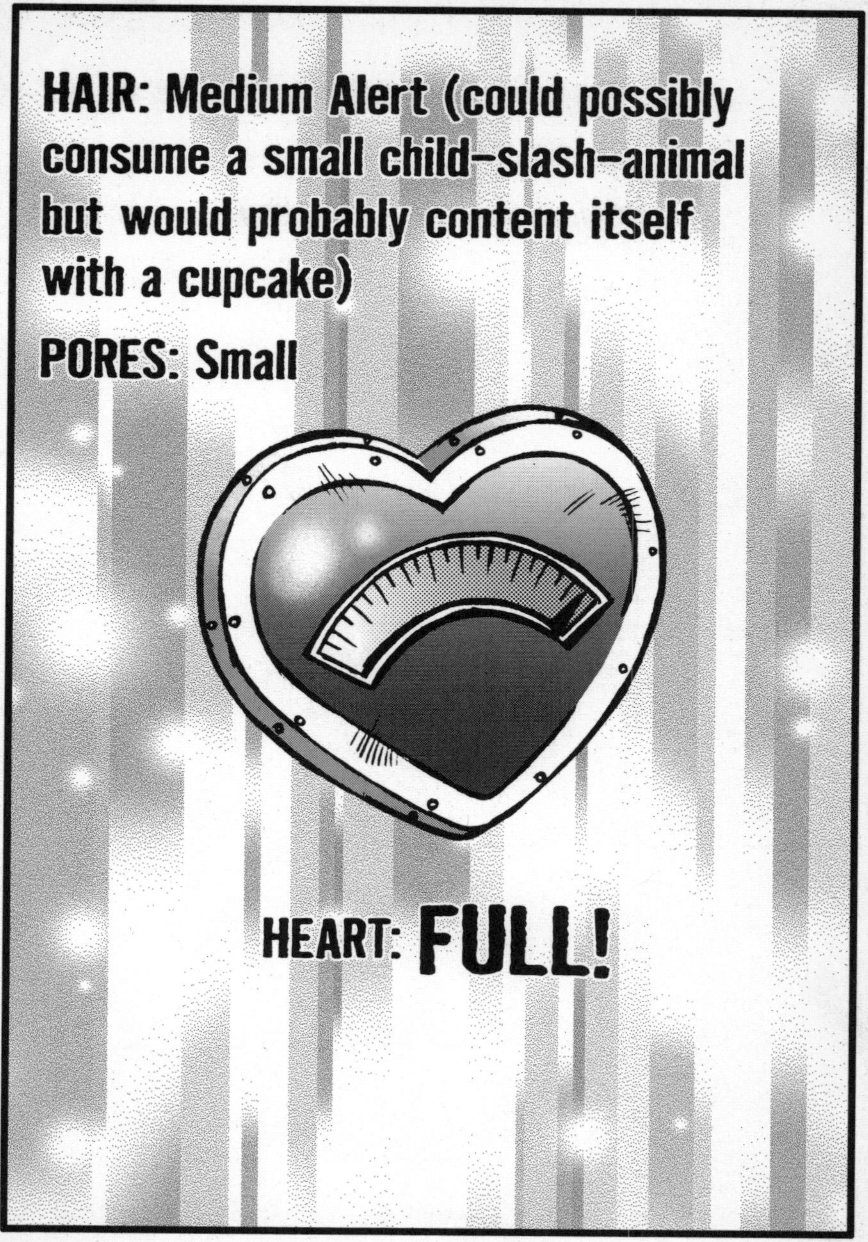
HAIR: Medium Alert (could possibly consume a small child-slash-animal but would probably content itself with a cupcake)
PORES: Small
HEART: FULL!

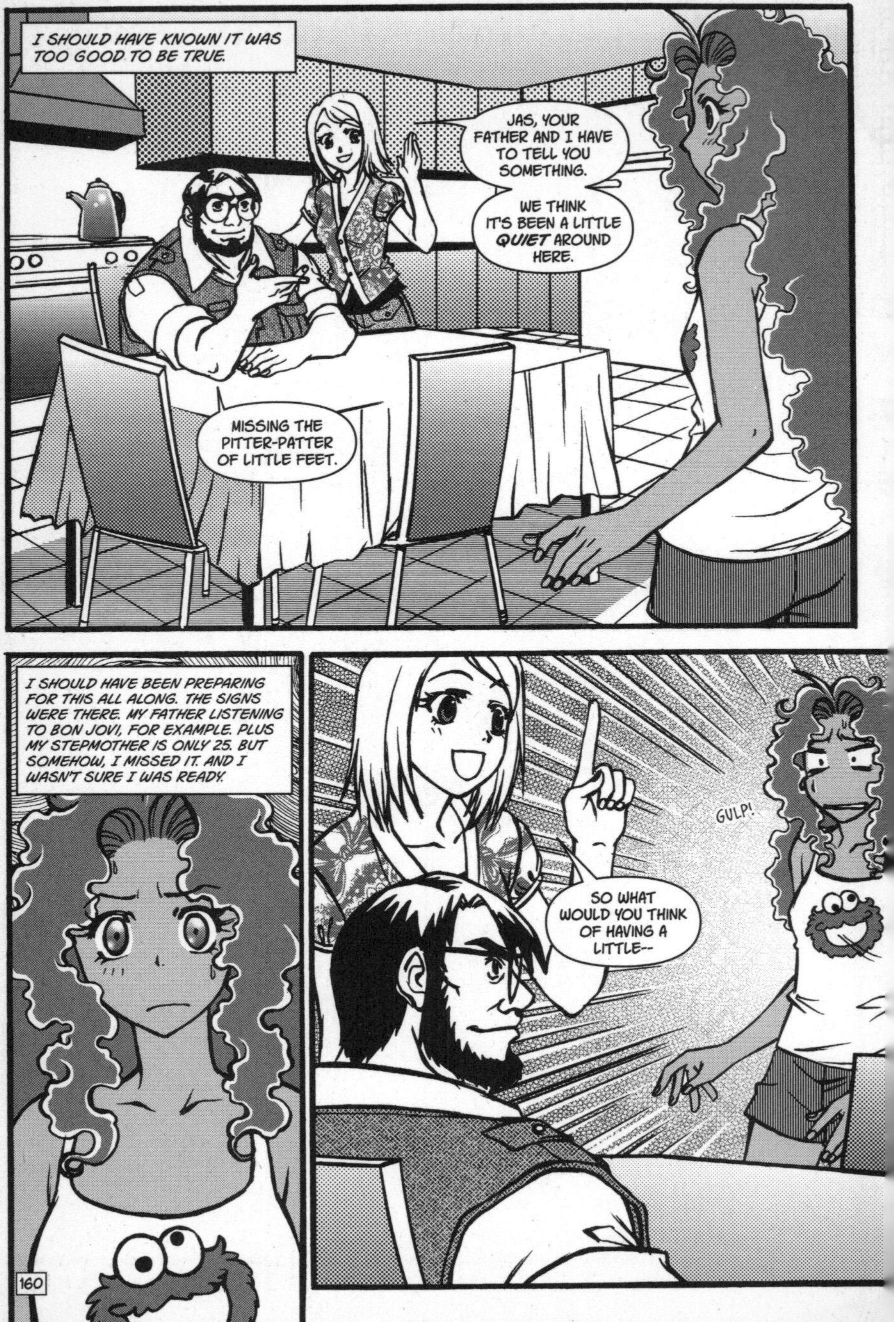
I SHOULD HAVE KNOWN IT WAS TOO GOOD TO BE TRUE.
JAS, YOUR FATHER AND I HAVE TO TELL YOU SOMETHING.
WE THINK IT'S BEEN A LITTLE *QUIET* AROUND HERE.
MISSING THE PITTER-PATTER OF LITTLE FEET.
I SHOULD HAVE BEEN PREPARING FOR THIS ALL ALONG. THE SIGNS WERE THERE. MY FATHER LISTENING TO BON JOVI, FOR EXAMPLE. PLUS MY STEPMOTHER IS ONLY 25. BUT SOMEHOW, I MISSED IT. AND I WASN'T SURE I WAS READY.
SO WHAT WOULD YOU THINK OF HAVING A LITTLE--
GULP!

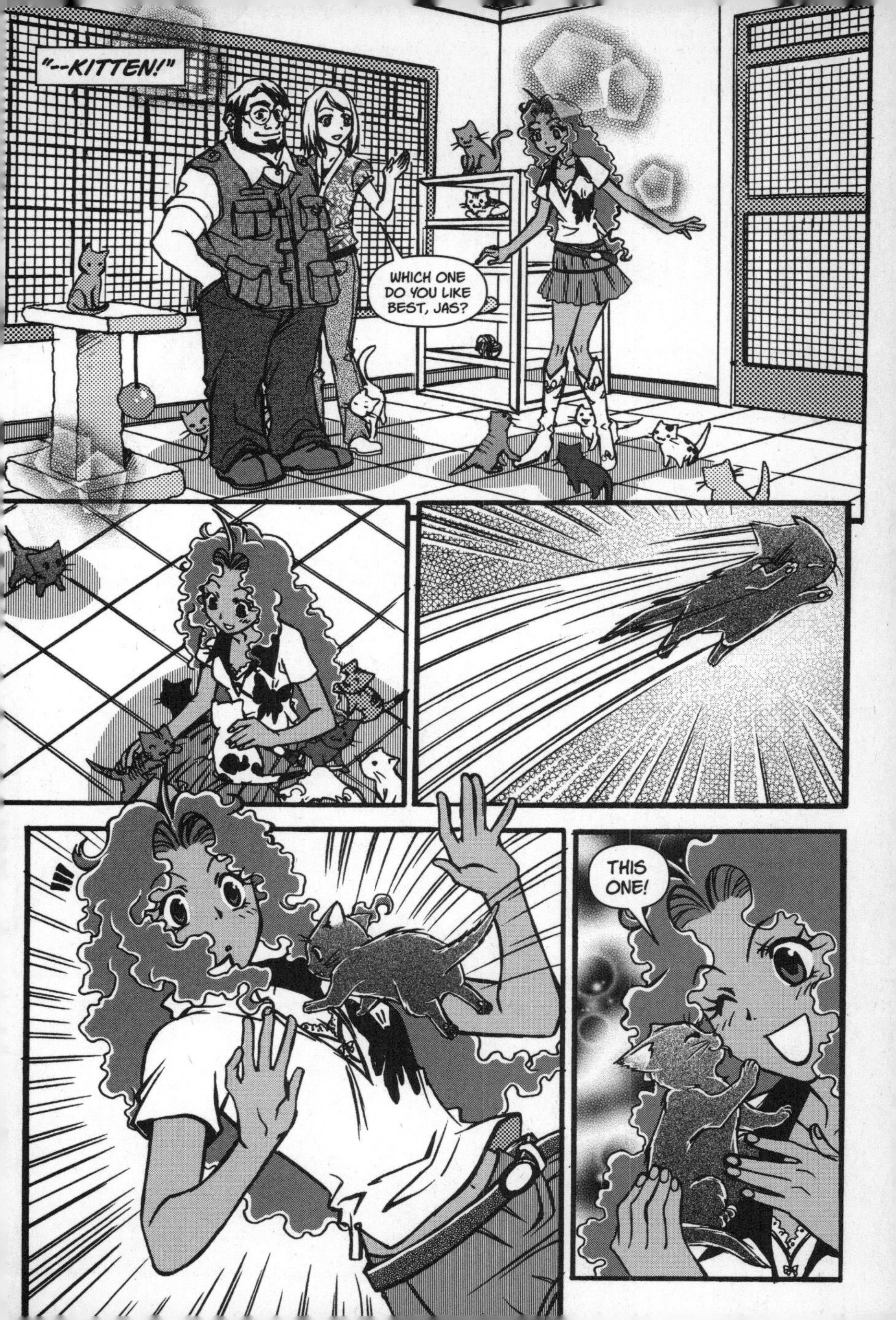
"--KITTEN!"
WHICH ONE DO YOU LIKE BEST, JAS?
THIS ONE!

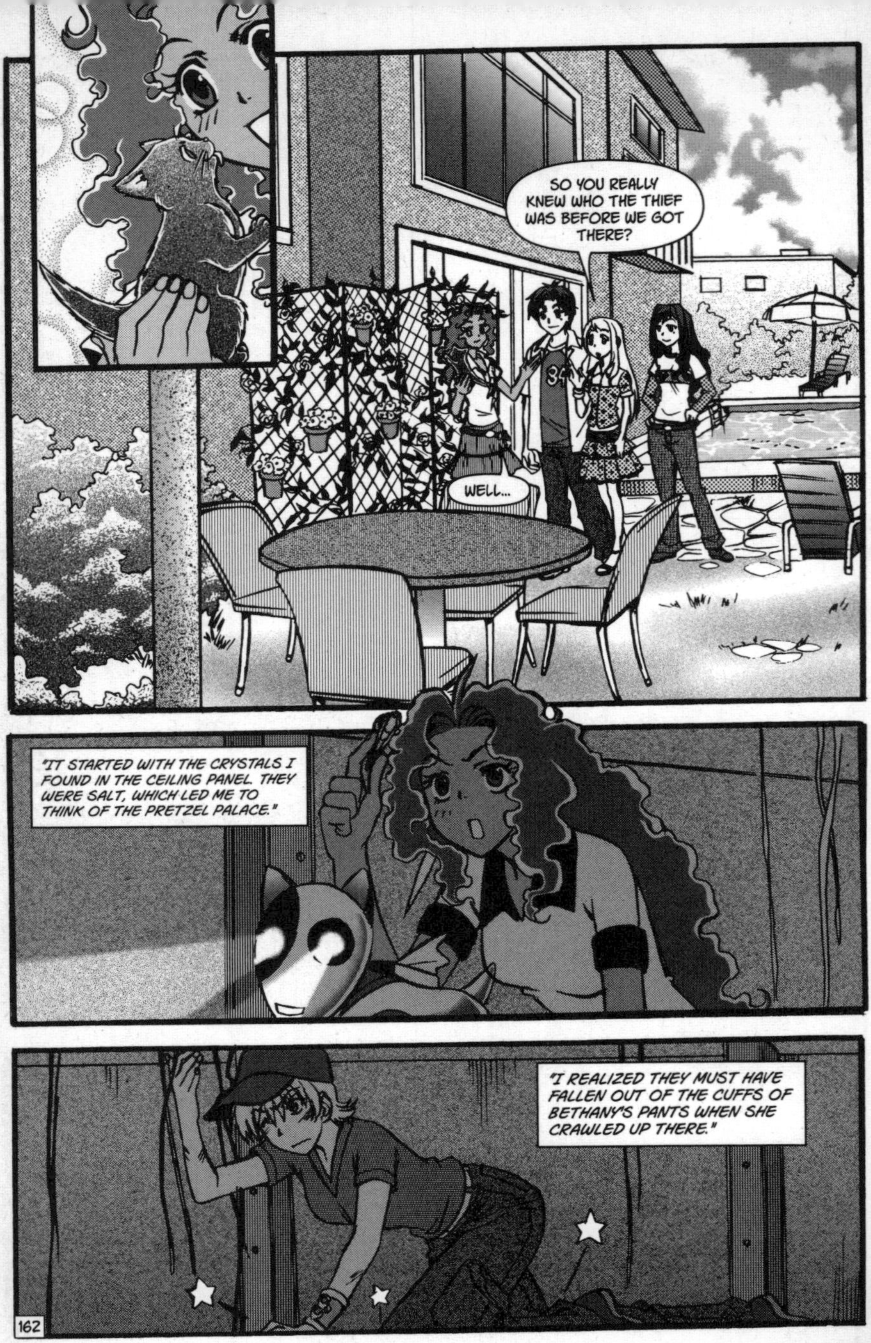
SO YOU REALLY KNEW WHO THE THIEF WAS BEFORE WE GOT THERE?
WELL...
"IT STARTED WITH THE CRYSTALS I FOUND IN THE CEILING PANEL. THEY WERE SALT, WHICH LED ME TO THINK OF THE PRETZEL PALACE."
"I REALIZED THEY MUST HAVE FALLEN OUT OF THE CUFFS OF BETHANY'S PANTS WHEN SHE CRAWLED UP THERE."

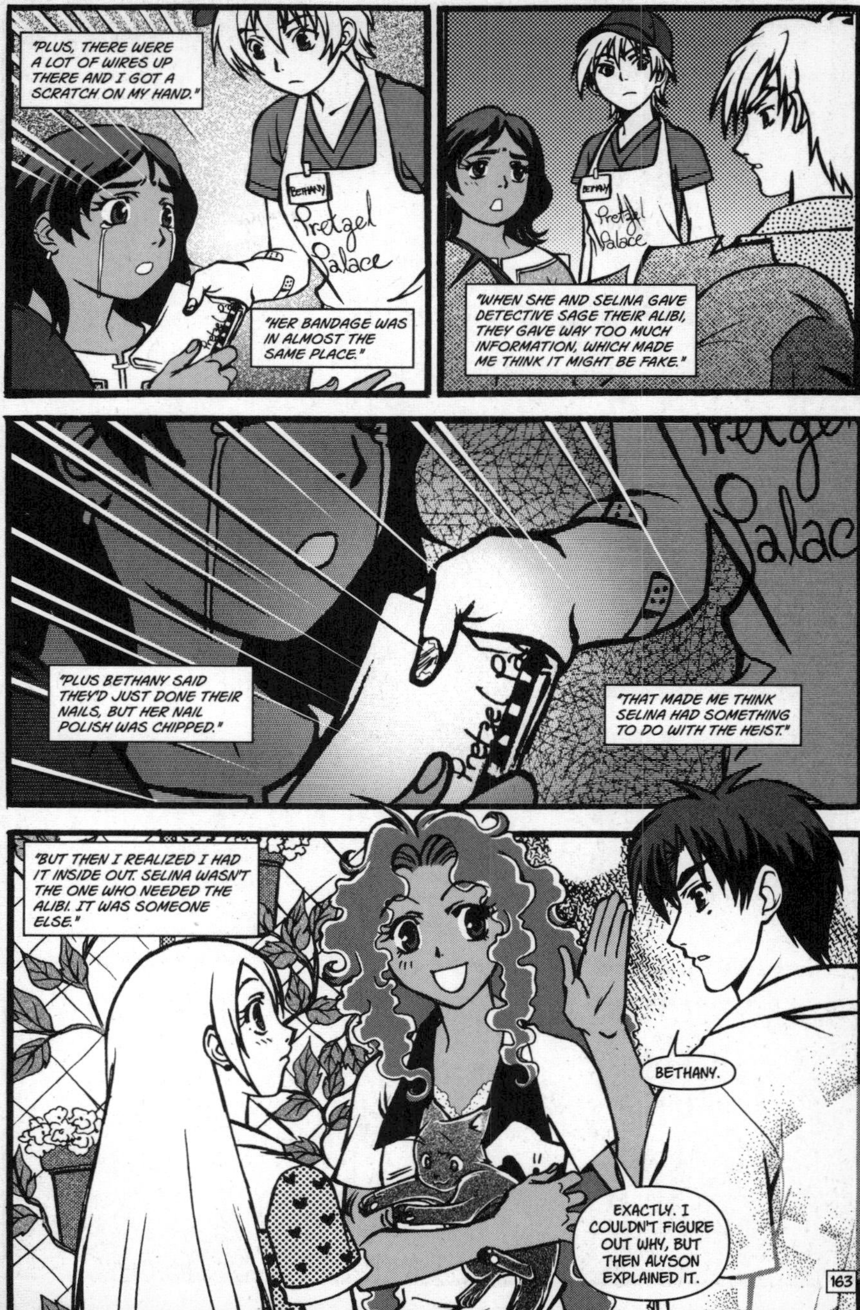
"PLUS, THERE WERE A LOT OF WIRES UP THERE AND I GOT A SCRATCH ON MY HAND."
BETHANY
Pretzel Palace
"HER BANDAGE WAS IN ALMOST THE SAME PLACE."
BETHANY
Pretzel Palace
"WHEN SHE AND SELINA GAVE DETECTIVE SAGE THEIR ALIBI, THEY GAVE WAY TOO MUCH INFORMATION, WHICH MADE ME THINK IT MIGHT BE FAKE."
"PLUS BETHANY SAID THEY'D JUST DONE THEIR NAILS, BUT HER NAIL POLISH WAS CHIPPED."
"THAT MADE ME THINK SELINA HAD SOMETHING TO DO WITH THE HEIST."
"BUT THEN I REALIZED I HAD IT INSIDE OUT. SELINA WASN'T THE ONE WHO NEEDED THE ALIBI. IT WAS SOMEONE ELSE."
BETHANY.
EXACTLY. I COULDN'T FIGURE OUT WHY, BUT THEN ALYSON EXPLAINED IT.

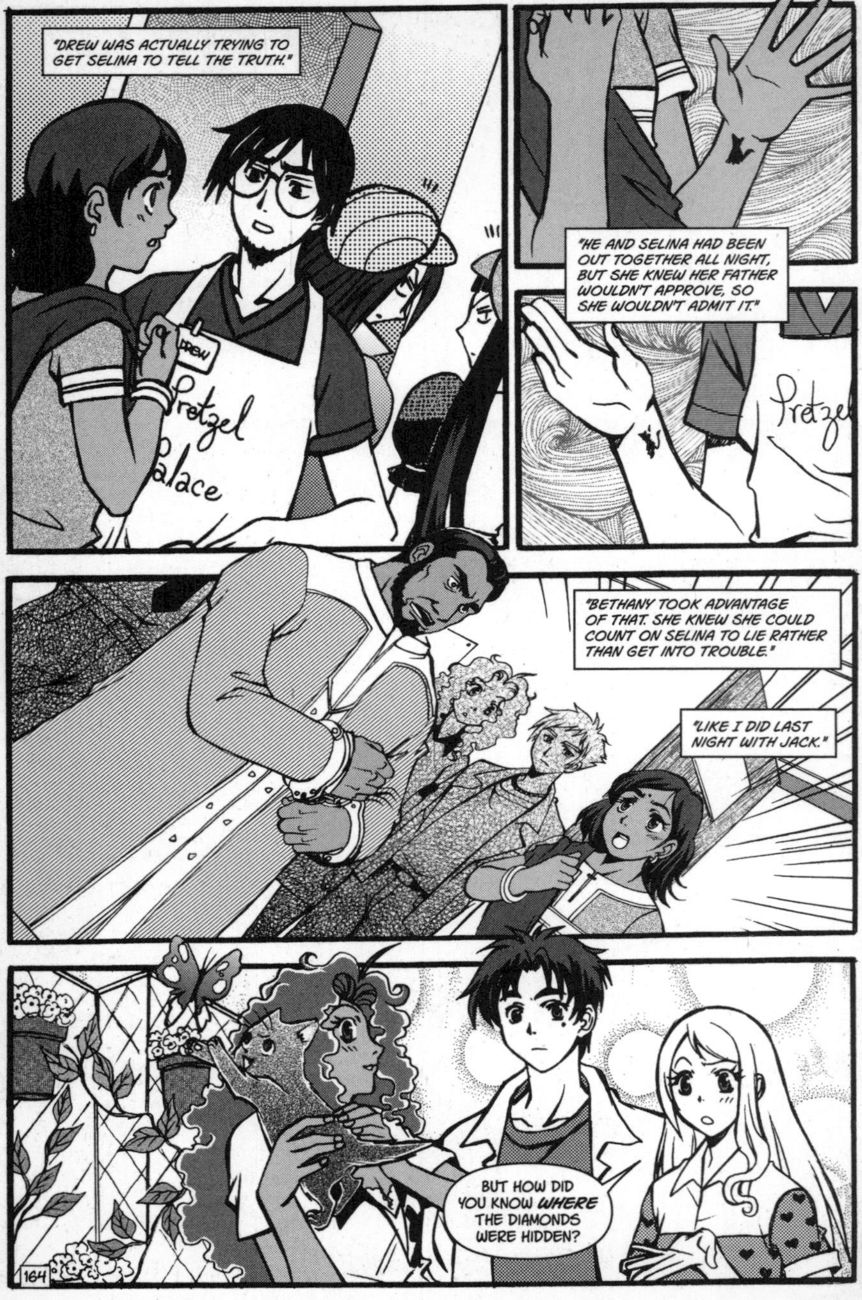
"DREW WAS ACTUALLY TRYING TO GET SELINA TO TELL THE TRUTH."
DREW
Pretzel Palace
"HE AND SELINA HAD BEEN OUT TOGETHER ALL NIGHT, BUT SHE KNEW HER FATHER WOULDN'T APPROVE, SO SHE WOULDN'T ADMIT IT."
Pretzel
"BETHANY TOOK ADVANTAGE OF THAT. SHE KNEW SHE COULD COUNT ON SELINA TO LIE RATHER THAN GET INTO TROUBLE."
"LIKE I DID LAST NIGHT WITH JACK."
BUT HOW DID YOU KNOW ***WHERE*** THE DIAMONDS WERE HIDDEN?

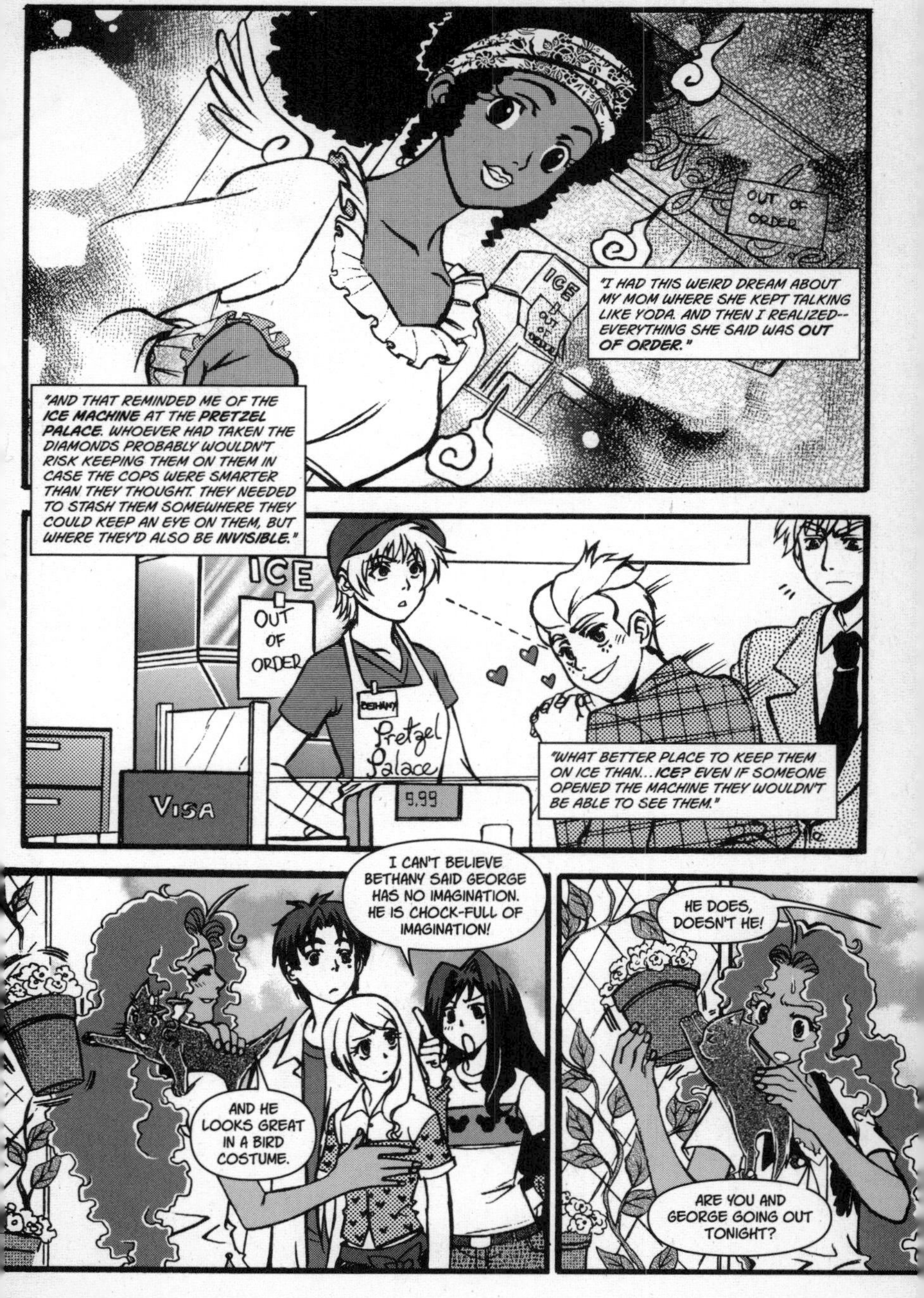
"I HAD THIS WEIRD DREAM ABOUT MY MOM WHERE SHE KEPT TALKING LIKE YODA. AND THEN I REALIZED--EVERYTHING SHE SAID WAS OUT OF ORDER."
OUT OF ORDER
ICE
OUT OF ORDER
"AND THAT REMINDED ME OF THE ICE MACHINE AT THE PRETZEL PALACE. WHOEVER HAD TAKEN THE DIAMONDS PROBABLY WOULDN'T RISK KEEPING THEM ON THEM IN CASE THE COPS WERE SMARTER THAN THEY THOUGHT. THEY NEEDED TO STASH THEM SOMEWHERE THEY COULD KEEP AN EYE ON THEM, BUT WHERE THEY'D ALSO BE INVISIBLE."
ICE
OUT OF ORDER
BETHANY
Pretzel Palace
9.99
VISA
"WHAT BETTER PLACE TO KEEP THEM ON ICE THAN...ICE? EVEN IF SOMEONE OPENED THE MACHINE THEY WOULDN'T BE ABLE TO SEE THEM."
I CAN'T BELIEVE BETHANY SAID GEORGE HAS NO IMAGINATION. HE IS CHOCK-FULL OF IMAGINATION!
AND HE LOOKS GREAT IN A BIRD COSTUME.
HE DOES, DOESN'T HE!
ARE YOU AND GEORGE GOING OUT TONIGHT?

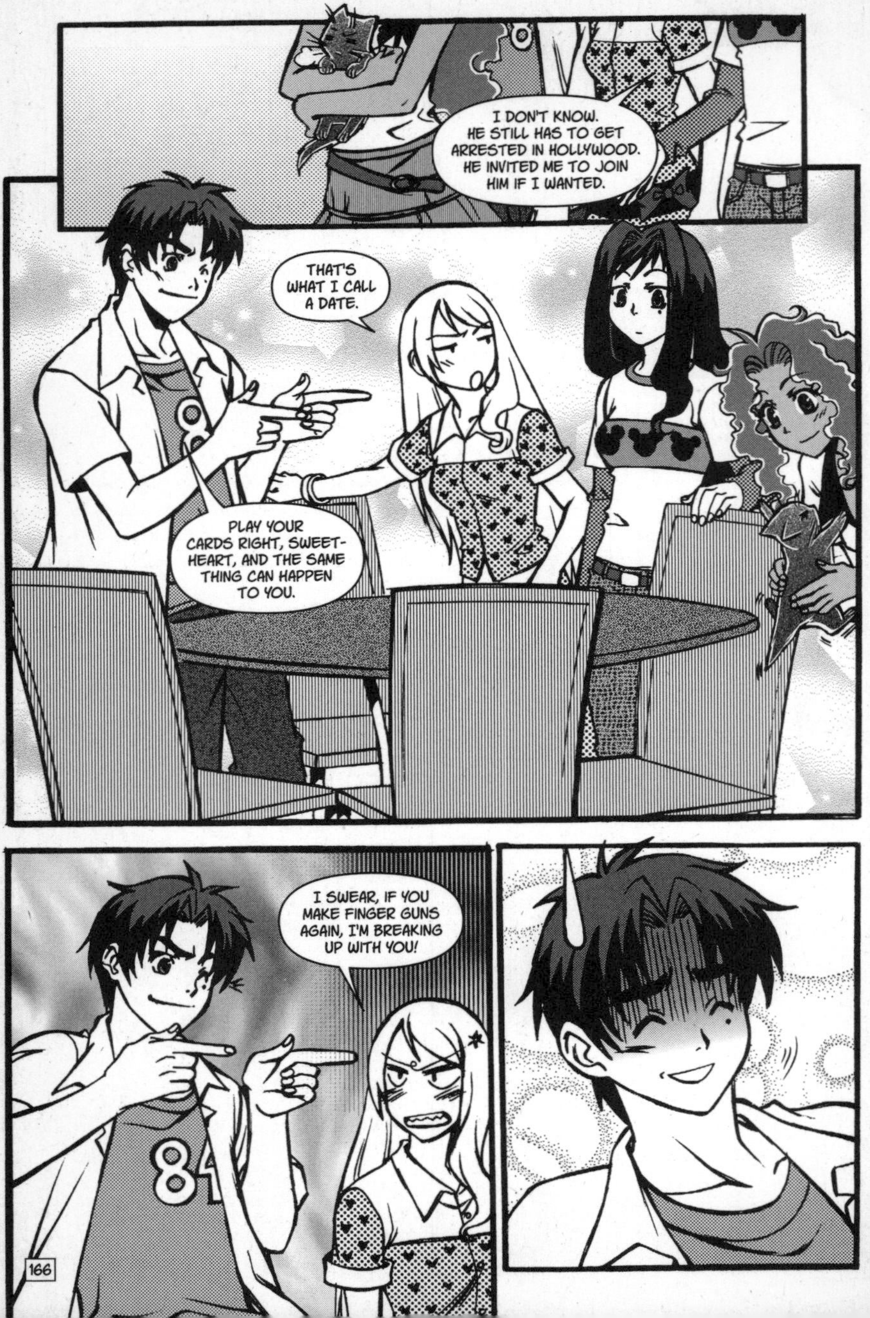
I DON'T KNOW. HE STILL HAS TO GET ARRESTED IN HOLLYWOOD. HE INVITED ME TO JOIN HIM IF I WANTED.
THAT'S WHAT I CALL A DATE.
PLAY YOUR CARDS RIGHT, SWEET-HEART, AND THE SAME THING CAN HAPPEN TO YOU.
I SWEAR, IF YOU MAKE FINGER GUNS AGAIN, I'M BREAKING UP WITH YOU!

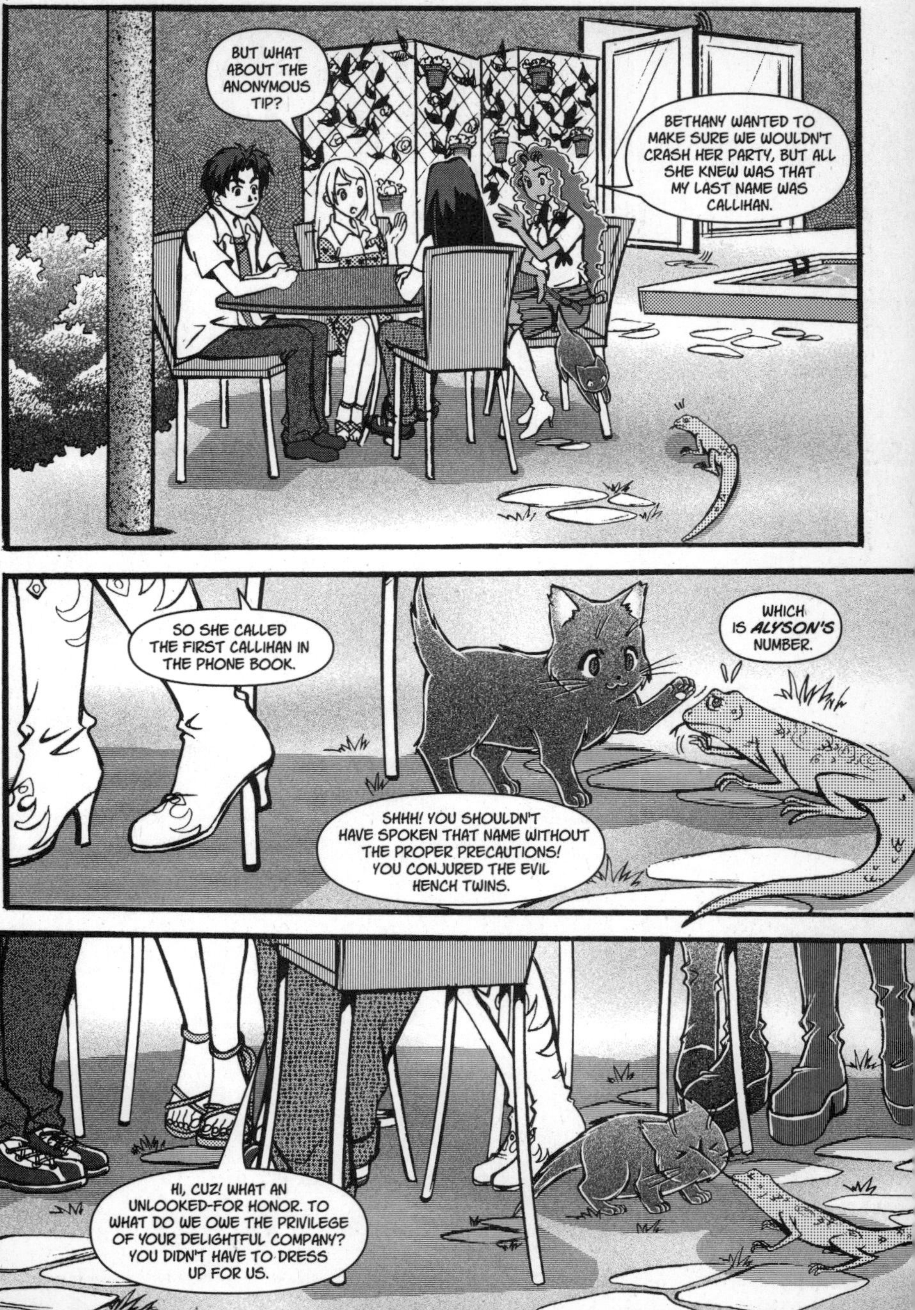
BUT WHAT ABOUT THE ANONYMOUS TIP?
BETHANY WANTED TO MAKE SURE WE WOULDN'T CRASH HER PARTY, BUT ALL SHE KNEW WAS THAT MY LAST NAME WAS CALLIHAN.
SO SHE CALLED THE FIRST CALLIHAN IN THE PHONE BOOK.
WHICH IS *ALYSON'S* NUMBER.
SHHH! YOU SHOULDN'T HAVE SPOKEN THAT NAME WITHOUT THE PROPER PRECAUTIONS! YOU CONJURED THE EVIL HENCH TWINS.
HI, CUZ! WHAT AN UNLOOKED-FOR HONOR. TO WHAT DO WE OWE THE PRIVILEGE OF YOUR DELIGHTFUL COMPANY? YOU DIDN'T HAVE TO DRESS UP FOR US.

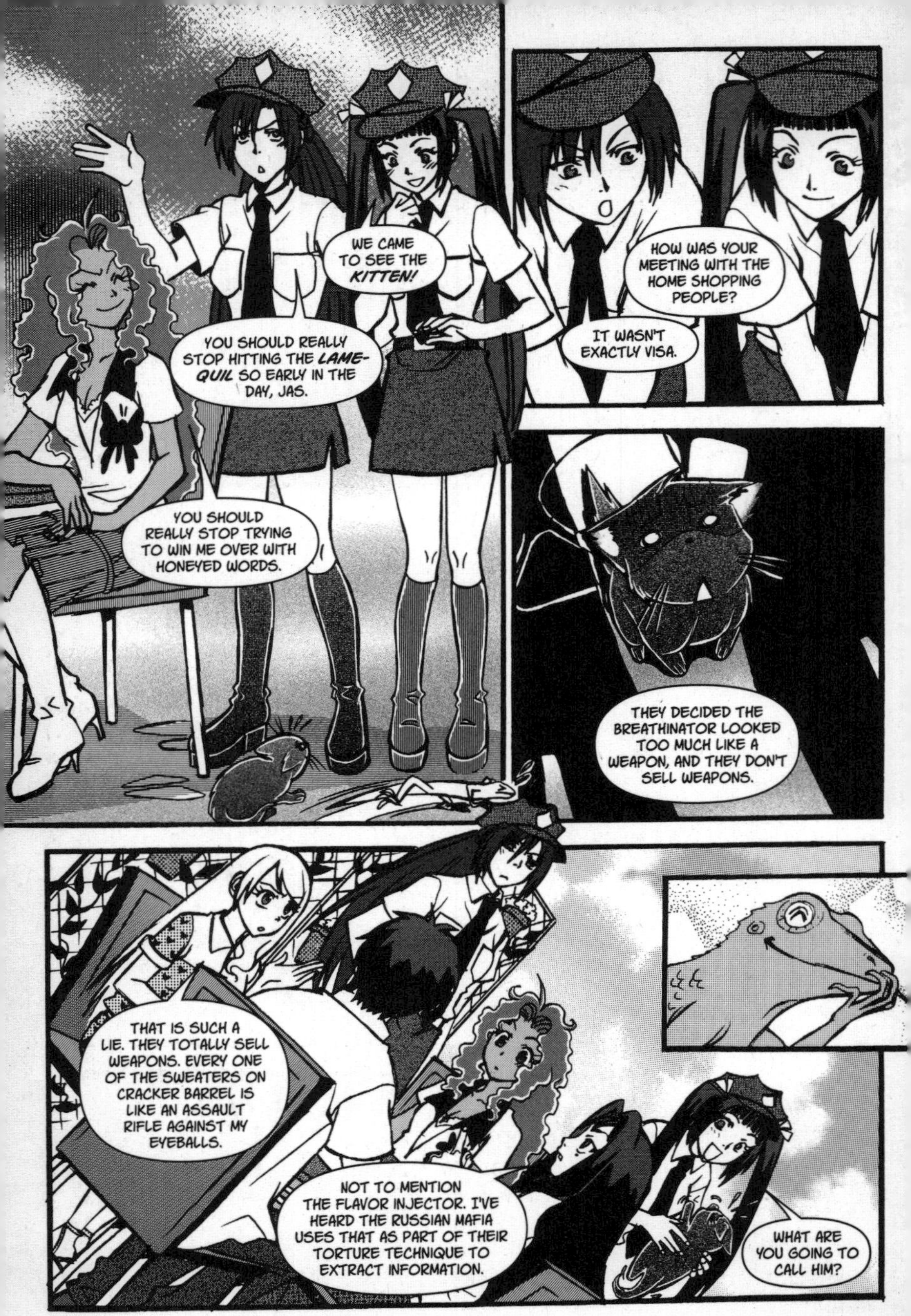
WE CAME TO SEE THE *KITTEN!*
YOU SHOULD REALLY STOP HITTING THE *LAME-QUIL* SO EARLY IN THE DAY, JAS.
YOU SHOULD REALLY STOP TRYING TO WIN ME OVER WITH HONEYED WORDS.
HOW WAS YOUR MEETING WITH THE HOME SHOPPING PEOPLE?
IT WASN'T EXACTLY VISA.
THEY DECIDED THE BREATHINATOR LOOKED TOO MUCH LIKE A WEAPON, AND THEY DON'T SELL WEAPONS.
THAT IS SUCH A LIE. THEY TOTALLY SELL WEAPONS. EVERY ONE OF THE SWEATERS ON CRACKER BARREL IS LIKE AN ASSAULT RIFLE AGAINST MY EYEBALLS.
NOT TO MENTION THE FLAVOR INJECTOR. I'VE HEARD THE RUSSIAN MAFIA USES THAT AS PART OF THEIR TORTURE TECHNIQUE TO EXTRACT INFORMATION.
WHAT ARE YOU GOING TO CALL HIM?

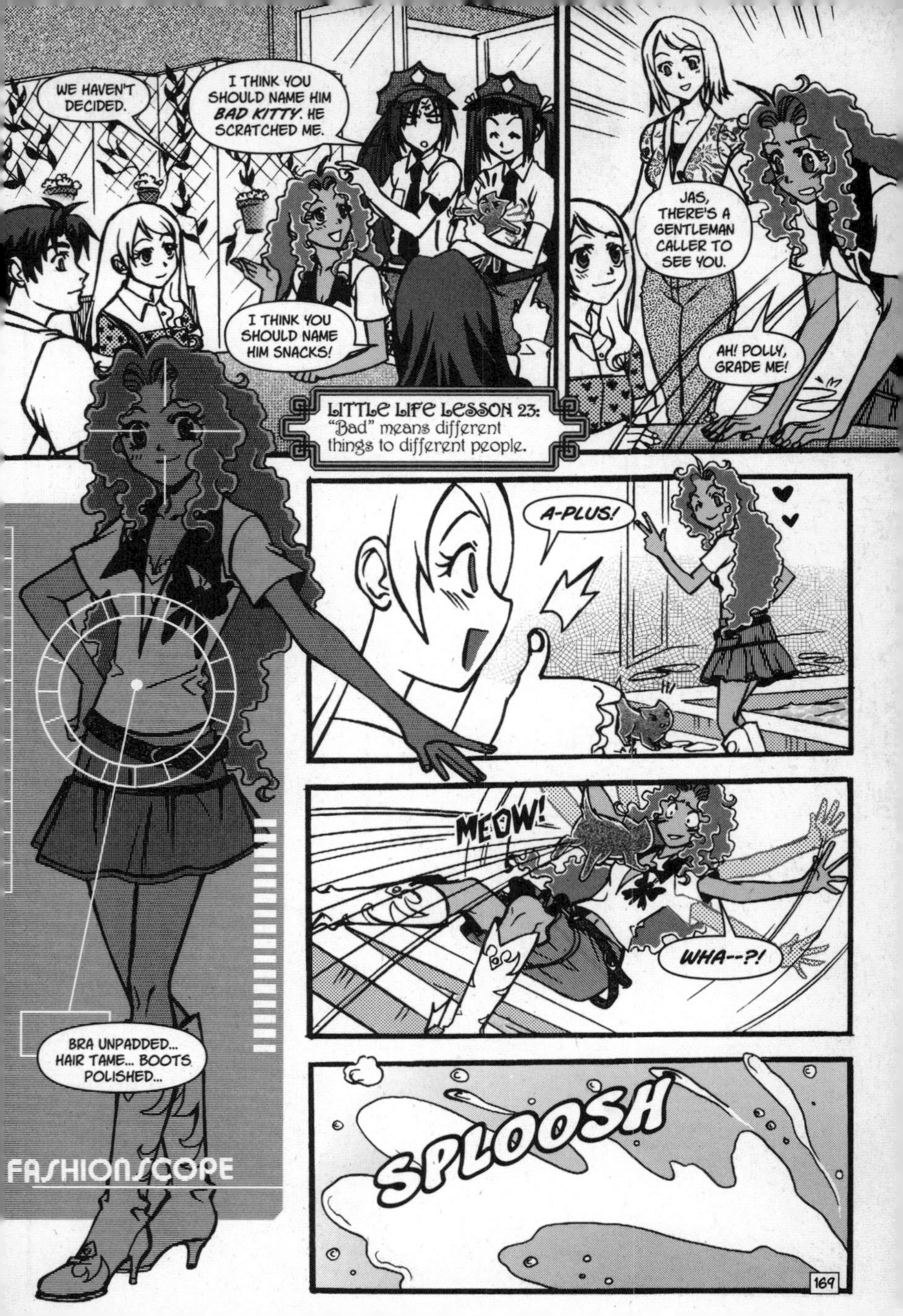
WE HAVEN'T DECIDED.
I THINK YOU SHOULD NAME HIM BAD KITTY. HE SCRATCHED ME.
I THINK YOU SHOULD NAME HIM SNACKS!
JAS, THERE'S A GENTLEMAN CALLER TO SEE YOU.
AH! POLLY, GRADE ME!
LITTLE LIFE LESSON 23: "Bad" means different things to different people.
BRA UNPADDED... HAIR TAME... BOOTS POLISHED...
FASHIONSCOPE
A-PLUS!
MEOW!
WHA--?!
SPLOOSH

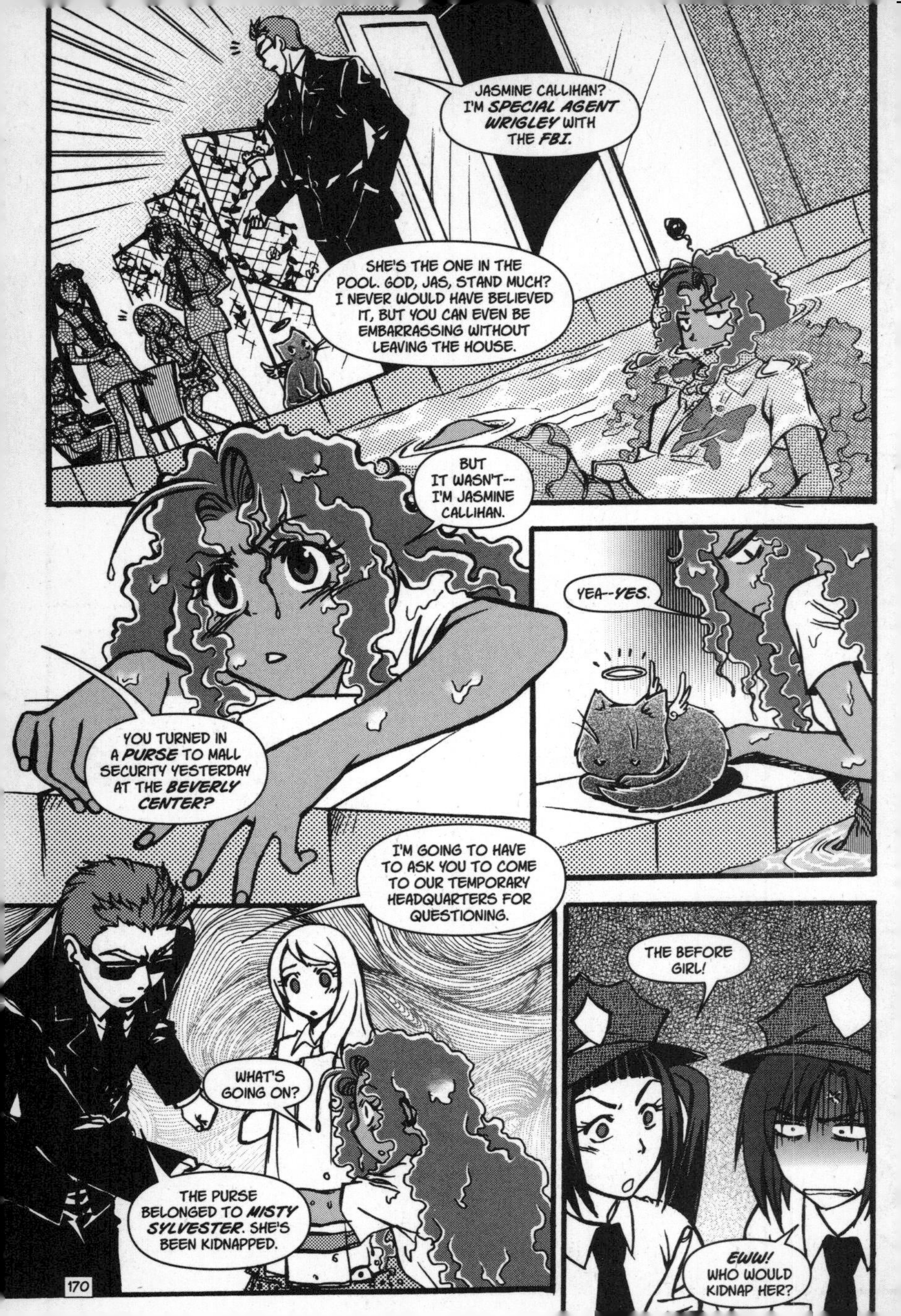
JASMINE CALLIHAN? I'M SPECIAL AGENT WRIGLEY WITH THE FBI.
SHE'S THE ONE IN THE POOL. GOD, JAS, STAND MUCH? I NEVER WOULD HAVE BELIEVED IT, BUT YOU CAN EVEN BE EMBARRASSING WITHOUT LEAVING THE HOUSE.
BUT IT WASN'T-- I'M JASMINE CALLIHAN.
YOU TURNED IN A PURSE TO MALL SECURITY YESTERDAY AT THE BEVERLY CENTER?
YEA--YES.
I'M GOING TO HAVE TO ASK YOU TO COME TO OUR TEMPORARY HEADQUARTERS FOR QUESTIONING.
WHAT'S GOING ON?
THE PURSE BELONGED TO MISTY SYLVESTER. SHE'S BEEN KIDNAPPED.
THE BEFORE GIRL!
EWW! WHO WOULD KIDNAP HER?

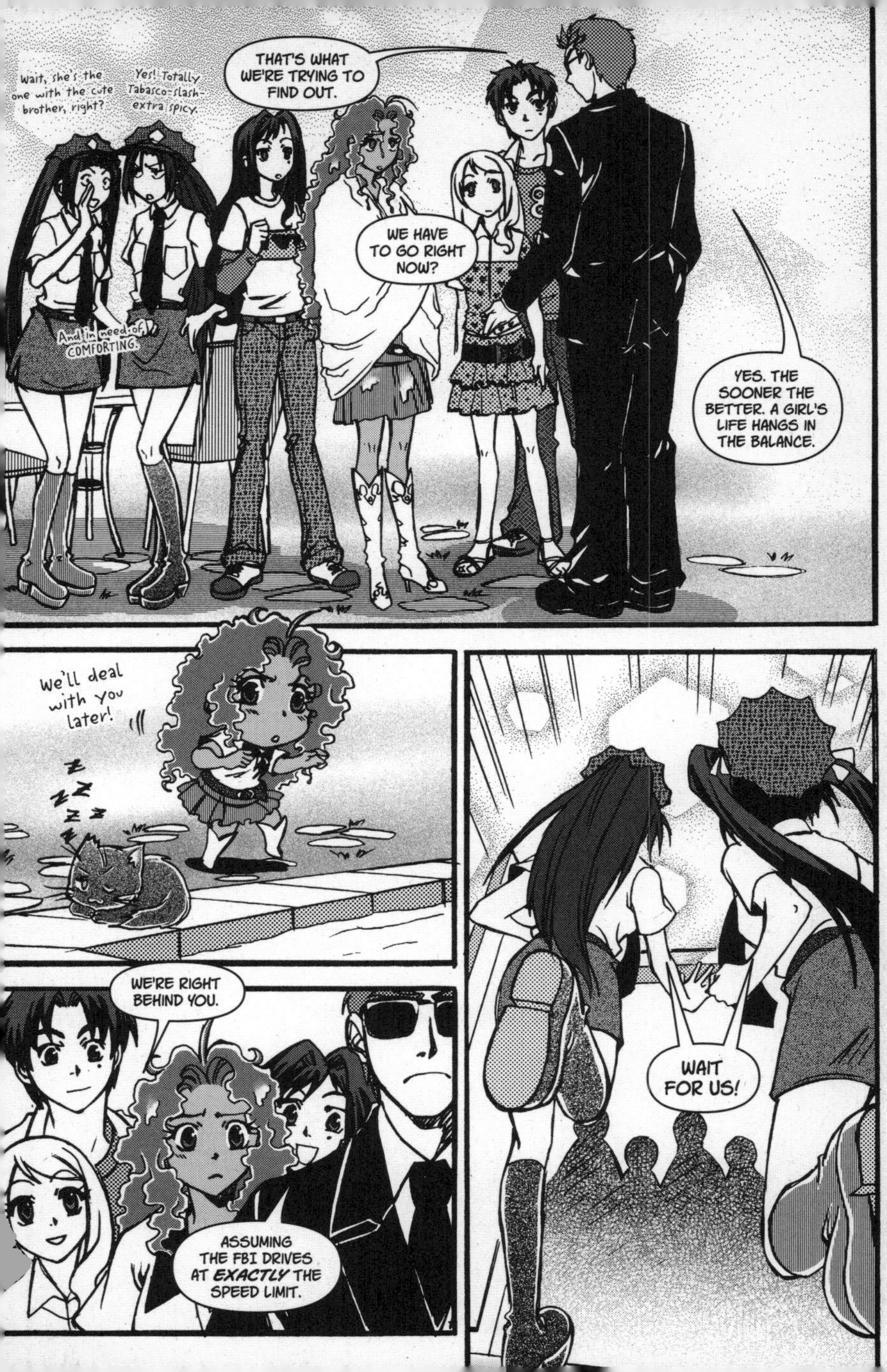
Wait, she's the one with the cute brother, right?
Yes! Totally Tabasco-slash-extra spicy.
THAT'S WHAT WE'RE TRYING TO FIND OUT.
And in need of COMFORTING.
WE HAVE TO GO RIGHT NOW?
YES. THE SOONER THE BETTER. A GIRL'S LIFE HANGS IN THE BALANCE.
We'll deal with you later!
Z Z Z Z Z
WE'RE RIGHT BEHIND YOU.
ASSUMING THE FBI DRIVES AT *EXACTLY* THE SPEED LIMIT.
WAIT FOR US!

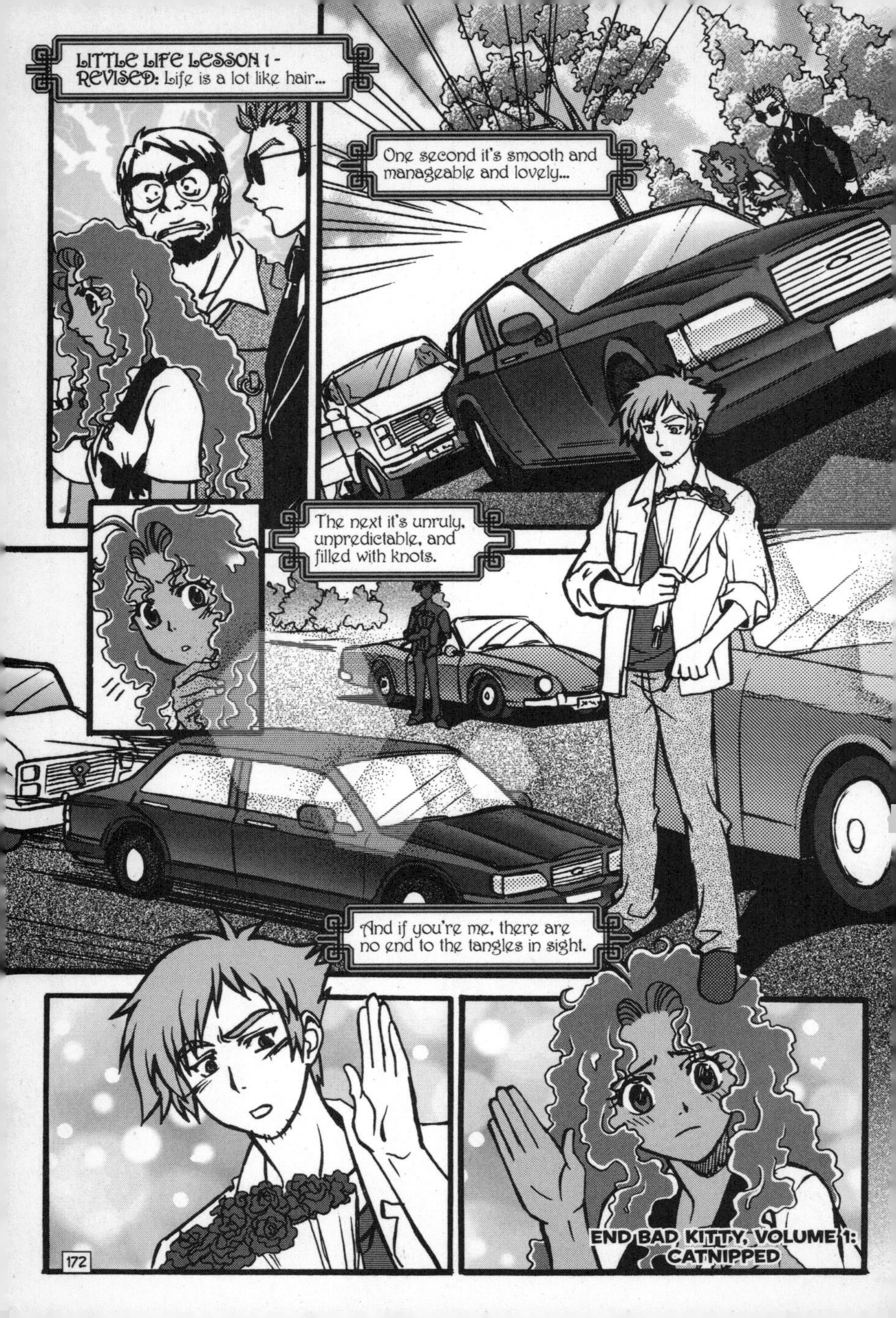
LITTLE LIFE LESSON 1 - REVISED: Life is a lot like hair...
One second it's smooth and manageable and lovely...
The next it's unruly, unpredictable, and filled with knots.
And if you're me, there are no end to the tangles in sight.
END BAD KITTY, VOLUME 1: CATNIPPED

Read on for a look at

KITTY KITTY,

the hilarious sequel to
the teen caper novel

BAD KITTY

While it might be unusual for most people to have others shouting "RUN!" at them, it happens to me pretty often. And I've developed a simple set of guidelines for these situations:

Little Life Lesson 1: Don't do it.

Little Life Lesson 2: Ever.

Little Life Lesson 3: Especially if you are trying to be a Model Daughter and the person who yelled it at you is a nineteen-year-old girl dressed like a homeless pixie whose life goal is to Write on Rice and who adds, with a quiver in her voice, "They're going to kill me, too."

They. Are. Going. To. Kill. Me.

TOO.

But sometimes doing What Is Right is not an option, such as when the homeless pixie whips out her Incredible Hulk strength and starts dragging you down the tourist-filled street at a rapid pace.

"Where are we going?" I shouted at Arabella as she bounced me off of two tourists.

"It doesn't matter," she said desperately. "We just have to get away from him."

"From who?"

"The man in the straw hat. He's following us!"

Without warning, she yanked me around a corner and started running faster. As she wove expertly between the people on the crowded street, cleverly using me as a buffer, I stole a look over my shoulder and had to admit she might be right: The straw hat was still behind us. And gaining.

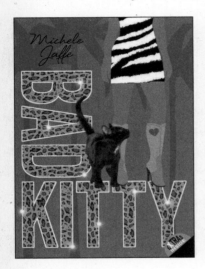